The Tymorean Trust
Book Four

EARTH MISSION

by

MARGARET GREGORY

Also by Margaret Gregory

TYMOREAN TRUST SERIES:

Book 1 - Power Rising
Book 2 - Great Ones
Book 3 - The Return to Earth

ATAPI SORCERESS SERIES:

Book 1- The Wild One

SHORT STORIES:

Graffiti Girl
Ghost Writer

The Tymorean Trust
Book Four

EARTH MISSION

by

MARGARET GREGORY

TAT Publishing

ISBN 978-1-925332-04-9

Publisher of record
TAT Publishing
www.tatpublishing.com

Chapter 1 - Disappearance

After slipping away from the prestigious Washington campus of the WSRA University, Tymos and Kryslie Ward effectively vanished into obscurity.

Vice Chancellor Gilchrist began an investigation when neither of them attended the formal, pre-graduation dinner, and no message had been sent to explain why.

He immediately thought back to the previous year when the two students, now the year's joint valedictorians, had prevented harm to the eminent physicist, Clement Emmanuel, and ensured that the precious data and crystals that were at the centre of the famed Grainger exhibit, were not stolen. He had thought that incident closed, once Emmanuel had published his findings.

Perhaps it wasn't.

Or was this something to do with the other agenda that he had felt those students had? They were Grainger's protégé's, and there had been pressure on them to solve the puzzle that the founder of the university had left behind. However, thinking back to that time, there had seemed to be something else in their single-minded determination to get Grainger's notes.

Leaving the dinner, he took several security guards to check the rooms assigned to the twins. There were no clothes or personal possessions, the beds were neatly made, study materials were ready to go back to the library. A check on their in-room computers showed that their email accounts had been cleared of all correspondence and contacts.

"What do you want us to do now, Sir?" one guard asked.

"Ask your superior to question the staff, very quietly. I want to know when they left and any if anyone knows why they left."

"At once, Sir," the guard left and Gilchrist returned to the dinner in a very thoughtful mood.

He had been angry at first, but then the doubts crept in. Everything indicated that they had left voluntarily - and since no CCTV record showed them leaving - they must have disappeared deliberately. Or someone wanted everyone to think that.

Gilchrist took a while to make up his mind, but eventually he called in the Investigative Committee - the enforcement arm of the United World Nations. The WRSA campuses were, like the World Science Research Authority itself, politically neutral - similar to a foreign embassy on American soil.

With no indications of foul play, the investigators said there was little they could do. However, they set some standard checks in motion.

The Washington Capital Police, asked questions at all the local transportation hubs, CCTV footage was examined - nothing was discovered. No person or camera had seen the twins, and their distinctive dark auburn hair would have drawn attention.

A search for financial and other records came back negative. The missing students had no bank accounts, no income streams; neither had a driver's licence or a mobile phone and the search did not turn up social security numbers or even birth certificates.

The investigators found this very irregular - and believed the students had been living at the campus under an alias. Gilchrist found it strange as well, for the university computer had all the information that was missing elsewhere. Moreover, it had been supplied by the late founder of the WSRA Tamir Grainger.

Even with the exact numbers to punch in for searches, there was no trace to be found.

When the Denver address given as their home address was visited by the federal police, they only discovered that the elderly owner had recently died and the young woman living there had no knowledge of the missing graduands.

Another dead end.

With nothing else to do, Gilchrist had the two un-presented Doctor of Astro-Science certificates placed in the vault of the university archive. Then, for reasons he couldn't fully explain, he arranged for all the computer records about the missing graduands to be sealed.

He told himself that if Tymos and Kryslie Ward wanted proof of their qualifications, they would have to come and speak to him and explain themselves.

Chapter 2 - Earth missionaries

The email had simply said, "Call home, urgently."

Tymos had known that it could only mean one thing and he had summoned his twin with a terse mental call.

She had simply excused herself from a casual conversation with a friend, moved out of sight, and transmitted to her brother's room.

For the past five years, they had been just like the other highly intelligent students - but the time was coming when their real mission would escalate in importance.

"Hillary wants us," Tymos had told his twin.

"Well, we have done all we need to here. I will go and see what she wants and come back." Kryslie pulled a device from her pocket. It mimicked the latest mobile communications devices, but was more than it looked and it had not been designed by human scientists.

She activated a signal on a frequency unknown to humans. "Hillary, activate the long range beam in thirty seconds."

Without saying goodbye, Kryslie transmitted from her brother's room to a secluded area of the university gardens. Her transmitter was a device that enabled her to move from place to place within seconds. On Earth, such a device was still in the realms of fiction. On the world Kryslie called home - only an elite subset of individuals could use one.

She and her brother were missionaries, from a distant world - Tymorea. More than that, they were Advocates of the Guardians of Peace who were powerful beings who worked to bring peace in the universe.

Her "home" as far as the university was concerned, was an address in the outer fringes of Denver City. It belonged to Rhyn, a great, great descendent of the previous Tymorean missionaries to Earth. For years, he had coordinated a group of other descendents, who lived spread out across the nations of Earth, observing, reporting and working to maintain the Peace that had existed for the past two and a half decades - since the end of the last war and the Peace treaty of 2057.

One look at Hillary, the brown haired woman who had tended Rhyn for over five years, coupled with what her own emphatic senses were telling her - was all she needed to understand the call. She used her communicator and spoke to her brother. "Rhyn is dying. Can you pack everything? I will re-activate the beam in an hour."

There was very little that he needed to pack. Both of them had only a small wardrobe of utilitarian clothing and one fancy outfit. Personal belongings were few and they did not need to take electronic texts. After stuffing his own things into a small backpack, he transmitted to his sister's room, and did the same there.

He tidied up the few loose ends, arranged for their electronic book readers to be returned to the library, emptied their university email boxes, and placed the room keys in an envelope that he left at the security desk. For the brief moments that he was there, the security camera was inactive.

As he walked out into the darkness, with two backpacks, he drew on his power and blended into the shadows. Exactly an hour after Kryslie had left, the long-range beam was reactivated. He saw the terminus clearly; an oval shaped mauve glow – high enough for him to step into before activating his transmitter. Normal human eyes would not see or sense anything.

Hillary, a brown haired and in her twenties, took the two backpacks when he materialised. Tymos paused only long enough to say, "If anyone calls asking for us, you haven't seen us," before hurrying to join his sister.

Kryslie's hands were glowing faintly with mauve light and she held one of the old man's hands.

Tymos went to the other side of the bed and touched the aged, dry skin on Rhyn's forehead.

With that contact, Tymos knew that the old man was on the pinnacle between life and death.

He glanced at his sister, who thought at him, "I am holding him here, but he was already in a coma when I arrived. Hillary said he was asking for us."

While Kryslie was able to start wounds and illnesses healing, he was able to speed heal. But even he could do little for the tired body that was already shutting down. The best he could do would be to hold back death long enough to hear the words that Rhyn needed to say. He sent a flow of energy into the old man.

After a few moments, the wrinkled eyes opened. They had gone from brown to black and although they could see nothing, the old man sensed who was with him.

"Prince Tymos, Princess Kryslie." The voice was like the whisper of a leaf being blown over dust.

"We are here," Kryslie assured gently. She increased the pressure of her grip, very slightly, as she willed her own healing energies into the frail body.

Rhyn's voice became a little stronger as he said, "I have seen them coming. The advance missionaries."

Memories of a frightening vision began to stir in his mind. Tymos concentrated on them as Kryslie urged, "Tell us what you have seen."

"The desert. They will come there," the voice dropped to a horrified whisper. Kryslie leaned closer, to hear him better. "But the army is there, doing tests. The dome that glows will be found."

Rhyn was not a scientist; he knew nothing of force fields and protective screens. Yet the old man knew the mauve glowing dome was Tymorean - for he was speaking words given to him by the Guardians of Peace.

In the mind images, were other glowing areas; blue-green in colour. One by one, these glows disappeared after blinding white flashes. Then white flashed around the mauve glow, and when the light faded, people began to trot away - only to be caught, interrogated, killed.

"Warn them…"

Rhyn's eyes closed once more, and his breathing became laboured. His agitation, caused by the scene in his mind of Tymoreans dying, sent a spasm of pain through him.

Tymos shared it, eased it, as Kryslie spoke to the old man's mind. "We know now that we must keep them safe - that is why the Guardians gave you this vision. They have given you a great honour."

As soon as Tymos was aware of it, Kryslie also sensed the energies in the old body stop swirling. The heart stopped beating and the lungs pushed out one last soft sigh or air.

Tymos kept his hand where it was for a moment longer as he uttered the words of an old Tymorean benediction.

"May the Guardians of Peace free your spirit, and make you one with them forever in Dirakee."

Kryslie released Rhyn's hand and murmured, "I will talk to Hillary."

Tymos nodded. "I will do what is needed here."

Hillary looked up from the vegetables that she was trying to prepare for cooking. One hand held a peeler, the other a carrot, but she had been looking down as if staring deep into the bench top. When she saw Kryslie, tears began to leak from her eyes and fell unchecked and she didn't protest when a gentle arm reached out to embrace her. Instead, she turned into the offered comfort.

"He knew he was dying," Hillary managed to say, although her voice was unsteady. "He was asking for you and he was so agitated. He was saying that they would be killed - the advance missionaries. That they would finally come here, and be killed."

Kryslie was aware of Tymos coming out of Rhyn's sleeping room, and going to where the clean sheets and towels were kept.

"We won't let them die," Kryslie said, drawing Hillary's eyes to meet her own. "His vision was a warning of what might happen."

"But - he was convinced it was real…"

"Yes, that is the way it seems - when the Guardians of Peace grant their faithful servants one final moment of enlightenment."

"But he was so agitated. Why did they do that to him?"

Kryslie urged Hillary to a chair at the still un-set table. She crouched next to her. "He was not in pain for long, and as to why, he knew his time was near. He was the nearest Elder to those who needed to receive the warning. The Elders who live on Tymorea know to expect such blessings and welcome one last chance to do the Guardians' work."

She let Hilary cry softly for a while, aware that Tymos was cleaning and bathing Rhyn's body, and sparing her that sad duty.

"He was old, and this was his time - you have taken good care of him and you ensured that we came in time. You should not feel as if you have failed him."

"I have to tend to him…"

"Tymos is doing that. What else must we do?"

Hillary straightened, as she focussed on her duty. "He made sure his affairs were in order and that I knew what to do. He wanted to be cremated…He said he wanted his ashes to be taken to the world where his great grand parents had been born. That maybe, since you and Tymos had come, it would be possible."

"It will be done," Kryslie promised.

"I had better call the doctor, and the other people." Hillary started to stand up.

"Not just yet," Kryslie gently pulled her back down onto the chair. "What arrangements did he make about …" she gestured to where the edge of a huge picture was visible through a door. There was a mauve glow about it.

Hillary glanced at the holographic picture that hid the room where Rhyn's computers and communications equipment were hidden from casual human eyes.

"Surely they can stay here? Rhyn willed the house to me," She turned her red-rimmed eyes to Kryslie. "I didn't know everything he did, just how to record messages and reports, but I learn fast."

Tymos came into the kitchen, moving very quietly. "I will take over as coordinator, and for that your help will be very welcome - but we will need to re-locate the equipment. Do you know of a suitable place?"

"My father, Raymon Diese, owns several properties. I can call him and ask him if he can make one available. But why not stay here?"

Tymos gave her an odd smile. "We have kind of done a vanishing act from the university. They have this address as home. If they were to catch up with us, here, we'd have more explaining to do than we are prepared to permit. So if you will call your father, I will go and start preparing the equipment for the move."

Kryslie stayed with Hillary while she moved to the telephone, dialled a number and left a message for her father.

"A kind of vanishing act," Hillary commented with a shake of her head. Now that she had things to do, she was showing her strength of character. "Why did you do that?"

"Last year we had to admit to an infringement of university rules. We were warned that if we ignored or broke any more, we would have to leave the uni. We could not explain why we acted as we had, and at the time, we had not begun to build the generator that the Earthbase will need once it is constructed. As a result, our inter campus travel permission was revoked and we had to adhere to a prearranged schedule so they could find us whenever they needed to. Well, even though there is only a week left of our time there, and we had finished our studies, we still left without permission."

"You could have gone back…" Hillary suggested. With the long-range beam, it took only seconds to go across the country.

"Studying at the university was the means to an end, and unlike every other student there, we were not aiming to walk into high paid jobs. If that had been our intention, we could have taken up any one of two dozen offers - including senior research positions at the WSRA itself."

"But why not at least graduate and take up one of those positions. Don't you still need to keep track of the progress of scientific research? Like you have been doing."

"There will be another way," Krys assured her. "But we don't want to go to work at the WSRA with the full fanfare and become too well known. We will wait several years and apply to work with them via the ground level entry. We will be less conspicuous that way."

"It's your choice," Hillary shrugged. "What would be your qualification if you graduated?"

"We majored in the astro-sciences," Kryslie told her. "So Doctor of Astro-science. It is more prestigious than a PhD."

Hillary finally understood why they didn't want to be well known. Too much would be expected of them and for a time, Tymos, as the highest ranked Tymorean, would be co-ordinating the missionaries.

Chapter 3 - Tymoreans in peril

After moving Rhyn's equipment to the warehouse, they had converted a small section of the top floor into a self-contained apartment. It was furnished in a very basic style, and was little more than two sleeping cubicles, a kitchen/living area, and facilities.

Rarely were both beds slept in at the same time, for since Tymos had taken over Rhyn's duties, he had spent more time visiting the Earth-born missionaries, than at the new base. His travels allowed him to gain an in-depth perception of the political situation within the area covered by the old Eastern Alliance, which was now being called the Imperium.

Kryslie monitored the progress of specific scientific groups including the WRSA and the Defence Development group. Her computer skills had yet to gain her access to the science conclaves of the Imperium, but her brother was keeping alert for potential trouble there. Though she had travelled to various labs in the United World Nations and infiltrated their databases from within their protected firewalls, and now could keep abreast of their plans and monitor their latest results.

In the absence of both, Hillary kept a watch on the warehouse. She also saw to the needs of the two new coordinators, as well as overseeing the financial affairs of the trust set up by the Tymorean missionaries who had returned to Tymorea before the war. The income from the trust funded the operational activities of the missionaries.

Both Tymos and Kryslie kept alert for the imminent arrival of the advance group of Tymorean missionaries. Tymos had devised portable devices to monitor the communications frequencies of their kin. Each now had a tiny receiver implanted in one ear as this might give them the only warning of the new arrivals. The transport ship bringing the missionaries would arrive in full stealth mode and cloaked, so that Earth's military detection systems would not see them. The newcomers would be transmitted down from the high orbit to some deserted and isolated area.

Using her high-tech data padd, Krys worked through Rhyn's computer to infiltrate the computers and communications systems of various military and government agencies in the UWN.

Her program was set to monitor all communications frequencies and to alert her to any indication of desert activity and secret tests. She could not be sure that the location would be within the United World Nations, but logic suggested that since the base was to be in the American region, they would choose to arrive relatively close by.

The first hint of the secret desert tests was the mobilisation of various military units to the New Mexico desert. Kryslie retrieved the full list of personnel being assigned there. In a very short time, she had picked out the perfect military officer to impersonate, and organised a temporarily debilitating accident to one of the senior military security officers. It was a simple exercise to infiltrate the relevant databases and forge the appropriate orders, so that Major Maddison became his replacement in the desert. The real major received ultra secret orders that took her to a remote region of India, to help track down a budding terrorist cabal.

The outstanding achievements of Major Maddison were well established and she already had a high-level security clearance. It had been a minor matter for Kryslie to change her own features slightly, as well as her eye and hair colour, so that her appearance matched the official records.

On arrival, her orders were not questioned. Kryslie took over command of the twenty-four men and women in the security detail and quickly proved her efficiency and skill.

Her team were extremely well trained marine recon officers or navy SEALs and their task during the three weeks leading up to the start of the tests, was to act as ground support for an air search. When indications of human occupation were spotted in the test area, they moved in to relocate the people. Major Maddison proved to have an uncanny knack for finding the fiercely independent desert prospectors.

When the test area was devoid of human presences, the boundaries were 'locked down', and the deployment of the test devices began.

By referring to a confidential list of GPS locations, Kryslie's team took the scientists to each of the designated test locations. There they kept alert while the devices were pre-programmed and secured to the ground. All would be activated remotely from the test command centre.

After all were in place, and the scientists had been returned, Kryslie's team supplemented the perimeter defences. The fenced perimeter of the desert zone was being patrolled by six troops of men, with dogs, as well as being monitored by the very latest security protocols. Should there be an alert, Kryslie's team, would spearhead the investigation.

The defence was not just confined to the boundaries. A security umbrella was initiated, with ground based and satellite detection systems monitoring the airspace over and around the test zone. Aircraft were on alert to scramble at a moments notice should unauthorised observers approach by air.

Major Maddison's team were professionals, but even so, they were curious as to the nature of the test devices. They tended to think they were some kind of weapon, since the security was so tight. Unlike the scientists, they did not think it wrong to keep scientific developments from the nations of the Imperium. They were realists - there might be peace now, and there may have been peace for several decades, but that could change.

Kryslie did not reveal that she knew what the devices were. She would only enlighten her team if they were sent into the test zone after they had been activated. The scientists knew, of course, but they had been sworn to secrecy - just as her team knew where all the units were, but they were not to reveal that knowledge. Even the commando squads, who had the task of locating the devices, would not know what they were seeking until just before they went in.

The secrecy was not just to prevent unauthorised people learning of the tests. It was also so that the search squads had no pre-conceived expectations. As things stood, the searchers had no coordinates to work from and a huge expanse of desert to cover. They would be told the targets, taught to use the detectors, and sent out to locate an unknown number of devices.

The devices were activated just before nightfall. From that time, Kryslie rotated her team between patrolling and sleeping in a prefabricated hut that was checkpoint twelve. From this position, she could hear the three search planes that were beginning the air sweep. Leaving her second in Command to monitor the radios, she went outside and used night glasses to scan the nearby terrain. This was not because she had any hope of seeing the activated devices, but because she had a sense of impending trouble.

The expected arrival of the Tymorean missionaries was on her mind, but so far, she had heard nothing on any of the Tymorean frequencies. The listening device in her ear remained silent.

She considered other possibilities, such as whether agents of the Imperium had heard of the tests. It wasn't impossible. Anything that the UWN military were doing in secret would be of vital interest to the leader of the Imperium.

The devices were force field generators, each creating a semi spherical dome of protection. Within the domes were the latest detector analysers, which would record any light or energy that came through both before and after each dome was stressed to test its strength and beyond.

The military were particularly interested in the force screens for defensive purposes, such as protecting important buildings. They assumed that in time, the Imperium would develop similar technology, or some sect in the UWN might try to use such a screen in a terrorist action. Therefore, in spite of the decades of peace, the military commanders needed to know if it were possible to neutralise the screens and at the same time, how much they could take.

During the night, Kryslie drove along the perimeter road, which was a roughly graded track, two kilometres inside the boundary fence. She stopped at one extreme of her patrol section and turned the truck's lights off. When her eyes had adjusted to the dark, she stepped out of the truck, and did a visual check with the night glasses. None of the sentries from the adjoining section were within view, so there was no chance of her being seen when she climbed onto the roof of the truck.

Using normal binoculars, she looked in the direction of the nearest of the test devices. When they revealed no sign of the force screen, she lowered them and adjusted her eyes to see into the distance. Her eyes were also able to see in the dark, showing the landscape as an even shade of orange, broken by the ridges of rock, which were a duller shade of red. One area drew her attention. Breaking the flat orange glow of the desert sand cooling down, was a pale blue dome - just at the distant horizon. She considered it for a time, and then slowly climbed down from the truck roof.

During the pre-operation briefing, a small-scale force dome was demonstrated. It did not glow, but was visibly perceived as a warping of the air. However, that had been during daylight. She wondered whether the searching planes would see a faint glow at night, or if she saw it only because she was able to see normally invisible energy fields.

The uncertainty worried her, as she drove back. On the way, she requested reports from her team. All was quiet along her section, as well as in all the other sectors.

Back at the checkpoint, she woke the resting marines so they would be ready to replace the next group that were due to have a break. By her own roster, she should be resting too, but she felt that she didn't dare sleep. Still, she handed over to her second in command and lay down on one of the just vacated pallets.

With her eyes closed, she continued to listen to the comms traffic between the planes and the control centre. As each test device was located, the coordinates were sent in code to the command centre.

A team of three commandos went to each location. They were tagged, so that the security sensors recognised them as authorised, and carried with them the equipment to analyse the properties of the force fields.

Anyone detected with in the zone with out a signal tag, would be neutralised. If they were lucky, they would only be arrested and held incommunicado.

Kryslie was keeping count, automatically decoding the figures and locating each set of coordinates on a mental map. Fifteen active devices located, nine were analysed and had the commando groups standing by. The planes had begun the search at the extreme end of the test zone, in the sector she had opted to patrol. From her private calculations, she knew the planes had missed five devices and would have to repeat the search.

Long before her rest period was due to finish, Kryslie was up and pacing the hut. The tone of the communications had changed subtly. Then the search planes were told to be alert. It was as if a warning tone had chimed. She stopped pacing, and waited to hear if her team was needed to investigate intruders. Her second in command was equally tense, and ceded the radio handset to her when she reached for it.

"Control, Maddison, check point twelve. Have you an intruder?"

The reply wasn't instant, and took a minute to come. "It seems not, Major. We had a brief signal from the heat sensors, but it soon vanished. It was likely several animals in a group together and they separated again. Air one is breaking off the search to check. Will advise."

She wasn't reassured. All her senses were resonating with warning. Not only hers; the resting marines were all awake and watching her.

So that her team would not notice anything odd, Kryslie took her night glasses outside and made a scan of the nearby area. She used this action to hide her distraction as she mentally called her twin. She heard the sound of a single plane circling over towards checkpoint 11.

Tymos was standing-by in their warehouse base, and answered her immediately. "I haven't heard anything, or detected anything that should have alerted the military," he told her in answer to her question.

"Something has got them edgy," Kryslie thought at him, and she shared the subtle sense of increased alertness with him through their twin bond. "They had a brief touch on the heat sensors, and then nothing. They think it was animals in a group."

Tymos sent back, thoughtfully, "I will check if the satellites picked up anything." He wasn't discounting her apparent paranoia.

A few minutes later, he sent, "The satellites did not pick up any suspicious transmissions, but two of them did have a brief signal dropout, as if something occluded it."

The same thought occurred to them both. The Tymorean transport ship could have caused it. The missionaries might have landed. The test commanders might fear an intruder.

Still, they had not issued a security alert…

Kryslie suddenly had the need to do something. She returned to the hut, and told her second she was going on patrol along the road. The resting marines gave up any pretence of sleep. This time she took a portable comm. link, and one of the two motorbikes that were for quick travel to either of the adjoining checkpoints. She started the bike and headed towards where the plane was circling.

Half way there, she heard the pilot give a negative report. He was over the test device and found only the three, tagged commandos. He was returning to the airstrip to refuel, change pilots and then the plane would rejoin the search.

Although the report was reassuring, Kryslie felt impelled to keep going. She wanted to check the area for herself - as best she could while staying on the perimeter road. She dared not move off it or she would trigger an alarm.

She stopped at the limit of her area, and found a sentry from checkpoint 11 there. After an exchange of code words, she asked, "Have you seen anything?"

"Negative, Major. Must have been a glitch," the man sounded resigned. "These tests have got everyone on edge."

Kryslie used her own night glasses to scan the area. She didn't have the same height advantage this time to increase her visual range, but she realised with a shock that she didn't need it. Slightly to one side of the line towards the nearest test device, she could see another force dome. This one had a mauve glow and she knew at once that it was Tymorean. She lowered the glasses. The plane had not detected it, but it had been looking for intruders here not a second force dome. When the plane came back to search for the still unfound test devices, it would be found.

The other sentry took his leave of her, returning to his patrol. Kryslie turned her bike as if to do likewise, but she was thinking at her twin. "They're down, under a force dome. So far they haven't been noticed, but it was close. They showed on the infrared, briefly, and the test commanders are wary. It was luck that the plane that came to check wasn't using the new sensors."

Tymos asked about the progress of the tests.

"They have only completed three quarters of the search area," Kryslie told him. "They will have to repeat it as they have missed several of the devices. How long the missionaries have to get clear will depend on where they start the repeat pattern. We don't dare send a warning."

Tymos agreed. "They won't be expecting any verbal communications nor will they send any. Can you try to reach Olassa? I know she isn't telepathic, but you might be able to make her hurry."

Kryslie flicked a rapid agreement, but decided to move back towards her checkpoint. After going several miles, she stopped again and turned the bike's headlight off. Without dismounting, she kept the bike upright, as she tried to get a message through to Olassa, who was the group leader of the advance missionaries. Nothing. The Tymorean woman was concentrating on getting the long-range beam projector assembled.

The memory of Rhyn's dying vision returned to her, and she saw the missionaries being killed. She would not allow that. Some of her desperation accompanied her attempts to reach Olassa. She sensed that the Tymorean woman was beginning to feel the need to hurry, and had translated it as a warning of danger. Kryslie was looking through the night glasses at the Tymorean screen and saw it flick off for a microsecond, and come back on.

Had they seen the other force dome?

Kryslie could not be sure, but she kept mentally urging Olassa to hurry. The Tymoreans would not be expecting to have arrived amidst a military operation. They would be expecting to be in an isolated area, and have time to disburse to the pre-determined coordinates. They would be feeling secure in the small bubble of the force screen because it would hide them from sight and be protection from solid objects.

Knowledge of the procedure for the missionaries came to her, and she instinctively timed how long it would take the skilled advanced missionaries to assemble the long-range beam, and transmit the individual missionaries away. Too long, she realised with dread. The power source for the beam would need time to recharge between sendings.

She dared not intervene to help them. If she left the road, she would bring too much attention to the area. If Olassa or the others saw her, she could create a time paradox. For the same reason, she could not try to signal the transport ship, even if it had not departed already. There may yet be no problem…but Rhyn had seen most of them dying…and before she had left Tymorea, so many years in her subjective past, she had heard of deaths…but not how many.

Kryslie travelled slowly back towards the checkpoint. The planes completed the search pattern and landed to refuel. The pilots were relieved, but others took over. They had five more targets to find. Dawn was less than an hour off.

She had the first inkling of dire trouble when the planes found the twenty-fifth target. A shiver of premonition ran through her as she heard the control room requesting clarification of coordinates, as they believed that one of the new targets had already been located. She didn't wait for the reply; she revved the bike to maximum speed and raced for the checkpoint. She was contacted just as she arrived.

"Perimeter leader," a burst of signal impinged on Kryslie's receiver.

"Perimeter leader," Krys acknowledged.

"Position?"

Kryslie gave it as the checkpoint.

"Possible bogey, sector 117. Coordinates…. Proceed to rendezvous with team zeta."

"Confirmed," Krys said.

The Tymorean force dome was the target of the investigation. As she raced towards the hut, she made a mental picture of Olassa, Xyron's niece, and projected a thought at her. The resting team of marines were now racing out towards the truck.

Olassa had a sudden, urgent, premonition of peril. As Bevan prepared to leave, she dared to drop the force field for another second and took a look around. What she saw through her scanning goggles confirmed the need to hurry. Vehicles belonging to the Earth military were rapidly approaching and they had weapons capable of breaching her protective shield. The shield went back up.

"Juve, go with Bevan. We have company coming. We need to get away, and we can sort ourselves out later."

It was pushing the limits of the beam's specifications to send two people, but she had no choice. With the Earth military preparing to surround them – they could not afford to be caught together.

There was no panic. The missionaries were highly trained, and prepared for every contingency.

The screen around them began to glow.

"They are trying to destroy it," Olassa said, calmly changing the coordinates and sending the next two off as if nothing was wrong.

The shield was not completely solid, because they had to transmit through it. And though it was well constructed and powered, it was not expected to be stressed like it was.

"Down!" she ordered at the instant that she judged that the shield would fail. A wash of heat passed over the eight remaining Tymoreans. Olassa raised her head slightly and saw the humans moving in, now that the barrage of energy had stopped. She counted them – nine – nearly even odds.

Kryslie stayed back as the three commandos of team zeta, and the six marines from checkpoint 12 encircled the dome and began to fire energy weapons at it. Her job was observer and reporting to field HQ.

The commandos approached the prone bodies that had been within the shield. The eight figures suddenly sprang up and began to fight like demons. The lead commando had a second to send a report, but the advantage was with the Tymoreans. They quickly disarmed and stunned their opponents, then set about ensuring the weapons were harmless.

"Power!" Kryslie thought at Olassa, as field HQ warned her of an incoming concussion missile.

She heard Olassa warn the Tymoreans that she could hear a missile coming. As one, they dropped the last of their opponents' weapons and began to run, drawing on their Tymorean power to increase their speed. Even so, the shock wave knocked them down.

Kryslie had dropped into a ball before the missile impacted. She was prepared for the compression wave, clinging to the ground, even as the pressure wave shoved her truck several metres further from her. The instant the effect passed, she rose and went to check her team. They were unconscious, but because they had been prone when the pressure wave hit, they would have escaped the worst effects.

Looking around to check she was unobserved, she continued to where the Tymoreans had fallen and felt for a pulse in the nearest — relieved to find it was strong.

She reported only that the infiltrators were stunned but alive, and her team and the commandos were unfit for further action. Already she could hear a helicopter approaching with reinforcements.

The back-up team dropped from the side hatch of the low flying helicopter and immediately began to immobilise the infiltrators. The helo continued on to land next to the unconscious marines and commandos.

A medical team tended the soldiers first and then went to check the prisoners.

Kryslie received orders to coordinate a search of the area. The military tests were cancelled until the following night. She waited as the helicopter departed with the injured soldiers, and a second helicopter arrived with a further dozen marines. That helicopter took off with the prisoners.

Chapter 4 - Rescue

Kryslie reported mentally to her brother, as the reinforcements sorted themselves into groups.

"I am picking up agitated signals between the missionaries that got away," Tymos told her.

"We have made a difference," Kryslie stressed. "Only eight were caught, not nearly all of them as in Rhyn's vision. They are all alive and being taken to the regional HQ, not the field HQ. Can you arrange for orders to be issued that will pull me, Major Maddison, in from the field?"

"Good as done, Sis," Tymos promised.

The orders were given several hours later – after the search was completed. No signs of other infiltrators were found. The devices located at the site of the destroyed dome, had been collected by Kryslie who knew exactly how to damage them so that they wouldn't work again.

She finally reached Regional HQ and after being debriefed, kept a low profile. Her orders were to fly out to the Eastern HQ on the first flight the following morning. Major Maddison's involvement in the desert tests was terminated. However, her personal interest was not, and she waited until after the next shift change to approach the security cells.

The guards recognised her rank, but challenged her authority to approach the prisoners. Kryslie was not perturbed, and asked instead if the prisoners had been searched and if so, where any confiscated items were to be found. She claimed to have orders to examine any objects carried by the prisoners.

The guards relaxed and told her exactly where to go. Kryslie thanked them and departed at a casual pace. When out of sight, she ran quickly to the secure storage location.

Kryslie entered the area stealthily and found the 'secure' safe easy to open. As she predicted, the missionaries had their created identification papers and a small amount of created currency. She didn't touch these, but took only the eight palm-sized metallic devices that the searchers had not been able to identify. She recognised them as Tymorean transmitters.

She closed the safe and used one of the devices to leave without setting off any alarms.

Then she approached the cells again, stealthily, and used her Tymorean power to hide her from human sight. She inched close to the guards and karate chopped the neck of each in quick succession. Then she had to move fast.

She already knew where the prisoners were, went quickly to the first of the two cells.

The four Tymoreans in that cell had recovered from the stun grenade. They were ready to take advantage of any circumstance to escape.

Kryslie transmitted into the room – surprising them with her sudden appearance on the far side of the cell. She didn't speak, as she jumped up and caught the base of the security camera. She twisted the lens upward before landing and going to break the metal restraints on the prisoners. She silently handed out four of the metal devices. The prisoners didn't recognise her, but intuited that she must be Tymorean. They wasted no time transmitting out of the building. Kryslie knew they would not have trouble blending into the human population. It might take them a while to link up to the others, but they were free.

Kryslie transmitted out of that cell as alarms began ringing. Knowing that she had limited time, she found the second chamber and transmitted in. In her haste, she hadn't scanned the space for more than a sense of Tymoreans. Fortunately, none of the three soldiers present saw her materialise out of the air but her presence was quickly noticed and challenged.

"Four of the prisoners have escaped," Krys distracted them. "I am detailed to back you up until others arrive." Since she was inside the locked room, they assumed she had the electronic code to get in. Her rank leant credence to her words, and the interrogators continued to work.

Kryslie quickly summed up the situation. The three Tymoreans were tied to chairs and wired up with the latest in lie detection equipment and 'incentive' devices to encourage them speak. However, their Tymorean power would neutralise most of those effects, and the three men were well able to confuse the interrogators. The main reason they hadn't yet tried to free themselves was the presence of a drug that caused intense physical weakness. In time, and faster than the humans would expect, they would metabolise the drug.

Krys scanned the room for the security camera, and moved to be under it and out of its range of view. She waited until the three questioners were looking away from her and gave a, "Do not move" command to their minds. An instant later, she had jumped up and snapped the camera from its mount.

Krys's main concern was that there might be orders to terminate the infiltrators if no information could be obtained from them. Either that, or they would be taken to some high security detention facility. While the soldiers were still immobile, she went to the bench containing the array of drugs and identified the one used on the prisoners to make them physically helpless. She filled another syringe and approached the nearest questioner. She injected him without warning. He toppled and Krys caught him and eased him down.

She repeated the action with the other two men and then spent a few moments, touching the foreheads of the three interrogators, to make their minds forget they saw her.

Then as thudding sounded on the locked door, she called her brother and in moments, a long-range beam was activated. She did not waste time freeing the prisoners, just hefted the first man and chair into the floating mauve beam terminus, transmitted to Tymos, and then returned for the next. As soon as she returned after the fourth trip, she slumped to the floor, apparently unconscious like the others.

Questions were asked when she awoke, cursing under her breath. Her answers were so logical and reasonable that for a time they accepted them. It helped that she was believed to have a very high security clearance - equal to the HQ Commander. On that basis, she was sent to ensure the safety of the remaining prisoner whilst the base personnel went hunting a man dressed in uniform, but with slightly incorrect rank insignia, that she had described in detail.

Olassa awoke - face down on a cold, slightly dusty, concrete floor. She hurt all over, and only the knowledge that the rest of her team were relying on her, forced her to move. She tried to use her power to dull the pain as she had been taught, but she could not make it happen. She had to get the others free – had to.

She was the most powerful, supposed to be the best, but there had been too many human soldiers and in the end, the humans had won. But why was she still so weak?

Her mind recalled the fight in the desert and then the concussion missile. She had recovered from the concussion while being driven in some kind of ground vehicle. She tried to take it over - there had been four guards, not too bad odds. She disabled the two guards watching them in the rear of the truck, and was fighting the driver and the other guard, then... the vehicle had swerved off the road and stopped. She had returned to the rear of the truck to help her fellow missionaries and...she recalled the pain, exploding through her. A projectile weapon, she realised. Then more guards had slammed her to the ground, and she had kept fighting, even through a haze of pain. They had kept punching her until she lost consciousness.

Olassa rolled onto her side and tried to sit up. The sharp pain in her right shoulder made it difficult. She dragged herself to the wall so it would support her. Her left hand felt for the wound. There was a dressing on it, but her fingers came away red. It was still oozing blood.

A lesser being would have given up, but she was Governor Xyron's niece and too many Tymoreans were depending on her. She had to think.

She let her weight sag against the wall. It felt like stone, except that it was too smooth. The only window in the six-foot square cell was high up, and had bars across it. It was too high to see through, even if she could stand.

There was nothing to stand on anyway, except the odd shaped personal waste disposal unit. If she had any strength, she would wrench it from the floor and use it as a weapon...but she was as weak as a small child.

Her mind continued to plan, and think of possible opportunities to get free. She couldn't give up. At least she had managed to get two thirds of her group away, but she had to help the others. She couldn't even call Homebase for help. She had lost the only comm. unit that was able to send that far. The others only had the short range, planetary comm. units.

Would the missionaries who had got away try to rescue her? She hoped not, but they had no way to get back to her and no way to find her. No, they couldn't help - she had to think of something else. The humans would come to question her soon, if they had a way to tell that she was awake again.

The sound of a lock opening made her glance at the door, but even twisting that much hurt her shoulder.

The door opened and two of the human soldiers entered with weapons poised. They were in mottled green coveralls, not dissimilar in style to what she was wearing. Both of the men had wrap around eye protection and kept their gaze on her.

Olassa sighed inwardly. If they had heard how well she had fought, they would be taking no chances. Instinctively, she moved her uninjured arm so that her hand could feel the pockets of her brown coveralls. The handiest pocket was empty. She glanced down and saw that all of her pockets had been cut open.

When she looked up again, two high-ranking soldier types had entered her cell and were watching her futile gesture. She studied the fancy stuff on the drab khaki uniforms, and recalled her briefing on the rank insignias.

Her first guess was confirmed when the tall man spoke. She ignored his demand that she tell him her name, and studied the shorter woman beside him. A shiver went through her. The woman was the same one who had witnessed the fight in the desert. She would have seen how well the Tymoreans had fought. Yet, the woman's face was betraying nothing - no emotion, no anticipation, no pity or even anger towards the prisoner. That made Olassa very uneasy. She could not read the woman's body language.

The man was getting angry. His edgy little movements were a give-away. He was an open book, and the higher-ranking soldier.

"What were you doing in the desert," the man was now asking. Olassa recalled he had said he was a general. "How did you get past our patrols?"

Olassa stayed silent. There was no safe answer to that. She glanced again at the woman, and saw for an instant that her face was blank - not merely expressionless.

"Who do you work for?" the man was persisting. "Who made that force dome that you were in? What organisation do you work for?"

Something cold swirled in Olassa's gut. How did the humans know about force fields and protective shields? Her briefing had not mentioned that humans knew of such things… but it had been a century since the previous missionaries had left. Homebase needed to know this…needed to be warned before the builders arrived. Yet even free, she had no way to warn them.

There was an interruption. A lower ranking soldier entered the cell and spoke to the General.

"Excuse me, Sir; the C-I-C is on the phone from the Pentagon."

"See what you can find out, Major," the General ordered, before turning sharply to leave the cell and return to his office.

Kryslie watched Olassa, hiding the sympathy she felt.

"Wait outside," she ordered crisply, not turning to see if the two guards obeyed her, but she kept silent until they had.

Olassa met the eyes of the woman defiantly. This one had 'presence', and ...what was happening?

It seemed like the air was vanishing from the room. What was the woman doing?

She had secured the door and taken something oval shaped from her pocket.

"What is your name?"

Once again, Olassa ignored the question. She glanced into every corner of the cell that she could see without twisting. The woman came closer, seemingly unafraid that the prisoner might jump up and fight.

The hand flick was so fast that Olassa almost missed it. The roar of an explosion followed immediately, as the woman fell onto her and began to reach for something in her pocket.

The sound was still ringing in her ears as she found herself lifted with ease. She had enough awareness to note that the rubble had come inward, before she felt a familiar sensation of being transmitted elsewhere. She fainted.

It was as well for her piece of mind that she recognised the red headed man leaning over her. Instinct made her turn around, and only the Great One's calm manner kept her from trying to attack the woman soldier, standing in front of a curtained window.

"Great One, thank you. How did you know we needed help?" Olassa said quickly, speaking in Tymorean.

"An Elder had a vision," Tymos told her gently. "Relax, Olassa, the others are safe. Three of them are here sleeping. The other four are fidgeting with worry about you. That is, in spite of my assurance that they were safe and I had the matter in hand."

Olassa noticed that Great One Tymos did not seem annoyed by the lack of trust.

"If you can manage a moment to reassure them, I will be able to do something about those injuries."

Olassa nodded and let herself sink back on the soft bed. She tried to relax, to ease the pain surging through her. She flinched when a gentle hand touched her arm, undoing all she had achieved.

The uniform was the same, but the face and hair were now different.

"Great One Kryslie," Olassa said with reverence.

"Just Kryslie. Now, lie still. I can ease the pain for you a little."

"Why are you both here? I did not think you were coming until later."

"It's a long story," Kryslie said casually. She was concentrating on controlling the flow of power into Olassa.

"You blew the wall out," Olassa realised. "And made it look like it blew in – that was impressive."

Kryslie grinned at her. "I had to make it look like humans rescued you. It wouldn't do to just disappear from a locked room. They may suspect Major Maddison, but the real major can prove where she was, and there is no way to link her to me. Not that it matters. They will not find me."

Tymos returned with his four active guests. They were still dazed by the fight, capture, and rescue but had changed into locally made clothing. Their relief at seeing Olassa was unfeigned.

When they had transmitted away from the military building, they had kept moving in line of sight flits until they thought they were far enough away to be safe. Then they had tried to contact the others who had transmitted away safely. Within moments of their signalling, a soft voice behind them had startled them. All four had spun around, ready for a fight. It was fortunate that Ewain had recognised Great One Tymos. They were all relieved to be taken to a place of certain safety.

The four Tymoreans expressed their relief that Olassa was safe, and were not surprised to see Kryslie with her. It took them a while longer to realise that she was the one who had returned their transmitters.

Ewain voiced his thoughts. "Great One, thank you for helping us. I apologise for not recognising you. I did not realise you were following us."

Kryslie smiled. Ewain wondered if it was disrespectful to think she looked smug.

"The Guardians of Peace warned us of the trouble, in time for us to act," Kryslie told him. "We accept your thanks and ask only that you don't mention our presence in any of your communications to Homebase. They do not know we are here and we would prefer them to think that you sorted out the problem without help."

Ewain grinned. If that was what the Great Ones wanted, it was fine with him. He preferred not to recall the recent embarrassing episode.

Kryslie shooed them out of the bedroom after Olassa assured them she would be all right.

Tymos had departed and returned after the men had retreated to watching a local tri-vid show in the sparsely furnished living room. He had what looked like a field medi-kit and she realised that he was intending to check her wound.

"Bevan is a doctor, Great One," she told him.

"Bevan is better off where he is," Tymos assured her. "We are not very far from a stingers nest of very angry human militia. If I can't deal with this, I can bring in a very trustworthy local doctor."

Olassa bit off any further comment; it was easy to forget Tymos was a Great One and that she had no right to question him.

Kryslie actually removed the dressing and washed the ugly wound that Olassa could just see if she lifted her head. The water, cloths and antiseptic had been in the room since Olassa arrived.

"Lie down!" Kryslie told her sternly. "It is a mess, but at least they had someone remove the bullet. That was our main worry. While we know a lot about medicine, we have never tried our hand at surgery. How does it feel now? Any pain?"

"No, it is numb, not painful at all."

"Good. I have discovered I have a talent for starting wounds to heal. Tymos can do more. You can help by lying very still. Sleep if you can."

Olassa closed her eyes and relaxed her body. It was easy now that the pain had gone. She felt gentle hands on her forehead and on her shoulder. Then she began to feel the tingling heat at the site of the wound and wondered what Tymos was doing. She opened her eyes and saw a look of concentration on his face.

In an instant of comprehension, she realised he was using his power to heal her. How did she rate that honour?

"Hello sleepy," Kryslie greeted cheerfully, bringing in a light snack for Olassa. "You have had a good long sleep and if you promise to take things easy – you can go."

"Where will you be if I want to call you," Olassa asked.

"Not here," Krys told her. "Our lease runs out in a week. Then we will be back where we were."

"Where is that? Home?"

"No," Krys shook her head. Instead of answering the question, she said, "When you are up to it, we need to have a serious discussion."

"I think I am ready now," Olassa sat up gingerly. Tymos seemed to enter as if summoned.

"You heard us tell the others that we didn't want them to mention our being here in communications back to home...?" Tymos asked.

Olassa nodded.

"That is because we do not want to cause a time paradox. This is going to sound strange, but we have not left Tymorea yet. We moved up the date for the rest of the missionaries to come – they will now arrive with the builders. We actually left with them, but we have been in this time for seven years now."

As soon as Olassa's mind accepted the time paradox, Tymos stunned her again with a brief outline of their transition. He saw her excitement when he told her of the Tymorean descendents still working on this world.

"We have reports from them, made over the past one hundred years. We have summarised the major events with commentary. I would like you to send the reports home. We will keep in contact with you at intervals. I have a written report of our transition. When the others arrive, we want you to give it to Vincent and Daniel and assure them we are well. We will contact them as soon as we can after they arrive. Please don't mention the descendants of the missionaries. I will arrange for the integration of the two groups. Finally, please tell Daniel that there is a vast cavern system under the site chosen for the base. When he goes down there, he will find a shield generator that needs to be activated as soon as possible. The base will be vulnerable to the human technology until he does."

Olassa nodded. The humans had found her, and her force screen had not withstood their weapons.

Kryslie added, "There is a second machine there, it is designed to extract energy from the isotopic emissions and transmute it into energy to power the base. Daniel knows we were working on the idea before we left."

Olassa had many questions and Tymos answered most of them. To some, he only gave her a slight smile.

Finally, "Great One, I will do all that, gladly, but I no longer have the means to contact Homebase. I must have lost it in the desert."

Tymos glanced at Kryslie.

"All of the equipment that was left at the landing site is inoperative," Kryslie answered the question her twin was thinking of. "I couldn't take it, and there was very little time. It wasn't in the secure lock up with their transmitters."

Tymos returned his attention to Olassa. "What frequency will you and your team be working on? Or are you using one of the Tymorean heterodyned and encrypted systems?"

Olassa gave him the specifications for both the local comm. units and the intersystem comm. unit.

"I will have one for you before you leave," Tymos promised her. He grinned as Olassa's mouth dropped open in surprise, and it broadened when she visibly stopped herself from asking questions about how he would get one.

Kryslie took pity on her. "Before we came here, we had free access to everything in your Uncle's scientific and technical archives. And we spent five of our years here filling in the gaps where we lacked data. Our helpers are using the same sort of technology now. Changing the specs…will probably take Tym less than five minutes."

With sudden passion, Olassa blurted, "Great One, let us help you."

Tymos understood her feelings, but he gently declined the offer.

"Olassa, you can help us most by doing as you originally planned. We have helpers, and even so, Krys and I can only be in two places. With your team dispersed, we will have eyes and ears in many more locations."

"As you wish, Great One," Olassa acquiesced.

"Then let us get your mission back on track. I will see to the communicator first, and then I will see to getting your people where they need to go. All the others have recovered enough to travel by long-range beam." Olassa mentally shrugged and resisted the urge to ask where he had obtained a long-range beam. No doubt he was capable of making one.

Chapter 5 - Dangerous Investigations

Once the missionaries were all safely away, having travelled first to the warehouse base where the long-range beam generator was installed, and then to their various destinations, Tymos and Kryslie returned to their interrupted tasks. They both knew that the builders who were coming to set up the base and the main group of missionaries would arrive within weeks but they could not be sure of the exact time.

Tymos returned to the other side of the world, where he was monitoring the activities of various groups that were controlled by Abdul bin Halil, the leader of the Imperium.

Kryslie kept aware of the after-reaction to the desert tests. She obtained the specifications of the detectors used to detect the test force-domes and kept a close watch on the radioactive zone where the Tymorean base was to be built. She knew the scientist that had developed the detectors; it was Dr Emmanuel with whom she had worked at the WSRA University. In fact, she had helped him create an earlier version, and from the specs knew that the new detectors were capable of much more than the creators yet realised.

When marines were deployed around the 350 km perimeter of the devastated missile-landing zone, Kryslie was instantly on the alert. It confirmed where the next series of tests were to be conducted, and even though she did not yet know the start date, it would be soon.

She would know when anyone actually entered the zone, for she and Tymos had placed several rings of detectors at various distances inside the official boundary.

The fence that marked the exclusion zone was five kilometres beyond the point where the ambient radiation was low enough to have no adverse effects on humans or creatures.

It was intended to keep unauthorised people from entering the zone, though occasionally people did - with the misguided idea that the government was hiding something there.

Until now, Kryslie had let the authorities deal with trespassers. Neither party would have found anything. Now though, with the arrival of the Tymoreans imminent, it was another matter altogether. She needed to be on the scene, to prevent inadvertent discoveries.

When the sensors detected people five kilometres inside the boundary, Kryslie was ready to act. She put all the equipment at the warehouse on automatic, so any reports that came in would be recorded, and took the remote access device with her as she transmitted by the long-range beam to the town nearest the radiation site.

It had only been eight o'clock in the morning when she left, but it was nearly ten in the time zone where Hope Valley was located. Her arrival point was the mouth of a natural cave, in the ridge of a rock upthrust across the valley from the exclusion zone perimeter. It was about two kilometres from the only official entrance gate into the blast zone.

She didn't need to adjust her eyes to see that a them to watch the purposeful activity. Civilians were unloading equipment from trucks, and storing it in the various buildings.

As she watched, she observed the security patrols and mentally timed their rounds. The military jeeps came into view along the only road into the area, and travelled in either direction along the "no man's land" dead zone that made up most of the valley. She saw them drive slowly, scanning the rocky ridge through binoculars. She had no concern about being seen, since she could withdraw into the cave, or stay still, and they would not see her.

From her knowledge of the security for the desert tests, she expected that the whole perimeter of the blast zone would be being patrolled, but that didn't matter. This small area was all that concerned her. Anyone foolish enough to try to penetrate the zone elsewhere risked being shot by the patrols.

That idea did give her a shiver of warning. Someone could possibly scale the fence and approach the scientist's camp along the narrow safe zone. They could be two or three kilometres in, and not visible from the fence.

She used her remote access device to send a message to one of the new missionaries who was recovering from a broken arm and living in the town.

He gave her the coordinates for house he was renting, and Kryslie transmitted from the ridge to his living room.

The young man, now going by the name of Jerry Hull, was able to tell her all she needed to know.

"Great One, the Earth militia arrived in force two nights ago. From what I have heard, they put in a huge order for supplies from the local food market. The truck that went to deliver it was stopped two miles short of where the sealed road normally ends. The soldiers searched it, and then took over the driving to where it was going."

"What about the scientists?" Kryslie asked.

"Them? They just got here this morning. Flew in by one of those hovercopter things. All their gear came yesterday by army truck."

Kryslie considered that - one of the scientists hadn't wasted time entering the zone. "You've been here about a month now," she said thoughtfully. "Have you noticed or heard of any strangers wanting to look at the zone?"

Jerry gave her a shrug. "I couldn't tell if people here are strangers or not. I've heard plenty of tales from the locals about the crazies that come here. What type of stranger do you want to know about?"

"Foreigners, ones who don't speak American."

Jerry shrugged again.

"The people I am concerned about would be skilled enough to blend in," Kryslie admitted, feeling frustration. "Get out and listen to the gossip, will you? Call me on the alternate frequency if you hear anything."

"Yes, Great One," Jerry agreed at once, and he went to get his jacket.

Kryslie concentrated on her twin and sent him a mental call. It made no difference to her sending and reception that he was halfway around the globe.

She told him where she was, and asked, "Have you had any hint of anti-UWN activity out here?"

Tymos didn't answer immediately, and his mind tone was thoughtful. "Out there, no. But I have had hints that activities are planned. Nothing concrete, but you should be alert for Imperium agents trying to infiltrate sensitive UWN places. They have heard of the desert tests and some of the odd events."

"And what is bin Halil's reaction?" Kryslie was interested to know.

"He wants to know who the people were," Tymos summarised. "My guess he thinks they are trying for a power play. Do you need me out there?"

"No, bro. The chief scientist is our friend Doc Emanuel. I am going to go and visit him, and monitor his experiments," Kryslie assured him. "I will have to go as myself, so he can vouch for me. I'll keep in touch."

It would not do to transmit past the security perimeter, but Kryslie did transmit to a point halfway along the road, intending to walk from there. She knew the area well and arrived in a compact clearing amongst the trees growing beside the road. From there, she emerged after checking that no other people were in sight. Her pace up the road was casual, as if she were just out for a day's hike. When she came into view of the sentries at the temporary road barrier, she did not attempt to hide.

Two of the duty marines were known to her from her stint in the desert, but they would never connect her to her Major Maddison role.

"Halt! This is a restricted area." The soldier challenged her with his weapon ready to be raised to fire. "No one is permitted to enter here without permission from Doctor Emmanuel."

"I am aware of what this area is," Kryslie told him calmly. "I am a former student of Doctor Emmanuel and I helped design the suits his people are wearing."

"ID papers," he directed abruptly.

She withdrew her outdated student identity card, as well as a fabricated ID that gave her a high position in an elite Government 'think tank'. "Please inform the Doctor that I am here."

A second soldier took the identity cards whilst the first continued to watch the woman who had appeared so unexpectedly. The first moved into a small hut just off the road, and used a radio to call the scientist's camp. Within a very short time, he returned, handing her ID card's back.

"The Doctor recognises your name. He is sending someone down to check your identity." He beckoned her forward, allowing her to pass the barrier, but go no further.

Five minutes later, a dusty jeep came roaring along road to the guard post. It skidded to a stop just back from the sentries.

Kryslie, standing in the open, recognised Dr Emmanuel at once and grinned as he jumped from the jeep with the vigour of a much younger man and strode over to her.

"It is good to see you again, Krys," he greeted, shaking her hand. His delight was unfeigned.

"Come up to the camp," he urged her towards the jeep. "I am trying to iron out a glitch in one of the detector programs – perhaps you can help?"

"Happy to," Krys assured him. She was aware of the guards relaxing.

"Here – you drive. I hate these confounded jeeps."

Krys drove at a more sedate pace along the road, and slowed even further once she reached the bulldozed dirt track.

"What the heck are you doing here?" Emmanuel challenged. "You caused quite a stir, leaving the Uni as you did. But how did you know I was working here and why come now?"

Krys ignored the implied question of her leaving the Uni and answered the second, but only partly.

"As it happens, I am studying the radiation around here. I have a ring of detectors in place. When I detected people entering the danger zone, I came to investigate. When I realised it was you and your team, I hoped you wouldn't mind me coming to see you."

"I am glad you did," Emmanuel admitted. Then scientific interest distracted him. "What aspect are you studying?"

"The possibility of transmuting the radiation into a useable form of energy," Kryslie said easily. She was quite prepared to discuss such a project with him and did so on the drive back as it kept his mind from other questions.

In fact, the idea intrigued him so much that it was only when he was on the verge of sleep that night that Emmanuel realised that she had not explained her abrupt departure from the university. He suspected that she wouldn't.

Kryslie was introduced to his team and was immediately drawn in to help fixing the programming glitch Emmanuel had mentioned. She made the process take longer than needed, since she was trying to delay Emmanuel's experiments. During the process, she learnt that the scientist was intending to insert detectors and force shields at intervals further into the radiation blast zone than anyone had previously. He had a range of shields, and he wanted to test how effectively each one blocked the radiation at the higher levels.

The detectors under the shields, would measure the amount of radiation getting through, and this would be compared to the levels recorded on unshielded detectors.

Emmanuel had plotted an arbitrary line from the camp to the centre of the blast zone. He told Krys that he intended to place them at three hundred metre intervals along that line.

Early the following day, Emmanuel was suiting up in preparation to enter the restricted zone, when Krys received a thought from her brother. "They are here already, Krys. They arrived last night. I just heard from Olassa."

"I am with Emmanuel and his group. He is going to place more detectors with protective force screens into radiation zone. I can't leave. His new equipment can do more than he realises. He is intending to set the detectors to record radioactivity levels. That isn't the problem. It is the screens on the detectors that give a picture image of the ambient levels," Krys thought back.

"I can't leave here either," Tym reported. "Let us hope Daniel activates the shield soon. Is Emmanuel likely to see the base?"

"His equipment is sensitive enough, and if he has it angled at the right direction there would be an outline," Krys reported. "He is intending to head directly into the centre of the zone, and there is not much in the way of vegetation to block his detectors. And after that business in the desert, if he detects something out here, he will report it."

"Well, keep an eye on him, sis," Tymos urged.

"Of course!" Krys assured him.

"Doctor, you are not planning on proceeding alone," Krys commented when it was apparent that no one else was going to suit up. "Who knows the dangers that may exist further in, besides the radiation?"

"I have great faith in this suit," Emmanuel eyed Krys, who had indeed helped him develop it. "However I will not force anyone to accompany me if they don't share that faith."

From the guilty looks on the dozen faces, it was obvious that all the members in this group had doubts. She forgave the youngest pair, who looked to be first year students from the university. The others were older and should have experienced the suits before.

"Do you have a spare?" Kryslie asked, knowing that Emmanuel had hoped she would offer. She hadn't wanted to seem too eager to volunteer.

A grin from the scientist indicated an affirmative, and he waved one of his students off to get it.

As Kryslie donned the borrowed suit, she asked, "Do you have any bio-monitors?"

"They will not be able to send signals through the radiation," Emmanuel reminded her. "Even the communicators will be useless after three kilometres."

"On the contrary, Doctor," Kryslie chose to argue. "The bio-monitor signals are carried on a highly focussed microburst. They should be receivable from further away, even through the radiation. I agree that the communications signals won't but with the bio-monitors, your staff will be able to monitor our well being even when we are out of radio range."

It was all very logical and hard to dispute its value. Emmanuel sent one of his students to find the devices and another to set up the receiver. Kryslie deliberately spent some time fine-tuning the receiver for greater efficiency.

While she delayed their entry to the zone, Kryslie was wondering what stage the base was at. They would be setting up the dome first and activating the first of the protective screens. She was delaying Emmanuel as much as she could without rousing his suspicions. But how soon would Daniel learn of, find and activate the extra shield she and Tymos had made?

Having no way to find out, and since Tymos couldn't get there, she would just have to keep herself between the base and his detectors.

Emmanuel intended to walk into the radiation zone, since it would be difficult to decontaminate a jeep. Krys ensured she carried the heaviest of the equipment since Emmanuel was not a young man. They entered through the barrier and followed original line of detectors.

"I checked these first thing," Emmanuel told her over the suit communicators. "They have been here since the fence was put up and are still operating properly. It was thought they were beginning to malfunction, but it seems that the radiation levels are slowly dropping."

Kryslie was keeping most of her attention on the track ahead, looking to see if she could spot the Tymorean base. She intended to keep her companion distracted. "The missile came down thirty or forty years ago, didn't it?"

Emmanuel didn't immediately recall her perfect memory, just that she was young and probably hadn't been born at the time. "Thirty years, nigh on. Looks like our guesses for how long the radiation would take to go were pretty well spot on. These readings will help us check if that has changed."

They considered that subject for most of the way to the end of the detector line.

Once they reached there, Kryslie took on the task of spacing the new ones using a hand held GPS to check their distance and direction. Then as Emmanuel recorded the equipment numbers for each shielded detector and unscreened control, as well as the location details of each placement, she set the devices up. Emmanuel tested each one, needing to use the screen to observe the diagnostic. Every time, Kryslie stayed between his detector and the centre of the zone where the Tymorean base was located. Then she took baseline measurements and read them to the scientist to record.

They were gradually descending into the area where the missile had landed. This part wasn't flat, but a series of concentric ridges and valleys - like ripples on a pond. The ground kept gradually rising and falling as they went in towards ground zero. Here they passed the petrified blackened remains of the once giant pine trees. Few were still vertical, most had fallen over, pointing away from the blast.

When they had extended the detector line a further two and a half kilometres, Kryslie suggested that was far enough. Any further and there would be a greater danger of the equipment registering an anomaly for they had almost reached the crest of the last low ridge. Beyond that crest was the vast crater where the ground had been molten and solidified, and there was nothing to block a line of sight detector.

Emmanuel was keen to place one more, while they were in there, but Krys had cautioned that they had spent long enough in the 'hotter' radiation and although the suits internal monitors still showed safe levels, they should return and recheck the suits to be sure they were not building up to an overload.

He had not protested too much, since they still had the seven and a half kilometre hike back to camp and after that would need a lengthy decontamination process.

When they were two kilometres out from the fence, Emmanuel used his radio to call the camp so the decon tent could be prepared. When he got no answer, he assumed the radio had been affected by the stronger radiation – or the higher levels his suit was emitting.

Krys did not propose any other suggestion, but her own view was that the radio should be working. She let her mind shield down fully and sensed ahead to the camp, and grew alarmed. Her mind told her that something was wrong. Only one person seemed to be there, and that person was impatiently awaiting Emmanuel's return. Nothing more than that. The mind was not revealing anything else.

A suited figure met them as they reached the boundary fence. Emmanuel did not find it strange and he must have recognised the suit.

"Omar, is the decon hut ready?"

"Yes, Doctor," was the immediate answer. The faintly foreign sounding voice confirmed the man's identity.

"This way, Kryslie," Emmanuel directed, as he walked towards a door at the far side of the hut from the gate.

She followed without comment, since she knew the standard decon protocol - enter away from where people might walk. They would emerge with the radiation neutralised, on the side nearest the gate.

The scientist had not sensed that anything was wrong, but it had been a very long day and for a man in his early seventies, she was amazed that he could still walk without teetering.

Inside the hut, they each entered a tiny cubicle where the spray soaked the outer side of the suits until the sensor lights cycled from dark blue down to white, as did the stripes on the wrists of the suit. Only then, did they emerge and stand over the draining grid and have a stream of air blowing the excess solution from the suit. As much as possible of the solution would be recycled for the next use.

Omar Harrison helped Emmanuel take his suit off, in an impersonally helpful way. He didn't ask how the experimental placements had gone, or make any kind of talk.

Kryslie deliberately brushed his mind with hers. Still nothing. She would need to make a deeper probe to get through his natural mind shields. All she sensed was his feeling of needing to hurry, that the old man had taken too long to get back. She considered that, did it have something to do with the mental silence from the rest of the team?

As they emerged from the hut, clad now I the light coveralls they used under the suits, Kryslie asked, "Where is everyone?"

"Jerry rolled the jeep," Harrison said, sounding unconcerned. "It went down into a dry creek somewhere along the clear zone. The rest are trying to right it and get it back to the road."

He spoke without taking his attention off Emmanuel, as if he was reporting a true fact. Kryslie knew he was lying.

"They should have called up the security guys for help," she commented, as if that was the most reasonable thing to do. "One of their trucks could tow it out in no time."

She sensed Harrison's spurt of fear at the idea. His face only twitched into a faint grimace. He shrugged to disguise the reaction.

"That's what I told them, but they all figured they could fix it," was his claim. He was lying again. He didn't want the security team involved.

"Is Jerry hurt?" Emmanuel asked with alarm, turning abruptly to go and see for himself. He tried to put on a burst of speed to return through the gate, but exhaustion was setting in.

"Not much. Just some painful bruises. He is sleeping off some pain killers though," Harrison lied again. He was calmly taking off his suit, and hooking it on the outside of the hut. He strode to catch up with Emmanuel, and offer the older man his arm.

Krys reached out again with her empathic senses. Something had attracted her attention, and she scanned the camp - stopping at the communal hut. Her sense of depth perception showed her the rest of the team bound and unconscious. One or two were beginning to stir.

She widened her area of perception. Harrison was up to something, and afraid he was running out of time. He had expected them back an hour ago. Was he in turn expecting someone to come or something to happen? Did he need to do something?

Emmanuel was trying to hurry, but Harrison was restraining him. Kryslie had a prickle of alarm, but could see no particular threat. She followed the two men, but when she would have locked the gate behind them, Harrison spoke over his shoulder, "Leave it open for now. I need to go back and turn off the solution filtering system."

Again, Kryslie knew he was lying. She made no comment about the fact that he was contravening the standard procedure. That gate was meant to stay locked except when people were actually moving in or out through it. Was he intending to let people through?

Even though the light was fading, Kryslie looked left and right along the inside of the fence. She adjusted her eyes for the dark and the distance. No one was in sight. Harrison was working to some schedule, and whatever his intentions were, it seemed that his grip on Emmanuel was to keep him restrained, not to help him. When he made his move, he would not want her to interfere.

Emmanuel began to pull towards the sleeping hut, but Harrison grabbed him roughly - yanking him to a stop. He turned towards Kryslie and she saw he had a gun in his free hand.

"You! Face down on the ground," Harrison demand of Krys. When she didn't immediately obey, he put the gun right against Emmanuel's head.

The scientist stunned by the behaviour of the man he had considered a trusted colleague. He tried to struggle.

"Keep still old man, or I will shoot you. And you, on the dirt!"

Sensing that Harrison was edgy enough to shoot if she didn't obey, Krys appeared to do as he ordered, but even with her back to him, she sensed his every move. She was aware of when he used the butt of his gun as a club to knock the old scientist unconscious, and she felt her anger rising. He was watching her, as he reached into a pocket for something to tie his prisoner up. Then, needing both hands to tie Emmanuel's wrists together, he crouched and put his gun on the ground. He kept glancing at her, but thinking he had her scared, he dared to take his eyes off her to concentrate on tying the leather straps.

Krys didn't wait for him to finish. With Harrison's attention distracted, she sprang up and leapt at him. He caught the movement as a shadow crossing the evening sun, and grabbed for his gun, but found it gone. He dodged her leap, and attempted to catch her foot and trip her. When that failed, he sprang up and twirled to kick out at her, only to feel an agonising pain in his jaw as Kryslie landed a solid kick to his face. He collapsed unconscious.

Without any sense of righteous satisfaction, Kryslie took the leather straps and used them to make sure Omar Harrison would not escape. When his wrists and ankles were bound, she looked at Emmanuel and saw he had roused, and was staring at her.

"How are you?" she asked, intending to distract him. Had he seen her take the traitorous Harrison down?

"What happened?"

Kryslie explained briefly, and moved to help Emmanuel who was trying to stand. He was shaking with the after reaction of the sudden attack. She carefully used her Tymorean power to help him recover.

After a few minutes, she asked, "Are you right to walk? I think we need to find the others. I am sure Harrison was lying when he said there had been an accident."

"I am not that frail!" was the scientist's stout declaration.

Kryslie smiled, "Can you check the communal hut. I am going to make sure this wretch stays put and gets no help."

"I don't think…" Emmanuel began to protest. Then he seemed to recall the short and effective fight he had witnessed, and recalled an incident in the past. "I will call the guards."

"I haven't lost my touch," Krys remarked. "But call the guards. I have better things to do than baby sit traitors. And if he had the forethought to wreck the radio, find one of the portables and adjust them to the next higher frequency. That's what the security team are using."

Emmanuel didn't think to ask her how she knew that, or stop to think how the pain in his head had vanished while Kryslie was supporting him. This was a crisis and he needed to act.

Once he had gone, Kryslie returned her attention to the man at her feet. With impersonal thoroughness, she searched him for weapons. In addition to the gun, she collected two knives, a stunner and a palm-sized radio. She slipped the items into pockets of the coverall. His personal papers, and the silver star on a chain around his neck, she left alone. Then she went to the gate and relocked it.

The rest of the team soon started appearing in the door of the hut, walking unsteadily as they tried to get circulation back in arms and legs. By the look of them, Harrison had treated them to a mild stun.

Krys could now hear the jeeps revving up the hill, but she stayed near her victim. The conversation amongst the ten other team members was about how they had been caught unawares. Harrison, it seemed was a patient, clever and ruthless man.

One of the team turned on the portable lights for the camp. Krys glanced down at Harrison and saw his eyes were open, but he quickly closed them again. She nudged him with a toe as two jeeps raced to a dust-raising stop.

"You are going to have to deal with the Investigative Committee," she told him in a conversational tone. "WSRA properties are neutral and any crimes committed there are investigated by them and their punishments can be harsh."

If that bothered Harrison, he didn't show it. He was good, Krys had to admit, or he was confident of powerful support. He was staring at her now as if memorising her face, but she had already done the same with his.

Krys let Emmanuel deal with the security team. She listened, and was grateful that he did not elaborate on how she had overcome the prisoner. He simply said that she had always been good at self-defence and he was grateful that she was.

When two of the guards took charge of Harrison, they requested that she make a statement about the incident. She agreed, but decided to suggest the possibility that he had accomplices.

"He had a communicator," she told the men, as she withdrew the device from her pocket. She also brought the gun out and handed both items to the guard. "I think he was expecting back up. He told me to keep the gate unlocked."

One of the guards spoke into his radio, ordering reinforcements. Then he demanded, "Did you leave it unlocked?"

"Then, but it is secured now. I don't know if anyone could have penetrated the fence elsewhere, but I could see no reason to leave it open, unless he was expecting help from inside the fence."

She could see the man considering the idea. "We have the perimeter secured," he assured her in a superior tone. However, his partner disagreed, "Remember that group in the desert? They got past us somehow."

The mention was enough. "We will check it," the first one promised.

Kryslie was satisfied with that, but she wasn't finished making suggestions. "I think the whole team here should go back to town and be checked over by the doctor, and stay there until you give the all clear."

Emanuel objected. "We have just got here. We have so much to do…all the observations…I have to check the detectors…"

"Doc, they can record data for three months with out you hovering. Once the area is cleared, you'll be allowed back. Harrison had friends somewhere, and he was attempting to take you somewhere," Kryslie said bluntly. "You can come back with stronger security. He might be connected to that group in the desert and is trying to steal your discoveries. I would hate them to torture you to get the information - or kill you."

She sensed his reluctant agreement, but not from the thought of danger, but from the thought of his discoveries being stolen.

"Captain, could you take us all back to town?" he asked.

In the town, after helping Emmanuel to move his important data storage equipment from the camp, and seeing all of the team settled into one of the town's guesthouses, Kryslie went to the small police station to make her statement.

By the time she arrived, several senior military officials had come to question Omar Harrison, and some World Council investigators were expected. She told what she knew to the officials, signed the statement, and all the while listened to the talk around her. She learnt nothing useful, and departed unobtrusively.

While she kept herself hidden from view, she leant against a tree in the patch of natural bush that was called a park. She watched the police station to be sure there were no incidents until Harrison was taken away. While waiting, she sent a thought to her brother, and reported on the recent events.

"I agree, with your contention that they had wanted him because he was the top man in the field and they wanted the force field specs," Tymos told her. "I am getting hints that bin Halil is making plans. And I know he has learnt about the desert tests. He will want to have anything that will help block anyone who wants to stop him."

"Have you anything solid enough to give to the investigative committee?"

Kryslie felt rather than mentally heard his frustrated growl. "All our people are trying to find something, but that man is so slimy that nothing sticks to him."

Chapter 6 - Hostile Welcome

Vincent awoke, and his mind was instantly alert. He sat up, and swung his long legs to the side of the makeshift bed. The side cavern where the beds had been placed was deep in shadow, but light reflected in the entrance from the main cavern beyond. He could hear the gentle breathing of several sleepers, and he rose quietly so as not to disturb them. Everyone had been working hard to get the base operational.

The previous night had been chaotic, and even now, Vincent did not know where his personal pack had ended up. He had fallen asleep in the clothes he had arrived in, a day and a half ago. He straightened his rumpled shirt and trousers and considered using the canvas-walled shower cubicle that was in a second side chamber. He wanted a change of clothes first and for that, he needed to find his personal gear.

He walked out into the main cavern where light from a multitude of bright portable lamps made it almost seem like they weren't underground. The power source for the lights would last a reasonably long time, but creating a power source for the base was a priority.

On the way to speak to the man in charge of all the materials and supplies, Vincent caught a familiar scent, and looked around.

Two of the building crew were sitting on empty crates in the area set aside for the camp kitchen. They had their hands around mugs of steaming hot beverage. He was startled to realise that they were drinking Earth coffee.

"Morning Doc," one of the men greeted him. "The water is hot and this brew is not bad. You should try it."

"Where did you get it? It's coffee!" Vincent was surprised enough to ask. He had developed a liking for the drink when he was previously on Earth and went to make himself a mug full.

The man shrugged. "It was here, so we tried it."

As he sipped the hot drink, Vincent observed the purposeful activity with a critical eye. In the six hours that he had slept, the utter chaos he remembered had begun to take on a semblance of organization. The huge pile of crates that had been hurriedly transported from the ground above, were piled wherever there was space. Some had been opened and their contents piled on the floor. Workers were coming and going, collecting what they needed of the tools and building supplies.

More crates of material were still in the outer cavern, the one closest to the tunnel leading to the surface. They had set up a force field between that cavern and this main one, to protect the personnel from the radiation absorbed by the crates. Every now and then, another case was pushed through, having undergone the decontamination process.

The shift of builders rostered to decon, had to wear their protective suits, but only while in the outer cavern. In the main one, everyone was able to wear normal clothing.

Vincent knew that being able to remove the suits in the underground caverns would make the idea of living there more attractive. Though once the bustle of setting up was finished, they would need to make the rock walls look more like the inside of a normal dwelling. He had seen the ideas that Great One Kryslie had proposed, and it almost seemed that she had known of this place before they left, but no Tymorean had been to this part of Earth before they arrived.

The Great Ones had chosen this site because the humans would not venture here and the Tymoreans would be prepared for the radiation. Besides, the reports of the area must surely have been made from the outer edges. Once they had arrived, Tymos and Kryslie had obviously come here, but before then, they could not have known what they would find. Surely then, Kryslie must have been gifted with ideas from the Guardians of Peace.

Thinking of the absent Great Ones, gave Vincent more things to ponder. He finished his coffee, washed his cup and went to where they had found the two generators that Olassa had told them about. It was still a wonder to him that Tymos and Kryslie had been back on Earth for some years, even though they had left Tymorea at the same time as he had. Yet it had to be true. The generators were technologically more advanced than anything yet developed on Earth. And the force field that had hidden the tunnel and blocked the lethal radiation was Tymorean and had to be the work of the Great Ones.

That was yet another point - how was the field powered? The extra field they now had between the two huge caverns was currently running off the portable powerpacks - same as the lights. If it came to that, how had the Great Ones carved out the caverns, and smoothed the rock faces? All that would have taken a great deal of time and energy.

They must have created the tapped spring that brought water down to the cavern too. Where that fed from was a mystery, but that wasn't important. An unpolluted water supply was a vital necessity.

Two technicians were studying the generators, and the provided schematics. Every now and then one scratched his head, and the other muttered under his breath.

"What seems to be the trouble?" he asked, after watching for a while. Both men looked at him hopefully.

"These instructions seem clear enough," the head scratcher admitted. "It says plug the cable into the power point in the wall. Well, as weird a way as that is to power anything, we did but it still isn't working. A green light should come on, and we should hear a faint hum."

The second technician added his opinion. "Daniel explained about how humans transport their power from the generators to the cities. Copper cables are strung either on pylons or in conduits underground. If there is a cable here, it has to come in underground, because there was no pylons topside. I checked the thing they called a power point, and my sensor tool gives me nothing."

From his time living on Earth a century before, Vincent understood what the men were meaning, but he could offer no solution either. Unlike his brother, Governor Xyron, he only really knew the medical sciences well.

"Daniel was just here, agitating about getting this generator working," the first said. "We have gone over the specs, and everything seems spot on. I just wish we could power it with one of the power packs."

Vincent was certain that the Great Ones knew what they were doing to make it as it was.

"It might require too much power to run," he proposed, while considering what else to suggest. "Double check the metal connections, to make sure there is no corrosion. I recall that can sometimes be a problem."

"We'll try it, Doc. Can't think of anything else."

Thoughtfully, Vincent retreated to the main cavern and went in search of Daniel. His mission-co-leader should have been on a sleep cycle if he followed his own rostering policy. He had to ask one of the workers where to find him.

The cavern system was indeed vast, and so far they had only explored a small part of it. The section where Vincent had been directed was new to him.

He found Daniel watching a sensor screen and fidgeting. Jonko and Keleb were with him, the former had ear buds in, and was manipulating a pressure pad at intervals.

"Daniel, there has been no change. All the activity is still on the outer edge of the zone," Jonko stated.

The older man would not stay still. Keleb spotted Vincent and shrugged at Daniel, who caught the movement and turned to see who had arrived.

"Have you any idea how to find Tymos and Kryslie?" Daniel demanded. "No one seems to be able to figure out how to make that generator work. It can't be connected to our portable power system, but we need to get that extra shield up! The sensors we left on the surface, are picking up intense activity not far away. Lots of radio traffic and aircraft overflying us."

Vincent recognised that Daniel was overtired, and needed rest. Likely he had not slept since they arrived. Yet he would not be able to sleep until he was reassured.

"I know where to start looking for the Great Ones," Vincent spoke with confidence. "And I do not think we are in danger of being seen just yet."

"Tymos said we needed to get that shield up as soon as possible. And we have all those military aircraft flying over."

"It is also still night time, and the dome is made of non reflecting black polymer, and protected by a vision distorting field. To have any possible chance of seeing it, they would have to be flying extremely low, and I doubt they would choose to do that so close to the radiating surface above."

"Olassa, said they found them under their shield in the desert," Daniel persisted.

Jonko pulled the ear bud from one ear, and made a suggestion, "I am no technical whiz, but if it should appear that the air force is getting interested in our specific location, instead of that spot on the boundary, we could collapse the dome. We don't need it now we are settling down here, and the earth sensors won't detect the polymer it's made from. We won't need the shields on it either."

"Yes, I will see to it," Vincent said decisively. "Daniel, where are we at with everything? I will take over, and you need to get some rest before you wear yourself out."

Keleb escorted Daniel to the sleeping cavern, with careful solicitude. Jonko waited until they were out of hearing range before adding his own comments to supplement Daniel's report.

"The builders are well ahead of schedule, even though they had to redesign their efforts on the run," he told Vincent. "They have found that a lot of the preparatory work down here has already been done."

"I see the hands of the Great Ones in much of what we have here," was the reply from the older man. "I am more concerned about this human activity that Daniel mentioned."

"From what Kel and I have heard, it seems like there was an incident at the scientific camp situated at the edge of the radioactive zone. The scientists were inserting sensors to measure the emanations. The activity has settled down, and there has been no additional agitation to indicate that our dome has been noticed. Most of the flyovers have been at safe height and after dark," Jonko summarised. "However, there is some merit in Daniel's concern about getting the extra shield up. Kel and I are monitoring the communications frequencies, and there have been several mentions of bringing in special detection equipment. We have no hint of how long that will take."

Vincent didn't dismiss the seriousness of the situation. "The Great Ones built that generator, and they said to get it working as soon as possible, they did not expect any problems."

An inspiration occurred to Jonko. "I was hearing talk of a storm front. That was why the aircraft departed. Maybe the storm put out the power supply and that is why the generator won't work."

"If that is the case, let us hope that the human technicians fix the problem quickly."

Keleb returned and re-joined the conversation. "He went out like a light as soon as I covered him. But he remembered something he forgot to mention."

Vincent raised his brows in surprise, since Daniel's report had been exceedingly detailed. He waited for Keleb to continue.

"It was something about there being a natural air flow or circulation in these caves. I have to agree, since I am sure I was smelling rain earlier."

"I do not doubt that is possible, and I would think the Great Ones had something to do with that too," Vincent said. "Though I wonder why they have not come here yet? Can it be that they are not aware of our arrival?"

"Olassa will have told them, surely? And she did say they will come when they can." Keleb reminded him. "So are we going to look for them?"

"As soon as I have checked everything here for myself," Vincent promised.

After telling her brother of events, Kryslie used her remote access device to check what messages had come in from the missionaries. Everything that had come in since early that morning was routine. Nothing that had been received since Olassa reported on her visit to Vincent and Daniel, needed her attention. Yet she had been expecting a follow up message from her group leader in the non-aligned countries. Louis Devalos had sent her a message indicating that he was onto a conspiracy that was aimed at destabilising the UWN - the United World Nations.

Now, with the actions of Omar Harrison on her mind, his report had taken on new urgency. He had promised a detailed report, and she felt he had meant to send it soon after his terse summary. That had been a day and a half ago. She would need to get back to the warehouse and check if he had sent it as a microburst transmission. Though if he had, surely he would have told her as much in his next report.

Still, there might be any number of reasons for the delay, and right now, with all the military activity around the Hope Valley exclusion zone, she dare not leave to check the warehouse. The safety of the newly arrived Tymorean Earth Mission was her priority.

The tiny earpiece in her ear picked up more transmissions, just as two air force jets approached from a low flyover of the zone, and powered up to climb to their normal cruising height. The transmission was telling their control tower that they were returning to refuel.

The jets' passage overhead made the ground tremble and the tree she stood under lose a scattering of leaves. Not far away, small groups of locals were standing around some picnic tables, talking and watching the sky.

News of the arrest of a supposed terrorist had them unsettled, and even having the army stationed nearby did not reassure them.

Kryslie did not think they had anything to worry about. Doctor Emmanuel had been the target and he was now in the centre of tactical security cordon. If Harrison had confederates, they would be caught if they tried for the scientist. They might try to free Harrison, and that was why Kryslie was watching the police station. The traitor had been convinced that he would get free.

It probably depended on whether anyone had been found within the fence as she had suggested to the security detail. So far, she had received no indication to confirm her idea.

From the intercepted communications, she knew that the World Council Investigators were due within the hour. They would take control of the prisoner, and escort him to their secure detention facility. Until then, Kryslie intended to remain where she was.

The night grew darker, and with the departure of the last of the jets, silence had returned to the park where Kryslie watched. None of the locals had noticed her, standing quite still under one of the aspen trees, and once the night started to come in cold, they began to return to their homes.

Six hours after she had begun her vigil, the dark sedan used by the Investigators, drove off in the direction of the county airport. Only then, did Kryslie slip through the darkness and return to Jerry Hull's rented house. He was still awake and waiting for her.

Without asking, he began to prepare her a warm drink, and started heating a pre-packaged meal in his microwave oven.

"What have you heard?" Kryslie asked him, after taking a sip of the hot drink.

"You will have noticed they have recalled the aircraft," he began. "The house shook every time they flew over. They had to refuel, and apparently, there is a storm front moving in from the north. I went to the local drinking place. One of the councillors was there, and he was saying that the army went into the zone and checked the inner perimeter. Apparently they caught four men, and there was some talk that they might have some kind of blind or hut in there - as a base for some terrorist plot. The army will be bringing in special detection equipment in the morning, and the planes will have something too."

Jerry took the heated meal from the microwave and set it at a table. Kryslie was glad to have it, since she had not eaten since that morning. She thanked him for his report, and used the process of eating to cover her intense thinking.

She was considering if it was wise to leave Hope Valley for a short time, to return to the warehouse to see if Louis's report had arrived. The long-range beam could take her there and back before first light. A lot depended on whether Vincent and Daniel had found and connected the shield generator she and Tymos had built.

"Jerry, that storm front - how severe is it?"

"Fairly intense. Our lights have been flickering a bit, and they went out for a while. It is meant to reach here sometime early in the morning."

Kryslie just nodded, and said nothing of her concerns. She hoped that Vincent had found the generator and set it working. They would be busy moving from the surface to the caverns, so that might delay them. She did not dare try to send a signal to the Tymorean base, since she knew that the security forces would still be blanketing the vicinity with communication detectors. She did not want to draw any more attention to the area. And for her to get to the base, she would need to return via the long-range beam to the warehouse, reset the coordinates and transmit to the base. But she had no way of knowing where to target the beam without risking it materialising within a group of people or a pile of vital supplies.

Jerry sat down in one of his chairs, and gave a large yawn.

"Go and grab a couple of hours sleep," Kryslie told him. "They won't do anything until it gets light."

"What about you?" he protested half-heartedly.

"I've been resting, while waiting for them to take the prisoner away," she assured him, but didn't say she had refreshed her energies from the energy aura of the trees in the park.

Once she was alone, she moved into the front room of the house and sat back in one of the armchairs. She sent a mind call to her twin.

"Tym, have you heard from Louis?"

"No. Why?" His mental tone seemed partly distracted.

Kryslie mentally calculated the time there. Midday, for the area of the unaligned countries was eight or nine hours ahead.

"He sent me a message, just after I left to come here. He said that he had finally found evidence of a conspiracy against the United World Nations. He said that they were planning to place agents in important places, to foster distrust within the Presidential Council, between the member countries as well as the scientific community. He was preparing a detailed report. That was almost two days ago."

Tymos's concern was clear to her through the twin bond. "Where are you?"

"Still at Hope Valley. They have removed Harrison and four of his cohorts, but there is talk of bringing in special detectors. All this has reminded them of the tests in the desert."

"Have you heard back from Olassa?"

"Yes, she has spoken to Vincent and Daniel."

"Then they should have the generator working soon," Tymos thought back.

"Except that we took a line from the northern power grid for it - and there is a storm front affecting the power there."

"We didn't plan for that," Tymos admitted. "Stay there for now, I will try to contact Louis or some of the others from here. I can't take the time to go in person, I need to keep watching two members of bin Halil's secret police."

It was the best compromise, but Kryslie was feeling jittery, although not yet strongly enough for it to be considered a premonition of trouble.

The helicopters arrived as the sun was just rising above the horizon to the east of the town of Hope Valley. From the communications she was intercepting, Kryslie already knew that they were setting up grid searches to cover the area five kilometres to either side of the boundary fence. If they stayed over the boundary, the base was safe. However, the jets were to return at full daylight to provide air cover and they flew high enough to be unaffected by the radiation. If they had the force screen detectors, the base would glow like a beacon.

Jerry woke when the helicopters flew over, and found her pacing his front room, with one hand cupping her left ear where she had the communicator earpiece.

"What's up?" he asked, sensing trouble.

Kryslie told him, as she pulled her transmitter from her pocket.

"Can't we warn them?" he asked. "Our transmission frequencies are nothing like these humans have."

"It is too dangerous. They will have a full spectrum detection system covering the area. If they detect any strange signals, they will have the origin triangulated in microseconds. I cannot even be sure anyone at the base is monitoring communications."

Jerry swallowed nervously; he did not want any attention from the human authorities. He still recalled his narrow escape from the desert.

"Can we do anything?"

"We may need to do nothing," Kryslie told him. "If they have moved underground, into the caverns there, they should not be found. However, I don't know how long it will take them. I am going to move closer, and watch."

Keleb came running from the chamber with the communications array and looked around. He spotted Vincent and changed his direction.

"One of the helicopters has left the search grid and is heading directly towards us. One of the jets reported seeing something glowing down here."

"Turn off all the fields except the visible distortion field," Vincent directed urgently. "I'll move the one at the tunnel entrance further in."

Jonko arrived as Keleb raced off again, drawing attention from the builders when he had to swerve to miss two who walked in front of him. He moved with Vincent and asked, "Can we drop the dome? So they won't see it?"

"Not from down here, and we don't have time. If we tried, and they spotted humanoid figures up there in the lethal levels of radiation, they will consider us dangerous," Vincent warned. "Go and get everyone suited up, just in case they decide to bomb the area. We should be safe in the deeper caverns, but I don't know if the rock over us can withstand a bombing attack."

"Or we could be buried alive," Jonko blurted, turning pale.

"It is a risk," Vincent admitted. "But I have faith in the preparations of the Great Ones."

"I just wish they were here now," Jonko said as he in turn trotted off to give the warning to the builders. He also wished there was an internal comm. system to sound the alarm.

After getting his own suit on, Vincent went to the communications chamber, a little side cavern that showed signs of being excavated by man not nature. Here they had a rudimentary monitoring system. He found Daniel there, suited up, staring over Keleb's shoulder at a screen that he hadn't noticed before. Something was buzzing in an urgent cadence.

"What's this?" he asked, and Keleb twisted his body to answer.

"When I got back here to depower the screens, a panel of rock had opened. All this was behind it. We have access to all sorts of sensors. I have a visual of the terrain above."

"That helicopter you see there is hovering right above the dome," Daniel said, sounding agitated. "They must be able to see us, but I don't understand how. Only the inner screen emits light and that should be screened by the visual distortion field."

For a moment, Vincent considered the problem. "It could be that the radiation is interfering with the screens. Keleb, have you taken down the inner screens?"

"Yes, Sir. Should be take them all down?"

"No, or the dome will be completely visible. Can you see it on any of your screens?"

"Yes, I can make out the shape, although it is like through a heat haze. Do you think they will think it some kind of radiation mirage?"

Daniel made a snort of disgust at such wishful thinking. "We need to prepare for the caverns to be breached. We have no weapons to defend ourselves. Can't we transmit away until we know for sure?"

It was a logical idea, and possible - except they had not yet assembled the long-range beam.

"Have faith in the Great Ones," Vincent spoke in a calm voice. "They surely know what is happening here. But even so, if the dome is located and destroyed, I do not believe that they will find the entrance to the tunnels. The force field over it cannot be seen by humans."

"The other fields should be invisible too," Daniel reiterated, recalling the truth of Vincent's words. He had been unable to find the way down to the caverns until Vincent had helped him. "But even if they do their worst, they will have to find a vehicle with enough protections, to get them here…that will surely give us time to act if we must."

"Tymos and Kryslie will know what to do," Keleb said to Daniel, because he was sensing the older man's fear of having all his work over the last months, coming to disaster.

Yet Daniel was maintaining a stoic façade, knowing that the builders might panic if he betrayed his worry. They were not missionaries, were not trained to deal with danger and disasters. They came, they built, and they left…usually. However, as for his children knowing what to do, they were not trained missionaries either. What could the two of them actually do? They were not around, and surely couldn't achieve miracles.

"We need to move deeper into the caverns," Vincent advised.

"I'll stay and watch what the helicopter does. I have their transmission frequency too," Keleb said. "They reported when they stopped seeing the glow…"

"That must be like a rocket flare going up, that someone is here," Daniel spoke under his breath.

"Or a weird effect of the radiation, due to the approaching storm," Jonko added, coming back to join the group. He earned a glare from Daniel.

"This is not a matter for levity!"

Keleb supported the idea. "There is an electrical storm coming. The atmospheric instruments on the dome are showing that."

The expression on Daniel's face changed from stern to thoughtful. "Perhaps that is why the generator Olassa spoke of is not working?"

"Of course," Jonko said, enlightened. "The storm must have caused a power blackout." He turned to Vincent. "Tymos must have managed to run a power cable from somewhere - heavens knows how - but it comes in at the wall socket. A local power outage would explain why we didn't get a power reading there."

"In that case, we should keep trying to start the generator. Though I think, it is too late for it to do any good. They have already found an anomaly here," Vincent considered.

"The winds are getting up - look at how they are buffeting the helicopter. They had to go up another hundred feet," Keleb remarked.

"If I were the pilot, I'd get the hell out of here," Jonko said, wishing the pilot would do that.

It seemed as if his wish was granted. The helicopter moved towards the ridge of the encircling hills. He saw Keleb glance at him with a grin on his face.

"The energy fields around here are going crazy," Keleb remarked.

Jonko moved to where he could study the screen. His friend had found yet another sensor, and it was putting a light grid over the visual picture, like isobars on a weather map - except the readings were energy levels. The effect reminded him of a time when he was working with Great One Kryslie back on Tymorea.

"The helicopter has been told to land," Keleb announced.

"So now we wait," Vincent summarised. "Jonko, monitor here whilst Keleb gets his suit on. I will go to check on the builders."

For an instant, just as he took the earpiece from Keleb, Jonko glanced at the screen. His eyes were still seeing the energy wash overlay of the base structure, but he thought he saw a humanoid shape of more intense energy. He looked again, more carefully, but the effect had gone.

"Wishful thinking," Jonko berated himself. "I wish Tymos or Kryslie were here, but perhaps it is better they are not."

He made a systematic study of all the sensor readings, and saw the storm was almost on them. He hoped it would stay over them, for that would mean the Earth air force would be grounded. However, common sense told him that would only delay events for a short time.

Chapter 7 - Hiding Earthbase

When the helicopter reported the anomaly to the search leader, Kryslie abruptly transmitted, vanishing from Jerry's sight. She used a memory of the terrain around the base to target her arrival point. The ring of hills around the flattened and slagged central valley, gave her some protective cover. She could see the hovering helicopter, and she was certain that an airstrike would be being prepared.

Returning her transmitter to one pocket, she took another device from a second. This was her remote for getting messages from the warehouse base, but it had many other built in functions. Now, she programmed it to link to the sensor array she and Tymos had built into the base and through that, she activated the network of sensors located throughout the blackened land. As soon as the sensor grid reactivated, she received a relay of whatever was on the screen in the base. As a passing thought, she wondered what the personnel now in the caverns would think when the protecting wall panel suddenly slid back.

Yet she needed the information coming in from the sensors placed in the ring of hills, and others within the cavern itself. For now, she adjusted two of the sensors to look directly at the base, the sensors were indeed detecting a glowing dome. She tried to link in the generator that she had helped Tymos build, to activate it remotely, but her device pinged an error message. She sent a command for a diagnostic, and it told her there was no power.

Then the glowing dome shape on the small screen suddenly disappeared. She looked towards the actual physical dome and adjusted her eyes. Five kilometres away, and three hundred meters lower, she could just make out the shape of the dome - black against black, and blurring at the edges - but now with only the faintest of energy glows.

"A good idea, but way too late," Kryslie murmured to herself. The helicopter pilot was already reporting the weird phenomenon. She considered possible options.

The most elegant idea was to convince the helicopter crew that what they had observed was a result of the radiation. Many ideas passed through her mind in rapid succession, each briefly considered and then discarded. The idea of a standing energy wave stayed. At the right frequency, and in the right conditions, standing waves could make you think you were seeing things. Could she work on that? The valley was circular…

Kryslie reached out with her mind to the sense the surrounding energy flows, she felt the energy of the storm about to reach the valley. With delicate care, she attracted the energy to herself and sent it elsewhere. A wind began to swirl within the valley, gently at first, but then with a violent blast as the storm front crested the western ridge and followed the ambient energy gradient.

She watched as the helicopter pilots became aware of the strengthening wind, it was buffeting them like they were within a whirlwind. They rose higher, trying to move above the swirling air. Using her outstretched arms like pointers, Kryslie focussed on different points around the helicopter, and the wind reacted to the changes in energy she created.

The turbulence made the helicopter drop suddenly, and then rise and almost tip sideways.

The pilot knew when it was not safe to stay. He reported his retreat to the search control, and flew to the south, to watch from there. However, that was not what Kryslie wanted. She needed it to be out of sight. Her tactics changed, and the winds obeyed her as she directed them to blow towards the helicopter. This time, search control ordered the pilot to return to is base and land.

The dangerous winds from the storm would also keep the jets away, but once search control registered them easing, the aircraft would return. She needed all the time she could get for the next part of her plan, and as soon as the helicopter fled for its landing pad, she began.

Transmitting to within touching distance of the dome, Kryslie glanced around quickly - just to be sure no one would see her. She was an odd sight. An unprotected human figure should not be able to tolerate the lethal radiation, let alone live for longer than a millisecond. If she were seen, then every fantastical myth about extraterrestrial beings would be recalled.

Even a human in a radiation suit would be inexplicable for at Earth's current level of technology, the radiations suits were not proof against this level of emanations.

However, Kryslie wasn't just anyone. She was a Tymorean Great One and during the war on Tymorea, she had survived conditions that were even more lethal than those around her now. The power given to her by the Guardians of Peace was exceptionally strong, and it protected her. It changed her physical being into a form that could use the roiling energies. Now, to an observer capable of sensing energy levels, she would seem like an area of denser energy.

In this form, a suit would handicap her. Her mind still directed her energy shape and a hand like a tendril of force, touched the dome. The matt black triangular plates hid the tubular struts of the dome's structural grid. The plates were of a polymer, resistant to the hostile atmosphere, the struts were an energy conducting organo-metallic polymer. She needed to touch the struts, but before she yanked off a plate to get access, she used her extra senses to check if the area under the dome had been vacated. It had. That the dome was empty, removed one concern. All the people and the materials must have been taken down to the caverns. Down there, they were protected from the radiation, and she could safely collapse the dome.

Through the hole she had made in the dome wall, she touched the nearest strut and sensed the structure of the rigid polymer, felt its strength, learned its weakness. Then, by drawing energy from the radiation into herself, she changed it and emitted it as sound, but at such a long wavelength that it was not audible. The sound travelled from strut to strut until the whole dome was resonating. The molecular bonds in the polymer began to weaken. Slowly, the dome began to collapse. Plates popped off and fell to the ground with a rattling clatter.

As the structure settled, Kryslie moved to spread the wall plates into an even layer over the blackened and slagged surface. Then she touched it again, and sent her power through the layered plates, until the molecular bonds broke and reformed, welding them together with the residual pieces of the struts into a huge plate of armour over the base.

The process had taken time and without her continued manipulation, the winds had returned to normal and were less intense now that the storm front had passed. With a flick of thought, Kryslie returned to the protection of the rock overhang on the ridge, and her form solidified back to human. From that vantage, the layer of fused plates blended into the slagged rock.

She could also see that the distortion field was still operating, giving a ghostly dome shape, and a shimmer to the air. She waited, listening to the radio traffic, until she heard the jets cleared for take off.

Minutes later, three jets roared over the valley on their run to line up the target. Instead of circling and retracing the line, the craft stayed in a wide circuit. The flight leader reported the inability to find the target.

From the response of their control, Kryslie knew they would not give up. She closed her eyes and evoked the energy field, and once again manipulated the energy tendrils, drawing energy into herself and then directing it elsewhere. In three different places, the radiation caused the air to glow unnaturally. Each of the places was well away from the location of the base. A short time later, three more areas began to glow, and she made these extra areas swirl and flicker.

The pilots were given new orders - to bomb each area that was glowing. Once again, the three jets lined up and did a targeting run - each concentrating on a different area.

Kryslie simply shook her head at the destructive mentality of the person who gave the order. If it were the radiation that was causing the glow - which is what she had tried to make the pilots think, bombing the area would do little more than spread the cause.

The first jet dropped a load of small bombs, spreading the destruction over a swathe of land around the first glow. The second jet followed on a line just out of the line of the first explosions, dropping its load and creating more fire and black smoke. The third added to the chaos and flew up and away to join the others in circling, and waiting for the smoke to clear.

The energy released by the explosions was powerful. Kryslie sensed the trauma to the Earth, by the roiling of the energy aura. Her body shuddered as the energy flowed into her, but she changed it and sent it out, partly neutralising the incoming energy waves, and partly making the air glow even brighter. When the smoke cleared, the observers would see that the entire circular valley was filled with a glowing mist like a ground hugging aurora. Let them take it as a warning.

The winds from behind the storm front slowly blew the smoke away, taking some of the glowing air with it. An agitated report from the flight leader resulted in the military force around the perimeter of the radiation zone being withdrawn, and an evacuation order given for the town of Hope Valley.

Kryslie knew that there was no danger from the glowing air; it was just the air molecules releasing energy as light, much as what occurred to cause auroras in the sky. She enjoyed the light show she had caused. However, she did not forget that she had friends in the caverns below the valley. Now that the ground had stopped trembling from the after shocks from the bombs, she reached out her awareness to sense how they had fared.

Naturally, there was fear and concern, but nothing indicating trouble needing urgent attention. It seemed that the base was intact, no sections of the rock roof had collapsed, nothing was blocking the airflow, or the water supply. The incoming power cable for the generator was still dead, but at least the other power cable had not been affected by the storm.

Looking over the valley again, she realised that someone had dropped the visual distortion field - for now, that was an excellent idea. When they flew over again to check the effect of the bombing run, there would be nothing to see. The black of the polymer armour shield, would simply look like the fused rock underneath.

She considered going into the caverns to see her friends again, but she felt her twin's mind calling her, and her fear for Louis suddenly peaked.

The caverns echoed with the concussions as bombs fell on the valley floor above them. The ground trembled like in an earthquake, and small pieces of rock fell amid trickles of dirt. As the bombardment continued, the group of builders began to move uneasily. By the time the barrage ceased, everyone felt deafened.

Daniel was the first to return to the main cavern. He looked around and saw the roof was intact, and sighed with relief. Jonko followed him, but he went directly to check the sensors. Keleb and Vincent began to check the builders, and reassure them that their hearing would return.

Jonko played with the sensor controls until he had a view of the valley. Visual sensors were useless - they showed a glowing fog. He changed the parameters and found a way to get a virtual image of the outside terrain. He wasn't sure that he was interpreting the image correctly. Above, all over the valley area, huge craters pocked the ground. All except directly above the extensive caverns, that was. There the ground there was almost perfectly level, as if no bombs had landed there. Maybe they hadn't, but it had sure felt and sounded like they had.

It took him a long while to realise that the dome was gone and that his assumption that it had protected them was false. The visual distortion field was still dome shaped, and registering as fully functional. He tried to get a closer look at the ground, but had little success. He would have to wait until the storm winds began breaking up the glowing fog. Then he might be able to link to the sensors set in the ring of hills, and zoom them in.

Finally, the air cleared but the distortion field still interfered with the visual. He dropped it. What he saw then, amazed him.

The panels of the dome had not simply collapsed onto the ground, nor had they been blasted everywhere by a bomb. They were neatly spread out, covering the maximum possible area, and fused together. The supporting struts - now spread out randomly on the ground, reinforced the fused polymer panels.

Within his own mind, Jonko was certain that either Tymos, or Kryslie, or both Great Ones, had been protecting them. He tried to project a thought to his friends, and for a fleeting instant, he thought he felt an answer. It was not in words, but as a fleeting sense of reassurance.

"Why?" he thought strongly, thinking of Kryslie and Tymos. "Why don't you come here?"

This time though, he sensed nothing.

Chapter 8 - Fleeting Reunion

"No one has seen Louis or his family, for two days," Tymos sent to Kryslie's mind, and through the twin bond, she knew her brother was worried. "Their house is being watched, too."

Knowing intuitively that her brother would have gone to Louis if his own current task was not vital, Kryslie knew that she would need to go herself. She sensed a touch of apology from her twin - they had not spoken of it, but the reason he was doing most of the work in the unaligned countries was so that there would be little chance that she would be recognised by any agent of Abdul bin Halil.

The chance was slight - it had been over thirty years since she had vanished from the hospital after giving birth to bin Halil's only son.

However, she never considered not going. She was a Tymorean Great One, not an inexperienced missionary. And Louis was Tymorean in all but the planet of his birth.

She could not go directly from Hope Valley though. She would need to return to the warehouse base and reset the long-range beam from there. In any event, she needed to check if any more reports had come in - and perhaps start a search though the recorded reports, maybe there was a clue there as to what Louis might have discovered - or who might have wanted to abduct him.

While she felt the urgency to go to Hadjibad, the city where Louis lived, she also felt uneasy. Hadjibad was an important city within the Imperium, and although it was not in the tiny country that Abdul bin Halil had once ruled, she would need to be careful.

In all the years since she had been openly in the Imperium, she had not aged, nor would bin Halil have forgotten or forgiven her. Maybe she should change the colour of her hair. Being recognised would hinder her search for

Louis and his family and if he was still alive, put him in greater danger of being killed.

Even as she considered such thoughts, she was transmitting herself back to Jerry Hull's house to collect the few items she had travelled with. He offered to prepare her a meal, but she thanked him and refused.

"Urgent matters have arisen," was all she said by way of explanation.

Jerry merely murmured, "As you must."

Within moments of programming her current location and activating the beam, the glowing mauve oval came into existence.

"Send a report if you learn anything of importance," she directed Jerry as she stepped into the terminus. He merely nodded, as she activated her transmitter. She vanished, and the glowing oval winked out of existence.

Kryslie arrived within the second floor apartment and immediately checked the security logs. It was a precaution, but here had been no attempted intrusions since she and Tymos and increased the security. Now, any would be vandals, thieves, squatters or inquisitive locals were deterred very quickly by the subliminal sonics.

The message recorder was her next priority. Still nothing from Louis. Her fingers flew over the touch pad, pressing keys in an intricate sequence. The search routine she input would search through all the records in all the formats and trigger an alert if certain keywords or concepts were mentioned. Copies of all triggering messages would be sent to a separate file.

While the computer searched, she went to wash and clean up. She was dusty and ashy from being in the radioactive zone - a fact that Jerry Hull had tactfully not mentioned. However, she could not appear in Louis's country in that state.

The computer pinged its tone for the completed search, just as she finished packing a small backpack. She travelled light, relying on the local missionaries to provide what she needed. She hoped Chave Zieman, Louis's second in command, would provide her with local clothing. This time, she would not be able to stay completely out of sight.

As she read the search results, and investigated some references in greater depth, the communications device chimed. The local wi-fi telephone system.

Kryslie grabbed it from its charging stand, and answered it with her customary terse, "Yes?"

Very few people knew the number, but there were occasional wrong numbers or canvassing calls.

"Hillary," was the return identification.

"Go ahead."

"I have some visitors - looking for you."

Kryslie had an immediate vision of the house Hillary had inherited from Rhyn, the former coordinator of the Tymorean missionary descendents. "Official?" she queried, thinking of the recent events at Hope Valley. It was possible that the authorities, if they had more questions for her, might link her to that address.

"No…" Hillary's tone sounded uncertain. "They are not saying much, but the one who spoke to me said his name was Vincent."

Suddenly, Krys was elated. "Bring them around."

The house wasn't far away, and it wouldn't take them long to walk the distance. Kryslie sped up the replay of the stored reports and finished scanning the last of them just as the intruder warning tones told her that people had entered the ground floor door. She turned off the sonics, and sent a tendril of awareness down below. Hillary, yes, Vincent…as well as Jonko and Keleb. She dropped the force field that hid and protected the second floor and trotted to the stairway to greet her friends.

To her, it seemed like a very long time since she had seen them - so much had happened, so much subjective time had passed. To them, it was less than three days.

She invited them back into the small apartment - though it sounded more like a command, because she really needed to go to find Louis.

When they were in the apartment, Vincent studied Kryslie carefully before speaking. "Great One, you look well - but tense."

Hillary's face betrayed confusion at the greeting. Then she turned thoughtful as if she now equated "Great One" with "Princess".

Jonko was less restrained. He strode forward and gave Kryslie an enthusiastic hug. He felt her tenseness, and released her - still grinning. "You've changed."

Keleb looked around, and didn't see or sense anyone other than the immediate small group and asked, "Where is Tymos?"

Kryslie gave Jonko a fleeting grin, before becoming formal, and looking at Vincent. "I don't have time for ten years of gossip. Have you spoken to Olassa?"

Vincent nodded.

"Good. Tell Daniel to get that extra shield up. Even though they bombed that valley and think nothing is there - you are still vulnerable."

Jonko, having found himself a wall to lean against, murmured, "You were there! I knew it. Why didn't you come in?"

Kryslie heard him, but shook her head, dismissing the question. "Dr Emmanuel from the WSRA University has been conducting experiments on force shields and radiation. If I hadn't kept myself between his instruments and the base, he would have seen it. The radiation interferes with the shields and makes them visible. Even the visual distortion one."

"You flattened the dome," Jonko stated.

"And you still had that one shield up," Kryslie pointed out. "It isn't as noticeable, but the government is now suspicious of that area. I don't think they will do another flyover just yet - but they might. And if they do, they will bring in the very latest force detecting equipment."

Keleb considered that. "How advanced are they? Earth had nothing like that technology before we left here."

"Did Olassa tell you how we helped her when she first arrived?"

Keleb shook his head. "She just said you helped her and the others."

"They arrived during seek and destroy tests in the desert - they had equipment to detect force screens."

"Oh," Keleb murmured.

"And Tymos and I might have contributed to the technology…"

Vincent's face betrayed alarm. If the Great Ones had innocently advanced Earth's technology in that area, the danger she warned of was very real.

"We have been trying to activate that shield, put the power input is inactive. Daniel thinks it is due to a power outage to the north of the valley."

"Surely that is fixed by now?" Kryslie said as she thought on the problem. "I can't go there and sort it out. I really need to be elsewhere right now. Hillary, get Edik here, would you?"

Hillary had stayed back by the door, but she obeyed the direction without a word, using the wi-fi phone to make a call.

"Vincent, all this equipment needs to be transported to Earthbase," Krys gestured around the room. "It should fit into the reception cavern, but you will have to transport it from there to its final place in working condition. Hillary knows what to do. She helped us bring it here. The backup batteries are fully charged. All records are backed up…"

Hillary turned, and when Krys stopped talking, said, "Edik is coming. But it will take him two hours to get here."

Keleb offered, "We could go and bring him."

"He's never travelled by the beam," Hillary blurted, but then her face paled as the eyes of all the strangers turned to her.

Vincent, studying her, remarked, "You are Tymorean."

Hillary turned to Kryslie as if pleading for help.

"Yes," Kryslie said firmly. She recited Hillary's lineage back to the missionaries that Vincent had worked with, back before the war, and who were still alive on Tymorea.

With a bow of genuine respect, Vincent spoke to the Earth born young woman. "I am honoured to meet you. Your many times great grandfather is a personal friend of mine, and I am sure he would be delighted to meet you, as I would be to meet all of the descendents."

Hillary's eyes went wide when she took in his meaning. "How can they be still alive?"

Kryslie interrupted, "Sometime, we might arrange a means for you to meet them, but not now. Edik, is another of the descendents. He and the others have been helping Olassa's group settle in."

"Great one, if I may suggest…" Vincent began to speak, but Kryslie spoke over him.

"I really must go. Tell Daniel that Tymos and I will report in person as soon as we can."

As she spoke, she took out her transmitter, and glanced down to touch the control pad. A brilliant mauve pole of light widened into the glowing oval of an active beam terminus.

"Use the beam to transport everything to Earthbase. Use setting one in the memory. Then take the generator. My transmitter is keyed to it."

Kryslie grabbed her backpack and strode to the terminus. Jonko straightened as Vincent glanced at him. Without a pause to consider, he followed, saying, "I'll go with you."

He met the eyes of the Great One, and sensed that she had changed from the person he'd known three days before. He had the feeling that Kryslie was looking right into him, and he was reminded of the President Governor back on Tymorea. It was more than just an aura of power, it was the sense that she knew her place and had settled into it.

She nodded as he reached her, took his hand and instantly transmitted away.

When the beam blinked off, Keleb smiled at Hillary in a friendly fashion and asked, "What do we need to do?"

The other end of the long-range beam seemed to be in a dark cave, as Jonko and Kryslie stepped out of the glowing terminus. To Jonko, their location seemed utterly and abysmally dark, until his eyes adjusted from seeing the bright light that accompanied the process of travelling from place to place. He knew that wasn't a problem for Kryslie for he heard her quiet movements. She touched his arm and held it, then spoke softly, "You will need to stay out of sight until I know what has happened."

Jonko stiffened, realising that there might be danger. He nodded, and he knew Kryslie either saw or felt the slight movement. "Where are we?" he asked as a mere breath of sound. His eyes were beginning to see a line of yellow light down near his feet. He slowly moved his free arm away from his body and felt a wall.

With as faint a whisper, Jonko heard, "We are in Hadjibad, that is the capital of Jafhabad. Louis, another descendent, lives in this house. Tymos told me the place is being watched. This is a secret room..."

Kryslie still held his arm, and Jonko guessed she was using senses other than just hearing to probe the house.

"This room has no windows, and I can't sense anyone in the near part of the house," Kryslie whispered, only slightly louder. "I will turn on the light."

"I can see light under the door," Jonko warned.

"Yes," Kryslie confirmed that she knew that. "Tymos said the house seemed empty. It was dark a few hours ago…" She moved away and he heard faint movement and a light came on.

Jonko had no idea what sort of situation he had stepped into, but from Kryslie's manner, he knew it was serious. He decided not to ask questions just yet. Instead, he glanced around the closet sized room and saw only a narrow fold-down shelf at one end and a fold up chair that was opened and angled towards them.

Kryslie still seemed distracted, facing one wall, but she spoke softly, "Louis coordinates a mixed group of missionaries and trusted humans. The latter have no knowledge of what Tymoreans are. They are just in sympathy with our ideas of peace, and know too well that the leader of the Imperium, Abdul bin Halil, is no saint."

Jonko quickly recalled the briefing on Earth's current political structure, as Kryslie went on.

"He sent me a message two days ago, and promised a report about intended espionage by the Imperium. It seems he was abducted, or arrested, before he could send it. I need to check this room."

"What of the rest of the house?" Jonko murmured.

"Whoever was watching, has been in the house. I don't sense unfriendly presences…"

Kryslie suddenly stiffened and turned to face him. She reached out a hand and grabbed his arm. Images came into Jonko's mind, as she whispered, "This room is only known to Louis, Tymos and myself. The room next to this is the formal meeting area. It is a mess; someone has been very thorough searching it."

Jonko could see the mess as if his own physical eyes were staring at it, then he was seeing the house as if he were walking through it - noting signs of the search.

"I have to look here," Kryslie insisted, "but I need you to go to the room at the very end of the house. There is a woman and child there - probably Louis's wife and daughter. Check every room on the way - quickly- just to be sure there is no one else here."

She was drawing a knife from an inconspicuous sheath pocket in the all-in-one suit she was wearing, and passing it hilt first towards him. "You have your transmitter on you?"

Jonko nodded, but didn't ask for confirmation that it would work on Earth. He took the knife and tucked it in his belt, as he removed his transmitter from a belt holster. He wasted no more time, just moved aside and transmitted to the next room, where he stilled and drew his power around him like a cloak of invisibility.

To call the damage that he saw in his line of vision a mess, was an understatement. Where he looked, towards the innermost corner of the room, there might once have been a home office. A desk had been overturned and smashed, the contents of filing drawers were strewn over the floor, and obviously, they had been rifled through. The communicator, a newer style of telephone than the ones Jonko had once known, was smashed into electronic components.

Jonko moved slowly to change his view. The door of a wall safe, set into the wall next to a decorative heater surround, was hanging open, blackened by the blast of some explosive. It was empty. All the ornaments that had once adorned the mantle over the heater were in fragments on the floor. Looking further, Jonko noticed the front doors hanging open, like the cupboard beside it. Of the entrance to the hidden room, he saw no sign. A huge, modernistic picture had been lifted from the wall and rested against it. The bottom of the frame was on the floor, and the canvas had been slashed. He concentrated on thinking a terse report, guessing that Kryslie would be listening for him.

She sent back, forcing the thoughts into his mind, "Louis reset the protective field on the entrance to this room, but not on his separate communicator and file cache. I think he knew who came, and didn't expect trouble, and didn't expect to be away from here for long."

Jonko thought a sense of agreement; not knowing the missing man, he really couldn't say. Without moving, in case an outside observer noticed the movement, he transmitted into the passage leading from the entrance room and began to make his way to the far end of the house.

Louis Devalos had designed his hidden room very cleverly. It wasn't large, only about two metres by one metre. The entrance, from the formal room, was under the large picture Jonko had seen on the floor, but there was no trace of the door, or a means to open it. That was due to the protective field that Kryslie had set up for him, using technology unknown on Earth. She had also given him some advanced equipment to record and preserve his reports.

That this room was undisturbed was a bonus for her, but she did not believe it would stay that way. If the searchers came back and attacked the walls, they would find the room.

Kryslie felt the need to hurry and wasted no time going to specific wall panels and pressing on the magnetic catches, and revealing Louis's equipment.

Everything in the room was compact - the communicator panel was set into the outer brick of the house frame, and hidden by one flap. A small wi-fi hand set was set into a neat recess next to the touch pad that operated it. It looked like the one in the main part of the house, but had extra functions built in by Tymos - calls made from it, and to it, were untraceable.

A second panel, when lowered, revealed the keypad and screen of a small computer with a picture tucked behind it. Kryslie checked and found a small optical disk in the drive.

Had the intruders found this space, found the computer and disk, they could not have read it. They would have no conception that the optical images were encrypted using Louis's unique thought patterns. He wasn't a telepath like Kryslie was, but that wasn't necessary to use this Tymorean designed equipment. However, any human trying to read the disk via the computer would think it was blank. Even if they put the headset on, it would not help. The headset and the computer encrypted spoken and visual data, using a particular memory chosen by Louis. For anyone else to read the contents of the disk, they needed the decoder and an identically designed headset.

Kryslie needed to discover what Louis had recorded, and was grateful that the disk had not been found and taken. She went to where she knew of a hidden niche in the floor and took out the decoder. The extra headphones were there, and she put these on before inserting the disk in the player. As a telepath, Kryslie could have understood the stored data without the headset, since she knew the thought image that Louis used as the encryption key. It was the picture of his wife and daughter that was tucked behind the small computer. However, the headset made it easier, and speed was important.

Starting at the beginning of the record on the disk, Kryslie saw Louis's face and heard his voice. He always recorded his calls to her this way. The image and sound came into her mind like a telepathic message and the start was the communication that Louis had sent to her two days before, and then she saw him disconnect the communicator and there was a break in the recording as if he had put the device on pause.

Then he began speaking again, explaining that he needed to clarify some points before stating the information he was to give her - background information to the events that led up to him finding out the information about the conspiracy. He was putting events into perspective, starting to describe the background of the person he was about to speak of, but as yet had not named, then he abruptly stopped speaking. On the sound track was a chime that Kryslie recognised as Louis's front door bell.

In her mind, she saw Louis glance up to where another screen was currently hidden by a wall flap. That screen showed an image from a hidden security camera set outside the front door. Louis stood, removed the headset and stopped the recording.

That was all that was on the disk, and Kryslie considered the expression that had been on Louis's face, as she removed the disk from the decoder. Mild annoyance, but not alarm.

Very quickly, she removed all the disks from the cache and put them in her pocket. Then, she re-hid the decoder and headset, and was about to re-hide the computer and screen when she felt the impact of Jonko's alarm and dismay. He had seen what Kryslie had sensed in the far room. Finishing her task, she transmitted to join him.

Kryslie knew the room from previous visits; it was the bedroom of Louis's daughter. Litzi and she had decorated the white and yellow painted walls with a frieze of galloping horses, situated at head height to the six-year-old girl.

Now, it was lit only dimly by the beam of Jonko's torch and the nightlight. Kryslie adjusted her sight to see in the dark, and saw dark patches on the floor carpet and the child's bedding. By the bed, Jonko was kneeling beside an unconscious woman, using the knife to free her from the bindings of wide, plasticised adhesive tape. She glanced around and saw the slumped form of a child in the armchair by the bed.

Adjusting her eyes again, this time to see the energy flows in the child, she was relieved to see they were strong. The woman, Louis's wife Jenala, was in a much more serious state, and had wounds that were still slowly oozing blood. Her nose smelt the metallic tang of blood, and the less pleasant smell that indicated both mother and child had fouled themselves.

Anger roused within her at the thought that they must have been lying tied up since Louis disappeared. She could not leave them there, nor did she dare call the local medics as she did not know who had attacked them. Still, there was a little she could do.

Jonko turned to her and hissed, "We can't leave them here!"

"See if you can find clothes for them both, particularly the child."

He stiffened at her tone, sensing the anger there, but moved at once to obey. He checked the drawers near the bed and the wardrobe next to the door. He needed the torch, but remembered to keep the beam pointing downwards, so it would not be seen through the window. As he took clothes out, he realised that Kryslie had placed her hand on the woman's forehead - and he recalled that she could start wounds healing. He wished Tymos was here; he could heal her completely.

Kryslie concentrated on the oozing wounds, speeding up the process of closing the them. Then she gently felt over Jenala's head, where she had seen indications of a head wound. She found the lump and concentrated on reducing the swelling.

As she sent healing energy there, she considered the reason that Jenala and Litzi had been targeted. Was it to make Louis tell them something? Did they think Jenala knew something? Knew where something was? The house had been thoroughly searched…

If Louis had evidence against the Imperium, did the intruders think he was working for the United World Nations?

She would need to find out if Jenala knew anything. More importantly, she needed to get them somewhere safe. If Louis had married a Tymorean descendent, she would have had no qualms about taking them to Earthbase - but Jenala was fully human.

A moan from the direction of the chair distracted Kryslie. She reached out her free hand and touched the child's leg. Litzi whimpered as if in pain, but did not come fully awake. Blood was rushing back into the freed limbs, and that could be painful - but most of the pain was from a headache.

To Kryslie, it seemed obvious that Jenala had been trying to protect Litzi. Had the intruders hurt her? Moving her concentration to the child, Kryslie reassured herself that Litzi only had a mild concussion and bruising.

Jonko left the room to go to the master bedroom that was next to the child's room. Kryslie made a decision. Human or not, she would send Jenala to Earthbase.

Releasing Litzi, Kryslie reached into a pocket for her communicator and remote relay device. She still had it set to the system at the warehouse so could send a message signal. There was no faint ping, to indicate the signal had gone through. She estimated the time and controlled a growl of frustration. Vincent and Keleb were probably in the middle of shifting the system.

Abruptly, Jonko ran back into the room and crouched next to Kryslie. He had a plastic bag stuffed with clothing, but he was alarmed. His soft voice warned, "There are people outside, walking around close to the house. I heard one try the window, and saw his shadow move past it. I don't think he saw me, I had the light aimed down."

Just then, they heard the window in that room rattle. "Why don't they come in? The front door is wide open?" Jonko asked.

One idea came to Kryslie - they could be watching the front and back door, and checking there were no other escape routes.

Her increased alarm surged through the twin bond. She felt Tymos reacting and heard his thought, "What?"

With rapid images, Kryslie showed him her situation, and told him that she could not raise Homebase. He in turn, was frustrated. He could not help her; his current task was both delicate and vital.

"Get the child, Jon," Kryslie said urgently. "Do you think those outside are police?"

"No," was Jonko's definite reply. He lifted Litzi and waited for Kryslie to continue.

She accepted his conclusion and said, "We'll go to Louis's hidden room - it will give us time to figure out where to go. Tym can't come, and I can't reach Earthbase with my communicator - I will need to try Louis's equipment."

Jonko nodded, knowing Kryslie would sense his agreement. He reached for his transmitter and dematerialised. In the darkened room, the brief period of dematerialisation produced a faint glow.

Kryslie lifted Jenala, and as she pressed her transmitter, she heard the window to Litzi's room shatter.

Chapter 9 - Defending the Innocents

After arriving within the tiny hidden room, Kryslie lowered Jenala to the floor - and left her propped against the wall at one end. Jonko placed Litzi beside her.

"What now?" Jonko asked.

"Go down to the other end; look for an odd shaped stain on the wall. Run your hand over it. That is where the distortion field around the communicator is activated. You will need to change the frequency setting on the unit to 512 omega. Call home base - hopefully someone is monitoring the system."

Jonko sprang to obey, but froze when the wall right next to them trembled from the force of a kick.

"Hurry!" Kryslie mentally urged him, before picturing a different person and sending an urgent thought.

"Chave!"

Chave Zieman was another of the Tymorean missionary descendents, and Louis's second in his group of agents. He was used to sensing Kryslie in his mind, but could not always answer immediately. He needed to be alone to concentrate on his reply. This time Kryslie found it hard to be patient, so she concentrated on sensing the nature of the four men who had stormed into the house, and who had already split up to search.

"Krys? What?" Chave's thought was in his mind for her to read.

"Louis is missing. Jenala and Litzi hurt. Can I bring them to you?"

Kryslie sensed his alarm and fear.

"I spoke to Louis two days ago. I might have been followed - I know I have people watching my house."

He didn't say that he had people with him in his house, but their presence now alarmed him.

"Be alert, Chave. Watch what you say," Kryslie thought at him. "I will deal with things here."

She sensed his regret as well as his sudden alertness. He would have to deal with his situation; she had to help Jenala and Litzi first.

Jonko was still trying to raise Homebase, and was twitching with agitation at not getting a response.

"Try the phone, Jon," she thought at him, as she drew out the stun weapon she had confiscated from Harrison back at the radiation zone in America. Into his mind, she inserted the area code and the phone number of the warehouse.

Even if the equipment was in transit to Earthbase, or there but not yet connected to power - Jon's calls should be recorded, but they needed an answer immediately. The phone at the warehouse would still be connected - Hillary would still be there, finalising other details.

Returning her focus to Chave Zieman, located several miles away in the centre of the city, she commanded, "Chave - send the local police here. Report an intrusion, but remain anonymous." She sensed him going to obey, as Jonko announced, "I have Hillary."

Kryslie left Jenala, she had no more time to spend helping her heal. She moved quickly to the phone, pressing her weapon into Jonko's free hand as she took the handset. "Cover us."

Speaking softly, but distinctly, Kryslie told Hillary what she needed, and was relieved that the long-range beam generator had not yet been removed. It made things easier.

"Set it to these coordinates," Kryslie continued, quoting a string of numbers. "The room here is constricted."

At the far end of the phone line, half a world away, Hillary dropped the phone and ran to do what Kryslie asked.

In the room, Kryslie held the phone and drew another weapon - this one emitted an energy beam. At any moment, the intruders, who sounded to be wrecking the room beyond, might try this wall again. So far, they had unknowingly kicked the area covered by the protective force field, but Kryslie knew it only covered the connecting door, and a limited area around it.

A different voice spoke over the phone connection, and into Kryslie's ear. "Vincent. Do you need me there?"

"No, this position is about to be exposed. I have two injured who need to be evacuated. One hybrid child, one human woman."

Vincent understood the urgency, and reported, "Five seconds to full power."

Kryslie terminated the call, and returned to Jenala. She sent power to her to make her rouse.

The woman began to struggle until Kryslie whispered, "Quiet, Jenala. It's Kryslie."

"Thank God! Louis is he…"

"I'll find him," Kryslie promised. "I need you to be very quiet, and I am going to get you out of the house."

Another loud thud, made Jenala whimper. Kryslie glanced at the wall beside her and saw a metal wedge protruding through the plaster. It was yanked out and another thud followed. Light came through the hole in the wall.

"You need to trust me," Kryslie urged Jenala. "You will see something strange, and you will feel an odd sensation - but you will be away from here and safe amongst friends. Tell Vincent all you can. He is a doctor as well."

The long-range beam terminus winked into existence and opened into an oval shape - barely wide enough for two people close together. It glowed faintly, to normal human sight. Keleb came through, saw Kryslie and trotted closer. At her pointed direction, he lifted Litzi, returned to the terminus and transmitted away. Jenala stood up unsteadily, eyes fixed on the place where her daughter had disappeared.

Vincent suddenly appeared, and Krys felt Jenala sway next to her. This was so very strange to her.

"This is Vincent," Kryslie whispered. "He is a friend of Louis, and myself. He will take you to Litzi and tend to both of you."

Vincent offered his hand, but Jenala was too dizzy to walk. Without wasting a further moment, he lifted her as if she were a child and took her through the beam terminus.

With Jonko standing watch, Kryslie began to jerk the communicator panels from the wall. They heard more thudding, and now, a steel bar penetrated the wall. Both of them heard a voice from the other side.

Kryslie understood, "There is something behind here." Jonko guessed the meaning from the tone of the voice. There was little time for finesse.

Keleb returned through the still active beam terminus, Kryslie gave him the decoder and the records, the most important things. He was gone and returned very quickly. His eyes went to where the bar was widening the hole, but he took the first of the communicator panels and obeyed her command of, "Hurry."

She gave the last panel to Jonko after taking her weapons back. "Go, and deactivate the beam."

One voice beyond the wall was exhorting others to break the wall down. Kryslie moved to get her small backpack, and just missed being hit by the next thrust of the bar. She holstered her weapon, and took out her transmitter. As she waited the few seconds for it to power up, a torch beam shone through the hole, catching her in the eyes. Then a gun was fired through the hole - they knew someone was in this hidden space.

As soon as the transmitter was ready, she activated it, calculating from memory an estimate of where she wanted to arrive.

She re-materialised in a shadow, beside the house across the street. She lowered her pack and edged to where she could see Louis's house. She could hear sirens approaching, and waited to see what would happen. Her acute hearing picked up the tone of angry disbelief from the house across the road. Everywhere else, close around her, was unnaturally quiet.

She heard a whistle, and then the four men in the house came racing out, carrying their axes and steel bars. They went to the dark van that had been parked close by, and slammed the door when the last man was inside. The van's engine revved and the vehicle's wheels spun on the tarred surface, leaving the smell of burnt rubber in the air when the van had accelerated away.

Lights came on in several houses across the street and the curtains in one twitched, but no one emerged from the houses. When the police car with its blaring siren turned into the street, all lights went out.

Two figures emerged from the car, once it stopped. In the vague light from the moon, a badge reflected light. Both figures drew weapons, as they cautiously approached the gaping door of Louis's house. While standing either side of the door, one called into the house, "Anyone in there?"

They waited, heard no sound, and entered - still alert for trouble. Kryslie watched as lights came on in the house, indicating that the men were checking each room. She wasn't concerned about what they would find, Louis and his family would not be going back there. She was, however, interested in what they would do. That the curious neighbours had doused lights when they approached, suggested that they had as little interest in having the police notice them, as they had in attracting the interest of the earlier group.

Eventually, one of the figures returned to the car, and used the radio. He was calling up reinforcements of some kind.

Kryslie decided she had seen enough, and adjusted her transmitter to take her to Chave Zieman's house.

He'd had guests earlier, and she had not checked to see if they were gone before arriving. However, her entrance point was a small utility room on the second floor of his house. There was just enough room for her to turn around, but it was usually empty and kept locked.

When Chave had first moved into the house, they had agreed to keep this room clear so she could arrive without being seen. He was a well-known figure in the city, and often had informal gatherings, where his guests might wander into even the private parts of the house.

Kryslie shrugged her pack off and sent a query to Chave's mind. His ability to sense her mind voice worked better if she sent words or short two to three word phrases. "Clear?"

In Chave's mind, she sensed him thinking, "Yes." It came with a sense of his current location and Kryslie, who knew the house, recognised the room as the one Chave used when he was alone.

She transmitted to arrive in front of him, and he rose to greet her, gesturing her to a chair.

Before she sat, she glanced around, checking that the heavy curtains over his window were fully closed. They were, so if there were watchers on the house, all they would see was a faint line of light around the edge, and no suspicious extra silhouettes.

"I'm sorry," he blurted. "I dared not let you bring them here." He stayed standing, and he was uneasy.

Kryslie shook her head to forestall further recrimination. "Jenala and Litzi are safe. What did you speak to Louis about when you saw him?"

Chave went to a side cupboard, and took out a bottle of the potent local liqueur, poured a small measure into a glass and drank it quickly. He was seriously alarmed if he felt the need of a strong drink.

What he, Louis and a handful of other people were doing, was dangerous. Treason was punished harshly in the Imperium, and even though the city of Jafhabad was not in the country ruled by the Imperium's leader, Abdul bin Halil, and the country had its own elected government, Kryslie knew who controlled them.

Returning to his chair, Chave sat forward, and seemed to consider where to begin.

"I was invited to an open discussion with a group of history students. Dev Klim takes history at the university. I often ask him questions when I need to consider the economic policies of various eras. I have been, at different times, asked to write commentaries on current or proposed economic policies of the government. This 'discussion' started on current policies. Klim knows I think the current government is weak. It led to a discussion of wartime policies. Now, in my classes, I try to avoid that era. The past few governments have insisted that this period be forgotten so that the country can move ahead - but, also because most of the records of policies from that time have been destroyed."

"Interesting," Krys murmured. "There was a purge of the wartime government, wasn't there?"

Chave nodded. "I would be interested to study that era," he admitted. "Because, as Klim commented, the policy – whatever it was, kept the country prosperous despite the depredations of the war. Other countries did not fare so well."

"What else did Klim say?"

"He asked if I felt the same policies might work today. I told him I could not honestly say. Without seeing the policy documents of the time, I can't figure where the prosperity came from."

"How did Klim take that?"

"Well, I think he was satisfied. I thought he might have been testing me – for loyalty to the government. But then again, I was not sure. He told me, after the students left, that he had seen microfilm copies of what seemed to be government documents of the war years."

"Really," Krys was interested in that. "Go on."

"I was properly sceptical," Chave told Krys. "But he said it had been in the vaults somewhere – as part of the evidence in the post war trials of government officials."

"Let me put this in perspective," Krys thought aloud. "The war, when these loosely allied countries over here attacked the UWN, then known as America, was led by the government of this country? How many other countries were involved?"

"Five," Chave said at once. He named them. "The leaders of those countries were executed and their governments disbanded. The World Council was involved with that."

In that immediate post war period, Krys had been out of touch with the policies of the region. She had been a 'guest' in the country ruled by Abdul bin Halil. That his country had not been mentioned in Chave's list meant nothing, only that bin Halil had been very clever. She knew he had been involved.

"Was there more? Even if only conjecture?" Krys asked.

"Nothing but feelings," Chave said. "I had the feeling that Klim knew or had known Claude Santon, the economics minister during the war. Santon, if he is still alive, would be about Klim's age – fifty something."

"Santon escaped?" Krys queried.

Chave nodded. "There is still a World Council bounty out on him. I did mention that feeling to Louis, and he implied he had heard other rumours about several other ministers being alive."

"You mentioned nothing that might point to a conspiracy?"

Chave shook his head, and then stopped, as if something had just occurred to him.

"I have been seeing a lot of my students wearing a silver chain with a silver star on it. All of that group of Klim's had them too. I assumed it was a fraternity thing, but I noticed that Klim had a gold chain and star."

"Have you seen others," Krys asked intently.

Chave considered that question for a long moment as he sorted out memories.

"I have cultivated a lot of diverse interests, and know people in a few elite circles. Yes, now I think of it, I have seen other gold star wearers." He named a few and added, "All those men have impeccable public images and are high up in industry, politics, science and the arts."

"That might be important," Krys said aloud. "How often do you visit Louis?"

"Only if I have a lot to tell him," Chave told her. "He is also my accountant, so that is my overt reason to visit him."

"I think from now on, you need to be careful. Do you see the others that report to Louis?"

"No, but I know who they are."

"It would be wise if you kept away from them," Kryslie said absently, for she was considering what Chave had told her. "I don't think you are any part of the reason why Louis was taken, but I don't have all the facts yet. Do you know if Louis knows Klim?"

"He never mentioned him," Chave said immediately. "However, he did have other academics as clients, as well as several low ranking government ministers."

"That may be significant, or maybe coincidence. What I do think is that Klim might be trying to cultivate you - recruit you for some purpose."

"To work for the Imperium? Against the UWN?" Chave shuddered at the thought. He knew too much about the disguised tyranny in the

Imperium. It went against every instinct for peace, equality and personal freedom bred into him by his Tymorean forebears. He was also a man who liked his modest affluence and prominent position.

"See how things play out," Kryslie advised. "Don't think of our work as being for or against any political belief. A safer opinion would be that you want to help your country become the equal of others in the world."

Chave thought on that and a faint smile relaxed his face. Put that way, Klim might think him anti-UWN - but those who disliked Emperor bin Halil's overrule, would think the opposite.

"How will I contact you?" Chave asked. "I don't have any equipment."

"You don't. I will keep in touch as I did today."

"How can I help find Louis?"

"Leave that to me. Just keep your ears open and wits about you," was Kryslie's advice.

"However, do you have any clothes that I might borrow to walk around in?"

"Of course," Chave agreed. "Upstairs, second door on the right. I tell people I keep the room for my sister. Take what you need."

Chave watched Kryslie dematerialise as she transmitted away. He did not have the power to use a transmitter, and was perversely glad. The idea of becoming a cloud of molecules did not appeal to him.

Kryslie returned looking very different now that she had changed from her all in one jumpsuit, to the attire worn by the local women. The style was more liberal than the traditional dress, but still quite concealing by UWN standards. The long skirt was a dark brown shade, as was the long sleeved top. And now, her noticeable red hair was hidden under the dark scarf that she had wrapped around her head and neck.

Chave rose, giving her appearance a critical survey. All he did was tuck the end of the headscarf in at the shoulder. It was the first time he had seen her dressed this way. He was used to seeing her in the jumpsuit, and did not consider it scandalous. His fellow countrymen, those whose ancestors were native to the country, would object to seeing a female dressed as a male, but Kryslie normally stayed out of sight.

"You will need to be careful," Chave warned. "That dress will give you a degree of protection, and make men think you are an adherent of the old customs, but they will also expect you to behave in certain ways."

He was about to add more when his doorbell, audible in his private area, announced a late visitor.

"I will see myself out," Kryslie stated, grabbing her pack. She didn't leave by the door, but transmitted away.

She didn't go far, just back to the utility room. Chave had been alarmed by the inference of Klim's interest in him, and further by the news that Louis was missing. The late visitor had made him very uneasy. Kryslie, seeing parallels with what had happened to Louis, decided to take no chances. She would wait to see who the visitor was. She linked her mind to Chave's - very lightly, so he would not sense her there.

Through that link, she saw the callers were a man and a female, and Chave instantly relaxed. He liked that woman very much. She withdrew her mind link, considering a surge of extraneous thoughts that passed through Chave's mind. The first was surprise, since it was past dark and women were meant to be off the street by nightfall. The second followed on, when he had noticed the companion. If women had to go out, they were meant to be accompanied by a male guardian.

That was a potential problem, in the off chance that she was seen and challenged. She didn't intend to be seen, but she could not use her transmitter if she did not have a clear idea of her destination.

Kryslie considered going to Earthbase before visiting the rest of Louis's team. She tried contacting Hillary using her communicator, but received no answer. The equipment, and Hillary, were probably away from the warehouse by now, and the equipment not yet reactivated. It meant, she could not arrange for the long-range beam to be located on her.

There was another way. "Tym?" she thought at her twin. "Where are you?"

His terse reply indicated that his mind was on some problem.

"Earthbase." The wordless image he sent was of his hand on Jenala's forehead.

"Has she told Vincent anything?"

"Not much. What do you need?"

"To know if Louis said he was going anywhere?"

"Wait."

Kryslie sensed that he had his full attention on Jenala. After a few minutes, his mind voice informed her, "No. When the doorbell rang, she was putting the little one to bed. Calls in the evening are not unusual. This time two men burst into the room, and threatened her. They wanted to know where something was. She had no idea what they meant, and said she knew nothing of Louis's work. They wanted to take Litzi, to make her husband talk. Another man said to tie them up for now."

He didn't put into words the sense he had that Jenala was still very traumatised, and if Vincent couldn't help her, Kryslie might need to use her own gift for mind healing. He was doing all he could to heal both mother and child.

"I need to visit the others who work with Louis," Kryslie sent back.

There was no sense of disagreement from Tymos, who had been doing most of the work in the Imperium. Nor did he allude to the danger she faced if seen. She would do what she believed to be important, and could look after herself.

"Should I send Jonko back?" he did ask.

Since she intended to stay unseen, and for that, one was better than two. Her friend might be useful as a 'male guardian' but not if he was in foreign style clothes.

"No, but can you keep the long-range beam located on me?"

Tymos sent an affirmative thought, but his mind filled with the need to get the long-range beam generator from the warehouse reactivated. It had several pre-set and direct coded coordinates - one was the locator signal from her communicator.

While still being within the small room at Chave's house, Kryslie entered the coordinates for her next destination into her transmitter, and then adjusted them slightly so that she would arrive outside the house.

Dequis and his wife Beth were both Tymorean descendents, and would not be surprised to see her materialise unexpectedly in their house, but Kryslie wanted to see if the house was being watched. She arrived in the open back garden area and immediately drew on Earth's energy aura, to hide her.

It was a wise precaution. She was no more than four metres from the house, and with her eyes adjusted, she could see a dark clad figure moving stealthily from window to window and finally pausing near the rear door to look around. He could have been a mere burglar, since all the windows were dark and the occupants might have been away.

The figure moved towards her, past her, and looked around the shared open garden beyond Dequis's personal back garden. All the houses in the square block shared the area for cultivating vegetables and fruits, and shared the harvest. He was making certain there were no late gardeners at work and which of the houses had lights on.

The dark figure moved back to Dequis's house, still oblivious to her, and met with a second dark figure.

Kryslie moved slightly, as she adjusted her transmitter, and was visible for a few seconds before she transmitted into the entrance area of the house. She almost had a knife thrust into her as she materialised. Dequis had caught the slightest movement, a silhouette against the dim light coming from a side room, and acted on instinct. Kryslie sensed how edgy he was, as she grabbed his arm and held it away from her.

"I'm Kryslie. You are obviously aware that your house is being watched," she said in Tymorean, and immediately, Dequis relaxed. Kryslie released him. He moved to look out of a small window beside his front door.

"Did anyone see you?" he asked, staring out into the darkened street. His twitchy movements betrayed his state of tension.

"No," she assured him. "How long have you known you were being watched?"

"Only since this evening. Beth saw some strangers out in the garden as she was bringing in the washing. She told me that Louis and his family were missing."

"How did she hear?"

"Beth knows some of Jenala's neighbours. They'd seen men go in with guns, and Louis dragged out. No one has seen Jenala or Litzi since."

In Dequis's mind, 'men' meant officials of the Imperium, and Kryslie agreed.

"I think you should leave. Will that be a problem?"

"No. Beth wants to, but we have no where to go."

They both heard a noise that sounded just outside the door - then the doorbell rang.

"I will take you to Earthbase," Kryslie said quickly. "Get Beth and hurry."

Dequis trotted off, making little sound. He returned quickly with his wife and their new baby, and he carried two bulging bags that had been hastily stuffed with clothes.

Beth whispered in awe, "The ancestors, they are back?" The doorbell rang again and this time it was followed by a very loud banging on the door.

"The ancestors have not returned. Younger missionaries have come, but they are still kin and you would be welcome. A moment," Krys told her. Then she thought at her brother. "Tym, can you locate a long-range beam on me? Can you come through and help three to the base?"

"Done," Tymos sent. The faintly glowing terminus appeared behind Krys.

Beth stifled a gasp, and Dequis stiffened until he recognised Tymos.

"Come close to me," Tym directed. "We will need to walk into the terminus very close together. It will feel a little odd, but it is safe and no one will see you leave. Daniel is expecting you and I think Jenala will appreciate a friendly face."

"Thank you, Krys," Dequis said just before they vanished from sight. The terminus blinked out.

Kryslie didn't wait to see what was going to happen. She knew that Dequis had nothing at his house to raise or confirm suspicions, and those at the door would not wait much longer before bursting in. She reset her transmitter and was gone before the door burst open.

Chapter 10 - Eluding Capture

Alen was one of the new Tymorean born missionaries, and he lived alone in an apartment in a building on the edge of the city. Kryslie materialised in his lounging room and found it empty. She moved quietly to his bedroom and heard his gentle even breathing. Needing to wake him without giving him a chance to raise an alarm, she placed a hand over his mouth and spoke in Tymorean. "It's Kryslie. Wake up."

Alen tensed for a fraction of a second and then relaxed. "What's the matter?"

He sat up and swung his feet off the bed, and turned on a bedside light. With a swift glance at her unusual attire, he reached for his jeans. He had been sleeping in his underwear.

"Louis is missing. It looks like the Imperium's secret thugs have him. When did you last speak to him?"

"Not for several weeks. I have been away and only got back today."

"I don't know how much they think they know," Kryslie went on. Alen knew which 'they' she meant. "But they roughed up Louis's family and left them tied up, and I just spirited Dequis and his family away to Earthbase to join Jenala and Litzi. Their house was being watched as well."

"What about the others? Chave, Rovan, Tomas, Ferdinand?"

"Chave is being watched, but he is staying. I think they are trying to recruit him, and are possibly checking him out. I will go to the others but you need to be careful."

"Do you need my help?" Alen offered.

Kryslie shook her head. "I don't want to give them suspicions about you. How well do you know Tomas and Ferdinand?"

They were the two of Louis's group who were wholly human.

"By sight," Alen admitted. "They don't know that I work with Louis too. Anything that I can do? I don't have to worry about a family, and I can get away if I have to."

Kryslie considered. "You work at the docks, don't you?"

"Shipping office," Alen corrected.

"Have you seen many people around wearing silver stars on a chain?"

Alen shook his head. "Not the labourers and I don't think any of my work colleagues or my boss do. But I know the sort of thing you mean. We had a VIP pass through. Governor Dhori. I saw one on him."

Krys stored that information in her mind. "Keep your eyes out for them, and try to identify who they are and what they do. I will call you periodically. If you need to reach me, call Earthbase on the same frequency you used for Louis. And keep alert. I need to talk to Rovan."

Krys sensed trouble as soon as she reached the little shop and residence where Rovan lived. The shop had all its windows broken at the front, and dark figures were going in and out, looting the shop.

She could not sense Rovan within, but her sense of trouble was strong.

Once again, she transmitted in. She arrived in the living area of the residence. She almost stepped on Rovan's body. He had not been dead for long; his body was still warm. Krys adjusted her eyes to see better in the dim light coming from the streetlights outside. She saw no bleeding and no other signs of violence until she rolled him over. The glow around his back told her he had been killed with an energy weapon. Single shot, close range.

Krys felt up and down Rovan's body, checking his pockets - nothing there to indicate his attacker. Then she felt his hand clenched loosely. In it was her first clue – a silver chain. She looked over the floor and saw the silver star. She took both with her and transmitted up to the roof.

She only stayed there a moment, long enough to program the coordinates for her next destination, and to report what she had found to her twin.

"Until now, I have learnt nothing to indicate those star wearers are involved," Tymos told her. "This may be a coincidence."

Kryslie told him about the man Klim, who wore a gold star, and who was interested in Chave.

"I'll look into things, and see about recovering Rovan's body," Tymos told her. "Where are you headed next?"

"I have to visit the non-Tymoreans."

Tymos knew who she meant, and knew that Louis used them to get information, but that they were ignorant of his covert activities. Rovan was a Tymorean descendant and had been more active.

Approaching the last two of Louis's informers was more of a problem, and the reason she had chosen to wear local style clothing. Since neither knew about Tymoreans, she couldn't just transmit into their homes and appear in front of them. Furthermore, they had never met her.

Tymos had checked both Tomas and Ferdinand and he felt they were sincere in their determination to undermine Abdul bin Halil. He had supplied details about each of them.

Kryslie went to Tomas's address first, knowing that his was one of the two ground floor units in a four unit building. He was single, and lived alone. Kryslie used coordinates supplied by her brother to transmit to the building, or rather, to a sliver of shadow nearby. She paused there to survey the scene. The left hand ground floor apartment where Tomas lived was dark. As she watched, a light in the unit above flicked off. The other two units were already dark. She was about to transmit herself across the open space to approach the door of the unit in the usual human fashion when a dark van drove up outside the building. The van's lights went out quickly, but Kryslie had seen enough to know it was the same make and model as the one that had been outside Louis's house. This time, she memorised the licence plate, and wasted no further time. The men would scout the exterior of the building, and then crash in. She had little time to act.

In spite of her reservations, Kryslie transmitted into the building, estimating distance and direction to arrive just outside Tomas's door.

A quick glance around the dimly lit foyer told her that she was alone. The area was empty except for two potted plants, two doorways and the start of a flight of steps. She transmitted again, to arrive just inside Tomas's unit.

Standing still, she listened for sounds and adjusted her eyes to see in the dark. She was in a lounging area with couch, two chairs and an assortment of throw cushions. Various cabinets stood against two walls, a bookshelf under a window against the third. Two doors led off, one led to where gentle snores were emanating from, the second led to a kitchen and other smaller rooms.

Aware of the men outside, Kryslie had a very quick look into the kitchen, and spared a moment to sense for presences in the small rooms.

Only the bedroom was occupied. She returned to the partly open bedroom door and sidled in, closing the door after her. There was an empty chair near by, and she soundlessly lifted it and jammed the back under the door handle.

In a quick sweeping glance, she surveyed the room. Faint light from outside penetrated the lightweight curtains over the double width, two-metre high window. The double bed had one sleeper, on the far side. The near side had the covers thrown back, as if someone had just got up. There was a bedside cabinet with a small drawer partly open, and a lamp on top. A similar lamp rested on a matching cabinet on the sleeper's side of the bed.

Kryslie was already moving, making no sound on either the polished wood floor or the scattered floor mats. She avoided the portable screen that mostly hid a cheap rail for hanging clothes, and stopped between the bed and the window looking down at the sleeper. It was a woman; Thomas wasn't there.

In an instant of consideration, Kryslie knew she could not leave the woman. She knew what the men outside would do to her if they realised Tomas wasn't there.

Placing her hand gently on the woman's mouth, she used her other hand to gently shake her awake. She saw the woman's eyes open suddenly, going wide and gleaming faintly in the dim light. The woman's body stiffened.

In the local dialect, Kryslie whispered, "You have to get out of here. Men are coming for Thomas."

The woman twisted and realised that the bed beside her was empty. She pushed Kryslie's hand aside.

"What have you done to him?" she hissed, drawing the covers up as she sat up.

"Nothing. He was already gone."

"Then why are you here? Who are you?"

"I am a friend of Louis," Kryslie told her, meaning to reassure her. "You need to hurry."

"I don't know you. I don't know anyone named Louis," the woman insisted. "Why should I go with you?" She was reaching one arm down beside the bed.

Kryslie tried once more. "Didn't you hear me? Officials are coming for him."

The woman was alarmed, but her reaction was not the expected one. She flung something cylindrical and solid at the intruder by her bed. Her aim was poor, but Kryslie plucked the object from the air before it clattered to the floor.

"If you don't get out of here, I will scream!"

Feeling frustration at the woman's refusal to believe her danger, Kryslie tried once more to convince her. "When they don't find Tomas, they will beat you until you convince them that you don't know, and then leave you tied up and helpless to rot." She knew that time was running out.

The woman drew in a sharp breath as if the truth finally reached her mind. She sprang out of bed, clad only in a dark negligee, and reached to grab clothes from the second chair.

A solid thud at the door rattled the chair jammed under it. Like an echo, the large window shattered and two black clad figures billowed the light curtain. The woman screamed and clutched her clothes; Kryslie drew a weapon and fired twice in rapid succession, the only sound being the buzz of the emitted stun beam. The figures that were trying to get free of the curtain, slumped to the floor, bringing down the curtain rod with their combined weight on the curtain.

The thudding on the door became more urgent as Kryslie tried to push the woman towards the window. Instead, the woman tried to get to her bedside cabinet, as the chair finally gave way and the door flew open. Kryslie spun around, firing at the balaclava wearing man that was half running, half stumbling into the room. From the subdued buzz, Kryslie knew her stun weapon was now low on charge. The man fell, as if he had stumbled, but he wasn't unconscious and would probably get up quite soon.

Something hard struck Kryslie's head, knocking her off balance before she could grab the woman again.

"Help! Someone! Hurry, before she gets up," the woman yelled at full volume.

It was abruptly obvious to Kryslie, in that instant, that the woman was not an innocent in this affair. She knew that the men were going to come, and had only been concerned because Tomas had snuck out on her.

Any anxiety for her as an innocent, changed to a need to get away. Kryslie did not want to be seen and later recognised. She grabbed the woman as she sprung back to her feet and threw her over one shoulder. The woman screamed and struggled, only to find that she was being gripped by a hand like a steel band.

Kryslie's free hand pocketed her weapon and reached for her transmitter as she stepped around the fallen men to reach the window. The woman kept struggling, but her efforts had no effect as her captor began to scramble through the frame.

A buzz from behind, warned her that another person was in the room she had left, but she kept going. The stunner beam must have hit the woman, for she went limp and silent.

Who ever was behind her was not waiting for his weapon to recharge. He was charging through the room. The dressing screen clattered as it fell. It gave Kryslie a few precious seconds, but then the dress she wore caught on some shards of glass still fixed in the frame.

She was aware that the man was calling up reinforcements via a microphone, probably attached to his clothing, and that even then, two more men were approaching from outside. Her hand reached for the transmitter, but an energy beam - hot and sizzling - lanced past her hand and burnt the fabric of her dress.

"Don't move! Step back and put the woman down."

Considering that the two men outside now had automatic projectile weapons aimed at her, she had little choice. They would likely shoot her, and Thomas's woman.

The voice betrayed impatience when it spoke again a second later. "You heard! Put her down or my next shot will cut your legs off at the knees." The sense of malice emanating from the man made his threat deadlier.

All the same, Kryslie did not move quickly, instead she seemed to be carefully manoeuvring so that her captive was not cut on any glass. She was actually using all her senses to study her situation, and looking for a way out that didn't involve vanishing in front of his eyes. Some of her options were limited, due to her need to protect the woman, even if she was a traitor to Tomas.

Once back in the room and clear of the window frame, she turned to avoid stepping on the unconscious men. She glanced at the weapon aimed at her. It was enough for her to know what it was, and its specifications and type of effect. She stared at the covered face of the man and studied his eyes - they were dark and cold, full of rage and soul deep hatred. A weapon like his had killed Rovan, might be used to try to do the same to her - as she, a mere woman, had outwitted three men.

Still moving slowly, she watched the man as she lowered the woman to a clear area of floor. The slowness was not due to caution or fear but to give herself time. The energy from the stunner was still jangling along the woman's nerves, and she would have been in agony if she had stayed conscious. Kryslie drew that excess energy from the woman, and held it within herself, augmenting her own power.

If the man had wanted her dead, he would have killed her right off. Therefore, he would want her alive - to take to his superior…it made sense. His target was obviously gone; she wasn't.

The woman began to stir and moan, Kryslie finished putting her down as her mind calculated where the three, armed men were. She could take them, because they would not expect her to be a skilled fighter. The skirt would be a slight handicap, but she had practiced fighting in all types of clothing. They would not expect her to be extremely fast…no, that would reveal too much of her skills and she did not intend to kill the men. If she let them capture her, they might take her to where they had Louis. She would be inside their base, with a chance to find out more about the cabal they were after.

A movement of the man's arm was the only warning she had. One of the men behind her was about to fire - a stunner, not his automatic weapon. She timed a fall, microseconds before the beam of energy struck her. The full energy charge did not hit her, much passed to one side, though enough reached her to send pain shooting along all nerves and make her body drop the rest of the way.

A normal fit and healthy human would still be fully incapacitated, even with the amount of disruptive energy she had received. It had been set just short of fatal. They knew she was dangerous, and were taking no chances. The difference between Kryslie and a normal human was that she didn't instantly lose consciousness. Instead, she felt the pain come and go in waves of agony. For a time, she would not be able to defend herself.

Kryslie wasn't completely helpless. She was able to direct her fall, so she landed onto Tomas's woman. Her cushion belatedly began to wriggle free, but during the contact, she confirmed that the woman had known that people were coming for Tomas, and she had been meant to keep him there. She was afraid of their anger at her failure, and it was why she had delayed so that the woman intruder could be caught.

Hands pulled her away and turned her over. A voice ordered, "Pull that scarf away."

Kryslie felt the hand that gripped her chin, but she kept her eyes shut, feigning unconsciousness.

"I want light here," the man said next.

Through the contact, Kryslie sensed his thoughts. He had identified her as the red head that had been at Louis's place.

"I want this bitch tied up, gagged and blindfolded."

Seeing her had freaked him, but he was not about to admit it. She had been in a closed room, without any exits he had found, and he had set an incendiary charge into that room and watched it and the house start to burn with fiery intensity.

"Clear out," the man ordered after he dropped her head back to the floor. "How are Aswad and Katar?"

"Heavy stun," was the report.

"Get them to the truck and bring these women."

"Shouldn't I stay? Tomas might return," the woman asked, defiantly, and hoping that she would not have to explain her lapse.

Her reply came with a vicious slap. "Silence! Explain your failure to the General."

Kryslie felt ropes being wrapped around her ankles, and then her wrists. As they yanked them tight, she flexed her muscles. That old trick would mean that her circulation would not be greatly impaired. She was lifted over someone's shoulder and taken out into the warm air of the night and then into the van. She was pushed onto a seat and a seatbelt was used to hold her in place.

Other men climbed into the van, each one rocking it. A body was shoved next to her legs - one of the men she had stunned. Finally the van's rear door was shut firmly and the van began to move.

As the vehicle began to accelerate, Kryslie felt her brother's mind, trying to reach hers. She sensed his concern at being unable to get her to respond.

"I will be okay, in a bit," she assured her brother. He was, she knew, feeling her pain as if it were his own. Now that she was not being handled, she was able to start a biofeedback technique to block it. "They won't expect me to be conscious for hours. If they take me where Louis is, I will have a chance to find out where they have him."

"How much of the stun caught you?"

"Enough so that if they search me, they won't suspect I am faking. Where are you?"

"Close. I have locked onto your transmitter signal. It is still on you?"

"For now."

"I have Jonko and Keleb with me. Just give the word and I will be there."

"I didn't get to Ferdinand," Kryslie warned him.

"I'm on it!" Tymos promised and his mind went elsewhere.

Kryslie concentrated on pain blocking, but was aware of the men talking. She heard the cold-eyed leader asking to see the weapon she had used. Rustling of plastic indicated that the weapon had been bagged for study, and was now being passed hand to hand.

"Looks like one of ours. We can account for all those issued to us?"

He received several affirmations, and then the men were silent.

"That bitch has to be one of the ones we seek. Perhaps a higher up."

"A woman?" one of the men expressed disbelief.

"An unnatural one, but our enemies do not take care of their women," the leader remarked. "The General will be pleased with this piece of luck, even if our other targets escaped."

Tymos sent a thought to his sister's mind. "I have Ferdinand away. I gave him no chance to resist, and now he has heard of this night's doings, he is grateful. I have him with one of our missionaries."

"That's all then - can you have someone watching out for Chave?"

"I put Olassa onto him, and Creedy is following the two men I was watching. What is your plan?"

"Originally, I intended to bring Tomas's woman back with me and question her, but the stupid creature decided to trust the assault team. She is having second thoughts now."

"Is she important?"

Kryslie send a picture of herself shrugging. "I doubt it. The people in this country don't consider women capable of doing work requiring intelligence. She had her chance, and my priority is finding Louis. Since they now think I am either an agent from the UWN, or the World Council, I should get to find out something about the higher ups in this cabal."

"I have you heading into the city," Tymos sent.

He was keeping some thoughts to himself, but through the twin bond, Kryslie knew he was worried.

"What is it?" she asked. "What are you afraid of?"

"We suspect bin Halil is behind this. What if he gets to see your picture?"

"I've been hiding from him long enough. If he is foolish enough to come in person, I will be ready for him. I will be dangerous once more in several hours."

"The other problem will be locating your exact position if they remove your transmitter. There are a lot of buildings here."

"This van has a licence plate of QA 2357X," Kryslie told him. "If you trace the registration, it might give you a clue."

In the rear of the van, it was too dark for Kryslie to use senses other than sight to make out the faces of the men even though she knew they had removed their face coverings. Their idea of gagging and blindfolding consisted of wrapping strips of duct tape across her mouth and eyes. So far, by keeping her eyes shut, the tape had not stuck to her eyelids or lashes.

When the van stopped and the door was opened, the ambient light was still too dim. She had the sense of an area - like a vast garage - for the leader's soft commands were swallowed up, but the opening of the van door had echoed.

First the men near the door stepped out, and then the two still unconscious men were lifted to the bench seats. Kryslie felt a man's head butt her thighs before someone unstrapped her from the seat and half carried, half dragged her from the van and let her slump to a concrete floor. Tomas's woman was told to get out, and she obeyed in silence, but her mind was thinking curses at the men.

The van driver was sent to take the sleeping men to medical help, and another man was told to bring "that woman" inside, into one of the cells.

Kryslie felt herself lifted and thrown over a shoulder and the man jogged a short way and then stopped. He moved one arm and then waited. A whooshing sound was accompanied by a breath of stale recycled air. She guessed it was an elevator opening, and when the door closed again, she had the sensation of going down, although she could not tell how many floors. The lift stopped with a clang, the doors whooshed open again, and she was carried out. At first, she only smelt the dusty smell of concrete and heard the sound of her carrier's boots squeaking faintly as he walked. He stopped again, and she was jostled a bit while the man removed something from a pocket in his upper clothing. This time, the man did something to open a metal door that creaked on its hinges, and when they were through, closed with a solid metallic clank.

Finally, the man turned into a smaller room, hitting her legs on the frame as he manoeuvred in. He dumped her onto a hard narrow bed, made sure that her legs were fully on the thin mattress, before he proceeded to search her. He took the knife she still had in a hidden sheath, her transmitter and communicator, along with the silver chain and star that she had found in Rovan's hand. She had no ID on her, or anything else to give them a clue about her.

The searcher was thorough, even to confirming she was a female, not a male. Only then did he leave her alone to sleep off the stun.

When he left and closed the door, it whooshed and thudded, an odd silence descended, for she could not even hear his retreating footsteps.

Even when he had left her, Krys felt she was being watched, but not from close by. She did not sense another presence in the small cell with her, so she guessed it would be by camera.

Since she was still feeling the effects of the stun, she lay still - giving the watcher no clue that she was not completely helpless. She concentrated on numbing the pain that had been roused again by being carried, dumped and searched. Then she sent a thought to her twin.

"Tym?"

"Can you tell where you are?" was his immediate reply. "As far as I can tell, you could be in any one of a block of tall buildings. I found the corporation that registered the car, but it has no link to any of those buildings." He wasn't frantic, just very concerned.

After recounting the little she could tell him from the arrival in the garage, going down in a lift, and the feel of the cell, she felt her brother considering how to narrow the search. His thoughts suggested that he had infiltrated various government databases. On another level, he was aware that if the need was desperate, he would be able to reach her, but if he arrived when others were around, he would blow their cover as mere human agents.

"They won't expect me to be conscious yet," Kryslie reminded her twin. "We have some time and I expect they will take me elsewhere to question me. I need time to see if I can sense Louis here."

She sensed his, "of course", and then, "I need to check some sources of mine," and his mind dropped the link.

After several hours, Kryslie felt her body begin to twitch spasmodically, a sign that the stun was wearing off. Soon, she knew, they would come and want to question her. Already she had deduced that she was in one of several secure cells, but Louis was not nearby. She had been trying to reach his mind ever since she had arrived. Now, she intensified her efforts.

"Louis?"

"Wha..." she felt the hazy thought.

"Louis – it's Krys."

"Krys?" the mind began to focus. "Can you help me?"

"Soon. Are you in a cell of some kind?"

"Yes. I can't move around."

Krys sensed he had been questioned. More like tortured, she decided, holding onto the weak thought as she sent a warning to Tymos. "Louis will need help."

She sensed his grim reply, "We have the building located. We finally got a lock on your transmitter, but it must be locked in a safe since it won't let us activate it as a beam focus. We are ready to move in - Jon, Kel and I will come when you say. Olassa, has a team ready to run interference. The building has a lot of people working, even though its night."

"I haven't located Louis yet, but they will be coming for me soon. The stun is starting to wear off."

Three men came, minutes later after she heard a snap, and whoosh. She was ready to remain limp when she was grabbed and dangled upright. A hand gripped her chin and forced it upright.

"Remove the tape," a voice ordered in the local language.

Both pieces were ripped off, mercifully fast.

Krys blinked in the bright light and pretended she was still having trouble seeing. If she were just coming out of a stun – her mind would be fuzzy. They would have no way of knowing it wasn't.

"Who are you?" a man in a quality suit demanded.

She didn't answer, feigning instead an inability to speak, because she was still dazed.

But she memorised the man's face and he was wearing a gold star on a chain. He was neither flaunting it nor hiding it.

"Bring her downstairs."

They dragged her out of the cell, along a passage to a lift. This needed an authority code to use. After ascending from the original floor, they dragged her from the lift into a more open area and to a wall. She was held erect while another man clamped a metal band across her chest and forehead. Her hands were then freed, but only so they could also be clamped to the wall. Her legs were freed and forced apart to be clamped at the ankles.

The original two guards were sent away. The new guard, if that was what he was, took a photograph of her, and then her fingerprints.

"Find out who she is," was the command of the well-dressed man. "Let me know when she is alert enough to question."

The guard left her line of vision but Krys couldn't move to look around to see where he went. She did however sense that Louis was close by.

"Tym?" Krys thought. "I am somewhere near Louis."

"We are in the building. I sense you are somewhere below ground."

Krys agreed, "I was brought up a level. What is the building?"

"The Justice Building. Can you get free?"

"Yes, but I am being watched. There is only one guard at the moment, and he could get to me before I am fully free."

"We will go for the power. Be ready."

Krys drew on the ambient energy to restore herself; the lights dimmed perceptibly. The guard moved into her view, glancing around warily.

The lights went out completely. Krys jerked her hands free, breaking the bolts holding the metal to the wall. She then freed her head, chest and ankles. The generator cut in and Krys saw Jonko leaning over the unconscious guard.

"I have Louis," Tym reported.

Jonko gestured to Krys. As soon as she was close, he transported them both to what looked like a private house. Keleb arrived moments later with Louis and gently lowered him into an armchair.

Kryslie wondered where her twin was, and tried to reach him, but his mind was busy. She only sensed he was doing a fast scouting foray of the lower levels of the building. Ten minutes later, he arrived and called up the long-range beam. The five of them traversed it to Earthbase.

Chapter 11 - The calm before the end

Their arrival caused a flurry of activity. Vincent immediately took charge of Louis, issuing orders to bring a stretcher to take him to his infirmary chamber.

Daniel hurried to Krys. "What happened?" he asked, forgetting to address her as Great One.

"I'm fine, Daniel," she said tersely. "I just need a wash, food and decent clothes."

The look he gave her suggested that he didn't believe her, but simply turned and bellowed, "Lexina!"

Kryslie glanced up in surprise as her former classmate hurried over and said, "Great One, this way."

"How long have you been here? I didn't think you had graduated yet."

Lexina grinned. "They hadn't finished testing us all when you left. Then Daniel requested some domestic staff, so the builders didn't have to stop with building the base to prepare food and clean up. I convinced father to let me go, though he told me I was a fool for throwing in my airspace controller studies. He said there were plenty of domestics available."

"But not missionary trained domestics," Kryslie caught on immediately. "I am glad you are here."

Lexina grinned then and revealed, "Stenn wanted to come too, but his father wouldn't let him."

They parted at the chamber now prepared as a bathing room, with Lexina promising to bring towels and clean clothes.

As Kryslie relaxed in the warm water of a real bath, she considered how quickly the base was being made liveable. The builders had to be working around the clock, carrying on from the basic functions she and Tymos had begun. Yet seeing Lexina, brought on new ideas - like the need to have space scanning capabilities. Earth had begun to make the move to space exploration with landings on the moon. Even though it had stopped there for decades, with the state of peace - uneasy as it still was, they were likely to start looking spaceward again. And there were dozens of satellites circling the globe. Someone would be needed to monitor their functions.

Kryslie smiled. Lexina would be perfect for the task of setting up the space scanning systems, once the rest of the base was finished. Perhaps Beth or Jenala would be willing to help with the domestic work until they were ready to return to their own country. She could also bring in some of the missionary descendents who were getting too old for fieldwork.

Vincent found her when she was eating, sitting with Lexina in the developing kitchen cavern. Lexina caught Vincent's glance of dismissal and excused herself.

"Tymos tells me you are getting over a stun, Great One."

"I'm over it, Vincent," Krys told him. "And I am over being annoyed at that stupid woman and being out of practice at fighting in a skirt and letting it hamper me."

"I am pleased to hear that, Great One," Vincent commented neutrally. "I still wish to check you over. Did you rescue the woman?"

"No. Louis was my priority and the woman is where she would have been without my interference. She betrayed Tomas."

She sensed his vague, unvoiced disproval and met his eyes, daring him to object.

He didn't, he simply waited for her to finish eating.

"Louis will recover. I have sedated him and treated his injuries. It was as well that he was not left there any longer."

Krys knew he was implying what would have happened to her – might still happen to the girlfriend of Tomas.

Vincent escorted her to a private room, in one of the smaller excavated segments of the base. There was a basic, unmade bed there. He had her lie down.

She decided to compromise with Vincent by admitting, "Tymos is looking for the woman. He went back to the building and is doing a more thorough search. He is sure that she is no longer there."

Vincent merely nodded and began to run a diagnostic tool along her body.

"Tymos told me that you had been on Earth for about ten tears before we arrived."

"Did he mention the bounces as well?" Krys countered, glad of the change of subject.

"Yes, but not in detail. I can't say that either of you look a day older than you did when we left Tymorea four days ago."

"I know," Krys agreed, relaxing to be a 'good' patient.

"You are in excellent health and the effects of the stun have gone, as you said." Vincent studied a reading on his medical scanner and stated, "You have had a child!" He sounded surprised.

"Is that relevant?" Krys asked sharply.

"Did the child inherit our power?" Vincent asked, in tones worthy of a brother to one of the Tymorean Governors.

"It was thirty local years ago," Krys muttered. "And the father was not Tymorean."

"Great One...," Vincent paused and then went on. "The general theories of inheritance do not necessarily apply to Great Ones. It is a fact you should keep in mind."

Krys finally answered. Thirty years on, ten in subjective time, did not make it easier for her to remember how she had abandoned her child.

"No. Tym said he made the power dormant. And before you ask, some of the missionary descendents were his early teachers."

"Who is he? I assume he doesn't know of us."

"The teachers would not have told him," Krys assured Vincent. "His father is Abdul bin Halil."

Vincent made no immediate comment.

To put it in perspective, Krys explained. "Bin Halil is the one who incited the last war, though he hid his involvement and fooled nearly everybody. He learnt of me and intended to use me against this country. However, he had a more intimate purpose first. I think the Guardians of Peace subtly influenced him. I encouraged him to think of uniting the non-aligned countries and start a dynasty of rulers. That was all I could do, since the Guardians moved us forward in time within hours of the child's birth."

"I haven't caught up on Earth's recent history," Vincent admitted. "Has bin Halil done what you suggested?"

"Yes, he is the leader of what is now being called the Imperium."

Vincent finished his examination before asking, "May I ask what you intend to do next? So that I may assist you?"

"I need to talk to Louis," Krys said. "He said he finally had proof of a conspiracy against the UWN. When I know what he found out, I will decide what to do. My preference is to hand the evidence to the World Council Investigators to take on. It is their role after all."

Vincent nodded, as if agreeing. "You may talk to Louis tomorrow, Great One." He nodded to her and left the room.

Kryslie joined her brother when he returned to Earthbase several days later. He was walking through and examining the underground garden she had begun to build.

"That woman is back in Tomas's house and playing the outraged citizen," Tymos said, aware of his sister coming up behind him. He had a faint smirk on his face as he turned around. "Tomas is safe. Something she said while they were, um, entertaining each other, spooked him. He called Ferdinand, and I went to fetch him. He's staying with Ferdinand and Markos. Anyway, Tomas is only renting the house, and he doesn't intend to go back, so the woman will be kicked out in a week or so unless she decides to take over paying the rent."

"Why don't you tell Vincent that," Kryslie told her brother silently, before changing the subject and asking aloud, "What new information have you got?"

Tymos sat himself on a boulder that had yet to be positioned in the garden. "Well, using that file you collated before you went to get Louis, and what he told you when you questioned him here, I am positive he was on the right track. Hillary has been transcribing the thought records you found in Louis's house, and I have been checking some details that he was unable to confirm. There is enough evidence to indicate a conspiracy. If you add the details I have collected, and the things that have been happening over here - like Omar Harrison who had to be after Emmanuel's knowledge of shields, the World Council will have to take us seriously."

As he spoke, his mind touched on a myriad of details, and Kryslie considered each, as she gazed over the unfinished garden.

"Any word about Chave?" Kryslie asked after a period of thought. She turned back to face her twin.

"Olassa and Alen are keeping an eye on him and Edik is working to infiltrate the communications system the other watchers are using. It is encrypted. Chave is going about his usual routine, as if he is merely the dilettante he is pretending to be. Naturally, he is indignant that his accountant was proved to be a traitor, and acting worried that unscrupulous people might be privy to his confidential financial affairs."

Before Kryslie could express her concerns, Tymos reassured her. "The conspiracy will find nothing to make them suspicious of him. If they dig deep enough, they will find indications that he thinks the current government of Jafhabad is stifling the region. I spoke to him briefly at the university. He has had an invitation, through that man Klim, to attend the sponsors' dinner for the upcoming Science Fair. Only the ultra, ultra of society are invited."

"Klim is an historian, not a scientist," Kryslie immediately picked up the anomaly. "They'll make the approach there, then?"

"That's my guess," Tymos agreed.

"When will you be going to the World Council?" Kryslie abruptly changed the subject. "Before that dinner?"

Tymos nodded. "I am taking Jonko with me tomorrow. Do you want to come too?"

Kryslie chose to sit beside her brother. "We still don't have any proof of bin Halil's involvement. Everything points to the conspiracy being based in Jafhabad, but Chave considers the government there to be weak."

"More protective camouflage," Tymos proposed. "But I have seen those star wearers all throughout the Imperium."

"Let me know how you go with the Council. We might have to find a way to lure bin Halil into the open."

Tymos considered the unformed ideas in his sister's mind, and sensed her unease.

"You are thinking of letting him see you…"

"Maybe," Kryslie shrugged. "Even though I am not convinced it is the best idea. However, if the conspiracy is Imperium wide, wouldn't it be better getting it from the top down?"

"I agree with the theory," Tymos paused, trying to think of a tactful way to express his concern.

"What? Is there something else?" Kryslie noticed his hesitation and guessed the reason.

Tymos grinned wryly. It was no use trying to keep things from his twin; they were linked at too deep a level.

"There seems to be a very thorough, but very subtle, hunt for you already."

"So? Louis said his captors wanted to know who he worked for. I know that they think I am involved too."

"They took a photo of you, and your fingerprints. And red hair is not exactly common over there," Tymos reminded her.

"And we haven't aged in thirty years. Surely bin Halil would not believe that I am his runaway wife." She had accurately deduced his concern.

"You could be a child of that runaway wife. One she had after leaving him. He may not consider the distinction. Is there anyway he might have some of your DNA from back then?"

Kryslie felt the blood run from her face, but she turned her mind back ten years in her subjective time to when she was bin Halil's captive. "I don't think he thought it necessary. He was going to eliminate me after I had discredited the American led alliance."

Kryslie knew there were periods when she had been drugged, but the assurance she had spoken had come from the Guardians of Peace. "Then I conceived his son. He had no reason to doubt the child's paternity, since he'd had a doctor check that I was a virgin before he even touched me. I don't know if the hospital where I gave birth has any records."

"I will get Edik to check," Tymos promised. He didn't need to add that should records be found, they would be removed. "You don't have to worry about your recent period of captivity. When I went back, I made sure that the tape and ropes they had on you were destroyed. I got rid of the bedding too."

"Are you trying to say that I shouldn't try to draw him out?" Kryslie challenged her twin.

Tymos knew better than to admit it. He could feel her desire to make the person, or people, responsible for torturing Louis and killing Rovan, and probably countless others, pay for what they did. Whoever those killers and torturers were, he agreed with her on the point that Abdul bin Halil was behind them. And Kryslie would be the one person he would want to question personally.

"May I suggest that you wait and see what the World Council Investigators say," Tymos proposed. "They may want to ask you more questions about Omar Harrison. He wore a star too, didn't he? And you can tell them about Louis's experience, and your own."

"What if they infer a connection to the desert events when Olassa and her team arrived," Kryslie countered, but sensed what her twin was thinking. "No, you are right. It might be a good thing if they did. We know how to cover our trail, and as good as he thinks he is, bin Halil does not. Right now, he is uncompleted business and I intend to see him finished."

Tymos made a motion of tossing something into the air. "Well enough. If you are so determined - who am I to stop you. Even Vincent has no authority to do that." He glanced around the garden but didn't ask why she was obeying one of Vincent's suggestions.

Kryslie stood up. "Give me a hand arranging these boulders. I am intending to make this a little piece of surface life - or at least a place where you can forget you are underground."

She shared her idea with her twin and for a little while, they both shifted rocks to create a basin for a pool and a fountain - something suggestive of the Garden of Peace in the Temple of Dira, back home on Tymorea.

"I am going to get Jenala to help me choose the plants and get them established. She loves growing things and now that she is assured that Louis is going to get better, she just needs to get over learning that we are aliens. It was a great shock, but Hillary, Lexina and Beth have been a great help."

As they worked, Tymos remarked with some amusement, that Vincent, like the Governors of Tymorea, knew how to manipulate even a Great One.

Chapter 12 - Investigative committee

Dressed in fashionable business suits, Tymos and Jonko blended perfectly with the stream of people entering the headquarters of the World Council Investigative Committee. No one gave them a second look, even though they passed through three discreet security portals before reaching the reception desk. Even then, they gave their name and the young man and he immediately sent them up to the fortieth floor.

The outer office of the Director, Marcus Chalmers, was overseen by a middle-aged woman, who received their credentials, and passed a message through into the inner office. On receiving instructions to bring the visitors in, she escorted them to the door and announced, "Mr John Goss and his associate."

Jonko had reverted to using his birth name when interacting with people outside of the Tymorean base.

Tymos stayed back as Jonko took the role of the instigator of the meeting. He greeted Chalmers, who had risen from behind his desk, with a handshake and formal words, and in turn, he and Tymos were invited to sit.

Tymos stared out through the wall to floor window that overlooked Lake Geneva, and listened to the Director sounding Jonko out.

"Sub-director Harlowe in Washington spoke to me about you. He would not discuss your business, even over a secured communications channel," Chalmers probed. "Yet he insisted that I should talk to you. What is so important and secret?"

At that, Jonko took out a large yellow envelope from inside the jacket of the business suit.

"My credentials, Sir, and my report of an extremely sensitive situation. Sub-director Harlowe insisted that I should discuss it with you." He leant forwards and passed it over the desk.

Chalmers opened the envelope, drew out a sheath of papers and began to scan read them.

Tymos and Jonko sat quietly, watching him, and not glancing at each other. Neither had any fear that Jonko's carefully forged credentials would be questioned. Tymos had created them himself, inserting his presence into some very select databases to provide substantiation. They were intended to give Jonko entrée into the Director's circle of acquaintances. The report, that had first been presented to the American-based Harlowe, was printed on official World Council letterheads. Only part of the report was known to Harlowe - the rest of the report was in the envelope.

Chalmers placed the last page down, and seemed to be staring past his guests, but his left hand was tapping on the desktop. Tymos knew, from a glance before he was seated, that there was a computer touch pad there.

"If what you allege is true, Mr Goss, then we are on the verge of war. Please tell me how you came to these conclusions - in your own words. There is much that is left unsaid in this report."

"Sir, I understand that you are aware of a recent incident on the American continent where an eminent scientist was nearly abducted by an agent of the Imperium?"

"Indeed," Chalmers agreed and then waited for Jonko to continue.

"It was seen as an isolated incident, but I have found multiple events that seem to link to it."

He had the Director's full attention, as Tymos had intended. There had been many, many more apparently unrelated but questionable incidents. Only a painstaking search through FBI reports, police databases in various sectors of the UWN, had brought to light a connecting factor. Tymos had brought in every missionary with any skill using computers and put them to work around the clock.

In each case they had highlighted, one or more of the suspects wore a silver star on a chain. The men were either overt exchange scientists or technologists, or supposedly American born. Until the 'star-league', as Jonko termed the group, had been identified in Jafhabad, there had been no way to link the wide-spread incidents.

As Jonko concluded his report, and presented a data disc of his findings, Chalmers' eyes moved focus to consider the quiet redhead. Jonko took that as an invitation to introduce his companion.

"Tym Ward was the one who alerted me to the connection."

"Mr Ward, tell me about yourself," Chalmers said. His hand was poised over the touchpad, and began to tap as Tymos spoke.

"I am a consulting scientist, specialising in computer design. I have many friends, both in the UWN and the Imperium…"

For nearly an hour, Tymos spoke of events within the Imperium, of scientists and technical experts being offered lucrative contracts to work there, and apparently never arriving. He mentioned specific names, and guessed that some of the tapping being done by Chalmers was a request for a data search.

"Their families receive regular income via the internet, but the men themselves are not where they were meant to be. Some of the wives are beginning to suspect that the communications they are receiving are doctored."

Tymos paused as Chalmers attention went to his computer screen. The hardening of his expression indicated that he did not like what he was reading.

"What else do you know, Mr Ward," Chalmers asked, looking at him to continue.

"I am aware of some other oddities. The Science Development Group in the capital of the Imperium, is working on a laser sighting device - supposedly an original design of an Imperium scientist. I saw the schematics - they are identical to a project underway at the Weisman Institute in Los Altos. Two years ago, there was an apparently unsuccessful break-in attempt there."

After Tymos cited a number of similar instances, Chalmers gestured for him to stop.

"Since the Peace Treaty of 2078, free trade and free transfer of information has been encouraged."

Tymos shook his head, knowing that Chalmers was testing him. "The treaty does not stipulate the free transfer of industrial secrets," he said.

"And how did you discover all these examples, Mr Ward?"

"As I mentioned, I have friends in many places."

Chalmers steepled his fingers and considered what he had heard.

"You are implying a conspiracy, originating at a high level in the Imperium. One that is performing acts of espionage within the UWN. Do you realise, Mr Ward, that you could be accused of a similar crime?"

"Perhaps, but I have stolen no secrets, performed no acts of violence or sabotage," Tymos spoke calmly, and he continued. "I saw a pattern, but you would rightly have turned me away if I had come to you with mere supposition and heresay. I was in a position to use my eyes and ears to find proof and I did so. However, all that I have told you so far is not the most unsettling aspect."

"It is not?" Chalmers revealed his steely nature, as he gazed at Tymos.

"No. You spoke of the Peace Treaty, Sir. It not only encourages free trade, it also lays down the rights of citizens. I believe those rights are being restricted within the Imperium. I believe that people who speak out in protest are being kidnapped and killed."

"In protest about what - specifically?"

"War. I believe that the Imperium is slowly gearing up for another war. One that may not need bombs and tanks or jets and massive armies, but make use of other kinds of twisted technology. We have long known how computers accessing data from everywhere can be compromised." Tymos's tone was sincere, and his body language betrayed no sign that he was not being truthful.

Chalmers had hidden his reactions well so far, but now his body was rigid, and he stared past his visitors, as his mind considered all the ramifications of everything he had heard over the past few hours. He would be checking as much as he could for himself, though he was sure he would find it all corroborated.

Finally, he returned his attention to Jonko and Tymos.

"Have you arranged accommodation?"

Since the sun had set while they were talking, the question was only a little unexpected. Jonko answered in the negative. Tymos wanted him to be seen as the leader.

"I will organise a suite on our accommodation level. I will need to have you both available. My assistant will show Mr Ward to the suite. Mr Goss I would like you to come with me."

Tymos allowed himself a period of relaxation, taking time to reflect on how the interview had gone. He had deliberately not mentioned Abdul bin Halil, or implied that he believed the Imperium's leader was behind all the events. There was no direct evidence pointing to the man, just as there had been none during the war that ended three decades ago.

Yet, when Chalmers had the chance to consider everything that he had heard, there was only one conclusion that he could come to. It was best that he came to it on his own.

Right now, he was quizzing Jonko, and having his team of computer specialists accessing the mammoth databases of the World Council and doing his own cross referencing and checking of databases in other parts of the UWN.

With his mind lightly linked to Jonko, he sensed the satisfaction his friend was emitting. In places where Tymos had not investigated, the same correlations were appearing, over and over. The suspects, photographed as a matter of course, were frequently wearing a silver star on a silver chain.

Jonko arrived at the suite when it was almost midnight.

"They are convinced," he said. "Chalmers has called video conference with the World Council Executive. By tomorrow evening, the Committee will have their mandate to go into the Imperium to investigate."

Tymos nodded, satisfied. It was the reason why the Investigative Committee had been established as a completely neutral body. The members came from all parts of the world, to investigate threats to peace. There would be as much emphasis on proving the allegations as there was protecting the honour of the country being investigated.

"They want you to stay here. They say, as you are known in the Imperium, they do not want it thought that you began the investigation. I will be going with them."

"A voluntary detainee," Tymos grinned faintly. He didn't comment further, as he expected any talking they did would be monitored as a matter of course. "Did they suggest how they would be proceeding?"

Jonko glanced around the room, noting places where listening devices could be, but seeming to be checking out the hotel like features. He went to a small fridge and selected a can of a local beer.

"They have made a list of people they have encountered who were wearing one of those stars. That's all I really know. However, I am likely to be leaving very early, so I will need to catch some sleep."

Tymos was summoned soon after finishing the breakfast that had been delivered to the suite an hour after Jonko had departed.

He was led into a room filled with monitor screens of which about half were active. Each showed some kind of office, the furnishings of which indicated that they were temporary.

Chalmers arrived and confirmed that offices had been set up in all the major cities of the UWN, and agents were picking up the people on their lists. The interviews would be being streamed via secure satellite links to the operations room.

"I'd like you to listen into the various info-feeds and tell me if you recognise any of the people. This is a long shot, but any insights you can give us will be useful. The first ones to be questioned are those living within the cities. We are bringing in others from the surrounding districts as we speak, and they will be questioned tomorrow."

As the day wore on, all the screens were busy, and Tymos rarely rested as he circled the room. Naturally, most of the reluctant interviewees were strangers to him, but he recognised some of the scientists, and local political figures. He was surprised to see so many American, or rather non-Imperium born members of the star league.

He was quite sure many did not realise the truth behind membership of the league.

His memory for names and facts astounded Chalmers, but the Director acted on his suggestions of questions to ask particular interviewees - particularly those with scientific specialities.

Not one of those questioned knew who had begun the 'star-league', though all claimed to have joined to 'bring equality at all levels between the UWN and the Imperium'.

The repetition of the mantra seemed more like a programmed belief, and while it was innocuous in itself, it could be taken to have two meanings.

To those who had not yet been asked to act, it was simply an ideal to strive for. Many of these were genuinely shocked at things other star-wearers had done. Others were not afraid to state that they believed strong action needed to be taken.

Of those questioned, the ones known to have committed crimes provided the most damning indications, even though they had no idea how much they were revealing. Each of the latter group felt that their 'crime' was insignificant and perhaps it had been, but add all the little crimes together and the overall picture was sinister indeed.

At the end of the second day, Chalmers invited Tymos back to his office, and provided refreshments.

"It is a cleverly run organisation," he said without preamble. "The old 'cells of agents' scheme taken to a new level. Each person we have spoke to only knows of three other star wearers by name. The person who recruited him, and the two they in turn recruited. Yet the skills and position of every new wearer are sent up the line to be stored somewhere. When they need someone with a certain skill set in a certain place - they have the data to call on. And the word is passed down the line…"

"I would surmise that the selected worker is watched by one of the higher echelon members?" Tymos said.

Chalmers actually gave a faint snort. "It seems that little escapes you, Mr Ward. Yes, and if he fails, he is allowed to be sentenced by the local justice system. If he objects and refuses to obey or prove his loyalty, he turns up missing."

"It is the overall leader we need to find, not these small fry," Tymos blurted. Even though he wanted the Investigative Committee to oversee the investigation, he was afraid that the leaders would be getting edgy once they learnt these people were being questioned.

"Have you any ideas? We were completely unaware of this cabal until you came to us."

"Have you thought to question the Gold star wearers?" Tymos spoke quietly, but he stared at Chalmers.

"We have no records of any of those outside the Imperium, which may be significant. But, yes, we have the names of a few of those, but they are men of impeccable public reputation. The wording of our mandate does not allow us to question them. How sure are you that they are involved?"

Tymos shrugged, frustrated by needing to have proof of guilt. "It won't be easy to prove anything against those that are. It is likely that there is a subset of rabid subversives and the rest are camouflage. Yet as I have seen these past two days, any that have been recruited were targeted for a reason."

He was thinking of Chave Zieman, recruited by the man Klim. The answer was there. "They are all important men in industry, finance, science, technology, education… every field you can name."

Chalmers breathed in and out slowly, seeing the implications. "They provide entrée into every level of society - would that be all?"

"Check their finances," Tymos said, the idea had only just occurred to him. All the wearers of gold stars were reputedly wealthy. "Every war needs to be paid for."

Silence fell in the office, Chalmers turned his chair as if to stare at the magnificent sunset, but Tymos knew he was not seeing it. After a while, he turned back.

"You cannot have found out all you did, by yourself."

Tymos met his gaze and admitted, "No Sir, there was a small group of us."

"Have you the skills to infiltrate databases?"

That question was a dangerous one to answer, but after a moment of consideration, Tymos said, "I am a computer systems designer and analyst."

Chalmers grinned faintly, aware that the statement was an evasion. He translated it as 'yes', but didn't ask for confirmation.

When Tymos gently probed the man's outer mind, he realised that it wasn't for reasons of deniability, but because he wanted to get at the truth, and his own hands were tied.

"Would your team be willing to keep looking for evidence?"

The question had been hovering in Chalmers's mind, but it was a breach of IC protocol to use outsiders.

This conversation was definitely off the record, Tymos realised.

"Sir, I am - absolutely. I am sure of several others. However, we have already been targeted by this conspiracy. One of us was caught and tortured. One was killed and another is missing - possibly dead as well. We have taken the ones with families to a safe place."

"I would like you to continue what you were doing," Chalmers said. "As private citizens, you can do things that my agents cannot. And at least, you know how dangerous this cabal is. However, I cannot give you any official sanction."

"I understand that, sir. Have you any particular direction for me, and are there any constraints on our actions?"

Chalmers relaxed back into his chair, faintly amused by the cautious verbal fencing.

"Your instincts have been excellent so far. However, I must caution you about the consequences of breaking the laws of the Imperium. If they object to your actions, you will be subject to their justice system, unless they refer you to us. And we will have every right to arrest you for espionage. However, I can assign an agent to you as a back up."

Tymos had not expected that offer, and considered it. There would be advantages and disadvantages.

"I can see some drawbacks," Tymos began to explain, but Chalmers interrupted him.

"Only if you break the law."

That was not the point that Tymos was thinking of - though the converse was that the back up might be a witness for him if he was framed for something he didn't do.

"I will accept the shadow, but only if he knows to back off if I say so. I will not put him into peril, or into a position whereby he must compromise himself."

"I will accept that," Chalmers said, but his mind held reservations. "However, I wish to meet the rest of your team."

"Very well," Tymos agreed. "It will take a day or two to get them all here."

"No! I will be travelling to the Imperium to oversee this investigation, leaving tomorrow. Are they all currently living there?"

Tymos shook his head. "Two of them are still there, but I have a female colleague who is on her way to meet me here in Lausanne."

"How soon will she be here?"

"If I could use your phone, Sir?"

Chalmers gestured to it, and stood to move away from his desk. He chose to look down on the city lights while Tymos made his call, seeming not to be listening.

Tymos used the actions of making a call to hide his distraction as he contacted his sister mentally. He finished the one-sided call and said, "Her taxi should be pulling up downstairs in ten minutes."

"I will have some one escort her up. What is her name?" Chalmers returned to his desk.

"Krys Ward"

"Your wife?"

"Sister."

Chalmers spoke to someone via his internal communications system, requesting the escort and ordering coffee. When he sat back at his desk, he began finger tapping again.

Tymos hid a grin. His own name had not rung any bells with the Director of the Investigative Committee - but his sister's had.

Kryslie arrived, dressed in a business suit and wearing a light brown wig. It was a precaution in case the IC building was now being watched by agents of the Imperium. Even at night, there was enough light that her red hair would have been noticeable as she strode from the taxi, to the entrance of the building.

When she entered the Directors' Office, her appearance, confident movements and firm handshake, impressed Chalmers. However, he did not rely solely on first impressions.

"Have a seat, Miss Ward," he invited. He also gestured to the refreshments, but she merely smiled and seated herself in the spare chair, after grinning at her twin. He had made a mental comment as she walked in, making a bet with her that the Director had noticed the wig.

As Chalmers re-seated himself, Kryslie removed the wig and took out the pins holding her hair up. She shook out her hair that now fell to her shoulders.

"Why do you feel you need such a precaution?"

With a slight shrug, she gave Chalmers an answer. "I would assume that the sudden interest the IC is giving the citizens of the Imperium, will result in counter measures. If I am to return to the Imperium, I have no wish to be linked to you."

Chalmer's hand had been tapping, almost idly, but he and his hand went still.

"Your brother did not mention that you had worked there before. In fact, he has not said much about you. I do suppose that you are aware that you are agreeing to engage in a dangerous undertaking."

Kryslie did not have to think about her reply. "Yes, I do, and to be honest, I have been working mostly in America. Not, I will stress, because of the danger, but because as a woman, I could not get access to places where I would need to be to get information."

Chalmers was nodding, but he said, "The standard of life for a woman in the Imperium has improved greatly in the past two decades…"

He was testing her, Kryslie knew, but he did not have an intimate knowledge of the place of women there.

"If what you stated is true, I would not have liked to have lived in the Imperium thirty years ago."

Chalmers would never believe that she had actually lived there at that time, but she had and she knew exactly how much and how little had changed. She told him so in terse statements, finishing with, "So yes, women are better educated, healthier, less restricted by day, but…even now they are not allowed out after dark without an escort. Further, any 'educated' woman with a true talent for an 'unwomanly' field such as science, or technology, must virtually choose between that as a career, and having children."

She shocked the man. Chalmers stared at her, his body quite still.

"You've been working mostly in America, you said. Yet you seem to know he Imperium quite well."

"I do," was Kryslie's terse agreement.

"You have been there recently?"

"Yes. One of our people was missing and I was the only one free to look for him."

Chalmers flicked a quick look at Tymos's inscrutable face, recalling things he had reported.

"Tell me about that," he invited of Kryslie.

"Yes, certainly, but I have another question first."

"Go ahead…"

"Mid-states, America, one month ago. What happened to Omar Harrison. The man who tried to abduct Doctor Emmanuel?"

"He was charged, found guilty and sentenced. Too bad we did not know of this star league then. He was wearing one."

Tymos suddenly leant forward and demanded, "Where is Harrison now?"

Kryslie shared the sudden chill in her spine that had caused her brother to react.

"Unfortunately, he escaped before he reached the federal detention centre. There is a council bounty out for him."

Kryslie flicked a glance at her twin, but said aloud, "Another enemy to watch for."

Chalmers echoed her statement as a question.

"On my recent visit to Hadjibat, that's one of the major cities in Jafhabad, I had a very close shave. I know I was seen, but they reacted to me with more virulence than I could explain."

Well, overcoming men who were bigger than herself was enough to make them angry, but there had been a suggestion of a 'higher up' who wanted to question her.

Kryslie gave Chalmers a terse report of how she had been captured and treated, but not how she had escaped with Louis.

"How did you get away?"

"I wasn't as helpless as they thought," Krys claimed, pausing to give emphasis to her next statement. "The guard didn't know me and I had no wish to be tortured."

Krys drew an envelope from inside her jacket. She gave it to the investigator. He took out a series of photos.

"Our friend Louis, after two days in that place. So, yes, I know the risks."

"May I keep these?" the investigator asked. Krys nodded, watching him typing more notes.

"Louis's wife, when I found her, had multiple knife slashes. His daughter – five years old – had concussion."

There was a hardening of the investigator's face. Krys sensed his abhorrence to such acts.

Something caught Chalmers attention on his monitor screen, and Kryslie glanced at her brother and mind-spoke to him. "What's with the finger tapping?"

"Notes, searches…my name didn't jog his memory, but yours did…"

When the Director turned his attention from the screen, after more finger tapping on the touchpad, his expression gave no clue to what he had just read.

"How old are you, Miss Ward?"

"Twenty-eight," Kryslie said, knowing her brother had claimed the same age.

"Twins?"

"Isn't it obvious?" Kryslie gave a wry grin, suspecting what was coming next.

"Washington University, eight years ago," Chalmers challenged.

She met it with a grin and a question of her own as she thought back to her first encounter with the Investigative Committee. "Oh, were you there?"

"We didn't meet," Chalmers admitted. "However, I heard about your martial skill then. I guess I should not doubt them now."

Tymos murmured, "I wouldn't."

"So, you are willing to return to Jafhabad. We usually don't send women agents there for the reasons you already understand. What do you think you can do? I have asked your brother to help us investigate the men who wear gold stars. If some of them are, as your brother suggested, high up in the conspiracy - we don't want to alert them to our interest."

He didn't allude to the danger, but that was in his mind. Kryslie addressed that first.

"I won't be going in looking like myself. I need to move freely and not be worried about being recognised. Other than that, the gold star wearers are all men who will not feel threatened by a woman, and will probably try to impress those they meet."

Chalmers accepted her words by continuing, "Like I told your brother, I cannot protect you from local charges, or sanction any action you take. I will be assigning an agent to shadow you as well."

Without looking at her brother, and looking as if she was considering the idea, she asked Tymos mentally, "You agreed to that?"

"A precaution," he thought back. "It might lead them to suspect your friend bin Halil."

He flicked a brief grin at her mental reaction to calling bin Halil her friend.

Aloud, Kryslie stated, "I don't find that idea comfortable. If anyone notices an IC agent shadowing me, they will start paying attention to me."

"I insist," Chalmers told her as Tymos was mentally proposing, "We could use that to our advantage…"

Chalmers continued, "He will be a witness to the fact that you will not be performing acts of espionage."

Kryslie decided it was not worth protesting further. "Then I request…an extremely discreet watch and the understanding that the shadow will not interfere…no matter what happens. He can run to you with tales, but he is to keep out of my plans."

She met Chalmers gaze and held it, not looking away. He warned, "You could be hurt or killed…"

"That won't come back on you. After all, our actions are not official. You are not responsible for us."

She won her point; Chalmers slumped back into his chair. She spoke again before he thought to add a proviso. "Nor will I wear any of your tracers!"

Chapter 13 - In the Imperium

Alen had arranged a place for them to stay, in a neighbourhood where people did not pry into their neighbours' business.

That this would make it hard for their shadows to work, was not their problem. If the agents were good enough, it wouldn't matter.

It was a furnished apartment, nothing fancy. The walls were painted a light brown, the curtains were orange and the furniture - a couch, some chairs, a low table and some cupboards - were in mismatched shades of brown. There was a trivision set, on one of the cupboards, with its antenna leaning over at an odd angle.

As a base, it would do. They would not be in it for an extended period. Kryslie lowered her backpack and went to check the other rooms, as Alen spoke to Tymos.

"Word soon gets passed on if people start nosing around here. I've moved into a small apartment downstairs and the locals know me. I would hear if anyone was asking about me." He was careful to speak in Tymorean.

Tym tossed his pack onto a chair and went to check the view from the window. It looked straight down between two nearby multi-storey buildings.

Then, gesturing for Alen to remain quiet, Tymos took a palm-sized device from his pocket, and moved slowly about the room, all the while studying its small screen. When he slipped it back in his pocket, Alen raised an eyebrow and asked, "Do you check everywhere you go?"

Tymos ignored the question and took out a second device; it that was slightly smaller than the other. He set it on the floor in the centre of the room and activated it. Almost instantly, the walls of room took on a mauve glow as a force field was generated.

"We need to stay alert. Things will be getting stirred up now that the IC is in the picture. This apartment is going to be our safe retreat and from now on, you come here by transmitting from your apartment - or we come to you.”

“Yes, Tymos,” Alen said, though he still had not become used to calling a Great One by his first name, without the honorific.”

“Okay, what’s the latest on that search?”

Alen saw Kryslie re-enter the room and gave her a grin. “At work, the government officials came to check the cargo manifests, but I heard they were very interested in the passenger lists and records from the cctv units in the embarkation lounge. Overall, I think it is dying down. The number of dark vans patrolling the streets has lessened.”

“Good,” Kryslie stated before advising her twin, “The two bedrooms, bathroom and closet sized kitchen are clear of monitoring devices.”

“I have food and other things in my apartment. I will bring them up,” Alen told her.

“Thanks. How is Chave?” Kryslie chose to sink into one of the chairs. It gave with her weight, betraying that the springs were old and weak.

Alen stayed standing until after Tymos had copied his sister’s example.

“He is keeping to his normal routine. Markos spotted several other watchers, who alternated in following him when he went out. Two lots were on foot, the other two kept to their cars.”

“Any odd visitors?” Kryslie asked.

Alen smirked slightly. “The Shirav woman and her brother have called after dark twice in the past week. One of the foot watchers made a point to walk past just as she was being helped from the car.”

“I knew he had a lady friend. Have you checked her out?”

“She is beyond reproach, and a suitable match for Chave.”

“I hope she is not drawn into our business,” Kryslie stated her concern. “Anything else?”

“Yes, he didn’t go to work at the Uni for two days. He called in sick.”

“Did he go out?” Tymos asked.

“We don’t think so,” Alen assured her. “Ferdinand had the night duty - he saw nothing out of the ordinary. Chave came home from work late, stayed up a bit, then went to bed. No visitors. Markos saw nothing either during the day. When he didn’t come out to go to the university, Markos rang me. I waited a bit and rang the Uni. They said he had called in sick and his classes were cancelled.”

“When was this?” Tymos was leaning forward, waiting for the answer.

“Two and three days ago, but he looks fine now and is back at work during the day. And come to think of it, the watchers were gone after that.”

"I think that means that they made their approach," Kryslie said. "If the watchers have gone, they must be sure of him."

Tymos sensed some doubt in her tone, and confirmed that he shared it. "The watchers might be watching from further away. They know he knew Louis, so they might be using him to draw you out. I will slip in and talk to him."

"Chave is solid," Alen said firmly. "He is very clever even if he is only a descendent."

"Yes, he is, but the descendents are not as highly trained as are missionaries like you," Kryslie told him. "Tymos and I have trained as many of them as we could, but only to make them better at what they normally do. They have not been trained in more than the basics of resisting hypnosis and mind coercion."

Alen, didn't contradict her, but his face went distant as if he had just thought of something. Neither Tymos nor Kryslie interrupted him.

"I guess that I shouldn't dismiss that possibility," Alen admitted. "I overhead a conversation between a couple of the dock workers. They were both petty thieves, and scared that they might have been identified somewhere they shouldn't have been. One was wanting to leave on the next ship in case the Imperium secret guards picked him up. He said, 'They can turn your mind inside out and make you believe that your friends are your mortal enemies.' At the time, I didn't think they were important enough for those creepy guards to bother with."

"Don't assume anything," Tymos warned softly. "What we are dealing with goes right up to the highest government levels. The people at the top would use even a petty thief if the man had skills they need."

Alen's eyes widened. He knew the Great Ones were investigating some underground cabal, but they had never before mentioned that they thought the government of Jafhabad was involved.

"The government here is…" he began to give an opinion.

"Higher," Kryslie interrupted his thoughts. "The person we want is …"

Tymos nudged her mind before she voiced the name of the Imperium's leader.

"…very good at hiding his role in this."

"Higher," Alen echoed.

Tymos smoothly inserted, "The cabal is not just in Jafhabad."

"Is there anything else you need me for? I'm due to relieve Markos in an hour, and I want to bring your supplies up." Alen seemed to want to end the discussion.

"Bring the stuff, and then see what you can find out about the Science Fair I have been hearing about. Get a list of all the exhibitors, where they are from, if they are locals or visiting from somewhere in the UWN. Every bit of information you can."

"I am on it Great One, "Alen promised, bouncing up from his chair.

"Cut the honorific, Alen. It means little here," Kryslie muttered.

Alen dared to say, "Not when you and Tymos look so severe." He gave them both a cautious look and transmitted from the apartment.

"Am I that transparent today?" Kryslie asked her twin after Alen had gone.

"I'm no judge. I can read you as well as you can read me. But we both know what is at stake here. We have to get bin Halil to come out of cover and betray his involvement and for the Earth authorities to be able to prove his guilt. It is frustrating, and as much as I would like to simply go and kill the man - that would create more trouble than we solve. This has been too long in the planning. He can't be working alone, and if we remove him, one of his closest underlings will likely step up."

Tymos sensed his sister's mind going quiet, he probed gently, but she had blocked him out.

"What?" he asked.

"His son?" Kryslie asked, and now some of the emotion she was blocking from him leaked through the deep twin bond.

All the blood had drained from her face. "My son. I don't even know what kind of man he has become. I don't know if he has come to share his father's views."

"He had Tymorean teachers," Tymos reminded her.

"Only for a dozen years," she said. "Then bin Halil had one of his purges of staff."

Tymos tried again, "He is only thirty. In this part of the world, they don't think anyone under fifty is fit to lead."

"Bin Halil can't have been even that old when he incited that last war. And not much past it when he …" Kryslie recalled the time vividly. She had used the man as much as he had used her.

"Trust the Guardians," Tymos finished. "It was their idea to create a child."

"I know…" Yet even remembering that, made that moment when she had abandoned her child, come flooding back to her mind in all its intensity. Never mind that she had no choice, that the Guardians had moved them forward in time, the emotional pain was as fresh as if it had just happened.

Tymos understood, and instead of voicing more platitudes, began to sub-vocalise a calming mantra. After a while, he saw his sister nod. She had pushed those memories back and she was calm again.

"I'll check on Chave," Tymos said. "Why don't you see what you can find out via the public media vids?"

He grinned when his sister gave a faint laugh.

"Fine. I will watch tri-v and play house. I guess someone has to."

When Tymos returned several hours later, he found that the apartment looked a little more lived in. Spare clothing was hung on curtained-off racks in the two small bedrooms and the two beds had been made. He looked for his pack and saw it had been emptied and flattened and was leaning against the wall in one of the bedrooms. There was no sign of any of the specialised equipment they had brought with them.

The bench in the little kitchen was set for a meal and Kryslie was making coffee. She handed him a cup and told him, "Everything is in the three-door cupboard in the main room."

She had sensed the question in her twin's mind.

"What's this?" Tymos asked as Kryslie dished up the simple meal she had concocted.

"This and that. Alen didn't bring a recipe book. Tastes alright - no worse than some of your experiments."

He grinned. They both could cook well enough, since they had needed to fend for themselves for a long time.

As he began to eat, he heard the distorted voice sound of a radio transmission. It seemed to come out of nowhere. Instinctively, he translated and then he asked, "What are you listening to?"

"I am scanning for official government frequencies. I have found the police frequencies, and most of what is on that is reports of people being picked up. Like you just heard. I haven't found the frequency that the secret police are using. What have you got?"

They both sat and began to eat, continuing the conversation mentally. "Chave now has one of the gold stars. Klim took him to see those wartime policy records, and had him analyse them. He wanted to know if the policies could be implemented by a contemporary government."

Tymos concentrated on his food for a moment, and Kryslie prompted, "And?"

"Chave repeated what he told Klim, and the details aren't relevant to us - except on one point. This country survived financially because all the people with the wealth placed it in the control of the Government."

Kryslie stopped eating and stared at her brother. "And most of the government was tried and executed, except for a missing few…did the other wealthy people get their money back?"

Tymos shook his head, and told her, "But those that survived the purge were given enough money to start their enterprises up again. Some did well, others didn't."

"Did Klim suggest anything like that to Chave? Putting his money in a war fund?"

"No, but I think he thinks that Chave would if asked. Actually, he told Chave that when they form a new Government, he would have a place in it."

"So how did Klim explain the star? Using the same rationale as for the silver star wearers?"

"Pretty much, just that Chave would be useful at a higher level. He played to Chave's sense of self-importance. There was nothing in the conversations they had that suggested anything more than trying to overthrow a weak government that was holding the country back."

Kryslie tried to fit the conversation into the bigger picture and could only decide that Klim was meaning one thing and had led Chave into thinking he meant something else. "There was no mention of Louis in the conversation? He had admitted knowing him, as a client of Louis's accountancy business."

"Not a mention. Chave thinks he settled that with his anger at the traitor."

"Something doesn't feel right," Kryslie said after thinking the report through.

"Do you think you should see Chave? You are more sensitive to the signs of mind control than I am."

"Not yet. If they have programmed him in any way, it is likely to be such as to get him to contact them if he sees me. And if they have, we can use that at a time of our choosing."

"And if they haven't? Or if they want him to do other things?"

"Either will work for us, with respect to him seeing me. As for other things they might want him to do, we can deal with that afterwards.

Anyway, second-guessing the cabal is not a productive use of time. We already know their real intentions, and what they tell their recruits. I don't think they will want Chave to do anything much yet, at least nothing that will go against his basic values. They will soon learn that their lesser recruits are being questioned. I think that will make them pull their heads in until they figure out what the IC seems to know."

"I think it is safe to assume that Chave will still be watched," Tymos said. "When I met him today I made it seem like a chance meeting in the university cafeteria. I merely said hello, and whispered that I would be in his room. Of course, no one saw me going there, and I set up a force field to prevent eavesdropping before we spoke."

"I did discover an interesting thing. I found out who is the patron of the Science Fair is."

Tymos shielded his thoughts so his sister was forced to guess.

Kryslie merely waited until her twin said, "None other than the leader of the Imperium."

Her eyes narrowed as she considered Abdul bin Halil's possible motives.

"Interesting! He has already stooped to sending spies to steal new technology, does he expect the UWN to give it to him now?"

"Ostensibly, he is interested in medical advances and technology to help with education - philanthropical things like that…"

"Pardon me if I doubt it," Kryslie countered. "He'd twist anything to suit his purposes. Anyway, will the patron of the Science Fair be attending it?"

Her casual tone did not deceive her twin.

"If he does, it will be a too public place to confront him…"

"Who said I would confront him. All I need is to find a place nearby, where I can try to pick up anything from his mind."

"Is that all you intend? We can't just take him on…we have no proof he has any part in this cabal."

"We have no proof yet," Kryslie corrected her twin.

"What if we suggest to Chave that he has a party? He could invite all the patrons, financial backers, the people who helped to organise the fair. Perhaps bin Halil might come. We could arrange to attend. I doubt if bin Halil knows of our interest in science."

"Devious, bro. There might be a lot of those gold star wearers there. We could actually do what the IC think we are going to do, and check them out. Personally, I would like to get close to that man Klim. He has got to be high up in all this."

"Right. I'll go and see Chave tonight and suggest this," Tymos told her. "We will make Klim our immediate target...agreed?"

"It is logical," Kryslie said, not exactly agreeing.

Tymos decided not to argue with her. She would tell him her ideas when she was ready.

Tymos was a silent observer, hidden in plain view by being dressed as one of the University café caterers. He seemed to be busy sorting cutlery and tidying the plate and utensil table. In his ear was a tiny receiver that was picking up the conversation at a table two metres away. He had planted a bug there when he had gone to Chave's table on the pretence of wiping it clean.

Professor Klim arrived with a crowd of students, but spotted Chave and went to him without getting food. Tymos was angled to watch the table, and was able to observe the history lecturer's body language.

Klim smiled widely when he heard Chave's suggestion of a social evening. He praised the idea extravagantly, and Chave began to sit straighter, and if he had been a cat he would have purred.

Tymos wondered what was going through Klim's mind, but it was not possible to try to read it. The man had seen some use for the idea. He spoke as if he assumed that the existing patrons of the science fair deserved to be rewarded, and so they would not have to pay to attend. He casually suggested that others could 'buy' and invitation - and these people would help cover the costs of the affair and any money left over would go to the Science fund. Did he have ideas about people who would pay to rub shoulders with all the rich and famous?

Probably. And possibly he would use this as an opportunity to entice other rich people to attend...perhaps to seduce them into the cabal? And get control of their fortunes?

Well, if he had ideas like that, he might not bother how many new supporters turned up, if they paid enough.

After Klim left, saying he'd be in touch, Chave remained at his table to finish his coffee. He gave no indication that he realised that Tymos was still close by. The conversation with Klim had left him feeling uneasy, so much so that he went home early. He had never charged people to come to his social evenings - he held them because he liked to be considered the equal of the rich and brilliant people he invited. After discovering how the country had stayed economically stable during the war - with the wealthy giving their fortunes into the hands of the government - Klim's proposal to allow people to buy an invitation to his party seemed ominous.

Back at his house, Chave paced his private retreat. The thought that he might have to give over his carefully accumulated wealth made him feel ill. He lived modestly, and his parties were his only extravagance. He had inherited the house, but little money. What he had, he had saved and invested to give him an income above that of a university professor.

Klim's approval had made him feel important, and had given his ego a boost. Now, he was feeling clammy and weak.

He felt so unwell that he went up to his bedchamber to lie down. As he hung his over tunic on a hanger, he sensed a presence behind him and he spun around. His heart was suddenly pounding as if it wanted to erupt from his chest.

Kryslie put a finger to his lips before he could utter a sound. She uttered a word, very quietly, "Klim."

In his mind, Chave immediately thought of the recent conversation, and all his fears. He guessed that Kryslie could sense them, but he had no way to hide his private worries. Then he thought he was beginning to imagine things - conversations he had never had.

Finally, Kryslie removed her finger, and he blurted in a whisper, "You shouldn't have come here. They want you, in a really nasty way."

With a grim smile, Kryslie said, "I know, and they won't have seen me arrive. However, I wanted to tell you that Louis, his family and most of the others are safe. Rovan, though, is dead."

Chave felt his galloping heart ease. He would not be able to betray his fellow Tymoreans, though they had never asked him about them, only about Kryslie - the redheaded woman they had seen. And then he realised that his 'imaginings' had been real - and he had forgotten them.

"Kryslie, you should not trust me, he said in a hoarse voice, and he was suddenly weak and needed to sit down. "I feel that I have to go and tell Klim that you are here."

In fact, it was taking every bit of concentration he had to resist the increasingly intense impulse. He was hardly aware of Kryslie speaking in the odd language that he had once learnt from his parents. The urge to do 'something' eased and he could not recall what he wanted to do.

"Trust your instincts, Chave, and have no fear for me. From now on, when you see me, you should not indicate that you know me. You will be wise not to mention that I have been here. Listen with your mind for instructions from me or from Tymos."

He nodded, no longer in conflict with himself.

"I have to go," Kryslie told him, and right before his eyes, she seemed to vanish.

Chave sighed, there were times when part of him did wish he was able to appear and disappear like that. Then, he shrugged and walked towards his ensuite bathroom.

"They tried hypnosis," Kryslie told her twin when she arrived back at their rented apartment. "Thanks to his heritage, they were not able to get him deeply tranced and so his mind recognised that the implanted commands were not his own desires."

"So, had he told them about you?" Tymos asked.

"Only that he had once seen someone like they described, when he had visited his accountant. Nothing about my visits to him, since he knew he'd have to mention how I arrived, and that would make him sound mad."

Tymos took that as an assurance. "What else?"

"They have various commands on him - or rather they think they do. Basically, he has to support Klim's ideas. They wanted him to report to Klim if he saw me, but I negated that."

"He might still be a weak link," Tymos warned.

"I reinforced his core values, and planted a few commands of my own, that will override any Klim put on him. When we turn up at his party, he won't mention that he knows us - and I will be disguised anyway, so he will have no qualms about not identifying me. Did you get a ticket?"

Tymos now grinned wickedly. "A copious donation to the science budget, and a generous one to the man Klim hired to help Chave organise his party…easy! I will be part of the catering staff."

"And my credentials?"

"Being organised. I asked Jonko to get onto it since most of the computers within the Imperium have limited world internet access. I tried to use the university wi-fi link, but there is an invidious official 'watching' net."

"The short answer?" Kryslie prompted.

"Oh that?" Tymos grinned even wider. "At first glance, you an authentic, brilliant, scientist…studying force fields."

"I thought we were not intending to be obvious?"

"Figure it, Krys! Layers of deception."

"So my supposed speciality is the carrot? I'm a woman, so the locals will find me something of an anathema, but if I really know the field, they won't be able to resist taking advantage of a mere woman?"

"Something like that," Tymos agreed. "Jon assures me that whilst your credentials are very good forgeries, there are just enough discrepancies that whoever checks them will get suspicious. However, they will have to work hard to prove that you are a fake."

"At which time they will start to believe I am an agent of the UWN - and want to bring me in. That will work…the high ups will want to question me."

Tymos turned serious. "Krys, I don't like this. We can't predict what they will do to you."

"I will have a personal force shield on and we are not mere humans. I don't intend to let them take me until I am ready. I want to get Klim on his own first. You want to search his house, don't you?"

"I've been through his house, his office, and his usual classrooms," Tymos growled with frustration. "He has to have a secret office where he keeps all information relevant to his subversive activities. I have checked his phone records. He has a wi-fi phone, and all his calls originate from somewhere within the city - roughly between the university and his house. All the calls are too short to trace."

"I will draw him out," Kryslie assured him. "He won't make a scene at the party. All I need to do is give him a hint, and leave. He will follow…"

She inserted into her brothers mind the image of a particularly eye catching blue outfit. It was demure by UWN standards, but on the edge on indecency for the Imperium.

Tymos simply shook his head. "I hope you know what you are doing."

Chapter 14 - The Party

Tymos was dressed in black and had his red hair dyed to dark brown. He was moving around Chave's large entertaining room with trays of drinks, or trays of empty glasses that needed to be washed. He sensed when his sister arrived, and easily changed his route through the guests to be near the door. Even then, he seemed to pay her no attention.

This wasn't the case with many of the guests. The glitzy blue fabric of the long sleeved over vest, caught the light and attracted attention. Kryslie kept her focus on the usher, with her invitation ready in her hand. She was smiling, and shifting subtly as if she were nervous. If he didn't know it to be an act, Tymos would have read her body language as being that of someone who was determined to pretend that she belonged in the presence of so many rich and famous people. It was a cross between how commoners behaved in the presence of Tymorean royalty back on Tymorea, and how he and Kryslie had been trained to act as the Heir Designates to one of the three Tymorean Governors.

The usher took Kryslie's overvest and passed it to one of the men looking after the cloaks of the guests. Tymos nudged Chave's mind, and he looked away from the man he was speaking with, apologised, and approached the usher.

More eyes were on Kryslie now, as she followed the usher, moving with sensuous grace in the high-necked, sleeveless thigh length slip. This white fabric was an glittery as the blue of the trousers and the overvest. The guests who were visiting from the UWN glanced her way, appreciatively, and went back to their conversations. Their partners may have eyed the shimmering dress and the slim form wearing it with an interest in the unusual style, having been careful to choose clothing that was less provocative.

The looks she received from the local guests, were more intense. As a visitor from the UWN, she would not be expected to adhere to the local code of women's attire. Her outfit was just on the edge of acceptable, but revealed more of her shape and form than was usual in the Imperium.

Chave waited for the usher's introduction, and greeted her with the same degree of politeness and courtesy as he had every stranger who had come into his house that evening. At first, he did not recognise Kryslie - it was the first time he had seen her with short light brown hair, and in anything like her current attire.

Kryslie sensed when he recognised her and warned him, mentally, to treat her no differently to other guests.

"May I call you Helaine?" Chave asked, using the alias Kryslie had chosen. His smile was gracious and he slipped an arm through hers. "You are a scientist? What is your speciality?"

He led her through the crowd of guests, with every sign of interest in what she was telling him. Based on her claimed speciality of 'shields' and 'forces', he introduced her to Imperium scientists working in that field. He stayed until he had to leave to greet his next guest.

Kryslie was perfectly capable of handling herself, and concentrated on learning about the local scientists and interesting them with her greater knowledge. Her interest in them, enabled her to discover where they worked as well as their specialities. The little group expanded as UWN guests heard her talking and came to hear what she said. Several of the newcomers were also knowledgeable about 'shields' and 'forces'. She actually recognised some of the men as being former students at the WSRA's Washington University, although they did not recognise her in her disguise.

Even while acting as drinks waiter, Tymos was keeping an eye on the proceedings. He was looking out for Dev Klim, Chave's history professor friend, as well as counting the number of people there that wore gold stars. So far, he had counted two dozen.

The two IC shadows were keeping near the buffet table, chatting casually but also with eyes scanning the room. They were not looking for anyone in particular, just anyone who might be taking too much interest in their 'charges'.

Kryslie felt a slight jolt as her twin finally spotted Klim, and then heard, "He's just come out from one of the small side rooms with one of the guest scientists."

Without betraying her distraction, she replied mentally, "What interest does a history professor have with scientists?"

"That one is a weapons specialist - and into rocket propulsion systems," Tymos told her. "I'm guessing he is being interviewed and will be a recruit soon. Anyway, I think you are his next target - I sent Chave to mention you to him, in your Helaine guise. Both are approaching now."

Kryslie felt a light pressure on her arm and knew it was Chave.

"Pardon my intrusion, Helaine. I would like to introduce you to another of my important guests."

After excusing herself, Kryslie turned and allowed Chave to lead her a few feet away to where a very distinguished man, who had greying hair and was probably in his fifties, was looking her way.

The man gave her a slight bow of greeting, as introductions were made.

"A history professor," Kryslie remarked, as she studied the man. "And you are also interested in science?"

"I am interested in many things," Klim told her, with a smile that seemed to be only for her. His mind seemed to be concentrating on what ever she was saying.

Chave stepped back and allowed Klim to take Kryslie's arm through his.

"I'd like to hear more about your work. Perhaps we could move to a quieter corner…"

As they walked, people seemed to move aside to let them through. Certainly, his UWN style evening dress with its expensive tailoring and exquisite fabric, set him above the rest of the guests.

Kryslie did not wish to leave the main room, so she suggested a corner near the buffet. It was within sight of the two IC shadows, and Tymos had a reason to hover nearby.

The small talk had moved on to, "Have you been in my country for long?" when they reached the table with the small plates for the guests to use for food.

"No, I only arrived yesterday," Kryslie claimed. "I do hope to have time to see more - the trip from the airport showed some lovely places."

Klim's next question was, "How did such a charming lady become interested in such esoteric subjects as 'forces' and shields'?"

It was the opening that she was waiting for and Kryslie launched into her topic with fervour. Klim had a basic understanding of many fields of science, but this was advanced physics - he knew nothing of the theory, but there was no doubt that the little he had heard on the subject, had aroused his interest. He wanted to know how the theory could be used for his own purposes.

His manner remained attentive, and polite, and he feigned delight at her intelligence, although his mind didn't completely hide his inner revulsion that a woman was his equal, intellectually. If Kryslie had not been able to sense the emotions he kept hidden, she could have easily believed that she had made a conquest of the man.

As she was slowly eating her way through a second plate of bite-sized delicacies, that Klim had requested from one of the caterers, a murmur of surprise rippled through the gathering. She looked up, and noticed that almost every head in the room was looking towards the door. From her current position, she could not see who or what was creating the sensation, but she could see her brother working his way around to get a look.

A group of dark suited men, all with shaved heads, surrounded a tall man with styled and gelled black hair. Chave had insinuated himself into the small circle and was using a quiet voice and hand gestures as he spoke to the new arrival.

Tymos sent a mental image of the man to his sister. "Know him?"

She studied the mental image while Klim was briefly distracted. "I have never seen him," was her conclusion. But she felt that she did know him - something about the shape of the face was familiar.

The group passed her position, and now she could see the back of this obviously important surprise guest. If Klim's tailor was the best in the city, whoever had made and fitted the newcomer's suit must be the best in the Imperium, or even the world. The fabric was, in her opinion, as far above that of Klim's suit, as that was above the off the rack suits in an UWN clothing store.

Seeing how everyone the man came near was either bowing stiffly, or in the case of the women guests bobbing a curtsey, gave Kryslie a prickle of warning. This man was important.

He wasn't Abdul bin Halil, for the Imperium's leader was much older and his hair was greying. But this could be his son...her son. The age was right. This man looked to be about thirty years old. Then the man turned and glanced around the room. For an instant, her eyes met those of the newcomer, and Kryslie felt her body go rigid.

Klim sensed the reaction, and asked, "What is the matter, my dear?"

Kryslie could not drag her eyes away from her son, but knew she needed to cover her lapse. "Who is he, Professor Klim? He is gorgeous..."

That she sounded like an infatuated teenager, amused Klim. He took her arm in his, and patted it gently to distract her. "That, my dear, is Prince Arthur bin Halil. His father is his Excellency Abdul bin Halil…"

She wasn't listening, and when she didn't react to the name, Klim added, "…Leader of the Imperium."

Kryslie felt Tymos give her mind a gentle nudge, and she forced herself to look away from the Prince. She gave a theatrical sigh, as if finally realising that the man was way too high in rank to associate with her. Then she turned back to where she had placed her half-eaten plate of food. She sensed that Klim was rethinking his own conclusions as to her initial reaction.

Using the action of eating more food, and selecting other delicacies, Kryslie managed to get her swirling emotions under control. She heard her twin's mind voice asking, "Are you okay?"

She replied mentally, "What do you think? No, I am not. I never expected…"

She didn't have to finish the thought. Tym would know that seeing her son had thoroughly rattled her.

"Could I get you a drink, my dear?"

Kryslie turned and gave Klim a smile, "I am fine at the moment. I am enjoying these little pastries. I have never tasted anything so delicious. What ever do they fill them with?"

Klim humoured her, and explained what was in the different varieties. His head was turned partly away from her as he spoke, and Kryslie knew that part of his attention was on the Prince.

While he was distracted, Kryslie glanced in the same direction. The Prince was walking with Chave, and speaking to various groups of people with the aplomb of a born statesman. She tried to fathom the reason Klim's interest.

"I take it that the Prince was a surprise guest tonight. His being here seems as odd as a history professor at this science gathering."

Klim returned his full attention to her. "Our host is a professor of economics," he smiled. "But he, like I, enjoy the chance to meet people from around the world." Again he patted her hand as if implying her, specifically. "My dear, you were trying to explain to me how something with no physical substance can block solid objects."

Krys allowed herself to be diverted, but for the next ten minutes she was still aware that Klim's attention was not where his eyes were looking. Tymos's timely warning allowed her to be in control when Arthur bin Halil moved up behind her. She sensed him there, waiting politely for a break in the conversation.

Krys saw Klim's attention move to behind her; she stopped talking and turned.

"Professor Klim, how are you?" the Prince greeted with a charming smile. Krys tensed as if nervous about being in the Prince's presence.

"I am well, your Highness," Klim bowed respectfully. "May I introduce Helaine Mesure?"

"Indeed," Arthur murmured, taking Krys's free hand and bending down to kiss it. Such an outdated greeting was very natural to him. "I see that my teacher of history has, as usual, found the most beautiful woman here." His eyes were the same blue-green as her own, and his features a mixture of Tymorean and Arabic. His hair was as black as his father's had once been.

"I am hardly that, Sir...Prince Arthur," Krys managed to sound nervous, but composed.

She sensed the 'connection' he felt to her like a powerful electric spark. It was much stronger than what she had felt looking at his face.

"You seem somehow familiar," Prince Arthur admitted, keeping her eyes on her.

"Have you ever been outside the Imperium, your Highness?" Krys asked, hoping to hint that he could not possibly know her.

"Alas, no," he admitted, politely releasing her hand.

Klim inserted himself back into the conversation. "Is your esteemed father expected this evening, your Highness?"

Arthur took his eyes from Krys and spoke to Klim. "He was disappointed that his duties did not permit. However, knowing of my passion for science, he allowed me to represent him. He still hopes to visit the Science Fair. It is an unparalleled opportunity to meet people from outside the Imperium, and to learn of the advances in science."

The waiters that had been unobtrusive were noticeably attentive to the Prince.

Arthur seemed to expect that and politely asked if Klim or Krys required a fresh drink. As there was only wine on the tray, Krys declined.

"I prefer water, your Highness," Krys said, earning an intent look from the Prince as if the comment evoked a memory.

Klim did take one of the offered glasses.

Moments later, Tymos arrived with a tray of other drinks that did include water. Now Krys took one, and used the action of sipping to hide the fact she was thinking at her brother. "Give me five more minutes and then distract the Prince. He is getting a bit intense. I dare not stay here any longer."

Tym edged closer and Krys risked a brief touch on the Prince's mind. She confirmed that he was trying to place her face. She did not dare let him – it would be a major complication.

Klim was helping to distract him by taking the conversation in another direction and keeping the Prince's attention off her.

That gave Krys the chance for a deeper probe, and with a sense of relief, became sure her son was not involved in any conspiracy. But that did not mean his father wasn't.

Timing the casual move of brushing hair from her face, with Tym's skilful insertion into Prince Arthur's attention, Krys released a tiny tendril of red hair from under the brown wig.

She used Klim's monopoly of the Prince's as an opportunity to excuse herself from his company, using gestures to indicate a need to visit the ladies room. She saw the faint tensing of Klim's face and knew he had spotted the red hair. His mind went immediately to the red headed woman who had escaped from the questioners. He was torn between continuing his talk with the Prince, and wanting to stop her leaving.

Krys went where she claimed, feeling Klim's eyes on her until she was out of the room. He would not be able to walk off on the Prince, so that gave her a slight head start.

Instead of returning to the party, she slipped out the front door after requesting her coat from the usher.

She went out to one of the chauffeured cars parked along the driveway of Chave's house. He had hired them to take guests to and from their hotels or local accommodation. She gave the nearest driver directions to one of the hotels being used by the Science Fair delegates.

The car moved off slowly, and as far as she could tell, no one followed her. That was hardly a problem. Klim would soon find out which hotel she had gone to, but she was not going to make the trail that easy, or that hard to follow. She had roused Klim's suspicions, and he would probably send people after her. So, after the car arrived at the hotel and the driver had opened the door and helped her out, she walked into the lobby and waited until the car had departed to return to the party. Then, she had used the courtesy phone in the lobby to call a public taxi to take her to the rented apartment.

The IC shadow had followed her, but she did not think anyone else had. Klim should be able to find her with a bit of effort.

Tym watched Klim's reaction, when he suspected Krys had slipped away. He excused himself from the Prince's company and moved purposefully away, his mind elsewhere.

Arthur bin Halil glanced after him and then turned as Tymos spoke to him. At first he simply saw one of the waiters, but his attention was riveted when the man switched languages to one he had learned as a child.

"I have not met you before, have I?" Arthur asked in his native language, studying Tymos. "I feel I know you."

"One like me," Tym said softly.

Arthur nodded. His early tutors had spoken that language. He still understood it, even if he did not speak it himself.

Tymos went on, "It would be wise, your Highness, not to involve yourself with the lovely, intelligent scientist. It could be dangerous, to you."

Arthur's expression hardened but finally, he nodded. Respect to those who spoke that language, ingrained in him at a very early age, won out. He had never identified that odd tongue, nor mentioned it to his father.

"We work for peace," Tym spoke softly in the Prince's language. "We do what we must...please do not get involved." Tym bowed then and moved away.

The Prince was soon distracted by another guest, and his training in statecraft took over again.

Tymos moved to locate Klim and found him talking animatedly to Chave. As he passed the pair, on his way to the buffet, he overheard enough to know that Klim wanted his sister found.

On his return with a plate of bite-sized edibles, Tym slipped his free hand into his pocket and activated a tracer he had requested from the IC agent shadowing him. He slipped it into Klim's pocket as he brushed past.

Chave noticed him, but said nothing to Klim.

"Excellent evening," Tym commented to Chave as he moved on, heading for the room set aside for the caterers. There he donned a dressy jacket, and became simply another guest.

Over near the door, Alen, unobtrusive in his guise of a security guard, drew a pager from his pocket. He looked at it, and then glanced around the room. His gaze rested on Klim and Chave. As the men moved apart, his eyes followed Klim. He made eye contact with Tym when he re-emerged and nodded slightly.

When Klim left the reception, Tym followed. His all black suit and shirt would help him blend into the shadows. His quarry took one of the chauffeured cars, and a short time later, Tym went to another.

Without needing to follow Klim closely, Tym asked his driver if he minded doing a short tour of the city before dropping him off. Since the man was getting paid by the hour and distance, he did not mind.

Heading off towards the university, where the Science Fair was being held, Tym glanced at his palm-sized receiver and determined from the tracking signal that it was not Klim's target. His next guess was that he was going home, but the tracer signal indicated that Klim was heading into the city. Tym redirected the driver from the university to one of the hotels where the delegates were staying. He left the car and walked towards the hotel entrance. When the car had gone, he slipped into shadows and waited.

Klim was nearby. Tymos looked intently around, studying the dark shadows and the magnificently lighted hotel entrance. He finally spotted his target walking down the front steps, and turning in the direction of the next nearest hotel - the one Krys had disappeared from. He entered that hotel and did not stay there long before emerging and walking further on. His mood, radiating from him like an aura, was a complex mixture of annoyance and determination of purpose. Tym decided he was trying to find where Helaine Mesure was staying, and had not wanted to assign the task to someone else.

Like a dark cloud of fog, Tymos followed him to each of the four hotels, and waited. After the last, he waited outside until a local taxi pulled up beside him. Tymos was close enough to hear Klim give the driver his personal address.

Tym transmitted himself to Klim's residence and did a quick reconnaissance of the expensive off street building before finding a place to wait. He did not go in, because the intruder alarm system was on.

When Klim returned and had deactivated the alarm, Tym transmitted into the front foyer and stood perfectly still in a corner where no one was likely to walk. He used his power to hide himself.

Klim relocked the door and walked out of sight. When his footsteps took on the cadence of one walking upstairs on polished wood, Tym waited for the sound of a door closing before moving like a wraith after him.

This was the third time that Tymos had been in the house. He knew where every room was and what it was used for. Now, he went directly to Klim's private sitting room. A thin line of light from where the door had not closed properly, confirmed Tymos's guess. He edged past the room to where he could listen for sounds from within.

Tym strengthened the force screen about the apartment when he returned. Kryslie was waiting for him, already changed out of her glittering suit and back to wearing the more comfortable dark brown coveralls.

"After checking the hotels, he went home. He reported to someone," Tymos told her with a hint of frustration. "He requested a check on the person you are pretending to be. I couldn't hear what else was said. He listened, agreed, and went to bed."

They had hoped he would go to his secret room.

"I guess it is not unexpected," Krys decided. "He is one of those gold star wearers and all of them are clean. Have you tried tracing the number he called?"

"I put Marco onto it, but I doubt we'll get anything. The man is too careful."

"Well, I left a trail to here. That should convince him that I am hiding something, and that I am not a scientist just visiting for the week. The question is now, whether they will try to hunt me out of this warren, or try to get me at the Science Fair."

"The Fair starts tomorrow and they have to figure that's your target even if they can't guess your reason. If they think that the Prince turning up scared you off, they won't think you realise that you compromised yourself," Tymos proposed.

"Don't try second guessing them," Kryslie reminded him. "We want them to find me…"

"And they will make sure that you are disabled…"

"I am already wearing a personal force screen," Krys responded to her twin's concern. "It will block a stun and they have no idea of our full strength. I suggest you wear a PFS too."

Chapter 15 - The Science Fair

The Science Fair was scheduled to last for five days and the first two passed uneventfully as far as Kryslie was concerned. She was aware of eyes watching her and it was not just her IC assigned shadow. Since she had come to the attention of Klim at Chave's party, anyone who wanted to find her simply needed to access the registration details she had given to the fair organisers. Her interests were stated clearly there.

Each building was dedicated to a different aspect of science. One was for the biological and medical sciences, one for the physical sciences and the third was for technology.

There were four places that Kryslie concentrated her attention, and coincidently, only two were in the same building. So during the first two days, she moved between the three buildings, spending time at the exhibits in each of her interest areas. She made a habit of travelling by the back ways, rather than the main public thoroughfares. After all, the people she wanted to draw out already thought she was trying not to be seen.

To add substance to that idea, she did not dress as well as most of the exhibitors and guests, choosing UWN style casual over 'business' and had changed the styling of her hair. Perhaps that might have fooled any from the cabal that were sent to find her, except that her IC shadow was not as unobtrusive as she had wanted him to be. He was just obvious enough to act like an arrow to his target. Still, that acted in her favour. If they thought she was an IC agent and he was her back up, it would make them cautious. That was fine, since it gave her time to thoroughly explore the three buildings each with their half dozen levels, the pathways between and around them, the various gardens in the area as well as all the exits and back stairs.

Her stated interests included 'forces' and 'shields' and she was an expert in those fields, but the other areas she mentioned were merely camouflage. Still, she visited many other exhibits, spoke to many people, and the extra watchers would be unable to decide her true motives for being at the fair. She doubted that they would realise that she was playing them like fishermen, with herself as the bait, while investigating the level of scientific knowledge within the Imperium.

Tymos was never far away, but he took no notice of her. He had his hair darkened to black and he wore an Imperium style suit. He was looking out for men wearing gold stars, and singling them out for an innocent meeting and a few moments of conversation. He learnt a great deal about each of them in the short time. He was keeping the IC happy, passing on what he learnt. The IC agents had no way of knowing that most of the information on the men was being accumulated by a group of tenacious Tymorean missionaries.

As soon as they arrived at the Science Fair on the third day, Kryslie felt a difference in the atmosphere, or rather, the intensity of the interest of her covert watchers.

"Tym?" she mentally nudged her brother. For a brief instant, their eyes met from across two sides of the fourth floor exhibition hall. "It will be today. I feel something, no someone, malevolent watching me."

His instant reaction was to scan the room, looking for the watcher. He had already identified a dozen men who were interested in his sister. His mind thought instantly, "bin Halil" but he dismissed that. The Imperium's leader was too well known.

"This person knows me," Kryslie emphasized. "Like they know what I can do..."

"One of the men who took Louis?" Tym suggested, flicking images of possible Imperium agents into her mind.

"Perhaps, but I am not sure. And none of the faces you are showing me are familiar."

"I will warn your IC shadow," Tym decided.

"Let him do his job," Kryslie suggested. "He has been very useful so far as a pointer to me. He is not to interfere...better for him to seem to be an impartial witness."

Tymos flicked a thought of concern and began to move closer to her, moving nimbly between other visitors. "If they are going to try anything here, they will need a distraction. It won't be easy to get you out from up here. Do you think you should amble down to the ground level?"

"Make it easy for them?" Kryslie thought back.

"Safer for bystanders. If they need a distraction, guaranteed to keep people looking away - innocents might get hurt."

"I will head down, but not by the back way this time. There is a local scientist I have been talking to who has some excellent theories about propelling objects faster than light. I just spotted him at the mini cyclotron exhibit. I want to be with someone until I am ready to hunt."

Tymos sent his agreement wordlessly, and waited a short time after she'd gone before leaving after her. On the ground floor, he stopped a few steps from the elevator, and looked for the source of the sudden hush. He concentrated on sampling conversations around him, which were all still, "What is happening?"

Then word began to filter through the crowd, "The Leader is here!" At the same time, people began to move towards the outside door.

"Krys? Where are you?"

"By the rear door, where the fire escape is."

"You know?"

"Yeah. News like that travels faster than lightning. What is happening?"

Tymos sent images of the pushing, eager spectators and the general exodus to the door.

"Anyone hanging back?" Krys asked.

The visual scan of the room gave no indication.

"That mind I felt is looking for me to come out. I am sure that he believes I will follow my habit to date and I will slip out the back."

"Can you pick up anything from bin Halil?" Tymos asked, although he was pretending to see over the heads of the crowd. More people were pouring down the stairs in an eager stream.

"I can, bro. I sure can. Smug bastard is drinking up the adulation, and feeling very self-satisfied at the success of the Science Fair."

Tymos pulled out his communicator and adjusted a setting. "My guess would be that one of his technical experts has succeeded in hacking into the computer net here. It seems, by the data stream I am detecting, that every little bit of data on every computer is being copied and uploaded. With everyone agog at his magnificence, there will be only a small chance of anyone noticing."

"That's one reason. The other is that he knows I am here."

"The woman who saved Louis?" Tym asked, but the level of emotion he was now sensing from his twin told him it was something else.

"No. Me. He saw the image of me from one of the cameras in that building - and he is convinced that I have to be his missing consort. The image was not very good. I can't get anything else from him - nothing about the cabal."

"He's coming into this building," Tymos warned, suddenly beset by a premonition of disaster. He looked around again. "There are guards coming in from all directions - did they see you?"

"No. They are walking obliviously past me."

That she was using her Tymorean power to hide was obvious, but that had not eased Tymos's bad feeling. "Someone is concentrating on you - wants you dead…"

"Bin Halil wants me dead," Kryslie said calmly. "I do not intend to oblige him."

"Someone else. Do you know any of these faces?" Tymos glanced at each of the suited figures moving deliberately through the crowd. They were studying the faces of all the people they passed.

"Trying to freak me into running," Kryslie deduced. "They will expect me to duck out the back way."

"Yes, that seems right…wait until I am positioned outside. Then come out. Does your IC shadow know where you are?"

"He has spotted me again. He lost me for a while…"

Tymos had allowed the crowd to pass him, and he moved back into a deserted side room. From there, he risked transmitting out into the open garden between that building and the next. He materialised next to the red brick wall and quickly scanned the area. It was empty of people. Like the 'find somewhere else to be' kind of empty. He let his mind move further out, and he sensed men waiting and watching. He tried to localise the malevolent mind he had sensed, as he felt his sister slipping out the back door, and walking purposefully along the narrow laneway towards the garden.

He shared what he had seen and sensed, and she in turn remarked. "There are cameras. One is panning along with me. I am not going to be able to use my full skill set - not that I intended to do more than give a good pretence, but someone wants to observe this encounter."

"That could work both ways. I am linking into the security net now, and recording the feed from the six cameras in this area."

The ambush was expertly laid. Tymos spotted the attacker, and had only time to send a brief warning, but his sister was already reacting.

Kryslie sensed the instant the malevolent presence spotted her. She scanned her forward and side view, but did not turn around. Movement, betrayed only by the faintest trace of a breeze teasing her hair, was all the warning she had. She was spinning around as her brother's warning echoed in her mind.

The furious face of Omar Harrison confronted her. He was less than a metre away, coming at her with his knife ready to stab. Kryslie reacted instinctively, her combat training on Tymorea subconsciously guiding her actions. She darted towards him, diving under his knife arm, twisting and grabbing the arm so that the knife dropped. He had been trying for a gut shot; had the knife been aimed at her legs, her move would have been different. She realised, too late, that the attack had been a ruse - the knife was not a stabbing blade. He had tricked her, and now he had her brown wig in his other hand. He kicked at her, as he gloated.

"They said you'd run away. Said you'd never dare stay near the Leader."

He jerked his arm free, and Kryslie let him. She dared not betray her full strength yet.

"So what?" Kryslie taunted him, as she trotted back out of his reach.

Tymos was telling her that the other watchers were just waiting. She wondered what for. Her to kill Harrison? Him to kill her? No, she was sure that bin Halil would want her alive.

Her considerations only took a fraction of a second, but Harrison was watching for his chance and drew another knife from behind his back.

"Freakish bitch," Harrison cursed as he slashed at her face. He leered when she leapt back to avoid him. "Can't hide with a face cut to ribbons."

He was trying to trick her, making her protect her face, but his stance was wrong. He switched the knife to his left hand and thrust it towards her stomach. His surprise when it did not connect turned to disbelief. He felt the bones in his wrist being crushed by the strength of the woman's grip. His hand lost strength and the knife dropped. His eyes met Kryslie's and he wanted to look away.

As he struggled to free his wrist, Kryslie kneed him in the thigh. Twice in as many seconds, Harrison felt the power behind the blow. His leg went numb. She gave him a powerful shove and he fell backwards.

She gave him a glance as she raced off, not at her full speed, just enough to seem to be trying to get away. It was a test, to see if Harrison or the others came after her. Harrison let out a vile curse in Arabic. He was climbing to his feet and stumbling into a run after her.

Tymos warned her, "Watch it."

A very young child suddenly dived out in front of her; she had to swerve to miss him. She ran into the apologetic parent, and used the encounter to trip and let Harrison get closer. Now she pretended a limp, glanced behind her and seemed to be trying to go faster.

She sensed Harrison catching her. Had she been really running for her life, looking over her shoulder would be mistake. As it was, it was what she needed for her next move. He launched himself in a flying tackle, aiming to get her pinned to the ground. Only he felt her go down, and instead of him landing on her, he somersaulted sideways. He could not believe that she had the strength in her legs to toss him aside. She began to scramble to her feet, but he grabbed her right ankle and held tight even though she was trying to twist free. Reaching with his other hand for his knife, he didn't see her other foot until it was about to connect. He felt his head lash back, and his world went black.

Kryslie picked up the knife, and tucked it into her belt. She didn't want a child to pick it up, and her watchers would expect her to take the weapon. She leant down to check Harrison was alive and then began to trot the rest of the way across the garden, but now, the six watchers ran into view, calling for her to stop. They had their weapons raised, ready to fire, and approached from three angles so that she had no where to run.

Their attitude and stance told her that they would shoot if she didn't comply. She was going to claim she was attacked, so she obeyed the order.

The one she guessed was the troop commander, came close. "Drop your weapon."

"It isn't mine. He tried to attack me, and I didn't want any child to pick it up."

"Drop it!"

Kryslie reached for it - keeping the movement slow, for the man was ready for her to try pulling the weapon or a weapon, on him. As soon as it dropped to the ground, one of the men grabbed it and placed it in a bag.

"Back!" the troop commander told her. She glanced from him to Harrison, and saw two men standing beside the prone body. She went slowly, keeping part of her attention on the man with the gun aimed at her.

He stopped her a few feet from Harrison, and jerked his head at one of the men in a gesture of questioning.

"He is dead, Sir. His neck is broken," she understood the man to say, but she pretended she didn't. When he said, "You are to come with us," she countered in English with, "That man attacked me. I insist that you arrest him."

Her captor switched to English. "I arrived in time to see that fancy move of yours. I saw him go down. Now he is dead. You killed him."

"He attacked me!" Kryslie protested as she felt her wrists grabbed, and her arms forced behind her. She expected metal handcuffs, but felt the unpleasant tingle of energy binders.

Her protests were ignored as the troop commander ordered one of his team to organise a team to investigate the murder and a van to transport the prisoner.

Kryslie had two men gripping her arms, making it difficult to get away.

"Neat," Tymos spoke to Kryslie's mind. "It all looks nice legal and efficient. The IC shadow saw the whole thing. Was he dead?"

"No," Kryslie told him, making mild attempts to shake herself free, and controlling her disgust. "But I bet his neck will be broken by the time a doctor sees him."

"And they will seem to be within their rights to charge you with murder, and keep you locked up," Tymos predicted. "What if they simply try to have you executed?"

"Then you had best be ready with an imperative reason for them to keep me alive," Kryslie countered. "But we know this is just a reason to keep me away from the IC. If they think me an agent, they might think I will claim some sort of immunity and that I might elude them. With a murder charge, the IC can't interfere."

"So Harrison was never meant to survive?" Tymos deduced. "You could easily have got away from him..."

"Harrison must have blamed me for his failure to get Emmanuel. It would not do anything for his reputation to have been defeated by a woman. Perhaps they convinced him that if he killed me, he'd get his honour back. If he didn't know who I was at the start, once he saw me, he'd be extremely motivated - for his own reasons as well. I agree though, I think they expected me to overcome him, since I managed to elude those secret police and escape from their prison."

"Yes, these guards watched until you got the better of him. Harrison failed to get you..."

"And bin Halil doesn't tolerate failures," Kryslie interrupted. "What is happening with him?"

Tymos used his communicator to contact one of the missionaries that were observing the Science Fair.

"Lording it over everyone," Tymos summarised. "People are starting to move off now they have seen him. Alen saw one of his personal bodyguards whisper in his ear… I'd say he knows his people caught a red-headed fish."

"I would consider that a safe bet. And if that is so, then these guards are not regular exhibition security guards, even though they are dressed like the real ones."

"Show me their faces," Tymos suggested, and he studied the four guards Kryslie could see.

"No, they are not regular guards unless bin Halil fired them. The oldest one, on the left, has the top of his ear missing. He was one of bin Halil's main guards when Arthur was born."

"Now he has seen me, he can't possibly think I am the me of thirty years ago. We haven't visibly aged."

"Don't count on logic, Krys. The man obeys orders."

"Yeah. I have just heard that my ride is here. They are to take me and Harrison out via the service roads."

"I'll be following," Tymos promised. "And I have your tracer signal at strength ten. I should be able to locate you, wherever they take you."

Kryslie had agreed to the safeguard of having one of the Tymorean devices inserted under her skin. Tymos had performed the minor procedure - making the incision, inserting the device, and then healing the wound so that the scar looked years old. They called it a tracer, but it was a passive GPS dot. Only the size of a button battery, the microelectronics received signals from the network of satellites circling the Earth, and when it received a signal on a certain frequency, it pinged back the most recent coordinates. It had the extra advantage of being constructed from non-metallic substances.

The grip of one guard was removed, as the man was needed to lift one end of a stretcher bearing Harrison. However, Kryslie did not use that as a reason to try to escape, for the remaining man pressed his gun into her side. If he shot her, the bullet might not kill her, but it would incapacitate her for a time. And fired from skin close, her personal force screen would not stop it.

Confined in the back of what looked like an armoured van, Kryslie was satisfied with her position. She knew that her 'capture' had been masterminded by bin Halil. His guards had captured her, and Harrison had been one of the silver star wearers. The secret police she had encountered before were bin Halil's spies. They had been hunting her, so surely her description was known to their superior. If they had managed to get a picture of her, and shown that - bin Halil would have recognised her likeness to his missing consort. Somehow, Harrison's encounter with her had become known and he was brought into the picture.

All that didn't matter; she was where she intended to be. If they questioned her about Harrison's murder, it would be for show - so the IC could not interfere. They would want to know what she was doing in Jafhabad - presuming her to be an agent of the UWN or the Investigative Committee. They would want to know everything the IC knew about their secret plans.

And sometime during the process, Abdul bin Halil would want to see her. He would want to know where his missing consort was. So, she simply had to endure the process until bin Halil showed himself. That was her goal.

One thing she had proved to herself that day - her connection to bin Halil still existed, even though, for her, ten years had passed since she had been intimate with him. Then, she had been able to read his mind, manipulate him without his awareness - today she had still been able to sense his emotions and the things on his mind. Yes, he'd eventually show himself, if only to gloat and demean her.

The van stopped abruptly. The drive had not been long, but that was not surprising. The exhibition centre was in the middle of the city. When the door opened, one guard stepped in to grab her, another kept her covered with his weapon. She was shoved out of the back, so she fell onto hard concrete. Another guard dragged her to her feet, and began to force her inside. She had a brief glimpse of a line of parked police cars, before she was inside the building and walking along a khaki painted passage. One guard preceded them and he opened one of the side doors. Her escort shoved her sideways, into the room, and then dragged her to a chair next to a table. He pushed her down into the chair, and one of the other guards attached a manacle to her leg. This was connected to the floor by a chain. Once she was secured, the guards left and the door clanged shut behind them.

Pretending to lean back in the chair, Kryslie used the opportunity to test the energy binders. She knew what they were, and that they were used in the

UWN, but had not realised that the technology had come to the Imperium. They consisted of a ring around each wrist, that when powered, acted like two powerfully attractive electromagnets.

She could, if necessary, force them apart. The police and the guards had no idea of her strength. A better option though, was to draw energy from the devices and use it to supplement her own power. No Imperial official would believe that such a thing was possible.

"Tym? What's happening?"

"You are in the police HQ building. I sent Markos in there to listen. He is lurking on the ground floor. Back at the science fair, the gossip is wild. Your IC shadow is trying to convince the police who were called in, that Harrison attacked you and you were defending yourself. Though most people are whispering that you were caught trying to assassinate the leader. Alen has heard all sorts of in-between rumours.

"Where are you?" Kryslie asked her twin.

"Down the passage from you in an empty room. I planted a listening device in the room where the police are debriefing the Leader's guards." His tone was grim. "They have been diabolically clever, and I am sure the security camera record will be doctored to back up what they claim. If I had to judge the evidence - it would take little persuasion to call it first degree murder."

There was a pause, and then Tymos sent, "That old guard just told the police that they were expecting an attempt on the Leader. He described you as being identified as a UWN agent and two weeks ago, you had been seen with known traitors. He mentioned that you had infiltrated Chave's party, and think you had wanted to get at the Leader if he had attended as originally planned."

"If I needed proof of bin Halil's hand in this - that just settled it."

"It is not evidence the IC can use," Tymos shared her frustration.

"Yet!" Kryslie emphasised.

"I am picking up low voices - like a private discussion between some of the police."

"I don't need to guess what they are saying. As soon as treason was mentioned, they will have to bring in the security police. In the mean time, they will charge me with this apparent murder, so that the IC can't have me extradited and I will be spirited away to where bin Halil's secret police can do as they please."

That was the part of the plan that Tymos didn't like. The sorts of things that they could do were not pleasant. Yet, this was his twin's idea, and she was not fragile. She believed that bin Halil would eventually want to meet her, face-to-face, and he knew the man would try to have her beaten into submission before then. There was no use in him trying to object. His sister was a Tymorean Great One, an elemental force when she was angry. And there were the Guardians themselves, who could step in and play a role - using their advocates - when they deemed it wise.

"I have some of the missionaries watching this building," Tymos said, changing the subject. "But I think they will have you taken to where they had Louis."

"Odds on," Kryslie agreed calmly. "And that is to our advantage. We know that place. The tracer is working?"

"Perfectly. My communicator is pinging it every two seconds."

They didn't keep Kryslie waiting much longer, and as soon as the group of bin Halil's guards had said all they could, or rather all they intended to, the police told them to stay available, while they questioned the prisoner.

Tymos took himself out of room where he was hiding, by transmitting outside into a van that Alen had hired. He checked in with the missionaries who were doing various tasks for him, and settled onto the floor of the van to listen mentally to what his sister was hearing. Since the van had no windows in the cargo section, he did not need to worry about being seen.

Kryslie had her own agenda, as she answered the questions posed by the police. Naturally, she was sticking to her story that she was a Swiss-born scientist, visiting the Science Fair. She admitted to being at Chave's party, and leaving early because she was feeling unwell. She admitted to being at the fair, representing herself and some of her colleagues that had been unable to attend. Of the incident with Harrison, she stuck to the truth. He had attacked her without provocation, she had defended herself, tried to flee, but he had come after her and tried to stab her.

When they began the questions again, trying to trap her into a different answer, she demanded representation. They ignored her, and tried to force her to incriminate herself. They had no chance. Tymos knew how strong minded his sister was and he agreed with her side thoughts to him. This session was merely a formality - the regular police were waiting for the security police to arrive.

Before they did, she was formally charged with the murder of Harrison. They tried to frighten her with the penalty she could expect, but she kept to the insistence of innocence.

When the three security policemen arrived, armed and armoured, Kryslie became mute. The regular police simply turned and departed the interview room. She had no qualms about reading their minds, and knew that no matter what she had said, even if she could have convinced them that she was innocent, the outcome would have been the same.

The three newcomers stared menacingly at her until the other men had gone. They were practically shouting their thoughts of satisfaction about having her captive. They knew how capable she was, hence the armour as well as the weapons. They knew she had escaped from them, freeing another prisoner as well - a situation that had made the Leader livid. Now they had orders concerning her and were going to ensure she did not escape again.

"The murder charge is the least of your worries, you freakish bitch," the spokesman told her. "Our courts might be lenient and only sentence you to hard labour for the rest of your life. The sentence for treason is death - unless you tell us everything you know."

Their words had no effect. Kryslie stayed mute, and did not try to plead for mercy. She simply stared back at the men.

After a full minute of silence, the spokesman gestured and one of the others walked behind her, and wrapped a strong arm about her neck. She knew instinctively, that if she tried to move, the man would break her neck. While she was held that way, another of the men freed her ankle.

While still with her head in the crook of the man's arm, she was dragged from the chair, and out into the passage. They didn't take her back the way she had come, but continued along the passage and deeper into the building. After a hundred yards, they came to an elevator, waiting open. Kryslie was dragged in, and when the door had closed, she felt the car going down.

Kryslie sensed that these men, skilled fighters though they were, had been prepared to take no chances. They thought they had her cowed this time, but even so, her lack of physical defiance was making them uneasy. When the elevator gave the slightest of lurches, the man holding her went tense. She played with their minds and drew energy from the lift mechanism, dimming the lights and causing the car to slow to a stop before the end. She heard the two men with their hands free, cocking their guns. She felt their relief and caution when the lift car began to move again.

In her mind, she heard her twin's concern. "The tracer signal is getting weaker. Where are you?"

She considered her location, taking clues from her captor's mind.

"Going down in an elevator, to some kind of tunnel. I think it is safe to assume it will lead to the lower levels of the Justice building."

"Can you delay them questioning you?"

She knew her twin needed time to set up their counter move.

"I'm tired of being dragged…" was her assurance to him.

Without any warning, just after exiting the elevator, she twisted into action, revealing a hint of her full Tymorean strength. Even that much seemed unbelievable when the tall, solidly built men considered her slight, five foot six stature.

One moment she was moving awkwardly, with her head twisted under the guard's arm, and in the next she was free and her captor had been tossed off his feet and onto his cursing partner.

Even with her hands secured behind her, Kryslie was not defenceless. While the first two men were trying to untangle themselves, she leapt at the third guard, aiming her shoulder at his chest to wind him and knock him over. He went down, cursing, and when he realised his prisoner was racing away along the passage, drew the first of his weapons to hand and fired.

He cursed more creatively when the energy beam did not bring her down. All it must have done was overload the binders, for he heard them clatter to the concrete. Her hands were now free.

He drew his second weapon as he clambered to his feet and began to race after his prisoner. As he ran, he adjusted the setting on the stunner to maximum. Normally, that was lethal, but the bitch was at extreme range. The guard ran faster, gaining slowly, but the woman was almost at the end of the tunnel. He fired.

Kryslie felt the buzzing as her PFS neutralised the stun beam energy. She allowed herself to slow to a stop and collapse to the concrete. She feigned unconsciousness as the guard approached with gun arm outstretched, ready to fire again. When the guard kicked her viciously in the hip and she gave no reaction, he risked touching her neck to feel for a pulse. He was freaked enough to fear she would suddenly leap up.

The man knew of her, and recalled that she had been stunned before, and had recovered unusually fast. He was more determined than ever that she have no chance to get away. Her escape attempt would have been recorded on the monitoring cameras, and his commander would be ready reprimand him. There had been special orders relating to this prisoner.

His breathing returned to normal as he waited for his colleagues to catch up to him.

"Get her to the cell," he directed the two men who had been attacked first.

He watched, stunner ready, as they holstered their weapons and hoisted the woman between them. They each had one of her arms across their shoulders, held by one of their hands, while their free arm went around her waist and gripped her dishevelled clothing. They dangle/dragged her along the passage that ran under a city block, and finally reached the lower levels of the Justice Building.

It was the perfect place for the security police to operate from, though few outside that elite force knew it. The building housed the offices of judges, barristers, solicitors and the officials that worked in the courts that made up the first three above ground levels. As far as most people knew, the only cells in the building were the few that held the prisoners currently on trial.

Kryslie risked a peek when the men stopped. All she saw was a solid wall, until the leader of the group opened a hidden flap and pressed on a keypad. Then the wall swung open and she was dragged through. A breath of a breeze blew from behind, as the wall swung shut.

She sent the information to her twin, and learnt in return that the tracer he had inserted in her arm had ceased to react to signals from his communicator. She was deep underground, so it made sense. However, for now, their mental connection was unaffected. Tymos promised that he would be in position near by before they tried to question her.

Kryslie did not need to open her eyes to know she was back where they had taken her the previous time. When the door closed with a clang, all sound in the room was muffled and the air was still.

The process was the same; they dumped her on the hard bed and began searching her clothing - this time finding her fake ID and passport. Just as they finished that, the door opened again with a whoosh, like air escaping. From her guards, Kryslie sensed surprise, mixed with apprehension. This was followed by the rustle and stamp of men coming to attention.

"Proceed," was the order from the new arrival.

Kryslie felt her head held and her mouth forced open. A finger, smelling of gun oil and the ozone stench of energy beams, felt around inside. The hands moved her head from side to side as her ears and nose were checked for micro comm. units. Then, for a few moments, she was left undisturbed, but she heard the rustle of fabric and the tang of synthetic rubber. Nearer, she heard the sound of stretched rubber gloves snapping back to size.

The gloved hands were not gentle as they stripped off her clothing, nor when they checked her lower orifices for tracers. The man was an expert, and didn't miss a trick.

"The scanner," the voice of authority demanded. She recognised that voice.

There was a scraping noise from the direction of the table that Kryslie recalled being in one corner. Then footsteps and the snapping of an object onto a palm.

Kryslie felt a slight tingle as the device was run up and down both her sides, her front and her back.

"Nothing." The voice seemed satisfied. "If this bitch is UWN or IC, they won't find her this time." Kryslie was now sure that this was the man who had not been able to question her the first time she had been caught.

Again, there were a few undisturbed moments, while Kryslie heard people moving about, and then she was rolled onto her front and her wrists were secured with fully charged energy binders. Two more sets were applied at knees and ankles.

Kryslie sensed the man moving away and heard the gloves being stripped off. Others came close, and she felt them lift her legs and slip a rubbery fabric around them, and ease her up so it came up around her shoulders and neck. Her feet felt the fabric and she guessed that this was some sort of sack. The idea was confirmed when they secured the fabric with a stiff collar around her neck.

"Call me when the stun wears off," the authority stated.

Kryslie had memorised the voice and recalled his face. She would recognise the man if she saw him again. He left first, the other guards followed, after making the sounds of collecting things from the room. She waited for ten minutes before cautiously opening her eyes a mere fraction. She was facing a wall, but that didn't matter. She was going to continue to feign unconsciousness for as long as possible. Ideally, until late evening - another eight hours away.

After assuring her brother she was able to deal with her situation, she analysed the treatment she had received. All things considered, they intended for her to feel degraded, humiliated, helpless and small.

"Let them think that," Kryslie told herself, and considered her situation in a different light. Being naked, did not make her feel vulnerable. She could wriggle out of the energy binders at any time she chose. They were meant to sap the captive's energy, but she was wearing a personal force shield, that was skin tight and invisible to the normal human range of vision. Instead of the energy being drawn from her, the force shield was drawing on that source of energy to maintain power.

She gave the binders at her wrist an experimental pull. She was still strong enough to break the attraction, and once her hands were free, she could free her knees and ankles and escape from the sack. The main problem would be in moving around. Being naked would attract attention.

However, she was not intending to escape - she intended to confront bin Halil. Until he decided to face her, she would have to endure whatever humiliating, debasing, or agonising treatment they chose to inflict.

It was two hours after full dark when Kryslie warned Tymos that her captors were getting impatient. They had been slapping her face trying to get a reaction, and had then received orders to transfer her. As she had suspected, the phone had been used to pass the message.

The two men who had stayed watching her, lifted her off the bed and put her on a trolley, sack and all, to move her along the concrete passage to a lift.

Peeking through a narrow slit in her eyelids, Kryslie reported what she saw to her twin, who identified where she was. When they took her into the large chamber on a higher floor, she recognised it from her first period of captivity.

She was still using her delaying tactic of being limp and unreactive, as they hung her sack from a hook that attached to the neck collar. It was rigid enough to retain its shape, so it didn't immediately affect her airflow. She now dangled a few inches off the floor. They would be able to make her spin around, adding vertigo and nausea to her discomforts and these might sap her will to be strong.

Tymos's plan to infiltrate the building during the night was already underway. His team of highly trained Tymorean missionaries, under the command of Olassa, had studied the schematics of the building, and the additional information Tymos had learnt from his initial foray. They knew the timing of the security rounds and would be ready for any guards or cleaners that they encountered. Two of the Tymoreans would be inserting a special virus programme into the computer network to monitor all activity. An umbrella of detectors was ready to intercept all types of communication - phones, radios, Wi-Fi.

Now, while he needed to wait, he stayed lightly in rapport with his sister.

When Kryslie told her brother she was 'waking up', Tymos gave Olassa the signal to begin the infiltration. Then he needed to concentrate, as his sister sent him vivid images of the two men who had entered the chamber. One was the officer that had almost let her escape, and the other was the man she had dubbed the 'General', from the way the guards in her cell had reacted. They would need to find out who the man was, since he was surely high up in bin Halil's favour.

The General began the questions, first asking about why she had murdered Harrison, and moving on to her association with traitors. When she stayed mute, they tried to scare her by telling her the penalties for murder and treason. That was not new information, and she disregarded it. She also ignored their promises of leniency if she talked and identified her fellow traitors.

Unable to break her determined silence, the General lost patience and slapped her face.

"If you will not talk voluntarily, you will experience pain until you do."

Still getting no reaction, he said to the other man, "Make her talk, when she is ready, call me. We need to know what she knows."

The man strode past where Tymos was standing pressed against the wall. A holographic screen distorted vision to make the passage look empty. The associated repellor field ensured the man did not blunder into the watcher. He warned Olassa that the General was abroad. She would warn her team and if possible, find out where he went. If he had an office in the building, they were to identify it and find out who he was.

While his sister had been feigning unconsciousness, Tymos had searched the lower levels, including the chamber where his sister was now being interrogated. The lowest level only contained cells - six of them. All were alike - sound-proofed and Spartan. He had followed the tunnel back towards the Police Building, and found the solid wall his sister had mentioned. The keypad was also hidden on this side, but he knew how to find it and he knew the code his sister's captor had used.

The next level up - was where he hoped to find information, but he had found no records, recording devices or computers. Yet he had seen cameras everywhere, and there was probably sound pickups in the same places. Each of these had malfunctioned for the brief time he was near them. The main room was the interrogation room, and what he found there was a nasty collection of devices for inflicting pain, and a cupboard of drugs. His scanner soon identified their purpose, and he warned his sister. He had found the phone connection and tried to ring out, but had failed. He suspected he needed a more sophisticated code than merely pressing '0' for an outside line.

The only important new find he had made on that level was the closed room containing the door to a gas-fired incinerator. With its door open, since the chamber was currently cold, his scanner had detected traces of charred human flesh and bone. It solved the question of how so many people had conveniently and permanently disappeared.

It could have been Louis's fate; might still be what they intended for his sister.

Even though this was her plan, Tymos felt a moment of unease. He shouldn't doubt her judgement, or her ability to take care of herself, but he could feel anger at the way these people were torturing and killing anyone who tried to oppose them. Kryslie knew what to expect, and was ready to deal with it - but he still felt like a deserter when he transmitted upstairs and then to the vacant shop where Jonko had set up the monitors for the communications umbrella.

He had only just greeted Jonko and asked for a report, when he felt his back explode with excruciating pain. He nearly collapsed as his right leg lost strength below the knee, and then his left arm felt as if it was broken. Then his head began to spin, and more pain blossomed in places all over his body. He knew it was pain being echoed through the twin bond, as his sister was being beaten with a long wooden rod.

Jonko, aware of what was likely happening to Kryslie, went to Tymos and gave his shoulder a gentle squeeze. When that did not get a reaction, he shook him slightly.

"She'd want you to block it out. That is why our President taught you to shield your mind."

Tymos jerked free. "You're right." He didn't obey the suggestion and his sister felt his surge of anger.

In is mind, he heard, "So I am the piñata at this party." He heard faint humour in her tone. "The PFS is blocking most of the force of the rod. I will have bruises, but nothing will break. This is no worse than some of our combat lessons with the President."

"They can keep this up for days!" Tymos thought back.

"They won't," Kryslie predicted. "The General told this torturer that they needed quick results, and the man is sweating from fear of failure. My near escape put him in trouble. And I am certain that there is an electronic voyeur somewhere."

Tymos glanced at Jonko before he answered, and whispered the question, "Are you detecting video uploads?"

"There is something," he told his twin mentally after Jonko had nodded. "I will put Edik onto trying to trace where it is going."

They both knew who the watcher had to be.

"Is it just a confession that they want?" Tymos asked. What he was hearing through his twin's mind suggested that.

"For now," Kryslie confirmed. "That is so the IC can't spirit me away, and they can justify the death penalty. Then they will want to know what my game is, and everything I know."

"What if they just decide to kill you and incinerate your remains?"

"I am not their ordinary traitor," she reminded her twin. "They set me up so that they had control over me. My stubborn silence is a goad to the watcher. He will want to question me himself, when he thinks me broken."

The strength of his sister's conviction came to him through the twin bond.

Yet it was his own conviction that this means to get knowledge from bin Halil would fail - and the man would escape from retribution once again.

"We haven't intercepted any incoming transmissions," Tymos commented. He winced as more blows struck his sister.

"It's too deep here for radio and Wi-Fi." Kryslie's mind voice seemed distant, as she was concentrating on pain blocking. "This man is not wearing a headset, or a throat mike. If he is to get messages, it will have to be via the phone."

"Keleb is monitoring bin Halil's estate in Karshada," Tymos told her. "He has access to the phone lines, and is working to get control of all electronics. If he gets into the internal CCTV, maybe we will get lucky and see that man making a call."

"He is not so stupid to let anyone oversee his private affairs," Kryslie thought back.

Chapter 16 - The interrogation

Within his palatial mansion, in his home country of Karshada, Abdul bin Halil reclined on a luxurious day bed, his back propped by soft cushions, watching a large television screen. He was receiving the CCTV footage of the Interrogation taking place in Hadjibad. The redheaded spy, who was the image of his traitorous consort of thirty years before, was now tied to a frame and was remaining mute in spite of the violently lashing whip being wielded by one of his secret police.

He had ordered the escalation of the punishment, and given his man incentive. If he made the piece of filth talk, he'd be forgiven for almost letting the gutter trash escape.

He revelled in the rush of sensual pleasure that surged through him with every whip stroke. His hands clenched and unclenched as he imagined himself in the place of the interrogator.

The filth was stubborn, but he didn't really care whether she talked or not. She would though, eventually. Few men lasted longer than a day before admitting to anything the torturer wanted to hear. No woman would last that long.

"Father?" Arthur bin Halil greeted as he entered the room. He was surprised to see his father awake there so late at night. Then his eyes were drawn to the screen and he made a sound of disgust. He recognised the woman, even without the brown wig.

"I see you recall her," bin Halil commented in a cold voice, not removing his eyes from the screen. "She is a spy and a dangerous agitator."

"What they are doing is barbaric," Arthur protested.

"If you are too weak to do what is necessary for the safety of the Imperium...you may leave."

Arthur forced himself to watch, impassively, but with each stroke of the cane, he felt pain in his own flesh. He couldn't understand it. Something had passed between himself and the woman when he had casually touched her hand. She was one like his tutors had been – a worker for peace, the man had told him. This was wrong – and he dared say nothing. His gaze wandered about the room and stopped on the picture of face of the woman who was his unknown mother and then returned to the pain filled expression of the prisoner.

Something uncoiled inside of him and froze him in place. However strange it was – the woman in the picture and the one on the screen – were the same. Deep within him, he knew it.

His father had told him that his real mother, not the woman who had tended him, but his birth mother, was dead. He had lied.

"Father! You must stop this," Arthur insisted.

"No!" bin Halil thundered. He stood, moving as fast as an attacking snake and turned his anger on his only son. With his eyes mere inches from his son's face, he said, "That woman is the image of the viper that birthed you. The witch that abandoned you mere hours after you were born. Ran away, fornicated with some common scum. My consort – the adulteress. That woman is the product of sins that will condemn the mother to hell. That woman deserves nothing from me."

"She must be my half sister," Arthur tried, and for the first time in his life, felt the force of his father's anger.

Lesser men cringed before his father when he raged. Now Arthur felt like he wanted to, but if he backed down now, his father would forever brand him as weak. "If it is her mother that you hate, find her and take your anger out on the one who deserves it."

"That filth deserves no consideration. It is a murderess," bin Halil said forcefully, moving closer to his son. "You will stay out of this or I will let you feel what that filth is feeling."

Arthur knew his father was not merely threatening. He would do it. He recalled in his mind the voice of the man at the party, warning him not to get involved. It caused him to say, "Do what you will then," before he stalked from the room.

Jonko nudged Tymos awake near dawn. His friend had only slept for two hours, ever since he had said Kryslie had blacked out. Even so, he stood up from the old dusty armchair and seemed fully alert.

"Olassa is here," Jonko spoke softly.

Tymos followed him from the darkened room that was the shop's back office, into the almost empty showroom that was lit only by two dim lights. Around the shroud draped to cover the display window, faint daylight was beginning to brighten.

"Great One," Olassa bowed as if she were greeting her uncle, one of the three Governor's of Tymorea.

"What did you find in that building?" Tymos asked without acknowledging the greeting.

"Nothing useful. All the physical files refer to unrelated business. Legitimate business, I would say. The program we added to the computer system is rifling through all the files on the network, and will flag the words and concepts you suggested."

"Someone in that building has to know what goes on in those lower levels."

"If not know, at least suspect," Olassa ageed. "We questioned two cleaners under hypnosis. Both had heard rumours, but knew nothing of a way down. It also seems that they know better than to be curious, especially when encountering people in the building after closing. They won't recall talking to me."

"What about the General?"

"Joshe followed him. He didn't go into any of the offices there, but left the building. Since he wasn't in any kind of uniform, he blended into the crowd of people coming out of restaurants near the science fair. Joshe lost him in that area."

"Damn! Have everyone keep an eye out for him. Did you find any strong boxes in any of the offices?"

"Five - we went through each one carefully."

"When they had Krys before, they took her transmitter and communicator - did you find them?"

"No, Great One," Olassa looked alarmed. Tymorean technology was meant to stay secret.

"I couldn't get a lock on them but I am sure they are in the building. Just as I am positive that there are records in that building. I should have given you my scanner before I left there," Tymos apologized.

"Do you want me to go back in?" Olassa offered. "I do have the latest model from my uncle."

"So did I, but I modified mine some time ago. We will leave that building for now. We can't search when people are there. We can check it again later."

"Anything else?" Olassa asked.

"Yes, tell me everything you observed while you were searching. And when you finish, I want you to get the others to add their observations."

Tymos listened as Olassa related the night's search, memorising everything she said. He saw in her mind every place. It did not seem she had missed anything.

"I found nothing downstairs either," Tymos said, as he unconsciously clenched his fists.

"Continue monitoring the communications into and out of that building. If there is someone there working with the General, we might be able to trace a call. Or discover if there is a separate computer network there. If there is, I want to know about it."

"We will find what you need, Great One," Olassa promised.

"Have some of the others concentrate on finding where the General went. He and that history professor, Klim, have to be high up in this conspiracy. There has to be somewhere they work from, or keep records."

Jonko had listened to Olassa's report whilst making coffee and toast in the little kitchenette of the shop - just a little alcove off the back office, next to the small bathroom. He took the plate and cup to Tymos just as Olassa slipped back outside. It was light now, and although she was dressed like the local men, with her height and solid build she would be mistaken for a man.

"Have you picked up on anything on the monitors?" Tymos asked after absently taking the plate. Jonko settled the cup next to the portable computer that they were using as the monitoring station. The screen had blanked out.

"Not yet, but it is still early. Most of the workers don't start until nine. Is Krys okay?"

Tymos sat on the chair next to the table and nodded. "She put herself into a deep trance before the PFS was fully drained. She was left alone after that, since her questioner thought she was unconscious."

"What if she can't recharge it? Can she last out?" Jonko's concern was evident.

Tymos looked up, met Jonko's eyes and gave him a quick grin. "She isn't that depleted yet. While she had the energy binders on, she was using the energy in them to power the shield. Before they removed them, they were drained almost to empty. She is storing more than her usual quota of personal energy."

That assurance allowed Jonko to relax. He knew he shouldn't need to worry about Kryslie, but she was his friend and he couldn't help it.

Yet Jonko had a point, Tymos realised. His sister would be drawing on that stored energy to pain block and to heal the swelling and bruising from the lash welts. So far, the interrogator had not considered why the whip had not cut into the flesh of his victim, just bruised and reddened it.

Tymos woke the screen, and the picture he saw was of the intercepted video feed from the cell. Kryslie lay like a limp weight from the metal frame. Jonko had been watching it, although small icons indicated that the other monitoring programs were still active.

"Jon, I want you to go to Chalmers and take all the stuff we have on the gold-star wearers."

"So, you want the IC to start picking them up?"

"Yes. The top echelon may not worry about what happens to the silver star wearers. They can write them off and find new people to do their grunt work. However, they might panic when they realise that they are vulnerable themselves."

"What if Chalmers asks about Krys?"

"Tell him we don't know where she is - that I can't get a lock on her GPS dot."

Jonko wasted no more time before transmitting away with the computer record of the information.

Tymos finished his breakfast as he turned his attention to the monitoring system. He saw for himself that little was happening. He turned his attention to a different program - the one that was monitoring the IC computer network. In moments, he had access to the list of silver star wearers that had been taken in for questioning from within the Imperium. He went deeper and sampled the residential addresses and statements for random people. There was nothing of use there - these people knew very little of the overall plan.

He used his communicator to call Keleb, who was in a van parked a mile from bin Halil's palace. It looked like an ordinary delivery van, but Tymorean agents had added some basic amenities, Keleb had been there since soon after Kryslie had been captured.

"I am doing my best, Tym, but the guy has some really advanced security protocols on his private computer. All I have accessed so far are the ones used for domestic management. They work on wi-fi and cable."

"Are you recording everything?"

"Yes, but I haven't noticed anything on an unusual frequency. I have only intercepted from admin and servant personnel."

"What about satellite communications? The Imperium agents have been stealing technology from everywhere."

"Sat phones have been available here for over a century," Keleb said as if Tymos should have known that. "I have got all twelve satellites covered."

Tymos had an instant of premonition. "I will get back to you about that. Keep working. I will send someone to help you."

He cut the connection and sent a call through to Earthbase. Lexina answered.

"I need confirmation of how many satellites are in orbit. Can you contact the transport ship and ask them how many they observed?"

"I will do it at once," Lexina promised.

He felt his sister's mind nudging his. "How much longer do you need?"

"I don't know," Tymos thought back. "Keleb's having trouble…I will have to go and see if I can help. How are you managing?"

"I have blocked all the pain," she assured him, but he sensed her energy was low. Too low. "The General's torturer is taking the chance to rest. What time is it?"

"Morning, nearly eight fifteen. So I expect they will be at you again soon."

"Yes," Kryslie agreed, but her mental tone held many nuances. "I can delay by fainting again…the man was not surprised when I seemed to. In fact, he was freaked that I had endured so much."

"How is your power level?" Tymos allowed her to sense that he knew it was low. He sensed in return a faint sense of malicious amusement.

"Not as high as it could be, but now that I am alert again, I am drawing on the energy of these horribly bright lights. I will have to stop when the guy wakes up. Apart from that, I have a full quota of anger and stubborn intent."

"They might use drugs. When I searched there, I found a collection on really nasty ones. Truth sera mainly, but some had additives to heighten pain."

"I am aware of them," Kryslie's mind tone was sober. "Pain, I can deal with, but only if my mind isn't addled by drugs. If they use them, I won't be able to pain block and I may not be able to metabolise the stuff fast enough. I won't be able to stop them injecting me, without betraying my true strength. And if they jab hard enough with the needle, it will create a point overload in the PFS."

A vicious jab was likely, Kryslie knew. Her questioner might be obeying orders, and might agree with the methods since they needed to know what she knew, but he wasn't naturally a torturer. However, he was under pressure to get results.

"And I am going to increase the obvious threat to bin Halil's plans. Jon's giving Chalmers the names of gold star wearers," Tymos warned.

"Chave?" Krys asked.

"Not yet - I will go with him to see Chalmers, and keep his name out of reports."

Tymos let the mental communication lapse.

Three of the infiltration team had materialised in the room.

"Olassa sent us, Great One," Devyn greeted him. "She told us of your concerns, but I can't add anything extra to what I reported earlier."

"Where did you search?" Tymos asked quickly.

"The third floor. Half of that is the records room. I couldn't look at every file and stored record, but everyone I sampled looked legitimate. I checked the computer for hidden files, but found none. I even checked the most recent searches and played with the results. Nothing. But the area is the size of this room, with a section at the front with desks and computers. The rest of it is racks and racks of files. They run right to the back wall. I couldn't detect any hidden spaces."

"What I want won't be obvious, as overtly, everything has to look legal, and it is looking more and more like they have a separate computer system for this conspiracy - but they have to have some connection."

"Olassa had me searching the top floor, Great One," Katya spoke up. "The Justice Minister has his office there. I found nothing that seemed out of order. He has three aides and they have desks in a partitioned off section of the outer area. I found a portable computer next to one of the desks. It was in a brief case. Olassa gave me a device to plug into it. When it is turned on, it will transmit to us, whatever data it is accessing, and will clone the unit's memory. She said there is a risk the owner will see it."

Tymos abruptly interrupted her. "What type of phones were they using there?"

Katya thought for a minute, reviewing what she had seen. Normal ones, with a cable and some without. And there was one empty cradle, but it was bigger than the others."

"Where was that?" Tymos asked, intent on the answer.

"At the desk where I found the computer."

"Did you try accessing the computer?"

"Yes, but it wanted a 32 bit decryption key. Should I have taken it away with me?"

"No," was Tymos's immediate and instinctive answer. "I will follow up on it, and this way no one will know anyone has been in there."

The third of the group was Ewain, and his normal exuberance was not evident. "I checked the ground floor thoroughly, Great One. The lifts there only go down to the garage level. I could find no sign of electronics to override the controls to force it lower. The stairs only go down to the garage level too. All the walls, except for where the lifts are, seem to be half a metre thick concrete with metal reinforcing. I'm sorry…"

Tymos didn't let him dwell on his perceived failure. "I know there is a way down from the garage, and you have indicated it has to be near the other lifts. That is something. I didn't expect there to be an obvious way down. They would not want just anyone going there. Thanks for coming."

After the three missionaries had gone, returning to the stake-out positions Olassa had assigned them, Lexina's return call came through. The transport ship had located thirteen satellites during its short stay in Earth's near space.

The news proved his hunch right. Bin Halil may well have his own private satellite. Tymos put the equipment in Hadjibad on automatic and contacted Olassa. She would send a missionary to monitor it. Then he called Lexina back and requested the long-range beam set to the shop, so that he could be relayed to the van in Karshada.

Tymos felt that time was against him. He was aware that his sister's interrogators were getting more desperate, and had increased the intensity of the pain they inflicted. And Kryslie was getting weaker, as she needed to use her personal store of energy to power the PFS. She was aware of the drain, and was drawing on the ambient energy, causing the lights to dim. This was making the interrogator and the General, very uneasy.

He let his sister continue the mind games, and nudged Keleb away from the computer. "Have a break, Kel. Get some fresh air. Let me at this for a bit."

As a protégé of Xyron, the Tymorean Governor who oversaw the sciences and technology, Keleb had a great deal of skill. Tymos, had more, and he had the wisdom of the Guardians of Peace to draw on. He thought of what he needed to do, and let his mind be receptive to their suggestions.

Keleb was glad to stretch his legs and have something to eat, but he found he could not stay away long. He was empathically aware of Tymos's focussed concern. He returned after ten minutes and found Tymos searching through the equipment in the van.

"We won't get anywhere unless we can send a signal through some kind of disruption field that he has around the fence. It might be some kind of electrical fence, or something more advanced."

Tymos found what he wanted, a spare communicator, and he programmed it to act as a signal relay. It would pick up incoming or outgoing signals, and boost the signal towards the Tymorean equipment.

"I am going to plant this inside the grounds of the palace," Tymos stated before he transmitted away.

From being still in the van, to being still in a particular area of the palace grounds, Tymos hid from sight using his power and the natural aura. He was in an open area, away from the path used by the patrolling guards, and had he been a normal human, he would have been seen. Had the guards looked his way, they may have seen a shadow where none should be. However, though they glanced left and right as they patrolled, their eyes would be affected by the brilliant glare of the sun even with glasses on.

When they had turned the corner, Tymos eyed a position on the palace roof that was close to where bin Halil had his private suite. With a deceptively slight flick of his wrist, Tymos sent the device flying towards the roof that was ten metres away. He adjusted his eyesight to follow its trajectory, and he saw it land and slide down into a gutter. He watched for a time, but no one came to investigate the odd clattering noise. He transmitted back to the van.

Jonko was with Keleb when he materialised. He instantly demanded, "What have you to report?"

"Chalmers has his mandate. Those gold wearers you identified are going to be picked up."

"Ok," Tymos breathed. "That should stir things up."

"He asked about Krys, and he's berating himself."

"He shouldn't. Krys told him she could look after herself. Anything else?"

"Olassa is watching the monitors - still nothing yet from that building. Those that she has staked out looking for the General and that man Klim have noticed that the number of people on the streets has decreased. I think word of the arrests is spreading."

"Okay, I want you to keep in touch with Olassa. Kel, let me back on the computer, will you."

Keleb watched as Tymos rapidly typed in a program from memory. He did not ask what it was for, because when Tymos finished, the monitoring program had an extra window, and there was a huge download of data coming from somewhere.

"I put the spare communicator on the roof of the palace. It is picking up signals from what I think is bin Halil's private satellite. Record everything, and run everything but the video stream through the decryption algorithm and the translator. You should be able to get the source or destination of any calls from the signal specs."

Tymos moved and let Keleb back in. He turned to Jonko. "Help keep an eye on things here, will you."

"Sure," Jonko agreed, but then he asked, "Are you alright, Tym? You look horribly pale."

"I'm fine. Just get into that palace system and get control of everything."

Jonko and Keleb exchanged worried glances. Tymos was staring off somewhere, as if he was able to see through and beyond the walls of the van. His fingers were warping the frame at the back of a metal chair.

Keleb, a sensitive empath, began to feel ill. Some of what Tymos was receiving was leaking past his mental shields. Jonko recognised the signs, although he sensed nothing himself. He dared to nudge Tymos, and in doing so, received a jolt of power. He ignored the painful sensation.

"Tym! Lock it down. Keleb is picking up whatever you are."

A flick of his eyes to glance at Jonko, was the only indication that he had heard. Keleb sighed with relief.

Jonko edged back to Keleb, but kept watching Tymos.

"That's why Tym sent me here, wasn't it?" Keleb murmured. "Kryslie is being tortured, isn't she?"

"As near as," Jonko agreed in a similarly low voice. "But she has a PFS on, though it must be getting very low on power by now. It is why Tym said to ignore the video streaming."

"Why is she letting them do it?"

Jonko shrugged. "We have to trust her. It has to have something to do with the Imperium's leader, but I have no idea what."

Kryslie knew the PFS was losing power and she had none to spare. The beating was becoming increasingly more painful; less and less of the force of the lashes was being neutralised or blocked. Now, it was becoming harder to maintain her stubborn silence.

Though there was no humanly rational reason to think so, they had connected the power dips with the intensity of the beating. They had decided that she was the cause, though neither man could offer a logical explanation. They had dimmed the lights in the cell, denying her that source of energy. To make the problem worse for Kryslie, they had also turned up the cooling in the cell. Now she was using up even more energy, because she was shivering, and that was also exacerbating the pain of the beating.

She heard the General order, "Get the syringe ready."

Kryslie tried to find the energy to warn her twin, but she couldn't seem to form the thought and send it. She was relieved when she felt her brother's mind in hers, strong and clear. Then all the power went out in the cell and she knew Tymos had caused it.

She enjoyed the shock and alarm the blackout caused in the two men. Both recalled that a similar blackout had occurred before this same woman had escaped the first time.

She heard the syringe clank back into a metal tray, and the rustling of weapons being drawn. A small bright light came on with a click, and something was pressed into her stomach.

"You are not going to escape this time. If any of your friends get in here, I will shoot you."

The interrogator sounded determined, but Kryslie knew that bin Halil wanted her alive - at least until she had revealed all her secrets.

The General spoke a moment later. "Stay here. Seal the door when I leave. I am going to see why the generator has not come on."

Kryslie sensed the interrogator moving away towards the door, but he returned quickly, and his hands began to press on her abused flesh, making the throbbing pain reach a peak of agony. Then, as darkness remained, his powerful hands began exploring her private places, as if he were considering a different kind of violation - one he dared not do while the leader was watching.

The light suddenly came back on, and he quickly moved his hands. The phone on the wall suddenly rang, and the Interrogator jumped as if it were an alarm going off.

Both sides of the conversation were audible in the room. "Continue with the drug," the voice of the General instructed. "I am going to check this power outage. It has affected the whole building."

"Yes General. I will start at once." After hanging up the phone, he returned to the table and picked up the syringe. Before he moved, he glanced at the prisoner again. The woman was unnatural - she should be screaming for mercy by now. Deliberately, he increased the dose of the drug to the amount for a large man.

Just as he turned to go to the prisoner, the lights went out again. He almost panicked. The syringe clattered to the table and he had to fumble to stop it dropping to the floor.

Then the phone shrilled again. Setting the syringe in the tray, he grabbed the phone.

"Yes!" he yelled into the phone, but then his next words were tensely proper. "No sir, there is no problem here. There is an external power issue. The generator will cut in soon."

In her mind, Kryslie sensed her brother's satisfaction. "Got him!"

The caller had been bin Halil himself. And he had been annoyed enough by the loss of the video transmission, that he had called to find out the reason.

In the silence of the room, Krys heard from the phone, "Continue. I will have security sent to guard outside the cell."

The connection went dead before the interrogator could say, "Yes, Sir!"

The power came back on.

The call had made the man's mind roil with apprehension. He put down the phone and returned to the table. He wasted no time in consideration. The tray clattered as he took the syringe.

His voice was harsh and angry. "You can only blame yourself for this, bitch."

With savage deliberation, he reached around her and jabbed her in the side. Then he walked around to where he could watch her face. He saw the blue-green eyes staring back at him, the face was a neutral mask. He hid how it unnerved him. It was freakish enough that such a small woman could remain mute after the harsh punishment he had given her. However, he had to make her talk, or his own life was in peril. The leader did not like failure; but the drug had never yet failed. The prisoner would talk, and he cared nothing if she was a mindless husk afterwards.

The drug was powerful, and it spread too quickly for her body to metabolise it. It sapped her energy, her concentration, her determination. It allowed the interrogators mind to force itself on hers. She was losing the ability to shield her mind. As her last mind shield collapsed, she called her brother. "How much longer?"

"We're almost through the security on bin Halil's palace…"

His mind was suddenly filled with a myriad of intense flashing images. He sensed that his sister wanted to tell him something, but her mind was fragmenting. Through the twin bond, he sensed, "Urgent".

However, the thoughts were jumbled, like they had been written on glass that had shattered.

He tried to interpret the sequence of images, but the strange feeling of the drug on his sister's mind was disorientating him. He did not realise that his body had gone rigid, as he fought to clear the fog and think back at his sister. The drug had her in its grip, her mind had no control over her body. She could betray him; betray all the Tymoreans. He willed her to stay mute, and for a time it seemed to be working. His mind, her mind, wide open to each other and acting like one. He was aware of the interrogator asking questions, demanding answers. He felt the man's terror of failure.

Kryslie began to speak. Her body reacting empathically to the emotion, and wanting to ease it.

Through clenched teeth, as he tried to force his sister's mouth to echo his action, he said, "Block that video feed. Do it here, and have Olassa do it in Hadjibad!"

Was he in time? Kryslie had admitted to working against bin Halil, wanting to get him. She was speaking in English, and bin Halil was fluent in that, but was the interrogator? No! He was demanding that she speak in Arabic, but Kryslie had no control over what came out of her mouth.

"Who do you work for? Who are you working with? Tell me names!"

They were still not asking about her supposed scientific knowledge, just what she knew of the people they perceived to be opposing them.

"Is it blocked?" Tymos forced out. He was not able to stop his sister speaking, and was trying to impress false information into her mind.

"With all the traps and firewalls, Kel has to be careful," Jonko forced his voice to sound calm. He spoke, since Keleb's attention was totally focussed on his task. Yet he only had to glance at Tymos to know the situation was dire.

Tymos had his fists clenched, his mind with his sister, over a hundred miles away, as he strained to control her. It wasn't working any more. She was speaking as fast as she could.

Then he felt his heartbeat become ragged and he found it harder and harder to breathe. His face grew sweaty and cold, and his vision began to grey out. In his mind, his sister's voice became sporadic.

"No!" It felt as though his sister was dying. He had to pull his mind free, but that would mean letting her go. He couldn't, she was part of him.

He had no warning when the next series of lashes began. The interrogator had lost control - he was desperate for his victim to keep talking. Tymos felt as if it were he that was being lashed, and he wondered how Kryslie had stood it for so many hours. He was unaware of how his body was writhing in pain, nor when he stumbled and fell.

His face stung with a more immediate pain, and then another, and another.

"Block her!" Jonko yelled. He was leaning over and holding Tymos with a grip to his coveralls, using his free hand to slap sense into his friend. "Block her out!"

"I can't…"

"You must, Great One," Jonko insisted.

"I have to help her…"

"The Guardians will not let her die!"

Another kind of slap, more like a flick of mental lightning, brought him to his senses, as the connection to his twin was abruptly silenced.

Jonko had evoked the Guardians of Peace, and they had come. Even on Earth, and so far away from Tymorea, they would help him.

Now that he was no longer sharing his twin's agony, or experiencing the echoed deterioration, his anger was focussed and his mind was clear and working at high speed once again. The jumbled memory images made sense, and his sister's message was suddenly clear.

He rolled out of Jonko's grip, and stood abruptly.

"Get a message to Chalmers at the IC headquarters in Hadjibad. Tell him that I want to meet him there in half an hour," Tymos snapped at his friend.

"What about here?" Jonko asked as he reached for his mobile phone.

Tymos moved over to the monitoring computer. "I want to have complete control of everything electronic and electrical in that bastard's palace, within the hour. Put a camouflage field around this van and move it closer."

Jonko nodded, indicating he was listening even as he waited for Chalmers or his assistant to answer his call.

Turning again, abruptly, Tymos paced back towards the door of the van. "Then contact Earthbase. I need to get the utility scanner that I put in the equipment store. I should have brought the one I improved. Also, get them to contact Homebase to send four stealth suits by long-range beam. I want them before I see Chalmers."

He paused as Jonko was connected to the Director of the Investigative Committee, made the request for a meeting, and then listened. When he spoke again, it sounded like he needed to convince Chalmers.

"Tell him that I know where they have my sister," Tymos stated, and Jonko passed the message on.

When he snapped his phone shut, and swapped it for his Tymorean communicator, Jonko said, "He'll meet you, but he will need evidence that he can take to the World Council before he can get the authority to enter and search."

"When you go to Earthbase to get the stealth suits, get copies of those photos that we took of Louis's injuries. I don't know if Chalmers has the others here, but when he compares those to the record of the video we intercepted being transmitted, he won't have any trouble identifying the place. You and I can both attest to where it is. Kel, I need a copy of the first hour of that video feed."

Jonko watched as Tymos made other calls. He spoke to Olassa, and to other missionaries he had doing various tasks. His friend had been like this before, during the war on Tymorea - working like one possessed, and with his power so strong that he practically glowed. He began to speak a warning, but Tymos spoke first.

"We have to time this carefully."

"What?"

"I will see Chalmers, and show him the video. He will have to contact the World Committee and organise his mandate to search the judicial building. That will take at least half an hour."

Jonko nodded, waiting for the rest of the plan. Tymos still paced the small open area in the van.

"I am practically certain that they will take Krys out of there before then. Bin Halil, will be spooked by the failure of the video link, and I am sure he will hear about the raid through his own devious channels. He won't be able to stop it and he won't risk Krys escaping."

"I thought you wanted him to come to Hadjibad," Jonko recalled.

Tymos stopped. "He won't. Not now. He will want to keep well away, for the purpose of deniability."

"So, she will be gone before the IC get there," Jonko summarised.

"As soon as I get back from speaking to Chalmers we will make sure of that. I will go with her," Tymos confirmed. "Give stealth suits to Alen and Markos and put one on yourself. When I'm gone with Krys, I want you to meet Chalmers at the building and offer to search. Use the utility tool. The records we need have to be somewhere and they will be well hidden. Start in the Justice Minister's office and then the records room. You should be able to find hidden places. Check with Olassa before you go in. When you finish, rejoin Kel here and have the other two ready to act."

"And Krys?" Jonko was aware of what she was enduring and he wished he could spare her from it, even though she was a Great One.

"There is more going on here than I realised. She has to get close to bin Halil, to do what she must."

"And what's that," Jonko asked.

"Keep that bastard busy while we search his palace." Tymos's grin was not at all friendly.

Although he sensed that there was more to it than that, Jonko smiled grimly as Tymos took out his transmitter and vanished. Very quietly, so Keleb only just heard him, he murmured, "It is not a good idea to anger a Great One."

Kryslie knew that she was babbling answers to every question the man asked, but was barely aware that she was speaking in the first language she had learnt - English. The man had demanded that she speak in Arabic, but her mind was too lost to translate her answers. Yet, from what little English he knew, he believed that her answers were important. He had heard her mention the Leader, so he persisted with his accusatory questions, knowing that the interrogation was being recorded. Someone would be able to translate.

Kryslie was beyond caring, her back and legs were on fire, and the welts were bleeding now. Her personal force screen had finally lost all power as her personal energy had waned. Now, she had nothing left, not even enough to try to move.

As the man began to feel that he had succeeded, his satisfaction exuded from him. When the phone shrilled once again, he had the premonition of praise from the leader, until he heard the voice. It was the General, his immediate superior.

"Get that woman ready to be taken out of there! Someone has hacked into the transmission, and blocked it. IC agents are coming to search the building - they will be there any minute. The leader is sending two of his personal guards to get the woman away."

He didn't even reply to the order, he dropped the phone and began.

Kryslie fell heavily when the restraints tying her to the rack were slashed. The man's sudden panic overwhelmed her mind, but she had no energy left to try to fight the danger she thought it meant. He had no illusions about his fate if the IC found him with the woman. Part of his mind told him, "At least the confession of guilt had been recorded and the Leader would have heard it," but then his stomach clenched into a knot - the transmission had been cut. How long ago had that happened? Did it matter, he asked himself. He'd broken the woman. She would repeat her confession, repeatedly, they always did after the drug. They were never the same afterwards - if the Leader let them live.

He stared down at the bloody mess that was the woman. Once he had what he needed, he didn't care to deal with the prisoner. With all the stress he currently felt, the sight made him queasy. However, if the Leader wanted this prisoner, he needed to clean it up.

Opening the door, he saw the two guards standing outside and gestured to them. They entered at once, and heard the order, "Drag that carrion over there."

He watched them shoulder their weapons and start to drag the woman where he had directed, over to where there was a grate in the floor. While they did that, he picked up the hose he used on the prisoners that had fouled themselves in the black sacks. He handed the hose to one of the guards and tossed an empty sack at the other. Then he fetched two sets of recharged energy binders.

The phone shrilled again, and he freed one hand to answer it. He listened, gave a terse acknowledgement, and looked at the progress of the clean up. His gorge rose as he saw one of the guards seeming to caress the bruised and lacerated flesh of the prisoner.

"You! Leave that alone! Go and show the Leader's men the way in from the tunnel."

Tymos sent another surge of energy into Kryslie, and felt her mind respond. Then he obeyed the command. He doubted that the interrogator would notice that the bleeding had stopped. He glanced fleetingly at Jonko, a tacit command to watch over Kryslie, and saw him nod slightly, confirming he understood.

Outside the door of the cell, there was no one in sight. The guards he and Jonko had overcome were in the room with the incinerator, and would stay unconscious for several hours. Tymos checked his communicator. Olassa had reported intercepting the message about the IC visit - it had come via a satellite phone to the Justice Minister who had then called an unregistered phone number. She had traced the call to a building near the university.

Keleb had left a similar message, he had intercepted a call from bin Halil's palace to the Justice Building and another to an unregistered number - the same as that Olassa had mentioned. They had him!

If the IC would be arriving in minutes, then Chalmers had not needed long to convince the World Council of the extreme disregard of civil rights in the country. Tymos wanted Kryslie away before they came and surrounded the entire block. She needed to get to bin Halil.

Since he was alone in the tunnel that had been pictured in the interrogators mind, he drew on his power and raced along it at Tymorean speed, pausing only to unlock and jam open the wall like door.

Bin Halil's special guards were waiting as the lift reached the garage level of the police building. He greeted them, recognising the ones who had arrested his sister, and urged them to hurry. When they reached the interrogation chamber, panting after the fast trot along the tunnel, Kryslie was within her black sack and on a trolley.

Sensing his sister's mind once again, he had no worries about letting the leader's guards wheel her away. He went back into the chamber and saw Jonko was filling a bucket with soapy water.

"I want this room cleaned," the interrogator ordered, as he went over to a table with drawers and began throwing things into a bag, starting with the drugs. He was getting ready to flee.

As he turned back to check on progress, he found both guards had almost come within touching distance of him. He saw a look of determination on both faces, and felt his guts writhe. He pulled his gun from his belt, but before he could aim it, his wrist was grabbed with a grip of steel. He glanced from his wrist to the hazel eyes of one of the guards.

"What is this?" he demanded, as the second guard, with blue-green eyes, wrenched the gun from his grip and forced his other wrist behind him. He held it with one hand, tossed the gun to his partner, and forced both wrists together. The interrogator's fierce struggles had no effect. He felt the unpleasant tingle of energy binders, and tried harder to get free. Normally he was strong enough to fight off any two other men.

As he tried to outstare the hazel eyes, he felt a numbing blow to his left shin and his feet were swept from under him. He fell heavily and before he could try to stand again, a second set of energy binders was attached to his ankles.

The second of the guards moved to stare down at him. "If you tell the Investigative Committee everything they want to know, they might not have you executed. They have seen exactly what you have been doing here. If it were up to me, you would be dead already."

The eyes now staring at him held no mercy. Those blue-green eyes were the exact colour of the prisoner's eyes. He felt all control of himself desert him.

"I will tell you everything," the man babbled. "Please, don't leave me here."

He was ignored. The two false guards turned and walked away. One moment they were there, the next, they were gone.

They were at the waiting van before the trolley arrived there. Tymos had changed his wig from light brown to black, and his uniform insignia to that of a junior member of the secret police. It had only taken a moment for Alen to bring what he needed from the apartment and leave again. He approached the guard waiting with the van. It was the old guard with the deformed ear.

"I have orders to go with you," Tymos told him. "I have a copy of the interrogation transcript to deliver personally."

He jostled the man as he turned at the sound of the trolley approaching. That contact was enough to force the man's mind to agree. There was no time to question the orders just then - they had little time left to get away.

Chapter 17 - Closing in

Jonko approached the police cordon and showed his temporary IC credentials. He was directed to the van being used by Chalmers to oversee the search. The Director was seated on a folding chair at a fold down table, talking on the radio. He finished giving orders and turned to where Jonko stood, waiting politely to be noticed.

"Why are you here?" Chalmers asked. His mind was on the search.

"Tym Ward sent me."

Chalmers gave the newcomer his full attention.

"He says that if the records you seek are here, they will be hidden - possibly in a sealed off area. He had me bring this…" Jonko drew out the scanning device and placed it where Chalmers could examine it. "It is a utility scanner that he designed and built. I have had a quick lesson on how to use it. Tym told me it should help us find anomalous spaces."

"I have experts going over the plans of the building," Chalmers stated.

"Do they show the lower levels, Sir?"

"My people are looking for them now. Why don't you go and see if you can locate the entrance. I am sure the elevator must go down there, but we can't get any of them past the basement parking level."

With a quick nod, Jonko turned to leave the van. He was allowed to approach the building and enter. Chalmers had radioed ahead. He had to show his credentials again at the elevator where guards were stationed, but he was allowed to take the car down to the basement. Once again, he introduced himself and explained what he was to do. The four men looking for the way down, let him get busy, but glanced at him as he ran the odd device over the walls.

He found the hidden elevator between the two upward elevators that were in plain view. He then had to adjust the settings on the scanner device to discover how to move the covering of apparently seamless ferro-concrete. When the third elevator was revealed, no time was wasted going down. In the short time between floors, the leader of the IC group expressed his interest in the scanning device, and asked where to get one.

There was only enough time to say it was a prototype before the elevator door opened again.

Jonko had been afraid that Kryslie's interrogator would have been found and released by the time the IC found the chamber. His fear was valid, and they arrived only just in time. Three people were just leaving the chamber. All began to run towards the tunnel, but the agents with Jonko fired weapons and the men dropped, stunned unconscious.

A cloud of smoke was blown out of the chamber, as an explosion detonated in the room. Jonko raced to the doorway, saw fire in several spots. He took a deep breath and went in, knowing exactly where the fire suppression canisters were. The fires died before the entire room was engulfed. He had time to note that not all the evidence of the torture done there had been destroyed.

The search team reported to Chalmers by radio, telling what they had found and requesting a security detail and a forensic team. Jonko was directed to a ground floor office, where he found Chalmers clearing off a desk and making himself at home. The Investigative Committee had locked the building down and were in control.

"You knew exactly where to go," Chalmers accused, as he sat behind the usurped desk.

"Roughly," Jonko qualified. "You saw the photos? Things weren't hidden the last time I was there."

Chalmers modified his tone. "You helped her escape last time? Too bad you were too late this time."

"We'll find her," Jonko said with emphasis. "We can't have missed her by much. Have your security cordon seen anything? Do you know where that passage goes?"

"We will look into it, and keep looking for your friend, if she is still alive."

Jonko kept his face inscrutable as he said, "She tough."

"I hope so," Chalmers admitted. "Meanwhile, we've identified some places where space may have been sealed off. We could use that gadget of yours upstairs. I heard it is quite impressive."

"Where do you need me?"

"Third floor. See Don Ypres."

Jonko nodded and went off at a run towards the stairs. He wanted this building to reveal its secrets quickly, so that he could rejoin Tymos in Karshada.

During the flight in the executive jet, Tymos stayed in his seat and maintained a serious expression as if he was aware of the importance of the prisoner. He asked no questions, betrayed no curiosity, and ignored the woman dumped unceremoniously on the floor in the galley.

Just from listening to the other men talk, he knew the flight would take less than half an hour. Karshada, the country bin Halil had ruled before the embracing of the Imperium, neighboured Jafhabad.

He also learnt that more of bin Halil's private guards would meet them at the airport, and that concerned him. He did not want to be forced to hand over the 'transcript' to them. He needed to be taken inside the security perimeter on the Imperial estate. So, during the short flight, he 'leaned' on the mind of the old guard with the deformed ear. He stressed the need for the transcript to be delivered to the Imperium's leader in person, and implied that the order came from bin Halil himself.

After landing, the aeroplane taxied to a secure area of the airport. Tymos spotted a truck waiting beside a building, before the plane turned again and stopped.

He followed the old guard out of the plane, ignoring the prisoner being carried down the mobile steps after him. He knew, however, that Kryslie was aware of him and the drugs were nearly gone from her system. The two guards, who had come from Hadjibad, manhandled the prisoner to the waiting truck. It appeared to be just another utility services van. Once they had Kryslie aboard, Tymos and the old guard followed, and sat on the bench seat along one side. One of the three new guards who had brought the truck entered and locked the door. Two more went to the driver's cabin.

Tymos expected the twenty-minute drive from the airport to the palace north of the city. The truck had the imperial emblem on the sides and back and so had right of way over everyone else on the road, so they stopped only once and that was at the palace gates. After that, there was a short drive over gravel before the van stopped again and the engine was turned off.

On emerging, the old guard directed the driver to take Tymos to the Imperial secretary, and turned to watch the prisoner being dragged out and carried towards a door that had opened in the rear wall of the palace. The door had not been marked on the plans of the palace that Tymos had located and studied. He stored the detail in his memory, as he followed his guide to the door used by the service staff.

As he was led through the service and administration sections of the palace, Tymos added what he saw to the mental image of the plans that he had studied. His knowledge of the palace was limited to the memories shared from his sister, and they were of thirty years in the past, and limited to the private sections of the palace. He studied the rooms they went past, and knew they were approaching the more official areas. So, while he was alone with his guide in the passage, he attacked the man, rendering him instantly unconscious. He took a moment to determine that the next storeroom had sufficient space just inside the door for him to transmit two people inside, before vanishing from the passage. He lowered the guard to the floor, and checked that the door was locked. The room contained cleaning supplies, and Tymos took the risk that no one would need to go there for a time.

As he stripped the guard of his uniform, people passed along the passage outside the door, oblivious to his presence. Once dress in the uniform of one of bin Halil's guards, he activated the stealth suit Jonko had brought from Earthbase for him. Now he could transmit out and not be seen by normal humans.

Before calling Alen and Markos to help him search, Tymos decided on a solo scouting foray to check the most likely areas. They would also be the most dangerous places to search. If he were the leader of a treasonous conspiracy against the UWN and kept records, he would want to keep them close by. That meant entering and searching the ultra-private rooms used by Abdul bin Halil.

He wasn't going to presume that was correct, though. The Imperium's leader was far too clever to leave anything to chance. He had been the instigator of the last war, but no one had been able to prove anything against him. He could potentially hide any records anywhere in his palace.

As Tymos moved along the passage from the storeroom, he let his senses tell him what was within each of the rooms he passed. Some were other storerooms, some were offices for senior palace staff, and some were tearooms or amenities. None of the rooms he considered even stirred a breath of a portentous feeling. For now, he ignored the passages leading to kitchens, laundries, ironing rooms and other servants' areas.

He knew he was approaching the official areas when the floor changed from polished wood to carpet. It added an extra level of caution, for while he could move soundlessly over any surface, the servants usually didn't. Now he would have to be more alert, and be ready to hold himself close to the wall if servants approached. They would not see him, but they could walk into him.

Even with the start of carpeted floors, the transition from servant plain to official opulent was abrupt. A servant, bringing a covered tray back to the kitchen, appeared through a swinging door, just before Tymos reached it. He had a glimpse of imperial purple furnishings, and sprinted around the servant to sidle through the door before it fully closed. He slipped to one side and studied the room visually.

Couches, groups of chairs, several low tables, a diorama of a proposed dam, various pictures of people and places - it made him think of a visitor's room. He was not surprised to find it empty of people. He had doubts that the servants would take dirty dishes through there if it were occupied.

Staying by the door, Tymos took out his scanner and checked the room. He found listening devices under each of the three tables, and two spy cameras, carefully concealed in flounces that were part of the carved fascia boards. Two passages led from the room, and from his mental map, he decided one went to the visitors' entrance and the other led further into the palace - probably to the Imperial secretary's office. Moving slowly around the room, Tymos tested the walls for hidden spaces. He found no other openings besides the unobtrusive servant's door.

Taking the passage leading further in, Tymos came upon a small open area containing three doors. One was marked private, a second as 'staff only' and the third was marked, 'Imperial Secretary'. The space was small, and contained only three armchairs. These too were in the purple fabric, and they were pushed back next to the mauve painted walls.

The third door drew him, and he put his ear to the wood. He heard voices, recognised the tone of one and decided to risk transmitting in. He used his memory of the palace plans to select what he hoped was an empty corner.

"…you must understand. It's absolutely vital that I speak to him. He must act. The Investigative Committee are making a mockery of the League to Improve the Imperium. They are arresting the members, accusing them of espionage and treason. My good friend Aldus Khazin was taken from his home as if he were a common criminal. He is eighty-seven and in poor health."

Dev Klim was red in the face, trying to convince the composed Imperial Secretary to announce him to the Leader.

"I am most sorry, Professor Klim, his Excellency left explicit orders that he is not to be disturbed under any circumstances," the secretary insisted politely. "And even I am not immune to his ire if I disobey."

Tymos wondered what Klim would think if he could see the memories in the secretaries mind. Abdul bin Halil had indeed given that order, and when he had, he had looked insane. His eyes had glittered with rage, and likely thwarted pleasure. Before that though, his ranting had been almost incoherent when no one at the palace could explain or trace the cause of the interrupted video transmission.

As he watched, Klim fidgeted. The secretary pressed a spot on his desk and said, "I have paged Prince Arthur. He might be able to help you."

Klim controlled a growl of disagreement and reluctantly sat himself in one of the visitor's chairs to wait.

Rather than answering the page, Prince Arthur entered unannounced a few minutes later. Tymos saw his face before he composed it to display the calm 'diplomatic' facade. It was a mask to hide a high level of inner agitation.

It had not occurred to Tymos that he would be able to sense the Prince's emotions so acutely. Kryslie was the more sensitive empath, but then, the prince was his nephew. He studied the young man, who was now much the same age as he was himself. Wherever the prince had come from, he had been very glad to get away. Under his normally tanned features, his skin was ashen pale.

Klim heard the door and jumped awkwardly to his feet. The secretary rose more sedately and bowed the ritual greeting. Arthur noticed Klim and moved closer.

"Professor Klim, this is a surprise. Are you here to see my father?"

"Yes, I am your Highness. My business is most urgent."

"My father is tied up with several crises right now. He has asked me to act on his behalf."

Now Tymos sensed that Arthur had been with his father who was obsessing about something to the point of incoherence.

Klim didn't answer right away, as if trying to decide if he should speak of his concern. Finally, his fear and panic won out.

"Your Highness, if you are able to speak to your father, in my stead, please tell him that I am extremely concerned about a breach of his Imperial Sovereignty."

Arthur's face creased into a frown. "Please give me what details you have." He seated himself in the most comfortable of the visitor's chairs, forcing Klim to re-seat himself as traditional courtesy and etiquette demanded. Furthermore, Arthur's outer calmness, sham though it was, forced Klim to take a deep breath to calm himself. He repeated what he'd told the secretary and added more detail.

"….and my classes are decimated. I have always encouraged my students to think wider than just one country. I have widened their worldview to consider future generations of the Imperium. I absolutely protest the arbitrary actions of the Investigative Committee. They are treating the Imperium's most respected citizens like slaves or serfs."

Arthur made a hand gesture, copied from his father, and Klim fell silent. "You are suggesting that the UWN are the power behind the Investigative Committee. They are not. The Committee does not act arbitrarily. They act to maintain the state of Peace we have enjoyed this past thirty years. They would act the same within the UWN to investigate any entity that might be set on destroying that peace."

"My Prince, who could possibly think that a respected scholar like Aldus Khazin could be a terrorist or a warmonger? He is a gentle, peaceable, old man."

"My esteemed teacher, I am sure that when these men are questioned, they will reassure the IC of their impeccable intentions. They will be released quickly, I am sure."

The assurance should have eased Klim's worry, but it actually made him more fidgety.

"Your Highness, please, I urge you to advise your father to intervene," Klim pleaded.

"My father is already aware of the situation," Arthur admitted. "He is convinced that a group of UWN agitators is behind this. Even now, he is attending to the interrogation of one of them. He intends to obtain a confession from this person, so that the IC will have no reason to continue the persecution."

While Klim seemed to hear something in that statement to ease some of his concern, Prince Arthur's controlled distaste had increased. He had not seen much of the video transmission, but his father's loss of control when the link had been cut - had disgusted him.

Tymos decided that he had heard enough, but he stayed a few moments longer, reacting to his nephew's unsettled state. Gently, he thought at the prince, "Go out, go away. You should not be involved with these acts."

He sensed that the idea had crystallised a decision within Arthur's mind.

"Professor, I think that if you have done nothing wrong by the laws of the Imperium, then you need not fear the Investigative Committee."

Again, Klim seemed to read more into that statement than Arthur intended. Tymos did not need to read the older man's mind to intuit his thoughts. The law of the Imperium, as things stood these days, was the law of Abdul bin Halil, whether it was written in the law books and constitution of the Imperium or not.

"Yes, of course, that is true," Klim admitted, calming further. "However, your Highness, sometimes theory and truth do not seem the same. You are still young and idealistic. With maturity, you will see things differently. I thank you for your time."

Tymos transmitted out while the two men followed the niceties of parting. He was making for bin Halil's private suite, but scouting at the same time. As he moved stealthily, he reached out to touch his sister's mind. He was relieved to feel that it had regained clarity.

"Krys, how are you?"

"I have been left alone. I am ready to act."

"Is he there yet?"

"No."

"Do you know where you are?"

"In a place I had only heard whispered of during my residence here. I never angered my master enough to merit a visit."

"It's below ground, accessed from a door at the back of the palace."

"I sensed that, but the aura that has seeped into the walls is so vile that I cannot bear to draw on it. Still, I have the present of the energy binders, and for now, I cannot do anything more than lie in a heap."

"Keleb has control of the electrical and electronic devices in the palace and your former consort was not pleased when the video link failed."

"I do not exist to please him," Kryslie told her twin forcibly. "I will tell you when he comes. It should be soon since my guards received orders to clean me up so that the fetid stench of pain and torture does not adhere to me."

The reminder that his sister was naked within the sack made Tymos uncomfortable. He did not think he could be as blasé as she was, about being kept that way. He did not intend to share that thought, it was.

Kryslie's response came with a sense of appreciating his concern. "When I think of what we were once, entities of pure energy, it made me realise that my physical skin is just another form of clothing. That notion gives me power over those who think it debases me."

"It does," Tymos realised. He added then, "Stay strong. I am not far away if you need me."

The awareness was always there, deep in the twin bond. "Find the bastard's secrets," Kryslie told him.

Tymos stopped just inside an enormous room - perhaps it was a ballroom, though it had probably not been used as one in over a generation. Somewhere beyond was the private suite of rooms occupied by bin Halil and another now being used by his son.

Before starting to search the room, he checked the area about him for listening devices, and then drew out his communicator and contacted Alen. After giving instructions for him and Markos to come in to assist the search, providing his current position as a locus to transmit to, he began a slow circle of the room. He used his scanner to detect any electronic devices and cameras, and his own eyes to look for anything that did not belong in this room of exquisite furniture all upholstered in red, of magnificent paintings and priceless antiques.

He found, and deactivated two cameras, just before he saw the glow of two stealth- suited figures arrive out of the air. Without giving them time for greetings, he moved closer and gave them instructions as to where he wanted them to search - referring to the palace layout they had also studied. He did not need to tell them how to go about it. Tymorean missionaries were trained to be unobtrusive.

Even though he doubted such an open room would hide what he wanted to find, Tymos began a thorough search - checking the walls for hidden spaces and all the furniture for any hiding places. Something was tugging at his mind, making him feel there was something here to find.

Hearing a door open, just as he had opened the drawer in an 18th century chiffonier, he turned around. Prince Arthur entered the room, and began to pace around. Tymos dared not close the drawer, but did move away from it.

For some reason, Prince Arthur was drawn to a painting of the desert that was hanging near where he stood. From studying the picture, the prince's eyes flicked sideways when Tymos edged further away. Testing an idea, he moved again. This time, the prince's arm swept to where he stood and he had to duck quickly. He transmitted from the crouched position to the far side of the room, wondering if the Prince was able to see a faint shimmer in the area of the stealth suit.

Arthur turned abruptly, saw the half-opened drawer, and slammed it shut.

"I won't...be sent away...like I am a child!" he stated to the empty room.

His thoughts were more intense and less controlled than they were earlier. He was broadcasting them, along with his emotions. He knew about the woman prisoner, knew what his father intended to do to her, and he abhorred the very thought. He wanted to march into that obscene room and stop it - but his father's very real rage, frightened him. On this subject, being his son, was no protection. His intended victim was possibly Arthur's own half-sister, and even if she were not, she was one of the people such as his early teachers had been. The men who had taught him to respect all people. He would stake his life on the woman not being an agent of evil, and every fibre of his being told him she did not deserve the brutality his father had ordered.

Tymos whispered and sent the thought of, "Do not get involved."

Arthur became rigid, seeming to have the words of the man from the party coming back to him. Was that redheaded woman, who was so very like his unknown mother, somehow playing with his father? That was more dangerous than teasing a snake. Did she know that his father would see her dead?

"No!" he said to himself, and with an abrupt turn, he strode from the room.

Instinct made Tymos follow him along passages containing alcoves displaying yet more priceless relics of history. He was deep into the private sections of the palace, coming closer to Abdul bin Halil's private suite.

Tymos was close behind the prince as he entered through one of the closed doors. His instant sweeping glance identified it as a lounging room, and was aware of the current occupant, moments before the prince saw her.

The young woman was sprawled on the long, single armed couch, and she adjusted herself to a very provocative pose when the Prince entered. Her physical assets were not hidden by revealing draperies worn bin Halil's concubines.

Arthur saw her and immediately ordered, "Out!"

The girl pouted, and insisted, "My Lord ordered me to please you, your Highness."

"You will please me by going back to your room. I am not in the mood for what you are offering. And if you have any intelligence, you will tell the other women to stay away from my father."

"I cannot disobey him…"

"Out!"

The girl must have seen something of his father in him. She fled.

When she had been gone for a full minute, Arthur moved from his position near the door, and began searching. He pulled open the drawers in a desk with a computer sitting on it, went through everything within them, closed each neatly before opening another. He flicked through papers, sorted through storage discs. He tried turning on the computer, and swore when the password he used did not let him activate it. He checked every drawer in the room, and did not find what he sought. Finally, he went over to the large screen hung on one wall. He found a rectangular remote controller and pressed various combinations of numbers and letters.

Abruptly, the screen lit up and displayed a deep blue blank image. He pressed more buttons and aimed the controller at the screen. Scenes from around the estate appeared, each staying on for a second. He stopped the progression when he saw an image of two men staring down at something.

Tymos ghosted up behind Prince Arthur as his sister's mind voice told him, "He's coming. I can sense him."

Prince Arthur drew in a sharp breath as one of the men dragged a woman up into view by her hair. She was nude, battered, bruised, but she held herself as if she were clad in the finest of gowns. She was magnificent.

Then he saw his father walk into view, shadowed by a bovine looking man - someone he had never seen before.

The man holding the woman's hair, pushed her down. Arthur fiddled with the controller and widened the view on the screen. The woman was on her knees, and her head was being pushed down to the floor - the position of absolute subjugation.

He moaned aloud, "Don't do this, Father. For the God's sake, don't do this."

Yet he couldn't tear his eyes from the screen.

His father sat on a chair that was positioned behind him by one of his guards. He looked down at the woman with undisguised hatred. At his gesture, the woman's head was dragged up so that she had no choice but to stare into his face. There were bruises on her face, scabs on her lips and forehead.

The woman seemed to shiver, but she neither pleaded nor tried to struggle free.

"I see you know who I am," Abdul bin Halil spoke in a tone that made Arthur shudder.

For the first time in days, the woman spoke. "You are the bastard that killed my mother."

Arthur saw the cane flick into view, and heard the thwack as it hit the woman's flesh. Only a tightening of the woman's face betrayed her pain, but somehow, he felt the echo of that pain in his own flesh.

Tymos sent an urgent thought to Keleb, still parked in the truck a mile away. "Kel, cut the power to the video screen in bin Halil's private lounge."

Instants later, the screen went blank. Arthur clenched his fists and hissed as if he had been lashed again.

"This has to stop! But I don't dare…"

Tymos spoke very softly in Tymorean, but stayed in stealth mode. "It will be over soon."

Arthur stiffened, recognising the language and the voice. "Where are you? Why don't you stop this?"

A gentle hand took his and held it, the phantom pain in his back faded into memory. "Do not look around."

A faint nod signalled that Arthur would obey.

"The question is, what are you willing to do to stop this?"

Arthur clenched his free hand. "He is my father. What can I do? I am expected to obey him."

"Do you know what he is planning?"

"He will torture her to death," Arthur whispered.

"If he does, it will not change things," Tymos said quietly. "She is but a symbol of the forces rising against your sire. It was her choice to confront him. Do you know what he is secretly undertaking?"

The answer was not immediate.

Finally, "He has not told me. But I have heard things, and I believe that the Investigative Committee would not come to the Imperium in force, without a compelling reason."

"They have come because I found sufficient proof of his conspiracy," Tymos said bluntly.

"And that woman…my half sister…is she a spy from the UWN as he claims?"

"She works for peace. To someone who does not want peace - she is a traitor."

"What can I do?"

"Tell me where your father hides his secrets."

Once again, Arthur fell silent. He was fighting a battle between what was right, and what he was expected to do as a son of his father. He wanted the madness to stop, but it would mean betraying his father.

"Are you out to destroy my father?"

"That is up to him."

"If he gives up this madness of wanting to control the entire world - will you let him live?"

"As I said, it is up to him. It is not I who is judging him."

"Then I will do this, so that in the eyes of our God, he will be spared," Arthur said with resolution. "He has a private sitting room, off his bed chamber. It once connected to the chief consort's suite. He had it sealed off many years ago. I don't know what is there, but in that place he spends many hours alone."

"Thank you. I must search and the Guardians willing, I will find what I am seeking and this madness will never escalate into war."

"Was my mother another like that woman with my father?"

"Yes."

"And you?"

"Yes."

"Will I ever get to meet you properly?"

Tymos felt the pang of longing from this nephew of his. "One day," was all he promised.

"What else can I do?"

"Do what you believe to be right."

"How will I know? How can I be sure?"

"You are your mother's child; taught by men of peace. Trust your instincts."

Arthur felt the hand touching his drop away, sensed the presence vanish. He didn't regret his decision. It had felt like the right thing to do and no one, not even the men watching the security cameras would know he had spoken. The disembodied voice had technology to hide him from sight. Oh, how his father would covet that knowledge. Better that he did not learn of it.

Tymos transmitted away, calculating the distance and direction from the memorised plans. He arrived in the room that Arthur had mentioned. The first thing he did was generate an energy pulse that neutralised the intruder sensors in the room. Only then did he use his communicator to call Jonko and send him the coordinates for transmission. In this room, bin Halil had allowed no cameras.

His friend arrived in stealth mode, but he knew where Tymos stood, for the suits had a face visor with the ability to project images for the wearer. Others in the suits showed up as glowing outlines.

"Did you find what was needed?" Tymos asked softly.

"Yes, but the names of the top echelon were not there," Jonko told him. "There were records in a sealed alcove of the records room. I found Krys's transmitter and communicator."

"Then check this room. Bin Halil spends a lot of time in here. You know what to look for."

Tymos moved away, concentrating on his sister's mind voice. It was once again in his head, but a sound like a rumble of thunder nearly drowned it. The sound was not audible.

"Tym, my plan won't work. I have touched his mind. He is quite insane."

"Will you leave?"

"No."

"Can you heal him?"

There was mental silence for a long moment. "No."

"Krys, what are you planning?"

"I know what I must do. Tell Keleb to seal this room and dim the lights."

She didn't explain, but her mind had the implacable hardness of the Guardians of Peace. The rumble, like thunder, had been the Guardians talking to her. Then her mind was blocked from his. She had the Guardians work to do. So did he.

He had to find the names of those bin Halil trusted with his most secret plans. He had to find these trusted commanders before they vanished into hiding.

Klim was one, and he had been here. He knew the IC was after him, and was trying to get the warning to his leader. Tymos had not dared to act against the man in bin Halil's own place. It might have warned the man of trouble, and vital records may have been destroyed.

"Tym!"

Tymos returned his attention to Jonko.

"I've found a computer, and some storage discs. I can't get access. Do you want to try?"

"We won't have time," Tymos said, feeling the truth of that. Instead, he called Keleb. "I need a completely blank hard drive for a XLC Systems ultra computer - is there another computer of that type in this place?"

Tymos listened, ended the call and then contacted Markos. Within five minutes, he arrived with the required drive. "It wasn't protected," was the report.

"Good, I took the drive out of this machine, while I was waiting - put that one in, then tell Alen that I told you both to leave. Wait in the van with Keleb."

Jonko hadn't been idle. He found a hidden cupboard and in this one were three drawers full of folders. His eyes met those of Tymos.

"Take the hard drive to the van - see if Keleb can clone the contents. Bring back a force screen generator and set it up to hide those filing drawers."

Jonko and Markos disappeared together. Tymos opened the middle drawer and looked at the file tabs; he pulled out one at random and glanced at the contents. He repeated the action several times before changing drawers to check some more. Until he could get access to the stolen hard drive, he could not be sure that these archaic printed files were duplicates of what was on the computer, but the contents were enough to implicate some very important men. Once the force screen hid the filing drawers, someone looking would think them stolen.

Chapter 18 - Manipulation

Krys met bin Halil's hooded dark eyes as she mentally spoke to her brother. Though on her knees, she held herself straight and proud, ignoring the leering looks of the two guards and the primal lust in the mind of the bovine man. Not one of those three was a potential ally. To the two guards, she was trash, one step away from death. If given permission, they would rape her without any trace of remorse. The bovine man behind her was sub-human, a brute, only a short step above a rabid animal. He had a dog like devotion to bin Halil. He waited there with his three-tailed lash, awaiting a gesture from his master. He was a perfectly obedient servant, doing exactly as he was told.

He had lashed her twice, not withholding any of his strength. He had not even wondered why her back had not bled.

Kryslie had been able to send power from the energy binders to her personal force screen. It had protected her, but the lashes had been intensely painful none the less. She had not been able to hide her reaction completely. Tymos had helped her recover from the previous days of torture, but her back was still very tender.

She refused to look away from bin Halil, and finally he took his gaze away, but only to scrutinise her undressed form from her eyes to her knees.

"You," he said with deliberation, "are an abomination. Born in sin and adultery, a murderess, a spy, a traitor. I have seen the evidence against you. As the highest power in the Imperium, I have judged you guilty on all counts."

Kryslie did not even try to argue that she could appeal to the World Council. The false murder charge had been concocted with devious thoroughness, and that alone would prevent help them giving her help. Bin Halil was within his rights to have her tried in the Imperium where the sentence for murder was death.

"Made up charges. Faked evidence," Kryslie accused him, defying him and not granting him the respect due to his position.

Pain lashed her again, but although she flinched, she made no sound, and continued to speak. "You will not be able to make me disappear conveniently."

She felt a momentary reaction of fear from the man in front of her. She knew he had made many people disappear.

"That is not my intention," bin Halil said smoothly, and his smile was malicious. "I will use you as an example of the Imperium's intolerance for your vile crimes. Equal opportunity - women will be treated with equal harshness to the men."

If he expected or wanted a reaction from her, he did not get it. She stared at him, and her face betrayed nothing.

"Do you know the penalty for murderers, adulterers and spies?"

Still no reaction, and bin Halil felt the beginnings of fear. He went on. "Death…but not a quick death. For adultery, you could be stoned."

He was picturing that option in his mind. It was giving him an almost sensual ecstasy. He was moistening his lips with the thought of rocks hitting her flesh. He drew his mind back to his prisoner.

"For murderers, I could make them give you poison – one that gives you a particularly painful death. For spies, once we have extracted all you know from your mind, we could choose many things. And what you have stoically endured so far is nothing."

A range of unpleasant options passed through his mind.

Krys felt her body freeze in terror, but her mind was still clear.

Bin Halil smiled a leering, unpleasant smile. "I think we will begin. I am told that you have already admitted so much. I believe my secretary has a transcript, but I think I will have you tell me all of it yourself. You have the choice of cooperating, or having another dose of that drug. My men must not have given you a full dose - or you would not be so stoic now. I will double that dose…"

"I don't think so," Kryslie murmured, lowering her mind shields to talk to her brother. "Tym, my plan won't work…"

Her eyes strayed to the two guards standing by the door, mute and ready to act. Let bin Halil think she was looking to escape, he could not know of the judgement against him. He could not hear the voices of the Guardians of Peace.

"Tell Keleb to seal this room and dim the lights." As soon as Kryslie sensed her brother's mind turning elsewhere, she blocked his mind from hers. She left it open to the four men in the room.

The loud 'thunk' of the door sealing itself startled the guards. They brought their weapons up, ready to fire, but she had not moved.

"Your friends have erred," bin Halil told her. "Now it will be impossible for them to rescue you."

Kryslie ignored him, concentrating her attention on the brute behind her. His mind was not much higher in intelligence than an animal. She had touched the minds of animals before and knew they reacted more easily to emotion. However, instead of inciting fear or terror, she used gentleness. Into his mind, she evoked the memory of a mother's love, of him being held, cherished, and protected by her. She gave this 'mother' her own face, and felt him responding to this long forgotten sensation.

Before he could reconcile this new revelation with his slavish devotion to his master, the only person who now cared for him, she inserted another emotive image - of her arms wide, standing between him and the two guards as if she were protecting him from them.

His mind was busy with the new thoughts, and his ears were deaf to bin Halil's orders. It took moments for the slow brain to understand but when he did, his reaction was instantaneous. With a roar of fury, he trotted from behind Kryslie and launched himself at the two guards who were glancing uneasily at the door, and then at the dim room. They turned at the last minute, realising that the brute was attacking, but having too little time to react. They both fell like skittles; two brutal punches saw them both unconscious. The bovine man picked them up, one in each massive fist, and tossed them aside like trash. Bin Halil was standing, barking orders at the man in Arabic. Finally, the man turned and listened to the order to break the arms and legs of the woman prisoner.

It was too dim to see his expression, but when the brute stopped between himself and the woman prisoner, his 'master' and his 'mother', and said, "No", bin Halil was momentarily speechless. The brute had never defied him.

Uncontrollable fury erupted from bin Halil. He saw the woman had not moved, was still kneeling, with her body erect. She had to be the cause of the strangeness. He did not know how, but it had to be her. The bitch was unnatural - how could any woman still be defiant after the torture and beatings. He moved so he could see her, the brute moved to keep him away from her, but not fast enough - to prevent him having a glimpse of the woman's eyes. In the dim light, they had somehow taken on a purple gleam. An atavistic shiver ran down his spine, and his mind dredged up memories of his childhood and the gleaming eyes of an attacking wild cat.

"You!" he accused the woman. "You have bewitched him." He spoke softly, and moved slowly, so the brute would not think him threatening. He came within arms reach and gave the woman's face a vicious slap. Before he could land the follow up, the brute was on him. Only the rapid drawing of a weapon from a hidden holster, and firing at zero range, stopped the brute from strangling him.

Kryslie recognised the energy effects of a stunner set on lethal. While bin Halil was avoiding the brute as he crumpled to the floor, dead, she snapped the energy binders off her wrists and ankles and sprang to her feet. Her movement made bin Halil spin around; when he saw her standing free, he activated the stunner again. The energy licked around her PFS and dissipated.

If sight was possible in the dim light, an observer would have seen bin Halil's face suffuse with blood. He moved towards her, determined to kill her. He should have been warned by her calm demeanour, should have remembered her defensive fighting skills, should have considered his own thought that she was unnatural, but he still saw her as a female - weak by definition. He tossed the stunner aside and took a knife from the belt sheath of the brute.

That he had a knife now, did not concern Kryslie. If he hoped she had not seen him take it, because of the dim light, he would discover his error. She could see perfectly well in the dimness, her eyes were seeing his energy aura - pulsing red-orange with fury. She stepped forward to meet him, balanced on one leg and used the other to land a powerful kick on his face. She sensed the bone in his nose breaking, and said coldly, "Now your face and mine are equal. Now you will learn that I am your master and I will learn everything you know."

Bin Halil fell backwards, landing hard, but no bones were broken. In spite of his age, he was still tougher than many younger men. He eyed her as he quickly regained his feet. He took her lack of a follow up attack to be a weakness - he would have killed her before she could regain her feet. He still had the knife, and he gripped it firmly, waiting for a chance to use it.

"What is this about?" he demanded. He moved slowly towards her, his mind whispering, "Just stay there, bitch. Just stay there."

Kryslie was not going to oblige, as soon as he was in range, she kicked out once more, this time causing him to drop the knife. She ducked, grabbed it and tossed it across the room. She was aware of him leaping at her, and timed her spring upwards to catch him without a defensive surface to brace against. She tossed him to the floor once more, and stood over him, as she began to insinuate memories into his mind.

The thoughts he began to recall were from his childhood, when he had been attacked by a large cat and had been helpless to fight it off. He squashed the thought. He wasn't helpless now. He threw up his hands and surged up, catching her by the neck and putting all his strength into throttling her.

It was a long moment before he realised that his hands could not squeeze hard enough, and there was an unpleasant tingling when he touched her. Then he felt her hands, like vice grips, holding him by the waist and lifting his feet off the ground. It shouldn't be possible.

While his mind processed the unbelievable truth, he felt her taking him backwards, and then felt himself pushed into the chair. A shock, like a mild stun, made his hands spasm open. He found himself unable to move. He wasn't bound, but he couldn't get up.

He glared with impotent fury at the woman, as she said without emotion, "How do you like being helpless?"

He didn't, and as soon as he could move again, he would kill her. She would regret toying with him this way.

Kryslie knew he was fuming, and planning to kill her and if he concentrated on breaking her compulsion, he could get free. She edged towards the knife, and began to insinuate into his mind the sense of dark shadows slinking around the room. She saw his head turn from side to side as the movement evoked memories of his childhood nightmare once again. She read his fear in his mind, and added the suggestion of thunder - that traumatic attack had happened on a dark thundery night.

When his body went rigid, his mind played out the dreadful memory, Kryslie went up to him. She gave his mind the suggestion, that she was the feline of his memory as she used the knife to cut open his clothes, and rip them to shreds. Several times the knife scraped his skin, causing blood to trickle down his chest.

While his mind was in the grip of his most primal and deep-rooted fear, he didn't realise that he was becoming her equal in stance - naked and vulnerable.

Long ago, when he had captured and used her, she had discovered how fastidious he was. He never appeared in public unless he was impeccably dressed. He never coupled with a woman unless she was recently bathed.

Now he was exposed to her scorn, he would have to experience the degradation he had imposed on her. He would have to suffer being touched by one who he considered in the same description as gutter trash, whose body was bruised, welted and stinking of sweat and worse.

The nightmare was almost played out - he had been rescued, he was in the arms of his mother, he was finally feeling safe - he was…

He was no longer in the chair, he was on his back on the floor and the woman was straddling him. She was rousing his body, just like that other red headed bitch, her mother, had done thirty years before. That woman had spoiled him. His future consorts could never bring him to the same level of pleasure. But this one was filth. Did she think that he would be disgusted by her touch, feel raped by it? Was this part of her revenge?

If it was, it wouldn't break him. He had no squeamish qualms about forcing his manhood on mothers and their daughters. This creature was offering herself to him. He could vent his anger at her and her mother. He felt himself beginning to be able to move again…

Kryslie was aware of his every thought, he was relaxing, enjoying the sensations that her fondling of his private places was rousing. He was thinking he had power over her revenge - and as he thought that, she deliberately grounded some of her power. Bin Halil's body went rigid as what felt like lightning jolted through his very manhood - the ecstasy he had felt, replaced by agony.

She felt no remorse. She knew too much of this man, and was learning even more as her mind once more blended with his, removing barriers, exposing the hidden knowledge that she sought. What she learnt, she whispered back to him as he tried to end the agony. With every dreadful secret, she jolted him again, and reminded him of the penalties for murder - the dozens he had ordered, for treason, for torture and inciting war. She moved her hand so that his whole body knew what it felt like to be whipped.

This was torture, Kryslie knew, as she continued in a systematic and impersonal way. A small part of her was enjoying it, revelling in it. The human part that he had deliberately debauched when he was thirty years younger, and had ordered tortured these past few days. She felt a flick of lightning through her mind, recalling her to what she was. She was not merely human, but an Advocate of the Guardians of Peace - their tool. They were using her to punish him, to make him feel what he had ordered done to many, many people.

She heard a voice in her mind, "Enough."

She rolled off her victim, and felt the body of the bovine man behind her. She had more remorse for that brute of a man, for he had been trained to love torturing and killing by his despicable master.

Bin Halil was a mewling wreck, curled now into a foetal position. "No more, I can stand no more," he was pleading.

Kryslie rose and stared down at her victim. "You disgust me. The minds of beasts are cleaner than yours. Why should I listen to a weak abhorrent piece of excrescence like you? You gave me no mercy."

She leant over and forced him out of his curled up position, straddled him again and reawoke the pains all over him. "This is my revenge - making you feel what so many young innocent girls felt when you ravished their virtue. You were not gentle with them; it was rape. Now you must suffer because I, the lowest most disgusting creature in your eyes, am doing it to you."

She made the pain escalate to excruciating, for less than five minutes, before her victim's mind blanked. It had not taken her long to drive him into this state of catatonia, his muscles rigid, and his mind stuporous. Now, he was literally broken, mindless.

Kryslie eased off him, now feeling disgust at what she had done. She was a mind healer, but knowing how to heal minds, taught how to break them. She had acted at the behest of the Guardians of Peace, and now, in her mind, she heard, "Make this man what he needs to be."

Their all-knowing wisdom filled her, and she understood why they did not let her leave him broken, and why they had not simply stopped his heart.

The thought of using her mind-healing gift on him made her feel physically ill. Yet she had promised to serve and obey the Guardians. In the dimness, she raised both arms high and wide. She would obey.

She paused to consider how the Guardians had used her intimate knowledge of him to reach his deepest essence to break him. They had used her thirty years ago to give him a son, a seed of peace. Her son was nothing like his father, but he was not yet ready to take over from him, would not be accepted as a leader for a score of years yet. So, she needed to heal him, for just as back in time he had been the only one able to unite all the little splinter nations, tribes and peoples - he was still the only one who could hold them together.

"Make him what he needs to be." Kryslie considered all of the implications that came with that command.

He had formed the Imperium, and maintained peace and order for thirty years before his desire to overthrow the western nations had grown again. Or had it ever been forgotten? Maintaining peace, that was what he must do. It would not be his fate to unite the Imperium and the UWN. The democracies of the west would never accept his belief in absolute rule.

Where she had been harsh and unforgiving before, now she needed to be gentle. She sat cross-legged on the floor with his head in front of her. She placed gentle hands on his forehead, felt the mind there, subdued, empty. There were no barriers to the compulsions she now began to set.

He would never again conspire to allow the Imperium to make war on the UWN nations.

He would withdraw all agents sent into the UWN to spy, create trouble and steal secrets.

Those who refused to withdraw would be identified to the IC who would deal with them.

He would allow everyone in the conspiracy to be questioned and judged by their actions, and punished for their illegal activities.

With each compulsion, she gave his mind the sense of sexual ecstasy - as a promise of reward for obedience. His essence responded to that. While he was still compliant, she questioned him about all the details of the conspiracy, asked for the names of the upper echelon conspirators and what each of them did for him. She asked after his secret records, in case her brother had not yet found them. Then, when she had milked him of all the information she needed, she began to train his mind. She added compulsions to make him closer to the man he should have been.

It all took energy, and as the last of her personal energy ebbed away, she gave his mind her final commands. He would let her leave, alive. He would never talk of this meeting to anyone. He would not seek her out, or send anyone else to seek her out, and he would not conspire to have her killed.

Then she sent him into a deep sleep, to allow all the compulsions to sink into his mind.

She had no such release - she had done her absolute best, but bin Halil's mind was essentially flawed. It would, in time, seek to circumvent the moral behaviour she had imposed. Even if he couldn't talk of it, he would remember what she had done to him - how she had debased him, contaminated him, humiliated and controlled him. Only time would tell if those poisonous memories would erode her controls.

She would have to leave the Imperium and never return, lest the sight of her was enough to break the controls. If she discovered that he was hunting her, it would be a warning that her work had unravelled and should that happen, the Guardians would not spare his life again.

From the dregs of her energy, no more that pure determination, she crawled away from bin Halil, away from the three dead men, and into a corner. There, what little substance was in her stomach heaved and erupted. She tried to draw in energy, but the aura seeping from the walls was too vile to use. All else was a slight energy from the lights. It was barely a trickle, but enough.

"Bro?"

"Krys!"

"Unlock the door…"

"I'm coming for you…"

"No! Don't come in here."

"What did he do to you?"

"Nothing. It's what I did to him… and the aura in here is vile…"

Tymos tried to analyse the emotion coming to him through the deep twin bond, but for the first time ever…failed.

"I found where he keeps his records," he told his sister mentally, deciding she needed time to regain her composure. "Kel is copying a hard drive, and I will need to return it. We are out of the palace, waiting near by. Is bin Halil dead?"

"No."

"Can we prove his part in this?"

"No. We cannot let him be tried and executed." His mind sensed that it was not her choice, but that of the Guardians of Peace.

Frustration caused Tymos to kick the side of the truck, with enough force to make a hole. With all that his sister had endured, they still had to let the bastard go free.

Jonko and Keleb stared at him. The latter, an empath as well, was sensitive to his emotional state. Alen and Markos were startled and alarmed.

"Tymos? What's wrong? Is Krys okay?" Jonko asked.

"Yes! No!" Tymos answered, shaking his head.

"Can we bring the IC here to find the stuff?" Jonko tried.

Tymos shook his head.

"You said they needed to see those files…" Jonko reminded him.

"I know…"

Jonko glanced at Keleb, something was making Tymos act strangely. Keleb shrugged, he had no idea.

"I need to talk to Krys…but she…needs some time."

Just then, Kryslie spoke to his mind. "Bring Prince Arthur here."

Tymos straightened, and spoke to his friends. "I am going back in. When I send the word, reactivate the screens in the private lounge. Send up a drone to monitor anything that leaves the palace."

Tymos vanished abruptly from the van, leaving his friends staring at each other with concern. They had been waiting in the truck for two hours since retreating from the palace. They had guessed that Tymos's incessant pacing had been because he could not contact his twin. Now, it seemed that Krys was alive, but not all had gone to plan.

"Could bin Halil have discovered what you did?" Keleb proposed, as he set about programming and launching the drone to spy from high above the palace.

"I don't know," Jonko had to admit.

Moments later, Tymos sent the word to restore all power and all systems.

Tymos was in one corner of bin Halil's private lounge, shielded and standing very still. The room was otherwise unoccupied, but he expected Prince Arthur to return, and did not want his nephew to sense him. He sent the word to Keleb to restore power to all systems, and now the black screen came back to life. He had a view of the room below, but all he could see was his sister's bowed head, and the top of her shoulders. He did not try to reach her mind, and she did not move or indicate that she knew he was seeing her on the screen.

She wanted him to bring Arthur there. Was she ready for company yet?

"No rush," came the thought in his mind.

Arthur strode into the room, his face was flushed as if he had been exercising strenuously, but he smelt as if he had just showered. He was dressed in an impeccable suit, one that smelt new. Had he felt the need to armour himself against whatever his father was doing? He was far from calm, even now.

The bright screen immediately caught his attention and he went closer to study it. Then he called for guards and waited for two of them to race into the room. Tymos sidled closer to the door, and listened.

"My father has an obscene interrogation cell somewhere. Where is it?"

The two guards stayed mute, and their faces paled.

"Where…is…it?" Arthur repeated his request with deliberate emphasis - sounding so much like his sire that the younger of the guards spoke. The older guard glared at his partner, but did not rebuke him.

"In the cellar, your Highness, but the entrance is outside. But we were sworn to tell no one."

Arthur did not miss the innuendo of, "Not even you."

"Take me there. Now!"

Tymos turned to watch the screen. His sister was so pale as to seem bloodless. This time, she looked at the camera, expressionless, but said in his mind, "I did what they wanted."

Since he could no longer hear the rumble of thunder, he knew the Guardians had withdrawn. Why had they left her so depleted?

He didn't ask that, instead he said, "Arthur is coming."

"He will see me like this…weak, battered. He will see his father…and assume he was the victor here."

"Was he?"

"No."

"How is that good?"

"Bin Halil will find that he cannot kill me, or order me killed. I want to see that moment. However, if everyone thinks he won, he will think he is still powerful. To do the Guardians' will, he cannot appear weak. But he will still know that I mastered him."

"What…what must he do?" Tymos asked carefully.

"He is still the only one that can keep the Imperium together. So, he will get to keep his rule here, but he will not conspire against the UWN any more."

"That is not the full outcome I wanted," Tymos thought back. "Now I must find a way for the IC to find all of bin Halil's lists and files."

"You will think of something. It concerns me what bin Halil will think when he finds them gone."

"If it were me, I would be pleased if they did not find it," Tymos mused. "Do you think he will ask his son? Blame him?"

Movement of his sister's head told him that Athur had found the room. Then the prince came into the camera's view, he stared at Krys for a moment, and then knelt down.

"Father!"

Arthur entered the room after the two guards. They moved to each side of the door and held their weapons aimed at the only conscious occupant of the room. He studied the condition of the woman, glad she was still alive, but more immediately concerned for his father.

"Father!" Arthur gently shook his father by the shoulder. He touched his father's neck and felt a pulse there. There were scabbed over scratches on his chest, blood had trickled from his nose, and that looked swollen. He was alive, but what had happened? Belatedly, he realised that his father was as naked as the woman, and he would not wish to be seen that way by others. Without a second thought, he took of his coat and covered him. Still crouching there, he spoke to his guards.

"Are the other men still alive?"

He had never seen violent death before, but the men looked like they could not possibly be alive. His thoughts were confirmed. Had his father killed them? Had the woman? He could not bring himself to believe that she had.

Just then, his father roused and began to sit up. The first thing he saw was the woman, staring at him. His eyes glittered with hate and he tried to form the words, "Kill her." Instead, what came out was, "Throw that piece of carrion into a sewer somewhere."

"Father, she's naked!" Arthur protested as the two guards moved instantly to obey.

As they dragged the unresisting woman out, bin Halil's voice gained volume, "Come straight back. Talk to no one."

When they were out of sight, he went on to ask, "What has happened while I was here?"

Arthur was confused by his father's tone. The fury had gone and he was calm, but somehow subtly different to normal.

"We have had power interruptions and Professor Klim was here, concerned about the actions of the IC."

Without commenting, bin Halil stood up and donned the coat that had covered him. He looked down at his shredded clothing. Arthur saw where he looked and immediately removed his trousers and let his father put them on. He would not let his father be seen in such an undressed state.

"Wait here. When those two guards return, have then deal with these bodies. Send someone to get you trousers. When they have cleaned up here - I want to see those two guards."

Arthur only nodded and watched his father leave. Then he studied the bodies of the dead and shuddered. Blood had leaked from their mouths, and they lay as if thrown against the wall. It seemed impossible that the slight redheaded woman could have done that. However, the staring bovine looking brute - could have, but what had killed him?

Moving around the room, Arthur tried to determine what had taken place here. He found a weapon on the floor, and a knife. The latter had blood on it, and he wondered whose it was. Had it made the scratches on his father's chest? Had the woman done that?

He turned when he heard boots on the concrete floor outside the door. A young guard stood there. He was not one that he knew by name, but the face was familiar. He stiffened when he heard the man speak in the language he had learnt from his early teachers.

A bundle of cloth was offered to him, and he realised that it was a pair of trousers. He took it gratefully and put them on. He missed seeing the new arrival aiming a device at the camera in the corner of the cell.

"My father is still alive. Thank you," Arthur said, correctly identifying this man as the one he had heard but not seen some hours earlier.

Tymos knew that he had very little time. "Your father has had his only warning. He will continue to live unless he reneges on keeping the peace and treating all with respect. If you wish him well, you should encourage the new aspects of his character."

"Did he hurt her?" Arthur gestured to where Kryslie had sat.

"Do not be concerned for her. Forget her. There are more important things."

"What must I do?"

"Your father has certain records and documents. Perhaps as his dutiful son, you should suggest that they do not stay here lest they be found if the IC search."

"If he thinks that I have been reading his private papers…"

"Even if nothing in those records mentions your father; finding them here will implicate him."

Arthur shook his head, "He will not want the IC here."

"Trying to stop them, will suggest guilt," Tymos suggested.

"He will think that I have interfered in his private affairs. That I know what he has been doing. I will not let him think that I condone what he has done."

"You do not have to convince him that you now approve of his deeds, only that you were protecting him from them."

"I understand. You should go. And when these bodies are tended to, I will bury this room so that no more atrocities will be perpetrated here."

Chapter 19 - Netting Traitors

When Arthur looked at the dead men again, Tymos reactivated his stealth suit. He paused a moment longer to evaluate the Prince's reaction.

Seeing that he was alone, Arthur did not try to control his expression. He looked ill. When Tymos brushed his mind, he felt the conflict there - the expectation of obedience to a father he no longer respected. Not wanting to keep seeing death in such graphic immediacy, Arthur walked out of the room to wait in the brick lined passage. This time, he went past Tymos without sensing him.

Tymos transmitted back to bin Halil's private sitting room, and positioned himself in a corner behind one of the armchairs. No one would be likely to walk into him there. He was merely watching the computer while Keleb was still out in the van copying the hard drive from the computer. He needed to know what bin Halil decided to do. If he came in and discovered the substitution, the plans would need to be changed.

Then there were the files hidden in the cupboard…his original idea had been to locate them so when the IC searched, they would find them. Now he had to get them away without giving any clues to his interest in them. He had to let bin Halil remain free, though the idea vexed him.

The situation at the moment was perilous enough, should the hard drive switch be noticed. The data on it would be most useful, but if it could be construed to have been tampered with, it could not be used as evidence.

What would be the best option was to get hard drive and files into the place where the General was hiding, but Olassa had yet to confirm that exact location. A better idea would be for bin Halil to send them there - but as yet Tymos had no idea how to cause that situation. He was giving the need some thought as he listened to bin Halil who was in the adjoining suite, being bathed and tended by two of his women.

The man was not in an amorous mood. He was curt with the woman who had expressed concern over the livid scratches on his chest, and made the other add more hot water. After a great deal of subdued splashing, and complaints that they were doing a poor job, he sent them off. One was to bring scented towels, and the other some of a strong locally made liqueur.

Tymos allowed himself the slightly malicious thought that a bath, even with the hottest water and staying in it until his skin was wrinkled like a prune, would not cleanse the man of the feeling of being 'dirty' and used. Let him feel the sense of degradation that he had inflicted on many young women. Women such as his sister.

The thought of Kryslie prompted him to check on her. "Where are you?"

She answered him immediately, but he sensed she was still weak.

"On the floor of a large black car, with a gun in my face."

"Can you get free?"

"A boy scout could tie me in a knot right now, but I will have a chance. They were told to dump me."

"They may still try to kill you out of their own misguided sense of loyalty to bin Halil."

He sensed his sister testing considering the emotions of the men. "You might be right."

"Do you need help? Keleb should have a drone following the car."

"No…I am drawing energy from the car engine…it isn't running very well. If they are minded to kill me, I think they will wait until they get where they are going. I will have some reserves by then. Anyway, you have things to do."

That she didn't ask about how the rest of their plan was going, told him that she was more concerned about her current plight than she let him see. But she was right, he had important things to do.

He heard bin Halil summon the women back to dry him. He heard one of them speak very deferentially. Tymos imagined her bowing low, overdoing the normal obeisance so as not to anger him further.

"Prince Arthur waits in the outer sitting room, Sir."

Considering his earlier waspishness, the reply was unexpectedly mild. "See he has refreshments and advise him that I will not be much longer."

Tymos let his mind delve into bin Halil's thoughts. It was a rudeness that he rarely committed, but the Imperium's leader had ceded his right to be treated with respect when he had ordered the torture of Kryslie. Those thoughts were in direct contrast to the polite façade. He was still seething, recalling the loss of face the red headed woman had inflicted on him, still trying to convince himself that he had won. He cursed in his mind for his inability to force out the command to 'kill her'. He hoped his guard commander would countermand the 'dump' order, with 'kill and dump'.

Tymos had warned his sister, but now he had confirmation. He tried to reach her again and felt no answer. With sudden alarm, he sent a message to Keleb.

"Where is the car that left here?"

Keleb gave a location and then added, "It drove into a building."

"Can you still pick up the signal from her GPS dot?"

"No. What is its range? The car is in the south of the city, near the flood containment system."

Tymos had the specs for the GPS dot tracer device come into his head. It should be registering.

"Tell Jonko to get to where you lost the car and look for Krys. Tune his comm. unit to the frequency of the GPS dot."

There was a very brief pause. "He's on his way. Someone left a power bike parked nearby. He's borrowing it."

Tymos withdrew from the contact. He sent a mental plea to the Guardians to keep his sister safe.

Bin Halil did not come to his private sitting room, but joined his son on the outer room. Tymos moved ghostlike, through the private part of the suite to where he could peer out into the room where the now dark screen hung.

"What is it?" bin Halil demanded, as he sat himself in the most comfortable of the chairs.

"Professor Klim telephoned. He wanted to talk to you."

"He was here, wasn't he? Where did he go?"

"He told Danik that he was heading back to Hadjibad by road."

"He only mentioned that the Investigative Committee had the border point blocked. He has stopped in a town on this side."

Bin Halil's face creased into a faint scowl. "Hardly a vital problem."

"I would venture to guess that he does not want to be questioned by the IC," Arthur said. "They have been questioning all the eminent men in the League for the Advancement of the Imperium."

"My very good friend has nothing to worry about. All he is doing is trying to improve the position of the Imperium with respect to the UWN."

Arthur held back from blurting his thoughts about the so called League. He was beginning to see its true insidious nature. Instead, he took a deep breath and went on to the news he expected would anger his father.

"Director Chalmers of the Investigative Committee has advised Danik that he will be calling to have discussions with you - tomorrow at ten."

"Very well. I will be able to clear up his misconceptions. Has that mess below been cleaned up?"

"Not yet. The two guards have not yet returned."

"Have my guard captain put them on report and have him assign two others to take over the task."

"I have already done that," Arthur stated. "And I have also ordered him to fill that foul cellar with rubble and seal it permanently." He stared at his father, daring him to object.

"And why did you take it on yourself to do that?" The mild tone belied the blazing glare in his father's eyes, and Arthur straightened and stared back.

"Father, you are the Leader of the Imperium. You shouldn't be dealing with …what did you call that woman…gutter trash?"

Bin Halil turned from facing his son, to staring at the portrait of the red headed woman who was his son's mother. "You have changed your tune, haven't you?"

"No, I haven't. I think it demeans you to be the one who must force answers from criminals."

"You are weak! Squeamish!"

"So you have said, Father," Arthur admitted, without trying to argue. His father turned back to face him.

"Send Danik in. I want to know what he can tell me bout the transcript of that criminal's confession."

Arthur betrayed his surprise. "What transcript?"

"Evidence that will convict that gutter trash if she gets out of the sewer alive. Get Danik and have some more food sent in."

Even though his father was treating him like a servant, Arthur went to the sideboard with the phone and made the calls.

As soon as Arthur had finished, bin Halil demanded, "Do you know what caused all the power problems?"

"Here?"

"Of course here!"

"No one seems to know."

Danik, bin Halil's secretary, knocked on the door and entered when told to "Come in." He bowed correctly and stood about six feet away.

"Where is the transcript that came from Hadjibad?" bin Halil demanded.

"I am not aware that there was one, Sir."

"The messenger arrived with Captain Yasu. He sent an escort to bring the man to you."

Arthur clarified, "That would be about when Professor Klim was here."

"I saw no one waiting when the professor left." Danik glanced at Prince Arthur for confirmation.

"Go and get a description from Captain Yasu, and tell him to instigate a search. If that man was trying to rescue that gutter trash, he didn't succeed."

Arthur, thinking of the man he had spoken to, hoping he had gone to help the woman, made no comment.

"I would surmise that the man is the cause of all the power problems. It is the same pattern as they used in Hadjibat. It makes this man predictable."

Danik departed at once, and Tymos watched him until he was out of the door, wondering how much of his master's business he was privy to. He returned his attention to father and son, when Arthur seemed to blurt out, "What if that man was seeking evidence to use against you? The security cameras were on in that obscene cell."

"It is of no concern if he saw that. The woman was a confessed spy and an assassin. I judged her guilty."

"That is not what I meant, Father. He could construe that as the woman being denied her rights as a citizen. The UWN is big on trial with a jury."

Bin Halil turned a steely glare on his son, who refused to look away.

"And can you be sure that he did not infiltrate where ever you keep your reports on your League…"

Arthur managed to control his face so he looked concerned, not repulsed.

"Have you been prying in my private affairs?" bin Halil interrupted.

"Of course not, Father. I am simply suggesting that these agitators you speak of may be trying to twist the activities of the League into something sinister."

Tymos edged to where he could study bin Halil's expression. It was thoughtful, neutral. His mind was admitting that his son had a point. Several excellent points. However, there was no mention in any of the records of his own involvement.

"If the IC have a mandate to search the Justice Building, what is there to stop them searching here? Finding records of the Leagues activities here will imply your involvement or at least that you condone all their actions."

"The League is not a subversive organisation."

Once again, bin Halil stared at his son as if daring him to disagree.

"Father, whether it is or not, I am not the best to judge. Unlike General Thek, Professor Klim, Minister Adwar and your other cronies, you've never invited me to be part of it. I just don't want your honour compromised by mistakes made by others in their enthusiasm to promote the Imperium."

"Are you suggesting that I should destroy all records of what the League has achieved, and disband them? Allow our country to slide back into barbarism?"

"No! That's not what I mean," Arthur protested. "I was thinking that maybe Professor Klim could take them somewhere - until this blows over."

As a listener to the conversation, Tymos had to applaud the Prince. Arthur had chosen exactly the right words and tone to convince his father of his ignorance and provoke bin Halil's own basic preventative paranoia. It was the older man's nature to distance himself from his own illegal activities. Surely the younger man had been inspired by the Guardians of Peace.

However, he had provoked ideas in bin Halil's mind.

Tymos moved back into the private sitting room and sent an urgent thought to Keleb.

"Set off an alarm in an obscure part of the palace, and get that hard drive back here, pronto."

It was an obvious conclusion, given the mention of an intruder, that the alarm would be linked to that person. Bin Halil immediately used a remote control to activate the big screen and to link it to the security system. For a while, his attention would be focussed on trying to get a picture of the intruder.

Arthur, with his father's unnervingly calm attention off him, felt shaky and decided to help himself to a drink of spirits from the supply his father kept in one of the side cupboards. He wondered what had possessed him to speak the words that had come from his mouth. He hadn't planned to speak, and at any other time, what he said would have inflamed his father's temper, not simply earned him a mild rebuke. He expected that any time soon, his father would revert to his true form and explode in anger.

Tymos had his attention on helping Keleb replace the copied drive in the computer, as well as listening for bin Halil, when his mind lost interest in the alarm. When the man gave his son instructions and sent him off, their time was almost out. Keleb finished connecting the inner leads and left Tymos to complete the rest, and step quickly out of the way.

Bin Halil strode into the room, then stopped abruptly, his eyes scanning the room. The desk and computer, along with the associated devices were the first objects he studied, then he glanced at the position of the other chairs, the pictures, and the rugs, before walking to where the three drawer filing cabinet was hidden. He opened the flap of the wall, paused to study the scene, and then opened each drawer.

Tymos knew he had replaced everything exactly as he had found them, but still, the Imperium's leader was spooked. He closed the wall panel, and slowly walked to a deep armchair, that was next to a table with a telephone.

There followed three interesting conversations. The first to Dev Klim, whose paranoia was evident in the higher than normal pitch of his voice. Tymos heard it as clearly as if he held the speaker next to his own ear.

Bin Halil reassured the Professor, reminded him of the claimed aims of the League, and instructed him to return and collect some things to be taken to what he called 'the crypt'. He also promised a guide to show him an alternate route to go south to Hadjibad.

The second cal was to General Thek, who unequivocally assured his superior that the 'crypt' had not been compromised. His subordinates were watching the area and there had been no interest in it.

At that, Tymos smiled to himself. Tymoreans could make themselves scarcely noticed, and some were keeping official interest away from the area. However, it was the General's, "We have a direct view towards the University tower and at the first sign of the IC forming a perimeter, the doors could be sealed," that elated him. He would get Olassa to check the reference and ensure that Klim arrived safely.

Then the Justice Minister came on the line. After the initial greeting, bin Halil chided the man, "You should have stayed."

"It was too great a risk, Abdul. The IC were prepared to take fingerprints and DNA. I covered my going to seem as if I were abducted. It will make those interfering investigators think their methods are flawed. They will have received an order to 'back off' or I will die."

"And then they will be sure of a conspiracy in the legal profession. Are you sure that your aides will not speak unwisely?"

"Only Wilhelm Gurney knows anything. He will not talk, for he is my son. He offered to remain and be openly helpful and he was quick to activate the virus to wipe the interface to the secondary computer system. I am sure that any suspicion will fall on the 'secret police', who have no official presence."

Tymos decided that he had heard enough, and in a moment when bin Halil had his head turned fully away, he transmitted out to join Keleb in the van.

Chapter 20 - Great One cast low

Jonko defied all the road speed laws as he propelled the 'borrowed' motorbike towards the city of Tarsa. The one police car that tried to pursue him was soon left far behind.

With Keleb directing him via an unobtrusive communicator headset, he was outside the building where the palace car had disappeared, within ten minutes. He slowed and found a place to park the bike, in the narrow lane way, before walking back to study the old brick building.

It was two stories high and the old brickwork was discoloured with mould or mildew. All the windows were covered with rusty steel grids. The drone's eye view of the structure had been kind. He and Keleb had assumed it was a carpark, since they had seen cars and vans going in and out fairly regularly. He tried to discern a name on the building, but if there had been one, it was long eroded. As he was about to pass the entrance, the front of a car emerged, forcing him to wait. The closed in sedan had writing on the door. It was in Arabic, and as he could not read it, he called Keleb.

"Can you get the drone to zoom in on the car and can you translate the sign?

Jonko heard the high-pitched whine as the cloaked drone came low enough to scan the writing on the now moving car. It rose back above building height as Keleb reported.

"It's a hearse of some kind, City Funerals."

In an undertone, he replied, "It doesn't look like any funeral parlour I have ever seen. But then, my memories of such things are a century old."

Keleb's voice came again through the earpiece. "The front of the building is more modern."

"So I am at the tradesmans' entrance? Why did they bring Krys here?"

This time there was a pause before Keleb answered, and hearing a police siren, Jonko chose to duck into the opening from where the car had emerged.

"I hooked into the city computer network. That building is the official crematorium - though I did not think that was how these people usually disposed of their dead."

"They might use it for other things. Garbage disposal…Shit!" Jonko activated the stealth function of his PFS and began to walk faster.

"You're right," Keleb's voice came through the earpiece. "That building is right over the main sewer tunnel."

"Can you get a plan of this place?"

"I have - where do you want to go?"

"Wait a sec, two guys are unloading a car like the one that just left."

The driver was out of the car and resting against it - smoking a cigarette. A second car was parked further in, but that seemed to be unoccupied. It had some kind of graphic on the door.

Jonko moved close enough to glance at the body being dragged from the car onto a trolley. It was dirty, emaciated, bewhiskered and smelt of stale body odour.

One of the attendants asked a question, and the driver shrugged and gave a casual reply. Keleb provided a translation. He was recording what came through the communicator, so he didn't miss any thing. "Some derelict that died on the street," he said tersely, and then he added, "Your communicator should be picking up the GPS signal."

With a start, Jonko looked at the signal analyser and involuntarily glanced in the direction it indicated. A section of the wall had opened, and the men with the trolley were heading that way.

Feeling an extreme disquiet and a sense of urgency, Jonko moved after the trolley. As soon as he was within the newly revealed tunnel, a putrid smell assaulted his nostrils. He wished he had a mask similar to the ones the attendants pulled on. He tried to breathe through his mouth as he followed along the unadorned concrete walled tunnel. The trolley wheels were making enough noise to mask the sound of his footsteps. At the end of the tunnel was a waist high parapet with a tilting board, and the men slid the body from the trolley to the board. Moments later, the body slid and fell into a watery place below.

As if it were an everyday event, the attendants began to wheel the trolley back along the tunnel. Jonko pressed himself against the wall, and when the men were gone, he dared to look over the parapet. He couldn't see the water below, but the increased smell told him all he needed. His communicator told him that he was almost right at Kryslie's position.

She had to be down there, alive, or the signal would have stopped. He tried to convince himself of that, and then the words he had told Tymos came into his head. The Guardians would not let her die.

Still, he had heard it said that the Guardians didn't interfere unless a task was beyond the ability of their servants. Jonko was going to have to go down into the reeking sewer...

His stomach heaved and he added more substance to the putrid river below.

"Kel, I sort of know where Krys is," he spoke softly into the communicator, and tried not to throw up again. "I have to get below this building. Is there a ground level entrance to the sewers somewhere nearby?"

"With Keleb directing and the drone acting as a lookout, Jonko transmitted from within the building to the street and from there to where the tunnel entered the vast treatment plant, several miles out of the city.

Keleb programmed the drone to do a sub-ground survey, to locate where the sewer pipe was biggest - then Jonko transmitted down into it, crouching as he did so, just in case.

He stood up carefully, and relaxed when he did not hit his head. According to the plans of the tunnels, this one went straight until the outskirts of the city. He began to transmit in stages along it, trying not to think of how his clothes would be when he finished. He was thankful that the PFS was at least protecting his skin.

After each section travelled, he checked the position pinged back to him by Kryslie's GPS dot tracer. Finally, it indicated that he was close. He looked around, but the dim lights were too far apart to give the area any detail and he hadn't known he would need a torch. He dared to call out softly.

"Krys?"

He heard no reply, just the gentle sloshing of the sludge.

The sense of urgency was increasing, so he concentrated on thinking at Kryslie, as he had learnt to do back on Tymorea. He couldn't project thoughts, but she could read them.

Nothing. He walked slowly along the tunnel, his shins pushing through the thick sludge until they encountered something soft and solid. Overcoming disgust, he reached into the sludge and felt around; he pulled on part of the obstruction and needed to exert his Tymorean strength to lift it. He had been fairly sure it was a body, perhaps the one he had seen dumped from the building but when he hefted it, he could tell it was too big to be Krys, and too solid for the poor dead derelict. Something caused him to drag it closer to one of the dim tunnel lights. The sludge completely coated the body, but the outline suggested a uniform, not the flowing robes preferred by most of the men of Karshada.

An unexpected surge of water shot into the tunnel, and washed some of the muck from the clothing Jonko held. When he finished wiping the splashes from his face, he realised that the watery effluvium had revealed an insignia. It was that of the Imperial Palace guards.

Jonko dropped the body, and wiped his hands on his clothes - above the sludge line. What had killed the guard?

"Krys!" Jonko called, louder now because he was desperate for an answer.

"Jon?"

It was the faintest of replies, and he couldn't decide if it was a voice or a thought.

Instinct more than anything else made him push the guard's body aside and continue on.

He found her, using one arm to cling to a maintenance ladder; only her head was above the sludge, though it seemed that she had been fully immersed. When his hand found her other arm, she moaned softly, and he felt some of his energy leeching from him. He understood what she needed, and willed her to take what she wished, praying to the Guardians that he had enough to spare.

"What happened?" Jonko asked, as he felt Kryslie stirring.

"Help me up."

Kryslie freed her arm from the ladder, but stayed slumped against the concrete wall. She held that arm out for Jonko to take.

"I'll take you to Earthbase."

"No. I don't want Daniel to see me like this."

"You are a Great One, you can…"

"Jon, I know what I am, and I know that no Tymorean would think to question why I chose to play in the sewer sludge - but Daniel doesn't see Tymos and me that way."

Jonko heard Keleb's voice in the earpiece. It was obvious that he had heard the conversation.

"Bring her here, Jon. Tymos sent Alen and Markos back to Hadjibad to assist Olassa. She can clean up a bit here and we have blankets and some spare clothes. Can you transmit this far?"

Jonko felt Kryslie shaking her head and his concern grew. She was so depleted, but couldn't she draw on the aura?

"No, it is too vile…not because of the honest abd natural waste that is here, but because this section has been used too often for unlawful deaths and unsanctioned burials."

"I'll get Tym…"

"No, he needs to be where he is. We can use the palace car if it is still up in the crematorium garage."

"Um…it was." The image of the body he had found came back to him. He didn't ask how Krys had known about the car - he guessed and decided not to think about it. "Kel, calculate distance and direction for me…" He read off the coordinates pinging back from Kryslie's GPS dot. "I want to go back up to where the cars park."

Moments later, Keleb had the information, but he added, "Wait five minutes. I am going to fake a fire alarm to get the people out of there."

The old style alarms were wailing when Jonko materialised with Kryslie next to the car. No one was around as he stood Kryslie next to the rear door and opened the passenger seat. He tried to ignore the layer of sludge, and the fact she had no clothes under it. Then he felt the water sprinklers coming on - he could have hugged Keleb for thinking of that. The water seemed to wash the sludge right off. He blushed as he helped Kryslie to balance; only now noticing that she was favouring one leg as well as one arm.

"The PFS has a repellor function," Kryslie whispered, to try to ease his embarrassment. Then she directed, "That's enough. Drive this car back near the palace and dump it. You can transmit me the last distance to the van."

Tymos materialised in the van just as Kryslie finished wrapping herself in a blanket. She was sitting on one of the spare stools. Their eyes met and they spoke privately, mind to mind.

"What happened?" Tymos asked.

"They thought I was unconscious when they took me to the chute. When they tried to toss me in, I had hold of them both. I needed the energy, and they came over me. They broke my fall, although I did hit my head and my right arm and leg are probably broken."

Aloud, Tymos said, "Let me look at your arm and your leg."

As he examined his sister's injuries, they continued their mental conversation. "The two guards were not told to try to kill you, although bin Halil hoped they would. In any event, they are two more casualties in his undeclared war. As it is now, they will never need to learn how their loyalty to their master would have been rewarded if they had returned."

"I knew that," Kryslie admitted. "It did not make my decision any easier. He would not have wanted them to recall seeing him in such a state of profound weakness."

"You were lucky, they were clean breaks," Tymos commented, still mentally. "Or did you start them healing?"

"No, I think I used up all my reserves trying not to drown in that sludge."

"Did you swallow or inhale any of it?"

"My mouth was full of it, but I don't think so."

Tymos was sending healing energy to the areas of the fractures, and where she had a bump on her head.

When she felt that her leg was healed well enough to hold her weight, she said aloud, "Enough! I can recover the rest of the way at Earthbase, unless you need me to do more here?"

Tymos shook his head. "All's good." He gave her the most recent update mind to mind. Then spoke aloud again, "Now that he assumes you are dead, it would be a very good idea if you stayed away from the Imperium, don't you think?"

Kryslie didn't even try to protest when his next words were, "Jon, help her back to Earthbase. I've healed the fractures - mostly - and even a Great One should rest the arm and leg until the mend strengthens."

"I'll come right back," Jonko promised.

"No need. I can call you if I need you. But while you are there…"

"What?"

"Take a bath!" Tymos grinned impishly.

Jonko glanced at his clothes and saw Keleb trying not to smell the odour that clung to him and Kryslie. "Yes, that might be an excellent idea. I can hardly creep up on people like this."

Keleb called Earthbase and requested the long-range beam to be set to their coordinates. Lexina answered him, so he asked her if Daniel was around, and was relieved when she said he was on his sleep period. She offered to get him if the matter was urgent.

"No, it isn't. Kryslie is on her way back. She will need to clean up and some clothes - better Daniel doesn't see her like she is."

Lexina admitted she had him intrigued, but the next instant the purple oval of the beam terminus appeared.

Kryslie insisted on walking into the beam terminus, but allowed Jonko to transmit her to Earthbase, since he had left her recovered transmitter with Olassa.

Lexina was waiting at the other end, and her expression when she smelt their odour was almost comical, but she made no comment about it.

"I have a bath filling in one of the small private chambers. Come on, I'll show you."

This time, Jonko lifted Kryslie and carried her. She sighed and kept still. "Tymos healed the leg well enough…"

"You've done more than enough," Jonko told her. "You also need food. When was the last time you ate?"

"You are starting to sound like Daniel," Kryslie grimaced, admitting privately that he had a point. "I don't think I can eat anything yet. It will all smell like…what's all over me."

"There is soup," Lexina offered.

"I need to get clean first, and then I will consider it."

"I will organise some perfumed bath salts - I brought some with me. Don't have anything suitable for you though, Jon. You should have warned me? You can use the bath in the next room."

Lexina left Kryslie to bathe herself, returning only to help her drain the first lot of water and replace it with fresh. She left towels and a soft robe nearby.

"Call me if you want me," Lexina offered, keeping her curiosity about what had befallen Kryslie firmly in check.

"Thanks," Kryslie acknowledged, and only referred to her arrival state by adding, "I'm glad Daniel didn't see me like I was. He'd have been upset."

Recalling, belatedly, that Daniel had raised Krys and her brother, she knew it was an understatement. "Yes, he would."

Trouble was, Kryslie thought as she gave herself another all over wash, her energy was returning and the memories of the past few days events were swirling in her mind, making her feel decidedly twitchy. And she was still feeling sullied in her mind. What she had done to bin Halil, even though it had been done at the behest of the Guardians of Peace, had not been nice. It had been rape, mental and physical. Even thinking of it as his just penance for the multitude of horrible things he had condoned, as well as for having her tortured and beaten, didn't help. It lowered her to his level. At least he wouldn't forget the lesson, but he would soon convince himself he had won. However, if the man no longer tried to make the Imperium into the government of the whole world, she had won.

Vincent announced himself moments after Kryslie had finished drying herself and dressing in the robe. With a sigh, she let him come in.

"Who told you I was back?"

"Lexina and Jonko confirmed it," Vincent admitted. "However, I did not need anyone to tell me. I could feel the power returning here."

"I was as limp as a dirty bath towel when I arrived."

"And now?"

"Better."

"The aura here knows you, Great One. You were a power void, ready to be filled…"

"I would rather be alone, Vincent," Kryslie suggested. Great One or not, she wasn't used to giving him orders.

"You have been through a great deal. Let me check you over."

"You are pulling rank as my physician?" Kryslie sighed and accepted the inevitable. "Where do you want me?"

"Lexina prepared a sleeping cubicle for you, just a few openings along."

The short walk along the passage carved from the natural rock, allowed her to feel the clean and pure aura around her. If the soft lights overhead had not been lighting the way, she would have seen the walls glowing mauve. No wonder Vincent had noticed she was back.

When she reached the bed, she lay down without waiting to be told. She thought in passing that Daniel had certainly sourced a high quality local made mattress. It was both soft and supportive. He must have been very busy in the short time since she had last been at Earthbase. The bedding smelt of lavender, which was a scent she knew Daniel liked, but which was not available on Tymorea.

When Kryslie returned her attention to Vincent, he was already using his diagnostic scanner to examine her. His face was completely neutral as he moved the scanner along her body. He was such a highly skilled doctor, that when he finished she was sure that he would know exactly how her body was feeling, and that was the aspects in addition to the healing trauma. He would also be aware of her twitchiness…

Still, he was the only person at Earthbase she could talk to about what she had done. He was after all the brother of one of the Tymorean Governors, would understand expediency, and most importantly, he would not offer judgement on her actions. She as a Great One sometimes had to take harsh action but she didn't know how to start talking of her feelings.

"The fractures, bruises, contusions are well on the way to being healed. The bruising is fading and your power level is coming back up. May I suggest that using the aura is fine, but you still need to eat. You body needs physical substance to maintain itself."

She knew he was right, but, "I really don't feel like eating."

"Do you feel like talking about what happened to you? It should help ease the twitchy feeling, since I do not advise a strenuous workout for a few days yet."

He was right, if she couldn't work things through physically, she needed to talk it out.

"The Guardians used me, Vincent." She glanced at him and saw the fleeting look of surprise. He had not expected that. Not here on Earth. He turned to draw up a chair and when he was seated, his face was composed.

"I let myself be caught. I was the only one who had any chance of getting close to the instigator of the escalating trouble."

"He? Do I assume it is the man you mentioned on your last visit?"

"Yes, Abdul bin Halil…that's why I had to be the bait."

Vincent nodded, he understood.

"I knew he wouldn't have me killed until had a chance to personally question me and torment me. He would have no way of knowing that the PFS neutralised the worst of the force of the beatings. To do what I had to do, I had to be close to him…"

Kryslie stopped talking, but Vincent merely waited for her to continue.

"I had to break him," she continued abruptly. "I made him a gibbering wreck…and then I had to mend him. I had to get right into his mind. He wasn't sane, although he masked it well. I knew that from when I conceived Arthur. At that time, I used his latent power hungry tendencies and channelled them into the idea of uniting all the then unaligned countries. I now know the methods he used. He is more than a little bit psychopathic. So I broke him and made him what he needed to be."

Once she had started, Kryslie found it easier to tell to Vincent everything she had done. It did not seem to shock him, and he accepted it without comment. Perhaps it was because she was a Great One acting on behalf of the Guardians of Peace. Whatever the reason, she was grateful.

When she finally stopped speaking, Vincent merely asked, "Do you feel that you succeeded?"

The question forced Kryslie to take a mental step back to think of her 'work' from a less immediate, distance.

"I think the experience profoundly terrified him. However, I think, with time, he will begin to revert to his previous ways. His current organisation will be neutralised by the IC. He is alive still, only because he is the only man able to keep the Imperium from collapsing back into individual states."

"Will you need to return there to maintain the man's attitude?"

"He will have no more chances - while he abides by the idea of peace, and allows his people their basic human rights, he can keep his money and power…and his life. And I agree with Tymos, I should not go back there. He tried and failed to order his guards to kill me, but his inferiors know his ways, and two of the guards tried anyway. He will come to believe I am dead, and his secrets are safe."

"If I may ask, Great One, as your physician, what has unsettled you?"

Kryslie looked away from Vincent before speaking.

"They used my intimate knowledge of him to get their message through. I know his weaknesses, what revolts him and what he craves."

"And afterwards?" Vincent asked.

"I did my absolute best to heal what I had done to him."

"Ah…" Vincent understood. "Perhaps you should talk to Jono. Of all of us, his connection to the Guardians is strongest since he bears the Sword of Judgement."

"Perhaps I should," Krys realised. The Tymorean President probably did know what it felt like to be used by the Guardians. "But right now, despite the long hot bath, I feel like I need to stay in the sonic shower for months and follow it with a very long soak in freezing water."

Vincent smiled faintly, Kryslie was reading her own state with great accuracy.

"I can assure you that you do not need to fear any after effects of your recent immersion, but apart from that, I do understand your current disposition. I offer a suggestion, and no one will judge you ill if you act on it. You need to purge what you are feeling…with one whose mind is relatively pure…and who is completely trustworthy."

Krys knew how she was feeling, and blushed. She was not innocent, and knew what he meant.

"And not my brother," Krys managed to tell him she understood. "Send Jon in, would you?"

Chapter 21- A traitor must live

Jonko returned to the Imperium after he had eaten breakfast. He called it that because his body was still on Imperium time. Tymos had passed on a request from Chalmers for him to act as secretary during the official IC visit to Abdul bin Halil.

He felt extremely pleased, for it meant that Chalmers recognised the importance of the work done by the Tymoreans, and that Jonko himself had impressed the IC Director. Tymos wanted him to be inserted into that organisation.

Yet those realisations did not eclipse the unexpectedness of the previous night. Kryslie had asked for him, and they had purged a mutual need in a very pleasant way. He knew it didn't imply any future commitment, because a Great One couldn't be tied down. But she trusted him not to betray her period of need, or to speak of what they had shared. He was fulfilled by helping her to regain her equilibrium.

"JON!"

Jonko jerked his attention back to the conversation he was having with Tymos in the vacant shop in Hadjibad. For a moment, he wondered if his friend knew where is thoughts had been, and he looked for any change of expression.

Tymos simply repeated what he had been saying. "We know that Chalmers won't find anything to use against him, but I want your evaluation of the man. Krys worked on him before he sent her off, but he's had time to sleep and get over the initial impact of his treatment."

"Right!" Jonko tried to sound alert. "Where will you be?"

"Chalmers is happy for me to go with the team interviewing the people wearing gold stars. The ones they brought in yesterday have had a night to consider their position. Their unguarded thought should tell me who are dupes and who are not."

"Can I tell Chalmers that Krys is safe?"

"No, I'll do that later."

"Okay, I'll go across the road and meet him."

Keleb wandered out of the rear room, rubbing his eyes and yawning.

"He didn't ask about Klim and if we had found the bolt hole."

"No," Tymos agreed neutrally. His sister had not completely shielded herself from him the previous night, so he was aware of where Jonko's thoughts had been.

"So, when will you be telling Chalmers?

"After he has spoken to bin Halil. Let the bastard think all his records are safe and he is in the clear. Before I do, I will have Olassa block any transmissions into that bolt hole and Edik can watch for transmissions into the palace in Karshada."

Belatedly, Keleb thought to ask, "How is Krys this morning?"

"Cleaner," Tymos said immediately. And much calmer, he knew.

Keleb laughed. "That's not what I meant."

"She is having to deal with Daniel's fussing, but other than that, she's fine. She said it is past time that she checked on the few missionaries that we didn't relocate to the Imperium."

"What do you want me to do?" Keleb had put a kettle on the tiny stove so that he could make coffee, and was in the process of getting bread out to toast. Olassa had only brought in very basic supplies.

"Just keep in touch with the people I sent to look for the rest of the gold star wearers. I'm hoping that the word won't spread as quickly to those who are not living in Jafhabad or Karshada, but I want them all questioned. Some of them have to be part of the elite in the so called League."

"Makes sense," Keleb agreed as Tymos's portable phone rang. "The Imperium covers a wide area."

Tymos glanced at the phone and muttered, "Chalmers" before answering it with, "Hello Sir, how can I help you?"

"You can come and join me in the Justice Building before I leave for Karshada. I am holding a briefing and I want to talk to you."

"Yes, Sir, I will be there quickly."

Tymos frowned slightly as he ended the call. He wasn't ready for Chalmers's questions, but he couldn't refuse to talk to him.

"Message me if you hear anything important," Tymos requested of Keleb. Then, without delaying further, he transmitted to a building several buildings away and walked briskly from there.

The borrowed office seemed full of people as Chalmers briefed those who were going to be questioning the important men who wore gold stars. He outlined the information he wanted and stressed the importance of politeness. He sent some of those present off to bring in more of the gold wearers.

When the room was almost empty, he introduced Tymos to one of his senior team leaders, Tarrant Yo. Then he challenged Tymos.

"There have to more of these top echelon members. Have you any more information?"

"I'm working on it," Tymos admitted, returning the intent gaze with one of his own. "No doubt you have considered that not all will be in this city."

"Indeed," Chalmers agreed. "Now, by you, I assume that means others of your group as well?"

Tymos nodded, aware that Jonko, who had been standing back out of the way, was staring intently at him. He touched his friend's mind and sensed, "Sorry, Tym, he tricked me."

Chalmers's sharp question dragged his attention back to the Director.

"I believe you found your sister."

"Yes, late last night. She was in a bad way and not very talkative. I was waiting for an update when you called."

Chalmers became more sympathetic. He didn't ask for details, just asked, "Do you think she can tell us any more if I sent someone to see her?"

"What say I have her contact you in a day or two?" Tymos countered. He didn't want to explain that his sister was half way around the world.

"Yes, it can wait. Do you have any more than that snippet of film that you showed me?"

"There's more and you will have it today."

"She let herself be caught, didn't she? Was it worth it?"

"I hope so," Tymos said soberly. "You will have to tell me. We hoped to draw out whoever was behind this business."

"General Thek," Chalmers suggested. "And did you hear that the Justice Minister disappeared from our locked down building?"

"Through the tunnel Jon mentioned?" Tymos proposed.

"Likely. We do not believe he was abducted, but rather he went voluntarily - not realising we already knew of the basement area."

Tymos nodded, not commenting. Chalmers had not taken his disconcertingly direct gaze off him.

"Is there more about this business that you haven't told me?"

Tymos did not look away as he admitted, "I have had people trying to locate the bolt hole that General Thek vanished into. We have a general location - somewhere near the university."

He wasn't lying, just not telling all the truth.

"What makes you think he didn't just flee the country?"

"How many people know that you found the hidden records and got access to the secondary computer network?"

"Two. Jon here and Don Ypres. Are you implying he thinks nothing can be proved against him?"

"That was one thought, but," Tymos looked at his feet and shuffled his right foot, as if feeling guilty.

"Hmm...I kind of had a communications detector set up around this building. Just before you arrived, a call came in - from that area - warning of your raid. I couldn't trace it though. And that video stream was going somewhere."

That did startle Chalmers. "I would like a record...if you kept one...of everything you intercepted."

"Umm, are you legitimising my interceptions?"

"You are being too modest. We would have been ignorant of many threats to peace and human rights if you had not approached us. Yes, I will say I authorised it, but...I expect you to help me update my present equipment to the same standard."

"Certainly, and I will redesign your portable analytic devices to increase their sensitivity, if you agree to keep my name and that of my sister, out of any reports about this business."

"I will need a statement from your sister."

"Will it be acceptable if she uses the name she adopted when coming back into this country?"

"That will do. And I will not ask how she came by such an excellently forged identification. Do you have concerns for her safety?"

"Partly. Those involved will not rest if she if free and able to talk."

A grim smile flitted onto Chalmers face. "That film is enough to put General Thek and his interrogator into the death cells." He paused thoughtfully. "I find it hard to believe that this cabal has been going for a long time with out the Leader of the Imperium being aware of it."

To detract from that line of thought, Tymos remarked, "It is insidious - a few rabid members of an organisation that purports to be highly altruistic, hiding behind dozens who are misguided dupes. I am sure many of the gold star wearers have no idea what they are donating to."

"We have judicial process to follow. Any who are innocent will be released. Though I will put the fear of their God into them, so they will not be so foolish again. They will think I will have them under observation for the rest of their days."

Chalmers glanced around and caught Jonko's eye. "I have a plane waiting. I will be eager to hear your thoughts after the interviews."

At the end of a long day, Tymos returned to Earthbase well satisfied with the day's work. Jonko and Keleb arrived later so they could discuss everything with Kryslie present. She was glad for their presence since Daniel was fussing and could not believe that Tymos had healed her. They met in the small private chamber she was using, and she had commandeered several extra chairs.

After hearing that Chalmers wished to speak to her, Kryslie said she would wait several days before contacting him.

"A good idea. He is likely to be very busy for a time," was Tymos's opinion. He went on,

"Jon, what is your analysis of his interview with bin Halil?"

Kryslie leaned forward in her chair to listen.

"Outwardly, he has the same derisive arrogance," Jonko began. "But it is bravado, no more than a memory of his former confidence. Lot's of little things betrayed him - his eyes kept flicking to each of us, his fingers were never still, and so on. I am sure Chalmers picked up on that too. He quoted the standard dogma that we have heard about the League. When Chalmers all but accused him of knowing that it was really a subversive organization, he denied any such knowledge. We couldn't shake him on that point. He offered to help the IC investigate the claims, since it was 'obvious' that 'they' were after his position."

"Which if we didn't know better, might be believable," Kryslie murmured.

"Then Chalmers brought you into the conversation," Jonko said, and seeing Kryslie eying him intently, hastily added, "He referred to you as Helaine, and claimed that you had made accusations against him."

"That's going to suggest that I got away from his men," Kryslie said. "Damn the man, I wanted bin Halil to think I was dead."

"That shook him. I could smell his fear. He demanded the opportunity to face his accuser…"

"I wish I could have called his bluff," Kryslie said. "I could tie his mind in tighter knots and no one would know it."

"He didn't stop sweating until Chalmers said you were missing, but he used that as a way of introducing the video to bring up the corruption in the Justice Department. Naturally, he acted like he knew nothing about a video. But that was another shock. I think he thought his private satellite link could not be hacked."

"Maybe not be anyone trained here," Tymos interrupted. "He's going to realise he isn't invulnerable."

"I really think he has begun to realise that," Jonko said.

"It won't hurt for him to think that there is a time bomb waiting to destroy him," Kryslie suggested. "It might help keep him honest. Anything else?"

Jonko shook his head. "Chalmers wasn't satisfied, but his hands are tied. He has no evidence against the man."

"I need binHalil to think that his man managed to kill and dump me," Kryslie told her brother.

Keleb inserted a comment. "Bin Halil has people looking for two particular guards.

"The two who took Kryslie from the palace are dead." Jonko knew Kryslie had killed them, but saved her the need to admit it.

"Well bin Halil will have to keep guessing," Keleb was satisfied with that idea. "I checked with Edik, he didn't make any calls out after Chalmers left."

"He knows his comm-lines are compromised, and may be expecting the IC to be monitoring anything he sends out." Kryslie hoped bin Halil was worried. "Tym, did you tell Chambers about the General's bolt hole?"

"Yes, when he got back. I sent him everything we found out about the place. He is organising a raid there."

"So do we just sit back now and watch?" Keleb asked.

"Yep!" Tymos shrugged. "We can't do all their work for them, and they have to proceed according to standing directives. And this way, when they find the records Klim took there, they won't think we had any part of it."

"There is something I want done - not necessarily now," Kryslie turned to look at her twin. "When you made that deal to keep our names out of the databases of the IC, have you thought about other databases we might be mentioned in?"

"Who else knows you by name?" Jonko asked.

Without facing him, Kryslie explained, "When we stopped skipping in time, we attended the WSRA Washington University for five years…"

Jonko guessed that had made a name for themselves, but so?

Kryslie sensed the question and sighed. "We had to drop out of sight after that because we had started to realise that we were not aging like everyone else. I convinced bin Halil that I was the child of someone he met thirty years ago, and that was logical since who would believe we skipped ahead twenty years. However, if people start taking too much interest in us, we'd lose the anonymity we need to do our work as missionaries. And if bin Halil were to accidentally find a reference to me, as me, my treatment of his mind may not hold."

"Do you intend to change your name and move around all the time?" Keleb asked.

"We might have to," Tymos admitted. "Any way, Krys has a point and I will create a robot virus to scan the internet and change any reference to us. But that can wait. I'm hungry and I am sure Chalmers will want Jon and me, when he is finished with his raid."

Keleb had the strangest feeling, like dread. "The damage may already have been done," he blurted. "What if bin Halil circulated your picture before you treated his mind?"

His statement made both Tymos and Kryslie go tense. They had no answer, but felt they needed to be back in Hadjibad soon.

Chalmers was still using the office in the Justice Building when Kryslie called to see him early the following morning. A sense of dread caused her to change her mind about waiting several days. She was heavily disguised, and clad in the long skirt and head covering that was traditional amongst the people of Jafhabad and surrounding countries.

She had entered when Chalmers's aide was on an errand and not available to announce her and slipped into the inner office with out disturbing the Director's concentration. In the short time that she waited, she had her hand in a pocket, manipulating a detector scanner device to check the office for threats. A faint vibration indicated that none had been detected. She sent a thought to Tymos, who had found nothing in the office being used by Tarrant Yo for interviews.

Jonko and several of the new Tymorean missionaries were covertly checking the rest of the building, even though the IC had checked the building thoroughly the night before, when they had received an anonymous warning. They had taken the threat seriously, and had sent home most of the staff who usually worked in the building. In the foyer, they had brought in scanners to detect weapons, explosives and signs of other terror devices.

Even so, there were still a large number of people coming and going. Many were silver star wearers awaiting their chance to convince the IC of their innocence, there were some of the gold wearers brought in from other places within the Imperium. These had come with their legal representatives and other retainers.

"Director Chalmers," Kryslie announced her presence by greeting him.
"Miss W…" Chalmers started to speak as he stood abruptly in surprise.
"Helaine."
Chalmers nodded and gestured to a seat. "Your brother implied that it would be several days before you would be able to see me. I feel bad about all you suffered."
"Director, I knew what I was doing and was acting on my own initiative. You have no need to apologise. Have you enough evidence to quell the unlawful subversive group?"
"We can certainly take the investigation from here. I will say that you seemed to be the catalyst that began to crack the façade of the conspiracy. You were taking an awful risk. If I had known I would have never…"
"That was why I did not tell you how I planned to threaten their grandiose plans. Despite the changes in the past decades, the men here do not expect women to be a real threat. They expected me to be the weak link in what they feared was a plot against them."
"I am impressed that you proved them wrong. They expected to be able to break you. I am impressed again, that they didn't."
"They were working under a misconception," Kryslie smiled faintly. "The first was that I was weak. I'm not, and I have a naturally high tolerance for pain. And, I had taken a large dose of slow release pain dampers."
That could be a description of how she had used Tymorean pain blocking techniques. However, the explanation satisfied Chalmers, and seemed to explain the anomaly that had puzzled him.
"It didn't give me any protection against their revolting drug. My brother knew that, so when he realised that I was likely to reveal our ruse,

he blocked that video uplink. By then, the General had vacated the room, puzzled by some odd power fluctuations."

"So how did you get lose?"

"Well, the General rang my interrogator and warned him of your expected visit, the bastard almost panicked. He had orders to get me away, and I took the opportunity presented by being out of the building to escape."

"We have your interrogator, and the General - both are being held in a high security prison. The interrogator is telling us everything we want to know, and may escape a death sentence. The General will not."

"Good. I feel some sympathy for the Interrogator - he was acting under orders. The general - he really didn't care what it took to make me talk."

"Perhaps you would be prepared to write a statement, and out in as much as you can about your captivity. If it does not upset you."

"I can do this," Kryslie agreed, then added. "I also picked up a great deal of information about the scientific community in the Imperium. I think you should investigate the Scientific Research labs in each region. They are probably legitimate, but there has to be others that are hidden."

"Your brother mentioned missing UWN scientists. Is this what you are thinking of?"

"Yes, but there may be another secret lab, because Tymos detected a data dump from every computer at the science fair. That was on the third day, just before Harrison attacked me."

She had no logical way to explain how Tymos had learnt that an extra satellite had been inserted into Earth's orbit, so she proposed it as a way out theory with the question, "Could the Imperium have deployed their own satellite?"

"Your brother did not mention the data upload to me, but perhaps that is understandable. Can you add anything else that you know that might ne useful, to that statement? I will have your ideas looked into."

It suited her to type slowly on the data pad Chalmers let her use, pretending her arm was more damaged than it was, for while she was there, she could be alert to threats. He was an obvious target, as director of the IC.

The detector in her pocket remained quiet, and so she was startled during the middle of the afternoon, when Tymos sent a mental shout of warning to her mind. "Get Chalmers out of there!"

It was like an electric shock through the deep twin bond. Without even pausing to ask 'why', Kryslie reached over the desk and grabbed Chalmers by the wrist, grabbed the data pad and shoved it in pocket in her dress. The same one that contained her transmitter.

The blast came as they were dematerialising.

Her destination had been instinctive, and she materialised again in the foyer of the building. Chalmers was leaning on her, disorientated by the blast, and the unfamiliar and inexplicable sensation of matter/energy transmission. Then, knowing that she could never explain how she had taken him from the first floor office to the ground floor in an instant, she stayed only long enough for the explosion and the showering of debris to subside before tucking his data pad in his hand and transmitting away. In that brief moment, Kryslie knew that Tymos had taken Tarrant Yo to safety in the same way, but had not tried to save the man they were interviewing. The bomb had been strapped to him, and Tymos had only sensed it in the instant he had detonated it.

They met amongst the milling crowd of onlookers, and people running out of the building.

"How did he get that bomb in there?" Kryslie asked. "What did we miss?"

The alarm bells of the fire trucks and ambulances were only now approaching.

"The stuff could have been in the building," Tymos said. "And the IC missed it. Even I didn't pick it up until the instant he decided to detonate the bomb. He thought in that moment that if he killed all the IC people, the League would be safe."

Tymos drew out a communicator and made a general call. "All team members report."

Jonko was the first to reply. "Thank the Guardians. Is Krys also safe?"

"Yes, where are you?"

"Second floor. I was checking the room where the gold wearers were and suddenly felt something was wrong. The last of the stubborn old goats obeyed my order to get down, instants before the plate glass wall blasted into fragments. I'm guiding them down the fire stairs."

"Chalmers is in the foyer near the door - when you get down, stick with him."

One by one the seven other missionaries reported. All were helping the shocked, dazed or injured to get out of the building.

"We need to blend in," Kryslie said quickly. She glanced around and removed the blouse and ankle length skirt to reveal an outfit suited to the local suit-wearing business men. Tymos glanced around and adjusted his eyes to see further. "There are some spare fireproof jackets hanging on the truck over there."

Moments later, two of the jackets vanished, and Tymos and Kryslie transmitted back to the first floor where a fiercely hot inferno had yet to be reached with hoses.

Tymos began on one side and Kryslie on the other, finding unconscious victims and transmitting them to the foyer. From there, other rescuers helped them to ambulances or the area set aside for triage.

The people on the upper levels were disorientated by the blast and the smoke rapidly saturating the air. They responded to the calm orders of the Tymoreans and were led down the stairs and out the back doors. from there they went around to the assembly points and identified themselves.

The Tymoreans immediately transmitted back into the building to look for more trapped people.

Tymos and Kryslie were unaffected by the fire's heat. It was energy, and they could draw on it and use it to create a protective zone around them and the victims they brought out. They stayed with each until someone came to the victim, and then went back again. Their mental count came to twelve dead and twenty-three badly injured, when they finally retrieved the last of the victims.

On one of her flits to the ground floor, a still dazed Chalmers had challenged her. "Where have you come from?"

He did not recognise her, "Upstairs. I heard this man calling out and helped him down."

"That's Martin!" Chalmers said. "Did you see a woman up there? Short, dark hair…"

He described what Kryslie had worn to see him.

Truthfully, although misleadingly, Kryslie told him, "No, I'm sorry. You should check the assembly area."

"She was with me on the first floor. She must have pushed me out of the way."

"Sir, the first floor is an inferno. If she didn't get out immediately, there is little hope that she is alive."

Chalmers watched her carry his assistant out to the doctors, and had no idea that the woman transmitted back into the fiery inferno.

Tymos stayed with the doctors after the last of the victims from the first floor were out. He noticed Thomas and Ferdinand, Louis's human friends, helping with the victims and gave them a nod of acknowledgement. He also spotted Bevan, the medic that had been with Olassa'a advance team, as he told the doctors that he had first aid training and could help. The doctors never questioned his statement, just set him to work covering the burns victims with sterile sheets and applying saline solution. Kryslie joined him later. After they worked with each successive patient, they were replaced by other Tymoreans, so that they could help as many as they could. The new missionaries remembered that Tymos could heal, and Kryslie had a touch of that gift, and they were giving them the chance to save lives.

Those who had been working in the Justice Building on various pretexts, continued to guide workers on the upper floors down the fire steps, through the thick smoke, and out to the fresher air. As soon as one group was safe, they returned to look for other trapped or smoke affected people. Then they joined Thomas and Ferdinand who were making lists of everyone who had got out.

When the fire was contained, all the people that could be saved were out, the Tymoreans slipped away. The Tymorean born missionaries who had met the descendents, invited them to join them at the shop across the road. While they waited, they exchanged stories, and the descendents heard what Kryslie and Tymos had been doing. When the Great Ones arrived, grime covered and smelling of burnt flesh and acrid smoke, everyone in the room bowed.

Tymos and Kryslie felt the sincere veneration of the new missionaries and the awe of the descendants, and felt their faces flush under the grime.

"We did not do it all," Tymos protested quietly. "Each of you helped, and each of you deserve the blessing of the Guardians."

Olassa spoke for all the missionaries, "I know what you were doing, Prince Tymos - it was thanks to you that more people did not die. And Princess Kryslie was keeping the bad ones alive until you reached them. The humans are speaking of the miracle that the injuries were not worse, and the death toll was not higher."

"Have you any idea why this was done? It seems so senseless," Markos asked.

"It was senseless! Though we should have expected something - this League for the Improvement of the Imperium, which was a front for an attempt at world domination, is finished. Those who hoped to gain power and importance, have failed. This was a last ditch attempt to stop the IC investigation." Kryslie's anger at the dead bomber was evident.

Tymos provided a further comment. "The fool behind this day's horror, thought he could frighten off the IC, but he made it worse. Every former sovereign state in the Imperium, will need to prove their adherence to the Peace Treaty of 2057. Administrators will be appointed for each regional government, until the IC and the World Council are satisfied."

"Is there more that we need to do?" Olassa asked, once again, including all the missionaries.

Tymos shook his head, beginning to feel tired and weak.

"Olassa, you Markos, Alen and Edik should keep monitoring events. Jon can keep tabs on Chalmers, hopefully quashing any weird ideas he may have got about us. The rest of you should go back to the tasks you were doing before we dragged you here."

Most of the Tymorean born missionaries transmitted away, but Olassa stayed, as did the local born people. Many in the latter group, including Tomas and Ferdinand, were still staring at where so many people had suddenly vanished.

To distract the ones who had never seen or experienced the transmissions before, Kryslie asked Olassa, "Have you met everyone here before?"

"Only some, Princess Kryslie. I would like to meet them all."

Thomas's eyes were so wide with surprise they looked to be bulging out. "What are you?" he asked Kryslie. Ferdinand was almost as bad.

"I am what you have always known - a worker for peace."

"No. I mean, I listened to what those others were saying you were doing. No one can do that - go into a fire like that and survive."

Tymos laughed. "The Imperium does not have the latest technology - and that is something that should be addressed. Krys and I have some special equipment - I'll show you something."

He pressed a spot on his leg and a fine wire mesh appeared over the exposed part of his skin. "This is what enabled us to do what we did. It wasn't magic."

Olassa frowned, since they were not meant to reveal Tymorean technology to locals, but she kept quiet. After Tymos had activated the force screen again, and it was invisible, he introduced the two humans who had worked with Louis, to Olassa. Then she understood. These two men did not know about Tymoreans.

"These two know all there is to know about Hadjibad," Tymos went on, and then he explained to the local men that he and Kryslie needed to be elsewhere, and would they object to working with Olassa, who would be taking over any further investigations in the city.

Both men agreed. For they both knew they owed their lives to Kryslie, and had been instrumental in discovering the conspiracy that threatened the rights of the people in the Imperium.

After Olassa had met all the locally based descendents, and they had left in twos and threes, she spoke bluntly. "You won't be doing any more work here?"

Kryslie shook her head. "We had to reveal our abilities to get Chalmers and Yo out of danger. They were targeted because of our actions. We have the perfect opportunity to disappear, without trace. Jon can take over, since we want him to be inserted into the IC. You and he can do any follow up that is needed."

"There was another consideration," Tymos added. "Bin Halil should not come after Krys, or send people to find her, but if there are any more zealots like the bomber, they might take up the crusade without being told. It is better that the IC thinks her dead, so that if anyone in the Imperium infiltrates their data base that is what they will find."

Olassa queried the mention of the Imperium's leader.

"Is he involved?"

"He is to be left alone," Kryslie said, speaking in a tone that to Olassa recognised as an order.

She merely murmured an acknowledgement.

"We will be following the IC investigation and the outcomes from Earthbase," Kryslie told her.

Tymos and Kryslie requested the long-range beam to get them back to Earthbase. Once there, they avoided Daniel until after they had bathed and eaten. He had heard some of the happenings from other missionaries as they passed through on their return to their normal duties.

"Tell me about it?" Daniel demanded.

"Daniel…" Kryslie tried to suggest he desist, but he didn't.

"As Coordinator, I need to keep up to date with world events. That bombing was on every video news network."

With a sigh, Tymos began to give the full, un-edited details. Daniel's face grew lined with the horror. He did not seem to comprehend the full degree of danger that they had needed to face to save people, just the deaths and injuries.

"We did what we could, Daniel," Kryslie assured him. "We have abilities and we helped many of the victims. And it wasn't just us. Did you send the extra missionaries to help?"

Daniel nodded.

"They were magnificent, all of them, even the descendents of the former missionaries. They all deserve recognition, and I have an idea. When the base is finished, I want to invite them all here. And I want to have a live video link between here and Homebase, so the missionary descendents can meet their many generations removed kinfolk. They deserve that."

As she had hoped, the idea distracted Earthbase's Coordinator.

"There is still so much to do," Daniel recalled.

"We will help, but we have time. The IC will be busy tying up details and then there will be the trials," Tymos reminded him.

"Yes, that is true," Daniel's worried expression cleared. Then he reverted to normal. "Both of you look like you should be in bed. I don't want to see either of you until tomorrow at this time."

They agreed meekly, but although they seemed to go to their separate sleeping chambers, Kryslie transmitted to her brother's chamber to await further reports from Jonko, Olassa or Edik. Keleb came in to wait with them. During that time, Tymos prepared the specifications for improved communications detectors and advanced portable scanners. He would have Jonko deliver it to Chalmers, to ease his grief at their perceived death.

Jonko returned for a short while, several hours later.

"Chalmers refused to stay in hospital. He insisted he was well enough and went back to his hotel. He has been teleconferencing with the Wold Council. They are sending a care-taker committee to Hadjibad, and an oversight committee to Karshada."

"Standing down the Imperium's Government?" Tymos stated with surprise. "On what grounds."

"That suicide bomber. He left behind a missive, which as well as saying it was a protest against those who would destroy the Imperium. He claims he was protecting the Leader."

"Damn," Tymos cursed, rising from a chair to pace the room. Jonko's report had sent a strong shiver down his spine - a premonition of something terrible to come. "Bin Halil won't stand for having his sovereignty threatened. Jon, I need you to get back, I want to know the bastard's reaction."

Kryslie and Tymos simply exchanged glances. They both knew too much about how bin Halil used to think. They foresaw another purge – like after the war. Back then, he discarded all those who had helped him to power, but who failed to deliver the UWN to him. Neither could tell how he would react since Kryslie had 'treated' his mind. They would have to wait.

A full day passed before Jonko returned. His expression was sombre.

"Bin Halil, he…the bastard repudiated every one of the group that were identified as leaders. He told Chalmers that they were traitors and he would personally see them all punished."

"No. They will be tried in the World Court. For the General, they have enough to get him the death penalty any way." Tymos knew that for a certainty.

"And the Justice Minister. I heard that they had discovered he was the Finance Minister here during the war. He had a bounty on him already."

Tymos raised his eyebrows in surprise. "I didn't realise that. What about Klim?"

"He was repudiated too, like the rest. Moreover, bin Halil was insisting that everyone involved in the conspiracy be tried in the Imperium. He meant everyone, all the gold star wearers and the silver star wearers." Jonko was truly horrified. "He wants them to get the death penalty too."

"It's what he did last time, after the war," Kryslie said.

"Is there nothing we can do?" Jonko pleaded.

"No, Jon. We can't interfere anymore. If the World Council has sent in administrators to oversee the Imperium, bin Halil has no say. They will follow the laws and policies of the World Council."

"But the leader, he will be back in power after all the trials are over," Jonko protested.

Kryslie went and took Jonko to a seat. "Jon, we have to leave bin Halil alone for now."

"Why?"

"We obey the Guardians, Jon. We are their Advocates, and they have seen that he is the only one who can keep the Imperium together."

"It doesn't seem fair."

"Tymos and I agree, but one day, he will pay for all his hidden crimes, his callousness, and for his very existence."

Jonko seemed to hear a rumbling like thunder when she spoke. It was odd, since they were underground, but he felt the promise in her words, and realised that this was a promise from the Guardians of Peace.

Epilogue

Earthbase's large hall was resplendent - brightly lit and decorated like the ballroom of some royal palace. At first glance, no one would think that they were below fifteen feet of solid rock and with a radioactive wasteland above. The carved rock walls of the cavern were disguised by wall screens that showed windows with a nighttime view of fabulous gardens. Several passages led to restrooms and the kitchens, and these might have graced the most expensive hotels in any capital city. One doorway from the hall led to a garden with real plants, and faint breezes that smelt like nighttime in a tropical garden. The lighting in there was set to emulate night, with a deep indigo sky full of pinpoints of light and lights at ankle level to light the paths that cut though the enclosed garden. This had been the self-appointed task of the Great Ones, who amazed everyone with how they had forced the plants to grow quickly.

Unobtrusive force fields blocked the other passages, so that no one wandered into the labyrinthine tunnels, or accidentally found the passage leading to the outside.

The Tymorean born missionaries transmitted to Earthbase over the course of the preceding days. Daniel put them all to work, inserting the finishing touches, and arranging accommodation for those who wished to stay over after the celebration.

Jenala, Beth, Lexina and a team of missionary descendents who were too old for active work, had spent days preparing the food, all of the ingredients were fresh and transmitted in by Keleb from local and more distant markets. As each new delicacy was finished, the trays were placed in racks in a specially made stasis chamber so that they would stay fresh until the time of the party.

Everything was ready when Tymos and Kryslie, clad in Earth style evening dress, left to escort the first groups of missionary descendents to the celebration. They believed it was to celebrate the end of the threat of war, and the new era for the Imperium, but they would find that they were to be the guests of honour.

All of the still living descendents of the former missionaries that had continued the work of their ancestors, as well as those who had retired, or who were still young and untrained, were invited.

Those with human spouses brought them too, having admitted to them a secret that they had kept for years. Some accepted it with amazement and excitement, others felt betrayed and apprehensive by the revelation that the mate they loved was alien. When Kryslie spoke to them, allaying their fears, disbelief turned to wonder.

Though the Tymorean descendents were escorted first, Kryslie did not forget Tomas and Ferdinand. They had been loyal to Louis, and indirectly to the Tymorean cause. Since learning of the Tymoreans, and seeing some of the abilities of Tymos and Kryslie, they had enthusiastically volunteered to continue helping them. It was not simply that they owed their lives to Kryslie, they had seen wonders and their minds had seen vistas that had never been available to the citizens of the Imperium. To them, alien was just another kind of foreign.

Meeting up again with Louis, settled the few lingering doubts and their eyes lit up with suppressed excitement when they accepted Daniel's offer of being special consultants, with respect to Imperium customs.

Once everyone had arrived and the Tymorean born missionaries were mingling with the descendents, and everyone was relaxed and enjoying themselves, and listening to the piped Tymorean music, Tymos and Kryslie slipped away from the party to change into their silver and gold 'robes of state'. These had been sent from Tymorea, especially for the occasion, and Kryslie had specified that the golden hooded cape have only a very short train, and her 'robes' consist of a split skirt, rather than a clinging skirt and the full long sleeved shirt, identical to that which Tymos would wear.The shirts, skirt and Tymos's full trousers, were all made with slits that revealed the silvery lining.

Lexina offered to help Kryslie with her hair, which was to be braided and coiled, and held in place by the silver and gold ribbons threaded through it. She returned to the party, leaving the Great Ones to wait for Vincent's cue to transmit back into the hall.

Vincent, acting as the Master of Ceremonies, walked onto a low podium, set in front of a wall screen displaying a series of scenes from Tymorea.

"I would like to have everybody's attention…"

Everyone turned his way as the screen behind him went to pure white. He began speaking, addressing his speech to the missionary descendents, as he spoke about Tymorea. The screen behind him began to show scenes of everyday life in the towns and cities of Tymorea.

He explained in general terms, the origin of the Tymorean Trust, and what it meant in terms of helping to maintain peace on all worlds. He moved on to talk of why the missionaries of nearly a century in Earth's past, had been recalled and of the recent war on Tymorea and the work of the Great Ones in restoring that world. As he mentioned them, an image of Llaimos, taken in the Great Hall of the High King's palace, appeared on the wall screen. Tymos and Kryslie transmitted to the podium and seemed to be part of the same picture.

"This celebration is not just because we succeeded in neutralising a dire threat to Earth's new state of peace, but because two generations of Tymorean missionaries united together, in a unique way. Those of you who were born here, and are the descendents of those who worked with me here before the war, may I formally introduce you to Tymos and Kryslie, Great Ones of Tymorea, Prince and Princess of the Royal House of Tymoros, and Heir designates to the Governorship of Tymorea."

Vincent stepped aside, and the wall screen blanked again to white. The Tymoreans had edged backwards, so that the descendents were in a group in front of the podium. As one, they were staring at Tymos and Kryslie as if they were strangers.

"We are still the same people that you have helped over the years, and because of what we are and the importance of our work, we want to give you the honour that is due to each of you," Kryslie explained.

Tymos continued, "When the missionaries were recalled to Tymorea, at our command, we had no idea that their children chose to remain and carry on the work of their parents. That this trust was carried on until our return is an act of faith unsurpassed in Tymorean history.

"Each and everyone of you deserves the highest possible accolade, and we, as the Advocates of the Guardians of Peace, are humbled by what you and your antecedents have done."

"When the original missionaries were recalled, nearly a century ago in Earth's time," Kryslie began to explain, "We needed their knowledge and experience to help fight a deadly enemy and to preserve our people from annihilation. That was achieved and all classes of Tymoreans slipped into a period of stasis as the world outside the protected places was cleansed and renewed. During that time, the people did not age, and so, those former Earth missionaries are still alive on Tymorea, and they wish to add their own personal tributes to you - their distant descendents."

Now on the screen behind them, the image of Llaimos returned, this time with the three Tymorean Governors, and the images were live, not static.

High King Governor Tymoros, introduced himself, then Llaimos and his fellow Governors, speaking to the group of people he saw on a screen set in front of him, in the Great Hall of his palace.

"You are all greatly honoured, to have assisted the Great Ones in their work, and I am honoured to present those who are your kin here on Tymorea."

A group of people assembled around Tymoros, and one by one, he introduced the former missionaries.

At Earthbase, the descendents looked as if they were seeing a vision of Nirvana. Everyone of them had learnt the names of their antecedents - all the way back to the people now appearing before them.

For the benefit of those who were far away on Tymorea, Tymos and Kryslie took turns at reciting the genealogies of each descendent in turn, beginning with the children that these missionaries had left behind.

Tymos made special mention of Rhyn, the former coordinator of the descendents, who had kept the faith alive, as had his parents and grandparents, and helped assure the success of the current Earth Mission.

Kryslie took over, and for the benefit of the Tymorean Governors, spoke of Tamir Janzoet, and the reasons he had remained on Earth, defying the recall. She explained that he had safeguarded his vital work, and after his death, his son had continued to do so, and had gone on to help forge the basis for a lasting peace.

They ceded the limelight to the Tymorean President, who spoke from Tymorea. Eyes were drawn to him as he stood with hands resting on the hilt of the magnificent and bejewelled Sword of Judgement. He held it with the point just touching the floor.

His words were an old Tymorean benediction, but as he spoke, the jewels on the sword began to scintillate with a light of their own, and the flashes of multicoloured light seemed to spread to the cavern on distant Earth.

Eyes followed the darting light flashes, and everyone began to feel the presence of the Guardians of Peace, as a sense of euphoria. It was the highest reward available to any Tymorean.

In the presence of the Guardians of Peace, Tymos and Kryslie looked upwards and raised their arms high and wide, and in that moment, they felt the essences of the Tymorean descendents who had died before seeing this moment.

On Tymorea, Llaimos was echoing their gesture, joining them in embracing those essences, sharing the accolade that they too deserved. The minds of the Great Ones joined in a benediction of their own, before they separated and the sense of the Guardians slipped away.

The new generation of Tymorean missionaries, being more closely related to those on the screen, exchanged greetings and sorted out family kinship with the descendents.

Tymos and Kryslie, no longer the focus of attention, moved from the podium and joined their friends, and the others that were born on Earth. This was a moment to celebrate peace, and enjoy it while it lasted.

This was not the end, or happy ever after…

The Earth Mission had begun, and already made its mark. However, to Tymos and Kryslie this time of celebration was transient. Their own mission on Earth was yet to begin, and the enemy they would face in the future, was even deadlier than the one they had just conquered.

*****

This is the end of
The Tymorean Trust Book 4

EARTH MISSION

The story will continue in
The Tymorean Trust Book 5

ALIEN CONTACT

Discover other titles by Margaret Gregory

NOVELS

The Tymorean Trust Book 1 - POWER RISING

The Tymorean Trust -
When peace rules Tymorea - Peace reigns in the universe.
Chosen to be the Advocates of the mystical and incorporeal Guardians of
Peace, twins Tymos and Kryslie must first learn to control and use the
power rising in them - or it will destroy them.
On Tymorea, only the ruling Triumvirate Governors are powerful enough
to guide the strong-willed alien-bred twins until they have mastered their
power.

The Tymorean Trust Book 2 - GREAT ONES

The peace of the Guardian Planet, Tymorea, is in deadly peril. War there
will create ripples of unrest and destruction throughout the settled universe.

Tymos and Kryslie, still adolescents, have barely mastered their power and
Llaimos is still less than a year old, but they are the three chosen to be
Advocates of the mystical Guardians of Peace, to safeguard the Tymorean
Trust.

The Tymorean Trust Book 3 - THE RETURN TO EARTH

Even before the war on Tymorea, the Elders foresaw that Great Ones
Tymos and Kryslie would have an imperative mission on Earth.
But as the Tymoreans prepare to build an Earthbase to support them, they
discover that specifications for two vital protective shields are missing.
Now, nearly a century later, Tymos and Kryslie must find his work and
build the generator before the base is found.

www.ingramcontent.com/pod-product-compliance
Lightning Source LLC
Chambersburg PA
CBHW070625170726
48291CB00003B/882